SKYLER PUBLISHING GROUP

MONTEGA

MONTEGA CHRONICLES BOOK 2

A NOVEL BY

KEON SMITH

Published by The Skyler Publishing Group

Contains explicit language & adult themes suitable for ages 16+ only.

Dedication

This book is dedicated to Tamyra Elias—the only one who stuck by my side like the rib that protects my heart. Girl, you are the best thing that ever happened to me in life, and I will forever love you.
"Right now, let's not waste any more time when we both know it's everything we ever wanted since the day we first met..."
(Kenneth "Kenny Montega" Carter)

Acknowledgments

It's the second time around, and I have to give thanks to my homies for their support, starting with, Taurean "Juice" Jewett, DeShawn "Barney" Rogers, Maurice "Kahlil" Cheathan, Timothy "LJ" Bickham, Samaj, Tyree "Whitey" Way, Ray Ray, Lamont Cooker, EB (Harrisburg), Travis "Pudge" Stanfield, Kareem Greenwood, Khem "B" Un, Mark "Biz" Johnson, Brent "Bee" Jenkins and Blackman, Laurence "L" Brown, and Charles "Poochie" White, the real Great white.

To the whole Danger Zone movement. My brother from another, RA Certified, Los Lansky, Kareen Shaw, Troy Spiz Wiley, and the rest of the Summerville mob. The time is near. Look over your shoulders, and you'll find me coming. **Beware Of The Wolf.**

To all the friends and family out there with good intentions but can't seem to shake the ongoing problems that life throws at them, Marcus and Michael Prater, Katifah "Tee-Tee" Bundy, Kaliah Bundy, Boo-Bop, Patrice Murphy, Roderick Wheatland, China White, Meiasha Mccoy, Kia Paschall, Reese Hall, Mahdi Bey, Cyril Woodland, my sister, Jameeka Prater, John "Pookie" Prater Jr., Shekiea P. Simson, Izzy Shaw, Tamara, Tasha, Neka and Tia Smith, Josie Drew, Jermaine Roper, Tamyra Elias, Emily Coleman, Regina Giles, Alex A. Smith, Detra "Mookie" Rogers, Alysha Ms. Pinup Jones, Crystal Scott, Khalid Johnson, Kevalaa Forsyth, Wavii Boii Mitchell, Jennifer Sumstud, Brittany Washington, Tia Mitchell, Sherrell Jackson, Pfhallon Sanchez, Earline Bryant, Joshua Martin, Shabree White, Gloria Howard, Whitegirl Keemah, Kesha Wright, Victoria, Workman,

Bihiyyah Smith, Ladetra King, Jayuana Bullard, Quille Ingram, Karimah Brown, Todd Dogtown Mull, Marcus Twin Mcqueen, Perry Kellam, Regina Smith, Kevin St. Felix, Whitney Beaurford, Ace Edward, Jahvion Dupiton, Quinzell Woodland, Keshaun T. Walker, Nysarah Jackson, Phillip Aye, Max Thomas, Jayda Kinard, Tyarrah Scott, Katieem Uptwon Representer, Aubrey Andrew Jackson, Andrea U. Riggins, Cara Williams, Ricquilla Cobb, Sha Donna Poe, Regina Bradford, Shatia Jackson, Mo Love, Muhammah Goode, Makkah Dumah, Ronetta Beckett, Haneef Jackson, Tajanee Glover, Chris Smalls, Denise Jenkins, Jason Taylor, Ranay Nurse Nay Herder, Tierra Harrington, Mila Shay, Uptown Ali, Reece 'Twin' Mcqueen, Shawnda Mitchell, Mory Hourouma, Latoya Lee, Kelz Spearman, Vaughn M. Bryant, Jo Peso Milton, John "Hook" Bryant, Latoya N. Martin, Danny Hammond, Qizzy Mac, Cain "Dip" Pharoah, Erica Wilson, Lashandia Walker, Junita Sissy Butss, Taheera Townes, Denise Hines, Akiem 'Cuzmoe' Mcneil, Shanta Thomas, Evelyn Lamar, Taieka Chamblee, Lala Taken byda Best G-Fam, Yazzy Beccles, Rell Ingram (RIP), Oliver Gladden, Curtis White Jr., Katima Jackson, Tanisha Johnson, Jon Randolph, Sheeda Johnson, Ophana, Walker, Hell Rell Jackson, Aunt Lisa Reaves, King Pharoah, Monique Thomas, Anthony Washington, Brandy Kenion, Nonchalant Jackson, Jimmy Young, Kevin Knight, Nonchalant Jackson, Ash One-Of-A-Kind, Julius West, Courtley Vinsion, Dee Dee, Sharita Gantz, Dominique Price, Alexis Ware AKA Bobby Headlines, Tirek Brooks AKA Reek (SP), Miranda Gore, Henry "Hindu", Jasmine Reid, Jamie at Lil' Miz Cupcake, Joseph "Yuseph" Reid, Karina and Aunt Donna Champmon, Kenya and Kyle Walker, Fice, Randy Jenkins, Streets, Nifice Fields, Antonio "Goose" Washington, Marc Ham, Prince Williams, Yalonda Jones, Tiffany, Yuckbird (B-More), Kareem Greenwood, James "Wazir" Mcnair, Kasim, Darrell "Butter" Giliam, D.C. Strikes, Tay, Black Ant, Goldie, Lil Geezy, Rickie Collier, Hasan "Breeezy" Mclean (BedRock Entertainment), Tiera "T-cup", G-Love, Alismall Small (Brick City), Little C (Tampa), Kennan Prince, and Edward "Freck" Colman, Doug Edward AKA K9 Boss Doug W.O.L., and Al Ferrell.

Special thanks to Joseph Raymos, A. Rodgers, Dev, R. Best, Skyler Publishing Group. My appreciations for tightening up this project. And to everyone else showing support for this cause, thank you.

Synopsis

The boss's nightmare is no longer a bad dream...It's a reality, and his name is Kenneth "Montega" Carter. Using a vigilante M.O., known as the Phantom, he is fueled with the desire to seek revenge on those who pose a threat to both family and friends. Little does he know, that threat could possibly be the end of him. All it take is the girl of his dreams and a seductive kiss of death. This is a story where pups become wolves and lions become sheep.

The Montega Chronicles is an endless maze of conflicts leaving blood and death in it's wake. Linking together man's strengths and weaknesses ultimately leads one to ask the question... can the thirst for blood, money and revenge be the prequel to Montega's ultimate demise or will the one queen in this game help him to become the man he is destined to be? The city of Philadelphia will never be the same. The chill of revenge invokes a thirst for blood money, and all who stands in its way will forever remember the name... ***Montega.***

Prologue

N*othing seems louder than the deafening sound of silence,* Diamond thought as she sat calmly Indian style, front and center on the wooden floors of the most secretive dojo in California—The Black Cloud dojo. The place was massive and so quiet; an item as small as a strand of hair could almost be heard from the back of the room where the traditional ninja weapons were mounted.

She took another deep breath, inhaling the incense burning from the shrine to her far left, and closed her eyes and listened shortly to the sizzling wax candles that barely preserved light to such a dark, dense environment. If one were to enter from the bright California sun, they would have been oblivious to the fact that there were fifty Black Cloud ninjas sitting Indian style through the entire dojo from the floor to the balcony before her, all waiting for one man.

Even in dead silence, Diamond didn't hear his approach until he appeared before her in the dense lighting.

"Diamond, my student," he said strongly.

Instantly, every masked ninja in the dojo pressed their palms together tightly and lowered their heads.

Diamond slowly did the same before saying, "Master Wong Lee."

Placing his hands behind his back, he looked down at his student and said, "You have been with us for quite some time—before and after the death of your father. You have honored my organization by bringing us into the fold of your own. For that, I am truly grateful. Never have I seen one so eager to learn the way of ninjutsu like I have with you."

From a distance, one of his trainees raised her head to look at him with disgust then lowered it again.

"You have completed your training and strategy, tactics, unconventional warfare, and guerrilla warfare, but you still haven't overcame your fear. Kim!" he called out.

The woman who had once looked up with disgust rolled to her feet and moved beside her master. Wong Lee didn't have to speak. With just the nod of the head, the woman made her way behind Diamond and tied a blindfold over her eyes then backed away with a bow.

Now Diamond was completely blind.

"Do you recall the story of Adam and Eve?" Wong Lee asked.

"Yes, Master," Diamond replied but as a whisper.

"And what did the devil use to corrupt Eve?"

"A snake," Diamond replied.

"Any reason why the devil would use a snake?"

"Snakes are cautious, beautiful but deadly creatures; this I know. However, I can't think of why the devil would use it over any other animal."

"Perhaps it is because a snake could sneak by a man and strike at the closest thing to his heart—his woman," Wong Lee replied, nodding to Kim to perform another task. "The snakes are still among us, only not in the form of the devil but in the form of Man, so I ask you, what should Eve have done when she heard the snake speak to her?"

"Kill it," Diamond whispered.

"Speak up!" Wong Lee said sternly.

"Kill it!" Diamond now shouted. Her voice echoed throughout the dojo.

"Show me," Wong Lee replied, stepping back.

No sooner than he did, Diamond spun to her feet with quickness. From the sleeve of her black Quora sprung forth a chained dagger in which she wielded over her head and struck like a bull whip.

All that was heard was the swipe of a blade cutting through air before silence sprouted once more. The lights in the dojo turned on instantly.

Diamond listened as Wong Lee Took a deep breath and exhaled. "Your training is complete. You may remove your blindfold."

Diamond snatched the silk fabric from her beautiful face and saw the dead, headless cobra before her that was soaked in its own blood. A devilish grin suddenly creeped across her face.

"Come, my student," Wong Lee said. "I want to speak with you before you depart from here for good."

Diamond followed the Asian man down a dark hall. They stopped by a large glass window where two Asian chemists wearing protective face masks were busy stirring a concoction.

"Allow me to speak freely about your brother," Wong Lee said.

"Go ahead, speak," Diamond replied, watching the man inside the lab.

"He is naïve and cocky. With two traits like this, his organization will not last long. When you leave here, remember this; the people around you are only as good as the one leading them."

Diamond nodded, soaking the words up in her memory bank. Her pretty, brown eyes, however, were focused on something else. "What are they making?" she asked curiously.

"It is a strong toxin made to deploy from one touch to another," Wong Lee explained.

"I'm not following you," Diamond replied, confused.

"What I mean is the toxin can be placed on your skin, and you won't be exposed. Only from the outer layers come its deadly venom. Like a snake, it releases venom from its teeth, yet the venom does not kill the snake. We as ninjas practice this, using the toxin on our two fingertips. One touch to a man's neck brings death in a matter of minutes. We call it *the touch of death*."

Diamond looked back at the two chemists then said,"Master Lee, with such a weapon like this, you're about to make millions." Turning to face him, she then smirked. "I want this toxin made in the form of black lipstick. I want my enemy to suffer, I want everyone to know that death is for certain from but a kiss, so that all will know that Diamond White has just made her mark."

Chapter One

"Where the hustlers roam and drugs are sold,
the dead walks amongst the living.
There's a place cold, where life has no soul,
and death is only the beginning..."

October 8, 2004
CHELTEN AVENUE AND ARDLEIGH STREET...

Montega sat on the playground bench inside the gates of the Lonnie Young Recreation Center outdoor basketball courts. He looked out toward the field of green grass, deep in thought. It was a boring Thursday morning on the streets uptown in Philadelphia. The weather was warm with a light breeze to it. The sun was on the verge of peeking over the East Germantown row houses, and the smell of trash truck juice that dribbled onto the road lingered throughout the neighborhood.

Montega was a product of an environment that natives called Topside Summerville. It was a dangerous, drug-infested place full of empty crack viles and bullet shell casings. The 'Ville was a danger zone for outsiders, but this morning, it was quiet. None of the hustlers were out on the grind yet, and no police cars toured the neighborhood to harass him. He was the only one up at the crack of dawn and the last to take it in for the night. He didn't mind being to himself. This early stretch alone gave him the time to ponder his next move.

Montega was a dedicated hustler, one who stayed on the grind. He and his homie Razor had been hustling ever since they graduated from Martin Luther King Jr High School. Poverty brought forth the goal of someday becoming millionaires. So far, their fate was the same as the others; they just couldn't get over the hump. Here he was, twenty-two years old and barely copping a deuce and a quarter.

As Montega fired up a vanilla Dutch of some of the stickiest weed that Ashmead Street had to offer, a local corner thug named KK approached from the gated entrance with both hands in the pockets of his black Nike hoodie. Montega looked on suspiciously. He had a good sense to know what trouble looked like, and KK seemed to be drowning in it.

"What's good wit' you?" KK greeted, giving Montega some dap before looking around the deserted basketball court for anyone else.

"Ain't shit but the weed," Montega responded while exhaling a cloud of smoke.

"You the only one here?"

"It appears that way, don't it?" Montega replied with a hint of sarcasm, shielding his eyes with his hand from the morning sun as he looked up at KK.

Montega couldn't help but notice the disturbed look on KK's face. His jaw was clenched, and his eyes were sharp and red. "You aight, bol?" he asked cautiously.

"Nah, man. In fact, I need you to take a walk with me. I gotta handle something, and I need someone to watch my back. Is you ridin' or what?"

Montega looked into KK's bloodshot red eyes but couldn't figure him out. As much as KK didn't like Montega, he was now asking for his help. Truth be told, KK had no choice but to respect his style. Montega was a calm, laid-back dude, but he had a hair-trigger temper that could catch people off guard. Not only that, the twenty-two-year-old was also a born leader with an aura way ahead of his time.

Without answering his question, Montega followed KK down Ardleigh Street, having no clue of what to expect. Passing KK the

Dutch, he tried once more to find out what the hell was going on. "Hold, bol. What up wit' you? What's all this about?"

KK didn't respond; he just continued to walk. When they got to the bottom of the block, KK stopped and turned to look Montega in the eyes.

"You got a burner on you?" he asked, making the hair on the back of Montega's neck stick up.

This shit serious, he thought. "Nah, I left mines up the street. Why? What's goin' on?" Montega asked again.

KK went into his waist, pulled out a 9mm, and cocked it back.

Montega quickly stopped in his tracks. "Hold up, main-man. You pullin' out guns and shit, got me followin' you down here without tellin' me nothin'. Fuck I look like? A crash dummy, KK?"

KK really didn't want to put him on game, because after he was done with what he was about to do, he would leave no witnesses. He just couldn't leave anyone alive to testify against him if things went sour. The way he saw it, there were two people in his way of becoming hood rich, and his plan was to eliminate them both. After thinking about it, he said, "I need you to lookout while I handle this rat ass nigga Smoke. You know he set to take the stand on a good dude in two days."

Montega let this bit of information marinate in his mind. He knew the person KK spoke of supplied all of uptown and most of North Philly, but when he went down for a homicide, a lot of hustlers suffered. Smoke, who saw the hit go down, got booked on some drug charges and immediately turned snitch in order to escape doing hard time. What ruined the hood's credibility, was the fact that Smoke lived directly down the block from where everybody hustled, but nobody laid a finger on him.

Truthfully, everybody knew that even though Smoke was a rat, he was still a cold wolf on the streets; and because of this, not too many people wanted to bang heads with him, but KK was different. He didn't care about a man's street credit. He was too busy trying to embellish his own. If a man wasn't made of Teflon and his heart didn't bleed steel, then he was getting dropped. He knew Montega was as tough as everyone said he was.

Too bad he won't live to see tomorrow, KK thought.

Montega watched as KK walked up the concrete steps to the enclosed porch. He then looked down the block to make sure the coast was clear. He did the same up the block as well. KK looked through the window for any signs of movement. When he saw none, he slid the window up, and climbed inside. He then unlocked the front door before taking a peek through the dark first floor. The lights were out throughout the house. Silence aroused suspicion.

His heart thumped fast. Hearing the floor creak in the other room, he drew his silver Taurus 9mm and began to initiate a search. Sweeping his gun from left to right, he checked each room, but there was no sign of Smoke anywhere. When he came back down to the first floor, he headed for the kitchen. As soon as he entered, he slowly lowered his weapon, cursed under his breath, and shook his head with disappointment. He had just seen Smoke go in the house a few minutes before he went to get Montega. *Did he just step in then leave?* he wondered.

Suddenly, KK heard the floor squeak behind him. He quickly spun around but wasn't quick enough to shoot. Smoke had gotten the drop on him, holding a .40 cal. with an extended ladder, locked and loaded. A shot was fired, and a hot slab of metal bore into KK's chest, knocking him on his back. KK's gun fell out of his hand, slid across the green tile floor, and stopped by the refrigerator. Holding the burning bullet wound in pain, KK watched with beads of sweat pouring down his forehead as Smoke raised his gun to finish him off. Smoke wasn't the dramatic type. He just aimed with one sinister eye closed.

KK shut both of his eyes and prepared to meet the devil. He had done too much wicked shit and contemplated too much evil in his life to even consider going to heaven. This was now his fate, and there was nothing else to do but accept it.

Rat-tat-tat!

Rapid fire exploded, causing KK's whole body to jerk. It wasn't from bullets, however, but from the loud sound of another gun. He opened his eyes to see Smoke's brains oozing out of his head. Blood painted the kitchen with tear drops of red. Smoke's knees buckled. His lifeless body hit the kitchen floor with a heavy thump before a puddle formed around him. Behind Smoke's corpse stood Montega impassively holding a fully automatic Ingram Mac-10. The barrel of the gruesome machine gun silently puffed a ghost-like white smoke from its nozzle.

KK knew then how lucky he was to have Montega covering his back. *Maybe I wouldn't have to kill him after all.* That thought vanished quickly.

KK sneered as he watched Montega pick up his Taurus and tuck it into his waistband.

"What the hell you plan on doing with that? That's mine," KK protested in pain.

Montega flashed a crooked smile then aimed the machine gun at him. KK's sneer quickly transformed into a confused frown. "Wha... What the fuck are you doing?"

"You know what's funny? Last night, I ran into your homie Ron while he was all drunk in Brickyard," Montega began. "It's amazing what dudes say when they got that yak up in 'em. He told me everything that you were up to. It was a good plan; I have to admit. Too bad you'll never carry it out."

"So what you gonna do? Kill me right here?" KK asked.

"You remember what you told Ron, right? The only way two men can keep a secret is if the other is burning in hell. That's the same thing I told Ron before the Phantom put a bullet in the back of his head. Now I'm telling you."

"Go to hell," KK spat.

"I'll see you when I get there, bol. But right now, hell is low," Montega pulled the trigger once more.

Rat-tat-tat!

Chapter Two

The Champ Is Back
Two Days Later...

"The state can't keep a rich nigga behind bars forever..."

— REEK

Inside the courtroom of the Criminal Justice Center on 13th and Filbert Streets, in Center City, Philadelphia, the room was packed with family and friends. The DA tried to paint the judge a perfect picture of Michael 'Million-Dollar Mike' Harris being a cold-blooded murderer. Everyone in attendance listened to the prosecutor's Academy-Award-winning performance.

Natali Brown was an exceptional prosecutor at the Philadelphia criminal justice center. Not only had she taken down some of the cleverest criminals in her career, but she was also fearless and put on one hell of a show for the jury.

Brown paced back and forth in front of the judge, dressed in a velvet pencil skirt that stopped just above her slender knee. She wore black heels and a satin blouse to match her hollow, green eyes. She was naturally blonde with a slender nose and thin lips. One might judge from the texture of her tan, speckled skin that she may have been cursed by sunburn, but truthfully, she was naturally freckled. When it came to her job, she was aggressive and relentless when it came to obtaining convictions.

After her speech, she strutted over to her seat, glancing over at the defendant. She took a seat beside a detective, crossed her legs, and waited for the witness to seal Mike's fate.

Across from them, dressed in a two-piece, blue county uniform that State Road's CFCF issued to him, Mike sat with his lawyer, LaTanya Gibson. He feared everything would go south the minute the witness showed.

Anyone from the streets that knew Mike could tell that he was stressed out. His deep, dark eyes showed all the more concern to whether he would survive or fall. Even his stocky build had slimmed down from the lack of food and nourishment.

Although he had the best lawyer in the city, he still felt he was doomed once the witness took the stand. Ms. Gibson didn't come cheap. In fact, she owned her own law firm in New York and was funded by a secret criminal society that ruled the United States black market. They called themselves the Underworld. The only reason she was there to represent Mike was because her boyfriend, Deshawn Butler, referred him to her.

Tanya was German, but her ability to fight in court came from her Israeli side. Her beauty reflected her reputation as one of the sharpest lawyers not just in the state but also the federal justice system. She was average with short, dark, terra hair, boomerang eyebrows, a slender face, with doe eyes the color of maple syrup. She had nice lips that were thick and an athletic figure.

As a representative of Mike, she stole the scene in a brown, two-piece Brooks Brothers suit, trimmed and tailored to her body perfectly, with dark-brown, leather-strapped Jimmy Choo heels to complement her look.

Mike looked over his shoulder and saw his girlfriend, Jasmine, sitting with her fingers crossed and a worried expression. Things had been shaky for her. She had never been one to ride for a man in jail, but for Mike, she had tested her endurance. Jasmine Whitehead was naturally beautiful, yet she took extra steps by applying light makeup and lip balm to her appearance. She had thick, dark hair that came past her shoulders. She had been riding with Mike for two years now, ever since his first girlfriend, Jennifer, took over a hundred grand from him and left him to rot in jail. Mike flashed a counterfeit smile, but he knew it was hopeless once the witness took the stand and told the story of how he killed Reds at TJ's bar. Just as Mike began to relive the scene, the judge called for the witness. Mike felt anger, hate, and fear at the thought of Smoke taking the stand.

He watched as one of the detectives came down the aisle and whispered something into the prosecutor's ear.

"Nat, we have a serious problem," Detective Whitehead said.

"Can't it wait? I'm about to nail this son of a bitch. Now, where's my witness?"

Silence never seemed so loud. She looked up at Whitehead. He looked distraught.

"I'm sorry, Nat, but I just received word from the 14th District. There was a double homicide on the 5500 block of Ardleigh. The witness was found inside. He's dead."

When Natali heard that, her shoulders sunk away as she sighed, deeply massaging her temples.

"Gary, what do you mean, he's dead?" the woman whispered in response.

"I just found out a moment ago. We have no suspect, no murder weapon. I'm sorry, Nat," Detective Whitehead explained.

The district attorney's face was contorted as she stood up to ask the judge if she could approach the bench. Once the two lawyers were standing in front of the judge. The prosecutor whispered, "Your Honor, we have just been informed that our key witness was killed yesterday. We request to postpone so we can deal with this setback."

"You want yet another postponement?" Tanya remarked before looking at the judge. She had heard this before declining with a client in the federal system. There was no way she would let that happen in the state. "Your Honor, you see what my client has to go through? He has spent two years fighting this case, and we've given them two years to get ready, and still, they are unprepared."

"She's right, Ms. Brown," the judge replied. "I will not keep wasting taxpayer's money on a case that is going nowhere. If there is no credible evidence against this man other than a dead witness's testimony, I am going to have to dismiss this case." He slammed the gavel down.

"No, Your Honor, please... jus..." the prosecutor pleaded as the courtroom erupted in celebration.

"Excuse me, Ms. Brown, but I have rendered my decision. This case is dismissed." The judge rose and left the courtroom.

LaTanya Gibson walked over to congratulate her client. After two years of being told what to eat, what time to lock in, and what time to take a shower, Mike was finally coming home. However, there was still one more pending case that he knew he would spank with his new lawyer.

No one was angrier at the outcome of this case than Dt. Whitehead. He and his partner spent over two years gathering information, paying off snitches, and countless late nights at their desks just to watch Mike Harris walk out the courtroom with a smile. His thick eyebrow squinted, and his old, droopy cheeks tightened. His teeth clenched under a thick mustache. *This was not justice.*

Seated beside him was his heavyset Italian partner who had dark and oiled hair slicked to the back. He was clean cut with dark eyes and a small nose. He and Whitehead shared cases together at the homicide division. His name was Detective Anthony Lucca.

"Can you believe this shit? The bastard is getting away with murder, just like that piece of shit cousin of his," Lucca stated in amazement.

"He'll be back," Detective Whitehead predicted confidently. "Besides, he has another open case with us, and a couple of my good friends in ATF are looking at it as we speak. What we need to do now is find the person responsible for killing our snitch," Whitehead said, rubbing his thick, cowboy mustache.

Once Mike was released from the county jail on State Road, Jasmine and Mike's righthand man, Reek, were out in the parking lot, waiting for him. Mike had put Reek in charge of his business while he was incarcerated, and judging by the brand-new, champagne-colored

S550 AMG Reek was standing in front of, Mike figured Reek had been cleaning up.

"I guess, for once, the rumors are true about what you were doing out here. They say you can tell a man's wealth from the way he carries himself, the people he keeps around him, and the car he drives. I see you looking like money right now… and you riding 'doe low'."

"The numbers don't lie, fam," Reek rejoiced.

"I see that. That Benz is all that too. What is it? A two thousand four?" Mike asked.

He circled the $90,000 Sedan with admiration for its sparkling coat of paint and creamy leather interior.

"Nah, it's an '05. It ain't even out yet. I'm glad you feelin' it though, my nigga, because it belongs to you. It's the least I can give you for puttin' me on, homie. The streets been missing the heavyweight champ. Plus, I don't think I could keep the wolves off my ass for too long with all the money that's been coming in lately. This right here ain't shit but a first down."

Mike cracked a wry smile and gave him some dap along with a brotherly hug. "Aye, man, I knew somethin' was gonna come up," Reek continued. "The state can't keep a rich nigga behind bars forever. It's too much money on the line. I knew that bitch ain't have no witness."

"Shit, I didn't," Mike responded honestly scratching the back of his head. "That was a close one. But yo, who killed Smoke's bitch ass anyway?"

"I don't know. When the neighbors heard the shots, they called the law, but no one came until days later. Turns out the cops found KK machine-gunned to death in the same room as Smoke."

"KK?" Mike repeated in confusion. "Black cousin?"

Jasmine watched as her man talked. She was so content with seeing the brown glow from his muscular frame; it had her soaking wet. He had a unique swag about him, despite the low haircut and thick beard. Maybe it was his confidence that attracted her to him. Maybe it was his reputation of being a hood boss. Whatever it was, she loved the ground he walked on.

"Yeah, bol, when the cops showed up, Smoke was stinkin', and so was KK," Reek went on to say. "I think KK tried to break into Smoke's crib and Smoke shot him. Then Smoke got wet up from the back."

"Damn, and nobody knows who rocked him?" Mike questioned.

Reek shook his head, no. "Man, it's a rumor goin' 'round that the Phantom had a part in it."

Mike shook his head in disbelief. "Not this Phantom bullshit again. Where do these dudes come up with this shit?"

Before Mike was incarcerated, he had been hearing rumors in the area about a vigilante killer who called himself the Phantom. However, no one he knew credible had ever actually seen the guy or girl for that matter, yet there were several stories floating around about him already.

As the guys conversed like two high-school buddies, Jasmine patiently waited her turn, folding her arms then clearing her throat. "Excuse me, but can I get some love too, daggg?" she complained.

Mike looked over to see her standing with her arms folded. He immediately felt guilty for ignoring his beautiful girlfriend. He wrapped his arms around her voluptuous figure. She was petite, and he loved her long, dark, lustrous curls and pretty, chocolate-brown eyes. He moved in and kissed her devotedly.

"My bad, babe. You know I love you, right?" he asked, looking deep into her eyes.

She flushed with desire and anticipation. "Well, why don't you show me just how much you love me?" she teased.

"Hold up, y'all. Why don't y'all take that shit to the crib? And don't be all day with him, Jazz. We gotta let the streets know that the champ is back," Reek stated.

Mike loved being called the Champ. He replied, "Oh, you ain't gotta worry about that. Nine out of ten chances, these dudes already know I'm back."

Mike got into the driver's side of his new vehicle. Jasmine took the passenger's seat, while Reek sat in the back. They pulled away from the prison, hoping to never return again. As they rode out of the parking lot, Detective Gary Whitehead and his partner Lucca watched from an unmarked, blue Chevy Impala. They swore an oath on that day. The oath revolved around one day bringing Mike and all his murderous associates to justice. That, Tony Lucca put on his kids, and Gary Whitehead put on his twenty-six years of marriage.

Chapter Three

Living Life Like It's Your Last Day On Earth
INSIDE A THREE-STORY ROW HOUSE...

"I'm a wolf... and wolves can't be tamed..."
(MONTEGA)

"Montega! Montega!" squealed the little girl with the two cap guns in her hands.

Five-year-old Kenny chased her around his mother's home, playing cops and robbers. The weird part about the game was there were no cops involved. The two had an agreement that neither one wanted to be the law; both would be the bad guy. Both were very young but very intelligent and caught on fast to what surrounded their youth.

Kenny fired his cap gun at the fleeing little girl. She had long, dark hair, which flapped like a cape as she ran for cover. "I still got your money." The pretty little girl giggled as she ran through the living room.

"Not for long," Kenny replied, trying to catch up to her.

He ran into the living room, aiming to tackle his new girlfriend, but he didn't see the piece of rug sticking out of the floor and tripped. Kenny tried hard to catch his fall, but his little feet couldn't control themselves when there was only air beneath his soles. He went head first into the corner of the coffee table. Everything went black after that...

Montega awoke in a cold sweat, which woke up his girlfriend, Tasha. "Baby, are you okay?" she asked with a tired, raspy voice as she sat up with him.

For some strange reason, he kept having the same dream over and over. He had no idea why he dreamt about being a five-year-old kid and blacking out, but it wouldn't go away. He felt as if the dream was a part of his past. Not only had his dreams been bothering him lately, but he also had survivor's guilt. He couldn't get over losing his mother. He felt she didn't deserve to die. To him, she was innocent like an angel. If anything, he should have died, not her.

It was also the reason he felt he had to protect those he cared about, fiercely if not violently. Rubbing his forehead where the mysterious mark remained, he wiped the sweat from his face and sighed in frustration as he looked over at Tasha. She was staring dead at him with hungry, silver eyes. He always thought those eyes were so cold in a way, yet she showed nothing but affection and devotion to him.

Tasha was a Milano with smooth, pale skin and dark naturally straight hair that fell well beyond her shoulders. She was a twenty-one-year-old beauty who studied law at an all-girls college in Atlanta. While on spring break, she decided to spend it at home with her mother and three sisters. She loved Montega because he was her first and was the only hoodlum who could capture her heart, but she hated what he did for a living. Tasha would always tell him how much she hated drugs, and Montega would always tell her how much he loved fast money. It was like two people speaking different languages. They represented two very different worlds, yet they came together so beautifully.

Tasha kissed Montega tenderly on the neck. "That better, baby?" she whispered before licking his earlobe and sucking it like a piece of candy. Montega closed his eyes for a moment as his dick bulged under the sheets. He then turned to kiss her. Tasha leaned back submissively while pulling the covers from her body to expose her firm, bare breasts and landing-strip-trimmed pussy. Montega's tongue traveled down to her ripe, quarter-sized nipple and playfully streaked across them.

"Umm, Kenny, stop before you start something, boy," she moaned.

Getting on top of her, he positioned his thick, long member at the opening of her swollen entrance and thrust himself inside. Tasha gasped as every inch of his shaft penetrated her. "Uhhhh!" she moaned as he stuffed the full length inside of her wet walls. "Oh shit, Kenny. It… it feels so good."

Montega slid his hands down to her curvy thighs and cupped them from underneath, pulling her legs up and around his waist. From there, his hands slid up the side of her ribs, taking her by her arms to pin her down on the bed. Tasha loved their lovemaking, but what made her go berserk was the thought of Montega being in complete control. He held her down by her wrists while pumping his member in and out of her wet tunnel. Tasha's eyes rolled to the back of her head. Her face contorted with each stroke. She didn't know what she liked the most about this street thug, but his whole persona turned her on. He had evolved from the young, smooth-faced pup to the peak of alpha male maturity.

Montega's face moved down to her neck. Using his teeth, he lightly bit her skin, causing her to purr like a cat. He gently licked her sweet skin while moving into her harder each time he delivered. His teeth moved to her ears. This drove her mad. Despite his ability to mask his thoughts and disguise his emotions, he was nonetheless a self-professed, clean-cut, romantic predator.

Tasha fought to break her hands. She wanted to feel him, to hold him. When he finally released her, her hands stroked across his scarred back, feeling every welt that was once done by torture. She adored him because he was caring at times, sensitive, nice, and instinctive. He showed her the very soul of respect and earnest ambition. What she didn't see was the darkness hidden behind his mysteriousness.

She cupped his face and stared into his eyes while he fucked her into oblivion. He was taking her every breath. To her, no man could grasp the thoughts she had stored in her mind and understand its reasoning better than he could. His handsomeness and irresistible smile didn't help either. He had a moon-shaped face with exotic, brown eyes, a thin, long nose, and full, pouting lips. Unlike his high-yellow brother, he had light-brown skin with a light mustache and full beard sprouting from his face like a lion's mane. Her hands stroked his short, wavy hair that was always shaped up sharply before moving down his chiseled back. His entire body was genetically blessed.

"Oh God, Kenny! You're making me cum!" she shouted while wrapping her legs around his waist.

Sure, guys came at Tasha in college every day, but no matter how much they threw themselves at her, she just couldn't find anyone who could match Montega's uptown swag.

"Let me get on top, baby," Tasha suggested while trying to catch her breath.

"You can try," Montega teased.

Tasha giggled as she rolled him over to his back. Montega took her by the hand and kissed her palm. She placed them against his rock-hard abs and milked him with rhythmic strokes. He reached behind her, taking a handful of her ass and squeezing as he pumped himself into her. Montega always admired Tasha's ass. For a white girl, she was holding. He watched her titties bounce as she rode him like she was a Kentucky Derby jockey. "Is this pussy good to you, baby?" she asked, picking up speed.

The warm feeling sent chills through Montega.

"Hell yeah," he grunted out while grabbing her waist to improve the leverage.

"Oh shit, baby." Tasha frowned as she felt him almost piercing her mid-section. "This dick is so big. I can feel you in my stomach."

I've heard that before.

Tasha rhythmically worked her body with his to a mysterious beat that only they could hear. Her love box was so wet; Montega felt he couldn't hold back his excitement any longer. Palming her ass, he deep stroked her until he could feel himself flushing out his seed. He quickly pulled her close, thankful she had just taken her depo shot two days earlier. He wasn't ready for a child and most certainly didn't want one out of pure lust and not love. He took a deep breath to regain his energy then slid out of her.

After the explosion, he slowly got out of bed and headed for the shower. "Kenny, put some clothes on before one of my sisters sees you," Tasha said, watching from the bed. She didn't want to move. The orgasm she just had left her paralyzed. Her hair was everywhere. She swept it from her sweaty face and pulled it back slowly. She was exhausted.

As Montega went to grab a towel, his phone buzzed in his jeans pocket. Tasha reached out from the edge of the bed to grab it. "Know your role, shorty," Montega said, approaching. "What you think you doin'?" he asked, grabbing his jeans before she got them.

"Damn, why can't I answer your phone?" Tasha asked suspiciously.

"Because it ain't your phone to answer. Fuck I look like? One of them tender-dick dudes you be meetin' at the college?" he asked before answering the phone. "Yo, bol."

"Yo, bol," Razor inquired. "What's the deal?"

"Ain't shit. Just got up for the day." Montega stuck his tongue out at Tasha, who had a pouty look on her face.

"Good, well, get dressed. I'm 'bout to walk around there. You know everybody hype because Mike just got out of jail. Shorties that ain't been around in a few summers poppin' up; dudes that used to beep the horn when they ride pass stoppin' to kick it—fake shit but expected. Anyway, Mike wants to see you. He said meet him at the playground," Razor informed him.

"Oh yeah? Aight, come on then. I'll be waiting," Montega replied before hanging up.

On hearing that, Tasha pouted even more. "Damn, bae, I swear you always ruin the moment with this crap. Why can't you say 'fuck the streets' for once and give me some more of that dick?" Tasha whined before flopping back on the bed.

Montega watched as her tender breasts bounced freely before his eyes. He sighed and said, "I can't, shorty. I gotta meet up with Razor."

Tasha sucked her teeth. "I never seen anybody like you. I come all the way from Atlanta to be with you, sleep with you, feed you, and fuck you, and you jump right out of the pussy then go running out in the streets the moment your friends call you. Or maybe it's *you* who doesn't have any feelings for me. Which one is it? Because I'm totally lost right now."

"Tasha, chill, yo," Montega said tiresomely. "Why we always have to argue over stupid shit, especially shit like this? Don't you know this bickering is annoying?"

"Because you're always leaving me; that's why." She folded her arms with an attitude. "I'm tired of this, Kenny. I really am."

"Maaan, I ain't going far. I'm only right around the corner. I'll be back before you know it. All this stuff about feelings and whatever else you got stored up, save it for a girls' night out with your friends because I ain't tryna hear that right now. You know I love you," he said, trying to get through to her. "But you can't keep me caged in like some dog you got on a leash. I'll never wear a leash. I'm a wolf... and wolves can't be tamed... not like that, shorty." He looked at his watch—a black G-shock sports with digital time. "Let me get ready before Razor get here."

Tasha rolled her eyes and looked up at the ceiling, thinking, *You must have never been to the zoo if you think I can't contain you.* Razor was Montega's best friend, partner, and brother from another mother. She knew that there was nothing that could come between them, not even her. The truth was, she wanted to keep Montega off the streets. She planned on marrying him once she graduated from college and possibly have three beautiful kids with him, but Razor was always interfering. If he could help it, Razor wasn't going to have his homie subjected to a spoiled, egotistical, control freak who didn't like drug dealers. Razor knew that his homie had a lot more potential than that.

"Why can't you stay with me? You know I have to go back to Atlanta in a few days," she insisted.

"Stop whining, yo! I told you I'll backtrack. Besides, Razor is on his way, and I can't tell him to go back now. Plus, I gotta meet with my man. He just got out of jail," he said, checking his G-shock again.

As he headed for the shower, Tasha wanted to ask him, *what do you love more, me or the streets?* She feared the answer she would get in return. Truthfully, Montega's lust for spontaneity and risk was a lot more than she expected. Even though he was loyal and protective, which made her feel special, he couldn't be faithful to just one woman. If that wasn't enough for her to realize, then his love for the streets clenched it. Tasha knew then that regardless of how much she loved him, Montega would never change, and that meant that she would have to end their relationship. To her, there was no future for a drug dealer.

She could still remember the sight of her father lying on the cold concrete with five red holes in his chest. She could still smell the gunpowder from the smoking gun, still hear the footsteps as they faded in the distance. Her father had been murdered all because he didn't want a few drug dealers selling crack in front of their home.

For standing up for his family, he paid for it with his life.

Five minutes later, the doorbell rang. Tasha, who was ripped from her thoughts, rolled her eyes, knowing exactly who it was. Throwing on some pajama pants and a T-shirt, she headed downstairs to answer the door.

When she opened it, a light-skinned guy with a small, curly 'fro and a thick beard stood before her, dressed in a brown, two-piece Dickie set, some tan Butters, and a Cleveland Browns fitted cap tilted to the side.

He had an oval face sunken in with high cheekbones. His strong jawline hung like the crescent moon and was covered with dark, sparkling facial hair. He and Montega shared the same slender nose and thick lips, which left those that didn't know them debating whether or not the two were related. Silky eyebrows were where the resemblance ended.

Razor was a hairy young man just like Montega's brother, Taliban, but there was no mistaking his charm, even for a woman who despised him.

"Oh, hi, Razor," she said, trying to disguise her distaste for him.

Razor could see right through her act. "Yo, where Montega at?" he asked as if he didn't hear her.

If it was one thing she hated, it was drugs, but the main thing was the name everyone called her man—Montega.

Where did he get that name from? She thought.

Even Montega didn't know why he took on such an attribute. All he could remember was waking up in a hospital bed with that name on his mind.

He grabbed Tasha by the waist, pulling her to him so that her boobs pressed against his chest, and her pelvis could feel the swell of his manhood. He dipped in and kissed her like a thirsty animal arriving to a waterhole. The kiss nearly took Tasha's breath away. He then pulled back from her succulent, cherry-red lips, kissed Tasha on the cheek, and headed out the door, ready to start the day, hoping it wouldn't be his last. Tasha watched him disappear behind the door, sucking on her bottom lip, wishing she could have extended the kiss a little longer. She hated having to face reality because behind it, there was always nothing but the truth. And the truth of the matter was that when Montega returned, she would be long gone… and so would their relationship.

Chapter Four

Too Far Gone

BASKETBALL COURTS ON ARDLEIGH STREET…

"It's a dog-eat-dog world… and I'm nobody's next meal."

— MONTEGA

It was a warm day in the city of Philadelphia. The golden sun rose high in the morning sky. A light breeze swept the streets of Summerville. Spring was fading away, giving birth to summer. Aside from the endless police sirens, the musical tune of Mr. Softy's ice cream truck played from blocks away. Young kids begged their parents for dollars so they could purchase a cone of soft vanilla ice cream with sprinkles from the truck. Those that couldn't get it from their parents ran to Ardleigh Street's playground to get it from the drug dealers.

Montega dug in his pocket, gave two kids a dollar a piece, then watched as they ran off back around the corner. He stood outside the recreation center with Razor, J-Black, and Taliban, surrounded by females indulging in ghetto gossip. They all took turns making sales to every crackhead that came through the gate of the basketball court. The Lonnie Young Recreation Center was a female magnet during the spring and summer seasons. Divas, smuts, and whores from all over Germantown drove through, searching for a future boyfriend or sugar daddy to take care of them during the lonely nights.

Taliban was Montega's biological brother on his dad's side. Only a year younger, Taliban had a lighter complexion than his older brother and sported a thick beard and curly hair that he kept cut short. He and Montega were the same height, but it was the weight he put on that made him look stockier than his older brother.

Besides weed, which everybody smoked, Taliban enjoyed drinking syrup—be it purple or yellow, it didn't matter. Many wouldn't know by looking at him, but Taliban had a low tolerance for problems. His emotions changed like a chameleon behind a face that was always a mystery. Like his brother, he was a ticking time bomb, and no one knew when he would explode. He was the type who did things out on the streets to show off his recklessness just to make a name for himself. Even though his irresponsible behavior always hurt those he cared for, he refused to stop until everyone knew who he was. Regardless of his notorious reputation, everyone admired him because he was considered one of the top hustlers on the block—one that could sell fire to a match.

He could hustle off anything he got his hands on, even sheetrock. J-Black was also a good hustlers, but he made his real money as one of Million-Dollar Mike's enforcers. Black's vice, however, was the club. While others were trying to stack their paper to get rich, Black was blowing his money, partying like a rock star and sporting expensive clothes to impress the ladies. One would think he was a model rather than a killer.

While the guys stood around in white tees, cargo shorts, ACG sneakers, or Dickie sets and Butters, Black wore white Gucci Linen with sneakers to compliment his angelic appearance. He wore gold-framed Marc Jacob shades to hide his dark-brown eyes. Even though he wore the latest gear, his wardrobe wasn't what got him in with the ladies. He was a slick talker with a bumpy face that only a mother could love.

"Where you been hidin' for the past few days, Tega? Shit been hot as fish grease around here after KK and Smoke got merked," J-Black stated.

"Why you think I ain't been around?" Montega asked, walking

through the black iron gates. "The Detectives been picking up everybody in the neighborhood and taking them down to the Round House. Reporters been snooping around, trying to get a private interview. I ain't never seen the news vans sliding through east G-town like they do now, so I fell the hell back." Montega shrugged before going to stash his bundle under a broken boulder of concrete.

"You sure you ain't been sneaking in nobody window with ya hammer out? You the one that play the early morning all the time," Black said with suspicion.

KK was his first cousin. Although the two had a fallout, Black wouldn't wish death on him, nor would he want to kick out money for a funeral his aunt didn't have the funds to pay for. Now he was on the lookout for the killer.

Montega remained calm. He placed his hands in the pockets of his black Polo cargos and said, "What I need to kill somebody for?" He spat on the ground. "All these killers I got on my team, I should be a motherfucking coach. I ain't making no noise. I been chillin', tryna stack paper, feel me?"

"You mean boo-lovin'," Razor replied as he passed the Dutch to one of the shorties sitting next to him.

Montega smirked. "You can say what you want, but when shit get hot, I fly to where the weather is cool. I ain't sticking 'round here so these cops can see my face. It's bad enough they be hopping out like Hannibal Smith and the A-Team on Blakemore. That's why we over here now."

"Shyit. After them murders, this block about to be the same way. On some real shit, who you think rocked them two down the block?" J-Black asked.

"Me, personally, I think it was the Phantom," Montega stated as he glanced at Razor.

"Man, you keep rappin' 'bout this Phantom dude. How come you the only one that seen 'em?" J-Black asked.

"Because like you said, I'm the only one that be out this muthafucka from morning to morning, feel me? I'm telling you, the bul was dressed in all black wit' a Phantom mask on."

"I know what you talkin' 'bout," Razor said, going along with his homie. "That's the same cat that rocked the old-head in front of the swimming pool. Everybody out there seen that. You can't tell me bul don't exist."

"Man, that was Mike who had somebody rock old-head in front of the pool," Taliban said after sucking his teeth. "That was just a power play to take over the hood. Tell 'em, Black."

"They already know what's going on. They got eyes. They know shit real. How you think Mike got the name *Million-Dollar*? Last I checked, it wasn't no Phantom on payroll."

"What's the Phantom?" one of the girls in tight booty shorts and a tank top asked.

As Razor told the females the stories that were spreading throughout Summerville, Black interrupted him. "Man, enough of that campfire bullshit. Ain't no such thing as no Phantom. You buls need to stop spreading rumors. By the way, I forgot to tell you, your homies came through here lookin' for you."

"What homies?" Montega asked.

"Some bul name Rider or something like that," J-Black replied.

Montega knew exactly who J-Black was referring to—J-Rider. He was Montega's homie from the Blumberg projects in North Philadelphia. He and his cousin Killa moved to Philly from California after J-Rider lost his mom. Both J-Rider and Killa were part of Montega's circle known as the Blood Money Mafia, which recently graduated to the Silent Kings. It was a circle that consisted of seven other members, including Razor. Montega knew they were up to no good.

He remembered years ago, having to be rescued by them from some kidnapping broads who liked to torture people. J-Rider and Killer were the first to respond with Razor. Only when they moved out, Killa had to bring his ten-month old son with him. They got into a shootout and even almost got pulled over by the police. Not to mention, they liked to burglarize homes. He really wasn't up to another failed burglary with his boys. Every time they broke into a house, it seemed like they would always come out with no money and a homicide.

As he got up and walked outside of the gate to call Mike to see what was keeping him, a white Mazda pulled up and parked just outside the playground. Montega paid the car no mind and scrolled down the list of numbers in his Blackberry phone. As he glanced over to where the car had stopped, his eyes got hijacked by nothing but hips, ass, and titties. Out of the driver's side emerged a new source of eye candy. Shorty was graham-cracker complexioned and pretty in the face, with curvy hips, titties, and an ass so big and round that all conversation came to an end. She had no stomach and a slim waist. Half her face was hidden behind big sunglasses.

The closer he got, the more majestic she became, sending off signals of sexual availability from the shift of her wide hips. She had soft, straight, mahogany Indian hair framing doll-like cheekbones and Asian eyes. She wore big, round, gold earrings with the name 'Breezy' cutting across the middle, encrusted in diamonds. Her T-shirt hugged her upper frame like a corset. Her Dolce & Gabbana shorts cuffed her ass cheeks and exposed her thick thighs and bow legs. She wore gold, thong-strap sandals by Versace exposing her pretty, black painted toes. Montega stood there with his mouth wide open until he saw her companion step out of the passenger's side. This one was blessed with an almond skin complexion, but she looked like a feminine version of his younger brother, Taliban. Her soft, shiny, shoulder-length hair and alluring figure rivaled her girlfriend, Breezy, who stood with her two cousins, Jasmine and Gi-Gi.

Kia, Montega mumbled as his sexual transmutation began to fade.

He changed his expression as his older sister approached him. "Me and you need to talk. Now," she said, grabbing him by the wrist and pulling him over to a large tree near the pavement.

Kia and her girlfriends rarely came around Summerville. They were a different breed of women who enjoyed the finer things in life. Although her mother lived in Summerville, Kia had her own apartment in the North East of Philadelphia. Ever since she moved,

Montega rarely got the chance to see her because he never left the block.

"What's up, sis? What I do now?" he asked with sarcasm, tilting his head to the side to steal a quick glance at her girlfriend.

"You know what you did," she responded abruptly. "What happened with KK, Kenny?"

"How the fuck am I supposed to kn—"

"Stop bullshittin' me, boy. I know you like an open book. You might think you have all these people fooled, but I still got spies who are my eyes and ears. Remember Tammy? Well, she said she saw you that morning out in the playground with KK. Next thing she knows, he's dead in Smoke's house. You so stupid, boy. That's your problem. You never leave the block. Plus, you and KK didn't even like each other anyway, so don't insult me. Now, what happened?"

Montega looked away from his sister's beautiful brown eyes as he took in some fresh air and exhaled. "Well, if you know me so well, you already know the answer to your own question." His voice was cold, his eyes heavy, his energy dark and challenging.

Kia took in all this and shook her head and asked, "Why would you do that?"

Montega shoved his hands in his pockets and spat on the ground before saying, "A few months ago, Razor got into it with KK's people and ended up rockin' one of 'em. Word on the street was that KK was plottin' on my man. He was plannin' on takin' me out the same time he got Smoke outta the picture for Mike. I found this out from Rom before I got him out the way," he said nonchalantly. "It's a dog-eat-dog world, sis, and I'm nobody's next meal... Neither are my homies—or my family for that matter. You should know that by now."

Kia shook her head and frowned, wondering where it had all gone wrong with her brother. She knew he was distraught about his mother's death, but the way he lived his life was scary.

"Kenny, you need to stop this shit before you end up in jail or dead like Daddy. Do you think you can continue to kill and not get caught? Newsflash, dummy, there is no limit on a murder. All they need is probable cause, and your ass is gone. You are twenty-four years old and still doing hand-and-hand hustling on the corner. When are you going to see that this ain't it? I expect shit like this from Rafeek but not you. Do you like your choices, Kenny?"

"Dead, maybe, but in jail? I don't think so. Before they put me in a jail cell, they'll see me in hell," Montega boasted.

Kia rolled her eyes disapprovingly. "See, that's what I'm talking about right there. You talk about trying to get rich, but from the looks of it, all you're looking to do is get booked like every other wanna-be gangster in Philadelphia. Breezy's father will tell you. The jails are overcrowded with stupid fools like you. Killing people doesn't put money in your pockets; it just puts money in the pockets of those greedy lawyers down at CJC, or if you're not lucky, it could put money on that hard head of yours. When are you going to see that?" she asked while peering into his cold, beautiful eyes.

Before Montega could answer, Gi-Gi interrupted, sizing him up seductively. "Why you ain't come to my birthday party, handsome? I know you got my invitation because your friend Razor was there."

Because I don't know you like that, he thought.

All of Kia's girlfriends admired Montega's swag. Truth be told, he could have them all except for Breezy, who was too into her boo, Kev from South Philly, to notice his potential. Montega slowly sized her up from her toes to her head. He admired Gi-Gi's mocha shade. She was thicker than her cousin Breezy, but like everyone else on her mother's side, chinky eyes and fat asses were their signature.

"I don't do parties," Montega admitted. "For one, my money funny, and two, I'm just barely makin' it. I don't want to be in there frontin' like J-Black, looking like I got it when I don't."

Gi-Gi put her hands on her hips and said, "Now, Kenny, you know you don't need no money to get a bitch. All you have to do is smile, with your handsome self."

Montega blushed unwillingly just as a car horn honked. He looked to see a champagne-colored Mercedes Benz double parked in the street. Reek stepped out of the car and got into his own. Mike signaled for Montega to join him, which caused Kia to suck her teeth and shake her head.

"I see your *boss* is home," she said sarcastically.

"Yo, watch your mouth, sis. Bosses give orders. Ironically, the only orders I take is from the man in the mirror," Montega said sharply as he turned to walk off.

"Yeah, *well*, I can't tell," Kia fired back with attitude. "It seems to me everyone uptown jumps to Mike's orders. When is he going to start jumping for you?"

Montega flagged her and said over his shoulder, "I'm a Silent King, pretty girl. I may not wear a crown, but I'm regal enough. Besides, you know what they say; success never happens when you want it to, but it will surprise you when you least expect it."

Kia watched as her brother got into the car and closed the door. She realized it was pointless to reason with him; he was just too far gone. She just hoped he didn't have to learn the hard way, because sometimes, the hard way ended up being a dead end.

Chapter Five

Crash Dummy
CRUISING UPTOWN...

"I liked you better when you was broke..."

— MILLION-DOLLAR MIKE

"Young! It's the life... Once again, it's the life... Yes! I don't know why I'm... so high on... so high on... so high... high off of life...

Montega sat comfortably in the passenger seat of the S550, zoning out to the old Jay-Z *Black Album*, while Mike cruised through each hood to be seen.

Summerville had never been known for a dull moment. It was a section in East Germantown broken up in four parts. Homicide Summerville extended from Wister Street to Marshall State's playground. Most of the blocks were connected to the main strip—a wide, two-way street of Chinese stores, motorcycle bars, pizza shops, and bootleg stores. Many of the row houses were rundown or abandoned. Others were broken down into slumlord efficiencies.

Then there was East Side SV, an area that extended to Martin Luther King High School. The heart of Eastside was decorated with a maze of row houses bunched tightly from one block to the next. A single Puerto Rican bodega rested in the eye of the neighborhood where most outsiders wouldn't dare set foot.

Bottom side SV was more of a darker area with a corner bar across the street from the projects. Row houses snaked up a block called Church Lane, and drug dealers took advantage of the zombie-looking crackheads that raced from the shadows to get high.

Montega was from Topside. It was a section planted in the heart of the 'Ville and shaped like a dagger, starting from the large playground, recreation center, and swimming pool. The blocks were long and full of row houses and intricate alleyways. They seemed to extend from Ardleigh to Wister Street, Matthew to Wister, and Blakemore to Wister. A one-way street called Woodlawn cut into those blocks and trailed up to the other side of Chew Avenue. Chelten and Wister Streets were the dagger's tip.

Looking over his shoulder at the up-and-coming wolf riding shotgun, Mike said, "Reek told me that y'all still movin' the same two ounces and a quarter that he been frontin' y'all from day one."

"He ain't frontin' me nothing. And to be honest, Reek need to be around when it's time to re-up. Bol be havin' us waitin' for like three to four days. What he expect us to do? Freeze time and not take care of our responsibilities? It's hard out here, and everything costs. The way he running things, you might as well call it slow money instead of fast money. It's like we working from paycheck to paycheck," Montega replied abruptly.

"I don't know about all that, but I want you to understand this; come next week, I'm givin' out nothin' but bundles if you ain't copping a point. Y'all wanna buy clothes and sneakers to impress these nothin' ass hoes out here, then that's on y'all."

"C'mon, man." Montega frowned.

"I'm serious. If y'all wanna act like young buls, then I'll treat y'all like young buls."

"Bundles, though?" Montega asked. "You serious?"

"Yeah, bundles. Fuck, you deaf? Unless y'all grabbin' four and a half, that's what y'all gonna be gettin' from now on. I ain't got time to be holdin' nobody's hand out here. Y'all too old to be hustling with the same amount of work. It's dudes buying half a joint right now. I'm getting too much work as it is, and I don't need nobody in my car that ain't trying to get rich with me. So if y'all want to be broke, this car pullin' off next week. If you ain't got thirty-five hundred to cop, you gettin' bundles, so tell all them dudes what I said!" Mike barked as Montega looked out the window.

"Where we goin' anyway, man?" He sighed with frustration.

"Reek told me that some dude name Money from up Locust Avenue been cuttin' sales around one of my spots. I need you to go holla at him for me. Let him know that if I catch his ass out on my block again, he might as well go casket shoppin'," Mike explained.

Montega twisted up his face. He was already pissed about the bundles; now he was being told to do something that he didn't want to do like he was some crash dummy. He knew who Money was and the reputation he had, but Mike didn't.

In fact, at one point, Montega was fucking Money's baby mom until Money found out about it and beat her ass. The only reason he didn't come after Montega was the rumors of some dude called the Phantom, who was supposedly affiliated with the Silent Kings. This was most certainly not going to settle well with him—this, Montega knew.

"Yo, man, why Black can't handle this?" Montega complained.

"'Cause I asked you. Fuck, you scared or something?" Mike shot back. "If you scared, I can drop you off and get Black."

"I ain't scared, big homie. Scared is asking someone to do a job that they can do themselves. That's scared," he said, glaring at Mike.

"You got a lot of mouth for someone who still ain't copping a point. I liked you better when you was flat broke." Mike turned the steering wheel right while mumbling, "Sometimes, I wonder why you ain't dead yet."

Montega snorted out a weak chuckle, drowning out Mike's comment with sarcasm. Mike shook his head, already knowing the reply. *I'm hard to kill.*

It was what Montega told everyone who asked that question. Really it was just an early invitation to the grave and a challenge for all looking to make a name for themselves.

Although Mike didn't see eye-to-eye with this ambitious hustler, he respected the man's ghost. Montega lived life like every day was his last with only one goal: to get rich or die trying.

When Mike pulled up to the block where Money hung out, he and Montega saw him seated on the steps of an abandoned house with his team and a few chicks from around the neighborhood. Mike pulled up in front of the crib, and Montega got out. At that moment, all eyes were on him. It was no secret how Montega rolled. Everyone who kept their ears to the streets heard about the Blood Money Mafia, who changed their name to the Silent Kings, mainly from the stories about J-Rider and Killa, who shot at the police task force from the high rises in the projects and got away. There was also Lil' Man, who rode on a Yamaha Banshee with an AK-47 assault rifle slung over his back. But the most recognition was given to the mastermind.

"Aye, Money, let me holla at you for a sec," Montega said, stepping onto the pavement.

Money puffed up with pride. "You can holla at me right here."

Montega looked at Money's entourage of would-be thugs and fake hustlers, shook his head, and replied, "Aye, Money, we ain't gonna do it like this, yo. You really want me to put your business out in front of all these people? Now we can talk like men, or you can dress up for a storm. Either way makes no difference to me."

"What's that supposed to mean?" Money challenged.

"There's a black cloud in this city, and it ain't that Chinese gang. You already know it. Anybody can get rained on, and you damn sure ain't untouchable. You can get caught slippin' while you're walkin' outta Patrice's crib in the a.m. Take heed to the forecast, and come with me."

Money looked at his boys who had his back if anything went down then got up to meet Montega. "What's up," he asked as they began to walk up the block.

"Look, homie, do yourself a favor and stay off Blakemore Street unless you got a death wish."

"What?" Money asked in a hostile tone while stopping midstride in the middle of the block.

"Relax, yo. I'm trying to save a life here," Montega said calmly, gesturing with his hands. "I ain't come here to rumble, and I ain't come here to shoot you. I came here to warn you. Dudes been seeing you directing sales from the top of Locust Street. What did you think was gonna happen? You thought we were gonna just sit around and not say anything?"

"Y'all act like we ain't from the same hood. We apart of the 'Ville too," Money said.

Montega's face tightened. "Man, y'all motherfuckas ain't never loved us, so let's be for-real here. You act like me and your BM ain't used to talk. She got a big mouth, dog. She told me how you and your homies be talking shit about us. I'm cool with that though. You got a right to speak freely in your own crib. And every man's crib is his castle. You got the right to act as if you didn't just throw a fucking rock at a giant, knowing you a little nigga and always will be." Montega spat to the ground to calm himself. It was slowly becoming a habit for him. He then said, "But when you step out of your comfort zone and wander… now, that's when you got a problem." He tapped Money on the arm. "Like I said, I ain't come here to fight with you. I just want you to think about what I said." Montega began to walk away mumbling, "The graveyards are packed as it is."

Money couldn't hear his last reply but knew it was something he'd rather not listen to. Montega calmly walked back to the car.

He was pissed, not at Money but at Mike and the way he'd been acting since he'd got out of prison. His sister's words were starting to hit even harder. He was no one's crash dummy. Once he got back inside the Benz, Mike pulled off. "So what did he say?" Mike asked as he noticed Montega's calm demeanor.

"He aight. I think we got a clear understanding now, but yo, don't do that no more."

"Do what?" Mike asked with a crooked eyebrow.

"Don't put me under the gun like that again. If Reek scared ass got a problem with bol, then he should have checked him, not me," Montega replied with an attitude. Mike didn't respond. He glanced over his shoulder and saw the anger coming from the man in the passenger's seat.

Montega was heated. He hated playing messenger because he usually pissed somebody off in the end. In this case, it was Money.

As they drifted to the red light of an intersection, the sound of tires screeching took a halt beside them. The horrific sound caused them to jump out of their skin. Montega's eyes grew wider than he dared to admit. Even Mike felt the thunderous beat of his own heart punching at his chest. Both had been in a lot of drama and done things to people that left them forever paranoid. Montega reached for his hip to find nothing there. He left his gun stashed in a car tire around Ardleigh Street.

The blue BMW 745 stopped on the passenger's side with the rapid sound of laughter. Montega's bright-brown eyes slowly hooded with annoyance. His thick lips pursed, and his jaws clenched.

"Did you see his face?" Jasmine asked her two girlfriends inside the BMW. They were all cracking up in tears.

Montega looked past Jazz to the passenger, who was an Italian girl with dark hair. She was cracking up, along with the pretty, brown-skinned diva in the back seat. Even Mike had to smile though he almost shitted on himself.

Before Montega could gain the emotion to curse them out, the light turned green and the girls peeled off.

Bitches, he thought. "I see everybody got jokes now," Montega said with an attitude. "Yo, you need to check your shorty and her girlfriends. If I was strapped, this wouldn't have been no laughing matter. By the way, who *was* her girlfriends?"

"They out of your league, young bol. One is the daughter of the mob boss Valentino. Her name Ebo. The other is Amber. She be all in them magazines and videos. Dudes in jail used to go crazy over that bitch's shots."

"What she do?" asked a clueless Montega.

"What you think? She showing off that phat ass of hers. You ain't never see her body? I ain't gonna hold you. I was half tempted to try and fuck her. I'm just not tryna mess up what me and Jazz got going on. Plus, they supposed to be best friends."

"Best friends, huh?" Montega said, rubbing his beard. "Aye, what's good with that chick that be with my sister? I think her name is Breezy. I ain't know shorty was so bad until now."

"Shorty fuck with Kev from South Philly. That's his lil' bitch. You might as well forget about her," Mike warned.

"I don't give a damn about no clown from South Philly. What was that supposed to do? Shake me up? That's just another place in the city with dudes who bleed just like us. Yeah, they might catch wreck, but you better believe they aware of us too," Montega said.

"Yeah, well, she don't want no broke ass nigga who gets bundles for a living; I know that. Plus, Kev my cousin's righthand man. Now, go 'head with that thug-life bullshit you be hearing in them 2Pac songs. Keep letting 2Pac put a battery in your back if you want. Your ass will end up somewhere stinkin'," Mike warned again.

"Picture that," Montega mumbled.

Truth be told, he did hear about Mike's cousin Shug from South Philly. He supplied most of the city, and his name was feared all over Pennsylvania. He had wolves on almost every block in Philly, from Tasker Street to Fern rock, and everyone knew he represented the Underworld, which had headquarters in New York and Los Angeles. It was controlled by two powerful people—Deshawn Butler and Clyde White. There were thirty heads in the Underworld, and Shug was one of them. That only meant one thing; Montega was way out of his league. He knew this; however, he was just too damn proud to admit it.

Chapter Six

Merciless Retaliation

"Sooner or later, dudes is gonna know you're the Phantom."

— RAZOR

Later that night, after coming from Buffy's bar in Nicetown, Mike dropped Montega off at the bottom of Blakemore Street. "Holla at me next week if you got the thirty-five hundred. Other than that, you already know what it is," he said before pulling off.

"Yeah, whatever," Montega mumbled as he went into the trunk of an abandoned car to retrieve his stash. He shut the trunk and stuffed the bundle of ten-dollar glass caps into his pocket. He went to cross the street when bright lights beamed at him. By the time he realized he was face to face with a black Range Rover, the driver beeped the horn at him as she brought the SUV to a complete stop.

Montega walked to the other side of the street as she rolled the window down.

"You need to watch where you're going if you don't want to get hit," she said in a sassy tone.

Montega turned to look at the light-skinned orchid sitting in the driver's seat with long dark hair and replied, "Obviously, I'm doing something right. I bumped into a pretty face like yours, didn't I?"

The girl smirked but rolled her eyes to keep herself from blushing.

"Please, boy. Your money ain't long enough for me. I'll have you ready to rob your plug with the appetite I have for nice things."

As cruel as she sounded, Montega found her interestingly true. However, he wouldn't give her the benefit of doubt.

"What makes you think I'm that easy that I would waste my bread on you?"

"Waste?" she repeated, feeding into his insult. "Boy, you better go play with one of them dirty bitches around here and be satisfied because dealing with a girl like me will only lead you two places—dead or in jail." She let her foot off the brake pedal and continued. "See, I just saved your life."

"My hero," Montega said with a sarcastic smirk as he watched her brake lights shrink in the distance. He shook his head before heading up Woodlawn. The bright-yellow rectangular sign shined like the North Star on the one-way intersection of Blakemore and Woodlawn. The smell of Chinese food could be inhaled even from three blocks down.

The Chinese store sat at the corner of the intersection like a house on a hill, looking out at all the activity going on around it. On the opposite side of the street, the row houses sunk down a hill that traveled almost a hundred houses down to the end where Wister Street met. It was dark and quiet. Most of the streetlights had been shot out to keep the police's task force from watching with binoculars. At the corner, in front of the Chinese store, Razor was the only one out. He sat on the concrete step with a white styrofoam platter rested on his lap. The platter was packed with three crispy fried chicken wings dripping with grease, salt, pepper, ketchup, and hot sauce, with a side order of savory shrimp-fried rice.

Razor bit into the tender meat, ripping it off the bone as Montega appeared. The juices and sauce dripped from his lips as a ball of steam faded into the air.

"Damn dog, you stay disappearin'," Razor said with a mouthful of food. "I know you ain't go back to that bitch crib."

"Nah, bol, we just broke up. She keep comin' at me with the 'she don't know if I'm gonna live or die out here in these streets, yada,

yada, yada' bullshit. Anyway, I went to get some drinks with Mike," Montega explained. "Did you know that this dude is talkin' 'bout givin' us all bundles if we can't come up with four and a half money? Fuck that, dog. I can't live like that. I need a come-up, and I need it like yesterday. Got me checking dudes like I'm J-Black. What the hell is wrong with him?"

"Man, Mike been on some other shit ever since he came home. You see how 'jo' dudes gettin', calling him 'Million-Dollar Mike'," Razor said sarcastically. "He know damn well he ain't have no parts in old-head gettin' smoked. That was all your work. Then you keep drawlin', talkin' 'bout the Phantom did it. Watch, sooner or later, dudes gonna know that you're the Phantom, and that's when you're gonna have real problems on your hands."

"Yeah, they gonna know, aight, right before I put 'em to sleep. Besides, the only people that got me figured out is you and my sister," admitted Montega.

"Kia? Man, why you tell her? You know her and Breezy like a Wendy Williams show. They gossip about everybody," Razor countered.

"Man, Kia ain't gonna say nothing. Relax. Besides, she my walkin' diary and the only person I can talk to when I be spazzin' out. Your ass, on the other hand, ain't gonna do shit but hand me a damn Dutch."

Razor smiled as he tossed the platter to the side, took the Dutch from between his ear, and sparked up the weed before checking his silver Movado. It was 1 a.m., and no one should have been out but the fiends. A stray alley cat came up and cautiously took a wing out of Razor's tray then ran off. Razor meant to chase the fur ball until he spotted two men walking down Woodlawn with cocked fitted caps. They were coming from the direction of the school.

"Yo, you strapped?" he asked Montega.

"I got a Mac down on Ardleigh on the tire of that abandon Buick in front of the playground, but the Tommy in the trashcan beside you," Montega replied nonchalantly.

He wasn't alert, nor did he think anyone would be dumb enough to try them. Razor however looked over at the can next to the steps of the Chinese store and shook his head when he realized how much time he could have gotten if the undercover cops pulled up on him earlier. When he looked back up the block, the two men had vanished. He was then able to calm his nerves a bit.

"What's up, bol? You aight?" Montega asked, following his gaze to two more men who got out of a dark-colored car up the block and were approaching.

Razor bugged out. *They look just like the two from earlier,* he thought. Before Montega could move to the trashcan, the two guys from earlier snuck up behind him from the alley with guns pointed. "Don't fuckin' move, or I'll blow ya head off your fuckin' shoulders," the one said, pointing a silver German Ruger.

Montega froze in a panic. He didn't notice it before, but the men who had their hats cocked over their eyes also wore stockings over their faces to hide their identities. *Maybe they won't kill us,* he thought.

By that time, the other two men had arrived with guns drawn. One had a Smith & Wesson .45 ACP revolver. The other had a Taurus PT2011 .40 cal semi-automatic. Another guy, with a sawed-off, double barrel shotgun, stood a few feet away from the action as backup. The one with the Ruger did the searching. "Get the fuck on the ground 'fore I pop ya dumb ass," he said, smacking Montega in the back of the head with the steel.

Montega groaned in pain as he fell to the ground, shielding the back of his head. "Ah shit, man! What the fuck?" he snapped before watching Razor get the same treatment.

Montega's heart raced with both anger and paranoia. He had mixed feelings of dying on the corner after the robbers got what they wanted. Besides the fact he had close to $1,000 in his pocket, he was even angrier when he saw his homie get smacked with the gun.

You motherfuckers better be about y'all work, he thought as he eyed the trashcan only a few feet away. It was impossible to try them now. He had gotten caught slipping again, messing around with the corner on the night shift, and there was nothing he could do about it. The first time was by three women who called themselves the Black Hornets; now it was four gunmen.

Once the men got what they wanted, the first two moved out while the one with the Ruger and the guy with the shotty stayed until they had the money tucked away. The goon with the shotty tucked the pump down his pants leg and slowly limped away. The last took a look at Montega and Razor long and hard as if he were debating whether or not he wanted to kill them. He then said, "If y'all get up, I'm rockin' ya both to sleep."

Razor sighed with relief as his heart beat up his chest. The gunman backed his way across the street. When he got to the other side, he turned to jog. Montega made eye contact with his homie, who was shaking his head, knowing what he was thinking. Every attack on Montega's family and friends was like a slap in the face. As soon as he saw an opportunity, he pounced up. One leap, and he was at the trashcan.

The man with the Ruger heard metal scraping against the concrete and turned around. When he saw Montega pulling out an old TA5 Thomson machine gun from the rusted can, his eyes bulged. It was an old fully automatic weapon from the 40s that Montega claimed after a successful home invasion. It was rusted black with brown wooden highlights and had a seventy-five-round drum of .45 hollow points. For some odd reason, the robbers froze.

"You want to take something, take these with you!"

Montega aimed and pulled back the trigger, causing eardrums to ring. Bullets and fire spewed out of the barrel. The quiet night was shattered by the loud crack of gunfire. Montega's victim took the hot lead into his stomach, ripping his white T into shreds. The gunman stumbled before his body hit the ground. His homies wheeled around and returned fire in an attempt to save their man. The .44 revolver barked, and so did the double barrel shotgun and the .40 cal.

Razor ran for his gun tucked on top of a tire of a parked car nearby. Stray bullets whizzed by, and sparks flew off the mailbox Montega took cover behind, trapping him in a tight spot. The Tommy suddenly jammed. He squatted with his butt to the concrete, back to the mailbox, trying to dislodge the shell stuck inside. The frightening sound of ricocheting bullets struck the iron mailbox.

The men began to walk them down with thunderous cracks of fire. Stray bullets pelted anything in their way, and copper shells flipped out and tinked as they hit the ground. The men knew where he was hiding. Montega was a dead man. Out of nowhere, Razor popped up and fired a Glock 17 at the goon with the shotgun. The first shot missed, but the second tore through the left side of his neck. He stumbled to the pavement, dropping the gun, and fled for his life. Montega finally got the shell out then popped up to spray again.

The other two shot it out with the two brave hustlers but quickly retreated after running out of bullets. The assailant with the Ruger alone would have to deal with an angry Montega as he approached with a smoking Tommy gun. He tried to crawl away, but Montega kicked him hard in the gut. The assailant turned over on his back and looked up at his assassin.

Montega was stunned when he removed the stocking cap from the wanna-be killer's face. It was Money from Locust Avenue. He looked shaken up and in pain. Montega's face turned sinister. "Oh yeah, Money? You sent those bols to rob us, you piece of shit?" he asked as he hovered over Money like a bald eagle.

The sound of police sirens was buzzing from the distance, and Razor grew uneasy. "Ay, Tega, we gotta bounce," he urged, but Montega didn't respond. He kept his eyes on Money, who was pleading for his life.

Raising his TA5 at Money's head, he proclaimed, "Didn't I tell you the storm was coming, main-man? Look at your ass now!"

With that, he pulled the trigger so that Money felt nothing but hard rain.

Rat-tat-tat! Click!

Razor watched as Money's skull splattered before his eyes. Montega lowered his weapon, his eyes glued to the murder scene. An instant flashback of his mother lying in a casket clouded his vision, followed by the corpse of Million-Dollar Moe. This really disturbed him.

Seeing the expression on his partner's face, Razor grabbed Montega by the arm and pulled him down the block to hide in Taliban's mom's house.

Taliban's mother, Stacy, welcomed them with open arms. "What the hell happened up there?" she asked as the two walked in.

"I don't know, Stacy, but we got the hell outta dodge," Montega lied.

"I know that's right. Oh my God, was your brother up there?" she asked, ready to flip out. "He hasn't been here all day."

"Naw, he wasn't up there," Razor replied before turning on the TV.

Stacy sighed in relief. "Well, y'all two stay in the house. I don't want y'all going up there tonight. It's too much shootin' going on," she lectured as if they were still children.

She then went back into the kitchen to drink some Bacardi lemon vodka with her girlfriend, missing the sight of Montega detaching the seventy-five-round drum, and stashing the murder weapon under her couch. Once she was out of sight, Montega looked over at his partner with relief. "Bol, you crazy," Razor said, shaking. "You gonna have to get rid of that old piece of shit now."

"I'll sell it to my man in West Oak Lane in the morning before I head to the Badlands." Montega eased back in the chair while reflecting on sending Money to hell. All he knew was that one day, he would join him. That was what he feared. Just then, his sister came to mind. She was right; he was too far gone. He had just killed again, and if he didn't lay low, he could very well be the star cast of A&E's *First 48.*

Chapter Seven

The Commission
CALIFORNIA...

"This is one vote you won't be getting..."

— DIAMOND "THE BLACK KISS OF DEATH" WHITE

On the west coast, in the beautiful hills of Hollywood, overlooking the city of Los Angeles, a meeting between both sides of the Underworld was held in a secluded mansion.

The room was large enough to hold a press conference and expensive enough to be an art gallery. Its tan limestone walls were decorated with expensive oil paintings and hand-crafted sculptures. An oversized stone fireplace took up nearly the entire end of the left-hand corner, while on the right, the floor to ceiling window with the immaculate view spread from one side to the other like an invisible wall. The sky had never looked so blue from inside. The smell of burning cigars, cigarettes, and oil burners filled the air with a ghostly white cloud of smoke. Silence consumed most of the men inside as business was discussed tediously.

Deshawn Butler was a man of power in New York. He ran the city's black market with an iron fist. Those that did not ride his wave of success drowned under it. He and his organization were the royalty of smuggling, which was the reason he changed his father's sigil from the Wolfpack to the Underground Kings. There wasn't a product that didn't touch their hands before it hit the streets—whether it be jewels, exotic animals, drugs, weapons, women... you name it.

Butler might have been intelligent and an extremely wealthy man; his looks, however, put fear in those he stood face to face with. The hideous scar running down the right side of his face was pure evidence of his diabolical appearance. He a Black man with a clean and shiny bald head. His eyes were dark and cold as a winter night. His lips were thick, and his nose slender at the bridge but wide at the nostrils. He kept his face shaved clean and smooth as a baby's bottom. He looked dapper in a dark-blue, double-breasted suit designed by Yves Saint Laurent and black Louis Vuitton shoes. He sat at one end of the fifty-foot long, rectangular, black marble table. His partner and head of the Great White Organization, Clyde White, was seated on the other side.

Like his father, Clyde was tall in stature but lacked definition due to neglect of exercise and dieting. He naturally had a slim build with light-brown skin and a high, squared-off head he kept sharply shaped-up with a fade in the back. His face was tightly drawn with high cheekbones like his sister. Sharp—brown eyes that could be mistaken for hazel in the light—gazed upon the members in the room. His small nose and extensive pale lips surrounded by a five o'clock shadow were the highlight of his features. He arrogantly prided himself in a tailormade gray Brioni suit with black-colored shoes.

Standing behind him stood his enforcer and commander of his army, Justin, flashing his typical stone face.

Seated amongst the well-dressed men in $5,000 suits was Thomas Gonzalez, better known as Tommy Gun. His drug operation, Guns and Roses, spread throughout the south and was heavy in Atlanta. He sat beside Semok Budinov, the head of the Russian Mafia in America. There was also Carlos Morin, the international designer drug's mastermind; Miami George, the boss in Florida who had the whole state on lock from politicians to low-level drug dealers; Stoney Williams, a Haitian leader who ran a huge exotic weed operation from the Florida coast to New York; and Chavo Garcia, who had connections with the Mexican Mafia. He sat next to the head of the Asian gang, known as the Black Cloud, who was seated beside the Pennsylvania bully, Shareek 'Shug' Burmington.

These men were all apart of Clyde's circle of bosses. Many had been with him from the start. Some were picked up along the way. All were rich and extremely dangerous.

The men listened as Chavo spoke firmly to the Underworld secret society. Chavo was a tan Mexican who acted as if he didn't have African American in his blood. He stood just under 5,5", stocky, with a haircut so close you would think he was bald. He wore a gray Salvatore Ferragamo suit with black shoes, a white shirt, and a hand-printed tie.

"The gap that we had in Mexico is closing," he said. "The war between the cartels has gotten so bad over the last few months that it will be hard to even consider getting our product through a pipeline from Bolivia." Chavo adjusted his collar and unloosened his tie a bit before folding his hands on the table. He shook his head and ended with, "It's a fucking disaster if you ask me."

"Facts, and let's not forget the problems in South America," Tommy Gun said, seated a few chairs down from him. "With all the terrorism going on, it's gonna be even harder for our suppliers to get the product out of the country."

"Deshawn," Clyde said, causing heads to turn. "Any way your people can help us out with this?"

"I wouldn't count on it; it's election time. Government officials and law enforcement agencies are looking to make examples out of anyone who would dare challenge them. They've got dogs that can smell drugs out of a smuggler's ass. I can't risk having that, hand-and-hand with the supply I already have. Sorry, but there's nothing my people can do to stop this."

"What about the South Africans?" a smooth baritone voice asked, commanding attention. Everyone turned to look at Shug. He was suited and booted as well and wore dark shades to hide his lazy eye. "They don't seem to have a problem bringing that work into the country. Maybe we need to pull up on them and see if we can't cut into their line."

Chavo shrugged. "Either them or perhaps Verningo Castor."

Tommy Gun shook his head, saying, "Whoa, Chavo. Let's think about this here. We both know those two names will be like opening a can of worms when Diamond finds out about it."

A wave of murmuring began as the men began to look amongst each other. Chavo snorted with disgust. "Do you hear yourself, Tommy? This organization is not based on one person alone."

"Understandable, but it takes every last member in both the Great White Organization and in the Underground Kings to make a decision like this. Without Diamond's vote, we're back to square one."

"Well, where's she right now, huh?" Chavo asked angrily. "She may be the new head of the Elcano Cartel in Cuba, but she's still apart of this secret society. Meaning she has to—"

Suddenly, the sound of clicking heels echoed off the marble floors outside the room, grabbing their attention. Everyone turned toward the door. Clyde's younger sister, Diamond, appeared, dressed in a tan Roberto Cavalli two-piece, form fitting business suit that complemented her curvy frame.

All eyes admired her as she walked in. Diamond White prided herself being the female version of her father—the late Charles White. She was strong, intelligent, self-made, and notoriously the most sought after. She was a work of art—heart-shaped face and sharp, beautiful eyes with full lashes so developed that they looked heavy when she would stare. She had a thin nose perfectly placed above her signature puckered lips. She walked in with perfect posture, shifting her hips evenly while planting one foot in front of the other.

Like an exotic candy bar dipped in sweetness, she sparkled deliciously with light, cocoa-butter skin. She raked the long, loopy, dark hair from her face and let it travel down her back. The low-cut blouse she wore showed off her firm bust, and the mid-thigh cut of her skirt accented the power of her glistening legs.

Not even Deshawn's girlfriend, Tanya, could match the Snow White Queen. When one thought of Diamond White, they thought of two things—gorgeous and deadly. Her beauty was more than skin deep. If people could get past her distrust and bitchy attitude, they would see that she was a strong, devoted woman who knew what she wanted in life. She loved being in control and being the center of attention. To her, her body was like a sacred temple made of gold, which she showed off every chance she got. But inside was a burning inferno of *do it yourself* masculinity.

"Sorry I'm late," she said, strutting to an empty seat with her seven-foot-tall bodyguard, Bain, following.

"Seems to me you're always late," Clyde challenged, irritated by her supermodel entrance.

"Well, if you don't like it, then start without me from now on. It makes no difference to me," Diamond replied, taking a seat in the vacant chair. She sat her Chloe bag on the table and then crossed her smooth legs. "So what did I miss?"

Deshawn watched her arrogance with disgust. A part of him wanted to crush her like a little bug; then there was the part that wanted to fuck her senseless, and he was sure that others felt the same way. Clyde quickly took the attention off his sister and began.

"We were discussing the problem going on in Mexico with the cartel pipeline. We won't be able to move the cocaine across the border if these cartels continue to wage war against each other. What we need is a new pipeline that will guarantee at least half of our product out of Bolivia and onto American soil."

Diamond played in her French-manicured nails, saying, "Has anyone thought of trying to reason with the cartels?"

Chavo grunted. "You're kidding me, right? Do you actually think the cartels will listen? Have you seen the news lately? They're chopping heads off left and right if they don't know who you are. They do not want to talk. They want to kill."

Diamond shrugged before glancing at Deshawn. "Well, I'm sure there are a few government officials you guys have on the payroll, right? Why not ask them for help? You guys are the *kings* of black marketing and smuggling, aren't you?"

"It's not that simple, Ms. White. There's an election going on. No one wants to risk their job helping—"

"But everyone wants to get paid," Diamond said, cutting him off. "I don't understand this shit." She shook her head and re-crossed her legs the other way. Taking a deep breath to relax while clipping a loose strand of hair behind her ear, she asked, "So how do we plan on resolving this?"

"The Agugbo Brothers," Chavo said proudly with a smirk. "Either them or Verningo Castor."

Diamond's face turned to stone.

"You guys gotta be fucking kidding me, right?" she asked, but no one answered her question. "Right?" She still got no answer. "Are you crazy? You have to be if you think for one second we're doing business with that snake. Have you forgotten what he did to our father, Clyde?"

"Look… Diamond, I don't like this anymore than you do, but this is busi—"

"The hell it is!" she fumed. "There's so many other cartels in the world that we can deal with, so don't give me that crap."

"Well, name a cartel then," Clyde fired back. "Who? Elcano? Oh, that's right, I forgot. You're in the same boat as we are. All that submarine bullshit is history with the technology they have these days. And if you continue taking chances like that, you'll find out the hard way. So who else then?"

Diamond was quiet.

When Clyde got the response he was looking for from her, he sat back calmly and folded his hands. "We need help. And Castor's the only candidate I can see that is large enough to feed our appetite. You don't believe him? Check the Forbes list. You'll find him ranked somewhere in the fifties."

"Well, if you ask me, I think it's a good idea," Chavo said, putting his two cents in.

Diamond's beautiful, ebony-brown eyes cut in his direction like a motorized tree saw. "That's the problem, Mr. Garcia. Nobody asked you anything," she retorted coldly.

"I think you need to mind your tone, Ms. White. I'm still the underboss of the Great White—"

"Fuck you," Diamond spat, causing the group to gasp.

"That's enough, the both of you!" Clyde said, banging his fist on the table.

Diamond pursed her lips at Chavo and slowly cut her eyes at her brother.

Over the years, Chavo had developed a lot of hatred for the Snow White Queen and would do anything to see that she got ignored. In his mind, besides her heroin distribution, she was a woman trying to fill a man's shoes. He hated to see a successful woman how didn't need help from a man, and most of all, he couldn't stand one with arrogance.

"Wait a second!" Shug boomed. "Have we even spoken to this dude Castor yet?"

"Not yet, but if we can have a yes vote from everyone at the table, we can send a message to Castor in Miami, telling him that we want to have a sit-down with him," Clyde answered.

"Are you guys even hearing yourselves?" Diamond asked in disbelief. "You want to make a deal with the devil? News flash. The reason I joined this organization is because you guys said that you would put Castor in a casket, not sit down and have fucking brunch with him."

Clyde looked at his hotheaded sister. "Diamond, we need this deal to go down. If not, we're screwed. Castor has everything this organization needs to stay on top—import/export mainly, crooked officers within U.S. Customs, trained smugglers. You name it, and he has it. You think that your smugglers in Cuba will last with the type of heat that's going on in this country? If we can't deal with him, then we'll just have to settle on the South African smugglers because from what I hear, they're names are ringing bells big time. Now, are you going to continue to work off your emotions, or are you going to vote with the rest of the organization? Castor or the Agugbo brothers? Which one is it?"

Upon hearing the names, Diamond's nose flared with rage. If there was anyone besides Castor she hated, it was the three South African brothers she had been trying to eliminate for over three years. She was now in a lose-lose situation. Fed up with the bullshit that had just been dumped in her lap, Diamond rose from the seat and replied, "My opinion would be to kill them both, not deal with them. If you guys are as smart as you all portray to be, you would eliminate them and take their resources for yourselves, but I see you're not." Diamond continued to look around at all twenty-nine members before continuing. "You know, there was something that my father once said when I was a little girl that stuck with me. When I was young, my father warned me about two things. He said never play with fire, and never pick up snakes, because they're both tools of the devil... Tools that cause death when you least expect it. I guess you guys have no problem selling your souls. Mine, however, is priceless, so this vote that you all have been waiting on is one vote you won't be getting from me."

The men watched in amazement as Diamond and her bodyguard headed for the door. Chavo hissed, "You see, this is the shit I'm talking about, Clyde. This is why bitches shouldn't get mixed up in a man's—"

Before he could finish his sentence, Diamond spun around with a small dagger in her hand. With a quick toss, the blade stuck in the table in front of Chavo like a dart hitting a board. The whole room went silent.

"That wasn't a mistake. Neither will the next one that pierces your Adam's apple if you don't watch your mouth."

Both Justin and Deshawn clenched their teeth as they watched her leave the room. Wong Lee smirked. Clyde shook his head and pinched the bridge of his nose in embarrassment. He thought to himself, *something has to be done about that bitch.* Judging by the unhappy faces around him, the feeling was mutual.

Deshawn was unamused by her performance as well. He really hated Diamond because he suspected her of killing his brother. Now she ran her own drug empire and was the head of her own family in the Underworld secret society. The only way she could be killed was if everyone agreed to it. With that in mind, he was ready to start an underground campaign to ice Diamond. However, he knew the first person he could convince would be Chavo.

Chapter Eight

Investigating A Ghost
ON THE CORNER OF BLAKEMORE AND WOODLAWN...

"It's no wonder the graveyards are so full of corpses."

— DETECTIVE ANTONY LUCCA

The crossroad of Blakemore Street and Woodlawn was cluttered with cop cars. An ambulance was parked on one side of the street. The news vans were on the other side. The crime scene was taped off, and well over fifty shell casings were drawn out on the ground and labeled by numbers.

In the area where last night's shooting took place, standing across the street from the Chinese store, Detective Whitehead and his partner, Detective Lucca, watched as paramedics placed the body bag on the stretcher. From there, it was shoved into the back of the awaiting ambulance.

"What do you think happened out here last night, Whitehead?" Lucca asked.

"Isn't it obvious? It's a robbery gone bad. My guess is that this guy took the money but forgot to check the victims for guns."

Detective Lucca snorted out sarcastically. "Genius. It's no wonder the graveyards are so full of corpses."

"Did you see the victim's face? Whoever slain him must have been very angry. Perhaps he knew the guy—because that's what you call overkill."

"Well, whoever it was, they better hope their prints don't show up on that shotgun we found, because if they do, somebody is gonna talk when I get through with 'em," Detective Lucca stated, letting his coattail flap while putting his hands on his waist.

Detective Whitehead hissed when he heard his cell phone ring. He pulled it out and answered. "Detective Whitehead."

"Hi, Detective, this is Detective Hasselback. I was calling to inform you about the John Doe that we found over in an alley on Locust Avenue. We have reason to believe that he was coming from your location."

Whitehead frowned. "And why do you believe that?"

"Well, when we searched him, we found four twelve-gauge shotgun rounds. Now, I just got off the phone with Detective Lucca a little earlier, and he gave me the impression that you guys recovered a shotgun," she said.

"That's correct," Whitehead confirmed, now knowing that all hope was lost on finding the others.

After he got off the phone with the detective, he frowned at his partner. "What was all that about?" Lucca asked.

"Looks like we gotta start from the bottom and work our way up. The owner of the shotgun was found dead on Locust Avenue. Must have gotten hit around here, dropped the weapon, and hightailed it up the block and around the corner."

"That explains the blood," Lucca added.

Whitehead shook his head. "Poor bastard must've lost too much blood while running."

Lucca pulled out a half empty pack of cigarettes. "Well, let's at least go find Michael Harris and probe him a bit about this. You know, break a little balls," he said before pulling one out and lighting it.

Before Whitehead could answer, his phone rang again. This time, it was his oldest daughter. "Shabree, not now. I'm busy," he snapped.

"Dag, hi to you too, Daddy," Breezy said. "Why are you treating me like a wet penny?"

"Because I'm frustrated right now. You want to know why I'm frustrated? Because one of your knucklehead friends is leaving bodies all over East Germantown."

"Why it gotta be one of my friends?" she shot.

"Well, it's somebody, and when I find out who he is, they're gonna wish they were the one being placed in body bags instead of their victims," Whitehead snapped.

"Okay, Daddy, I see you're in your bag right now, as usual. So I'll just get to the point. I didn't call for another one of your interrogations. I called for the money that you were supposed to give me like two days ago."

"Shabree, I'll call you back. Bye," he said, hanging up on her. Whitehead didn't have time to keep track of all the promises he made. To him, his job was far more important. He was a devoted officer of the law. Work came first for him, even before family. The way he saw it, if the streets were protected from drug dealers, murderers, and rapists, his family would be safe.

Detective Lucca, on the other hand, was a different story. He used his badge to intimidate and oppress people wherever he went, whether they were guilty or innocent. He grew up an outcast with his peers, and all his life, he wanted payback. At first, he harassed people to make them feel what he felt growing up around a bunch of slick Italians. But after years on the force, his abuse became a source of entertainment.

Looking at his partner, he shrugged his shoulders and said, "Kids. You gotta love 'em. Now c'mon. Let's go make someone else's life miserable."

Mike sat on the green steel bench inside the outdoor basketball court with Jasmine, Ebo, and Amber. The girls had just come from Rita's Water Ice and brought him back a strawberry Gelati. Mike had been sitting there all morning, watching the cops race up the block nonstop. E and J-Black walked into the gates and saw them chilling. They approached, shaking their heads. Mike thought it was about the cops, but truthfully, it had something to do with Amber and how fat her ass looked in a pair of army-green shorts that looked painted on.

"Police still up there parked," J-Black said, holding his phone to his ear although there was no one on the line. "It's hot as fish grease right now."

"You still ain't find out who it was that got rocked?" Mike asked before tossing the empty water ice container in the trash can. He sat back beside Jasmine and looked up at his enforcer.

"They said it was the bul Money from Locust," E explained.

"Money?" Mike snapped.

"Yeah," J-Black said with a chuckle. "They said he was trying to rob somebody and got his ass aired out."

"That's crazy. I just had Montega check that dude the other day. He must have felt some type of way and tried to rob the block. Who was out last night?"

Before E or Black could say anything, a blue Chevy Impala pulled up and stopped in front of the gate. Whitehead and Lucca got out, dressed in cheap suits but wore priceless smiles. The sound of sucking teeth and hisses followed amongst the guys. Mike looked over and hooded his eyes with pure irritation.

"Here we go." He sighed.

"Well, well, look what we got here, Whitehead. Ain't that Michael Harris, the big-time punk who thinks he's the fucking Teflon Don?" Lucca asked with sarcasm.

Whitehead looked past him at his niece-in-law and said, "Jasmine, get out of here and take your friends with you, now." He then pointed at E and J-Black. "You two, beat it."

Everyone began to walk off except for Mike. Whitehead watched Jasmine walk away before he turned to look at him. "I don't know what that girl sees in a scum like you, but it's nothing good," he said.

"You come to be her eye doctor, Whitehead, or you got something you want to say to me?" Mike asked calmly.

"Hey, watch your goddamn mouth, Harris," Lucca warned. "Don't think for a second that you got off scot-free because of that hot shot lawyer of yours. How about I let you in on a little something? I had a little talk with the United States district attorney, and they are pretty interested in your case. How about that? Whether you like it or not, you're going to do time. Trust me."

"Is that all? Because I have places to go and people to see," Mike said, stretching before he stood.

Whitehead smirked. "Oh, you definitely have some place to go. Downtown for questioning."

When Mike heard that, his cocky manor faded away altogether. He wanted to spit in the detective's face and run, but he knew he wouldn't get far, especially with a trigger-happy Lucca, who would just lie and say he thought he saw a gun. Instead, he followed them to the car. It was going to be a long ride to the Round House and an even longer waste of time and questioning.

Chapter Nine

Dead Cracked

"Send karma back around on somebody else."

— LIL' MAN

On a quiet summer evening in the heart of the Badlands of North Philadelphia, on the streets where the Hispanics flourished, a single row house stood amongst a line of abandoned houses. Inside, Lil' Man sat on his mother's brown, leather sofa, cleaning one of his AK-47s. Lil' Man was probably one of the most dangerous Puerto Ricans ever to roam the streets of North Philly. Shorter than most with dark, short, spiked hair and no facial hair, the twenty-three-year-old was highly respected by his peers and feared throughout his community because of his hot temper.

On the opposite side of the coffee table, searching through the internet on her tablet, was his fine nineteen-year-old sister, Faith. She had dark hair like her brother, but hers was long and shiny. She sat with her legs crossed as the touch screen had her full attention. Faith was an exceptional young lady who enjoyed learning new things. If people looked past her innocence and beauty, they would see her need to be accepted by men as an equal. Faith would also downplay the female cause and often side with the men out of pure admiration.

It took a second for Montega to realize this and recognize her desire to win. All day, she played strategic games like Chess, Battleship, and Risk, carefully studying her opponent's moves. She spent her whole life trying to fit in with her brothers, waiting to distance herself from her feminine side, which she felt was her biggest weakness.

Upstairs, a bed was squeaking from some extra-curricular activities. "Damn, I wish they hurry up with that bullshit," Lil' Man said, irritated with the sound of the bed thumping in tune with the moans and shouts of pleasure coming from upstairs.

Faith paid her brother no mind. She was too into her portable computer.

She secretly wished she could do the same as her girlfriend upstairs but knew that was impossible. She was trapped in her mother's house with two over-protective brothers for prison guards. Lil' Man's reputation was so notorious; it was impossible for her to even have a study-buddy. If it wasn't Lil' Man scaring her boyfriends away, it was her powder-snorting, tall, lanky brother—Ski-Mask.

More thumping upstairs caused the ceiling to fume with dust. "What the fuck, yo? Could ya keep it down a little!" he shouted up the steps in Spanish, but the thumping continued.

Up inside the bedroom, Faith's best friend, Montega, held Juicy by the waist, watching her soft, cushioned ass roll from the arch of her back into the direction of his pelvis in a reverse-cowgirl position. The headboard slammed against the walls with every thrust she delivered. Montega closed his eyes and bit down on his bottom lip to the warm, tight sensation of Latin pussy. His smooth hands squeezed her succulent ass cheeks while she looked back at him with lust. Her hair, long and wet, swooped to one side, and her face countered. She was a gorgeous half-Mexican, half-Puerto Rican redbone who had a thin nose that sported a stud nose ring, pouty lips, brown eyes, and a tattoo of red lips on the left side of her neck with Montega's name above it.

Montega's hands slid up her washboard stomach, cuffing up her breast. Juicy placed her hands over his as if guiding him to her sensitive places. He softly pinched her nipples then lightly tugged on them until they were rock solid.

"Owww, Kenny!" Juicy moaned to the stimulating feeling.

What Montega loved about her besides her pretty face and

bangin' body was the fact that she was a rider he molded from a young age. Juicy was only a year older than Faith, but she had more street smarts than the average hustler in his mid-twenties. Her youth fueled her spontaneity. Finding a husband, having babies, and being responsible weren't the first things on her mind unless she saw Montega in the picture with her. She cared deeply about her first love. Even though he wasn't committed to her, she preferred to stay on good terms with him. Aside from her big heart and healing nature, she had the unwanted gift of drawing men to her beauty even while appearing uninterested in them. Her love for Montega was dangerous. He had saved her life once, and for that, she was forever indebted to him.

Heavy breaths of passion continued to fill the room. Montega's hands slid from her C-cup breasts up to her neck as he watched her apple-shaped ass grind. It was no wonder everywhere she went, car horns honked, and tires screeched to a halt for her. Juicy grabbed his wrist and brought his hands to her face. She took one of his fingers and sucked on it with a lustful hunger. She aggressively sighed from his penetration.

"Fuck me hard, papi. Matter fact, put it in my ass," she demanded through clenched teeth before easing out his dick to slide it in her tight hole.

Juicy may have had only one partner in her entire life, but her sexual experience was extensive. Montega had corrupted her with porn videos and scandalous sex tapes that she studied and imitated. No one would have guessed that Montega was the only man she had ever been with. He held her by her curvaceous thighs, watching her drop down on his swollen shaft.

"Umm, yesss, uhhh, papi, do me dirty! You fucking animal!"

"You like fucking this animal, don't you?" Montega asked through clenched teeth.

"No!"

"Yes you do. Stop lying, bitch, 'fore I bust this ass wide open. You want me to put all this dick up in you at once?"

"No, papi, don't! I can't take it all. You know I... uhh!"

Montega slammed his pelvis into her ass, burying his entire manhood into her. Juicy moaned with pain and pleasure.

"Shut up and take this dick while you got the chance," he grunted.

"I am... I am taking it," Juicy growled out while trying to throw it back.

Montega felt himself reaching the point of no return. He had been there so many times, and every time was just as good as the first. "I'm 'bout to nut," he grunted while bouncing her up and down on his exploding erection.

"Oh, yes, papi, cum for me," Juicy whined as she came instantly with a white discharge that oozed down her inner thighs.

"Yeah, mami, this is my ass, ain't it?" Montega asked while still pounding her from the back while softening up.

"Yes! Yes, it's all yours!" Juicy shrieked with a delightful smile, knowing that she satisfied him so much, as he did her, every time they fucked. "We make a damn good team, don't we?" she asked after he finally pulled out her ass and lay on his back.

"Like Bonnie and Clyde," he replied as she lay on top of him. That was Juicy's favorite song. She had bought *The Blue Print 2* just so she could play the song with Jay-z and Beyoncé, imagining that it was Montega and her instead. Montega, however, liked the 2pac version better. To him, the song explained both his gun and his girl, and there was no better feeling than bussing a shot off except bussing a nut. He ran his fingers through her long, silky, auburn hair, breathing fiercely.

Although they weren't a couple, Juicy was Montega's ride-or-die chick. She would do anything for him at any given moment. He was her first, and as she always told him, he would be her last. After the two got washed and dressed, they headed back downstairs where Lil' Man and his sister were chilling in the living room.

"Y'all need a hotel for all that noise y'all was making," Faith said with a giggle.

"Nah, fuck that," Lil' Man disagreed while assembling his gun. "They need a fucking habitat for all that shit. They sounded like two wild animals. *Uh! Papi! Uh, put it in my ass*," he mimicked.

Juicy stuck her middle finger up at him as she walked over to the couch and sat next to her best friend. Ignoring her, Lil' Man looked over at Montega as he took a seat in the corner to read the newspaper, and said, "Yo, you tryna roll with me tonight, cabrón? Me and Ski-Mask are goin' out on *a robbin' spree... We'll make mon-ey?"* He did a poor imitation of Biggie Smalls. "Besides, I was doin' some thinkin', and if you need four and a half, this is your chance. I know you're dead cracked after last night. That's why we need to return the favor, nah-mean? Send karma back around on somebody else. You just gotta be ready for her when she come back around." Lil' Man cocked back the machine gun and placed it on the table before sitting back like a mastermind.

"Beto, why are you trying to get Kenny involved in your bullshit? He don't need no detectives lookin' for him the way they do you. Besides, y'all don't bring back no real money anyway," Faith said, looking away from her iPad.

"Look, bitch, these detectives ain't got shit on me. Now mind your fuckin' business. Montega, you comin' with us, or are you gonna listen to this bitch, who never had to worry about money a day in her life? Fuck she know what real money look like anyway, she's a dependent?"

"Where we going?" Montega asked calmly. He set the paper on his lap while looking at his deranged homie.

"I don't know. I was thinking about some big-time projects that's making a lot of money. You know how I do, something out of the ordinary. What do you think about Tasker projects?" Lil' Man asked.

"Oh, hell no," Juicy spat, throwing her hair over her shoulder. "You ain't takin' him back to no South Philly with that crap, Beto. Them guys don't play around. My brother told me that—"

"Fuck ya brother, with his bitch-ass," Lil' Man stormed. "I rode up on that fool the other day on my Banshee while he was at the gas station, and the puta almost shit himself. Fuck he know about anything but fixin' fuckin' cars and plantin' stash spots? When I need a new muffler or a fuckin' tire change, I'll ask him. Now, will y'all let Montega make his own decision? Damn!"

Montega gently rubbed his chin, contemplating the odds of making it out alive or having to sell bundles next week. "I got a question, and it's not 'cause I'm bitchin' or nothing, but why Tasker projects and not someplace else?"

"Because it's the only place where they won't expect a robbery. I mean, c'mon now. Who would be crazy enough to rob somebody from Tasker? Wait a minute... I'm crazy enough," Lil' Man said, pointing at himself.

Montega gave Lil' Man the signature smile that Juicy and every other girl he came across loved so much and said, "So am I. In fact, I got an idea of how we can do this and get away clean without losing our lives or being identified. It's all about the element of surprise and... I have the perfect disguise for the job."

Chapter Ten

Take Money
TASKER PROJECTS, SOUTH PHILADELPHIA...

"Break bread or play dead..."

— SKI-MASK

It was ten at night on Tasker Street. The weather was hot and humid, and the fiends rushed to cop from their favorite dealers. The half-moon was covered by dark clouds. The sound of thunder grumbled in the distance; then instantly, the clouds started to choke the sky and it started to rain. That, however, didn't stop the activity on the block. In the words of a true hustler, 'the block was poppin', and the Avenue was full of drug transactions.

One guy in particular was Kev. He pulled up to the block in his white Infiniti FX45. His windshield wipers swung left to right as raindrops pelted his vehicle. Kev was Shug's number-one lieutenant and was his best friend growing up. He had a dark-chocolate complexion and a close-cut beard, was tall, and always wore the finest designer jeans. Kev had just picked up the money to re-up with Shug, who was on his way back from a meeting he had with the Underworld in L.A. Not only was Kev getting money throughout South Philly, but he also had a rep in the Underworld as a potential boss.

As he pulled up to the corner, Kev gave his young bol TJ a nod before answering his phone. "What's good, baby? I was waiting for you to hit me up," he said smoothly.

"Don't *what's up baby* me, Kev. I thought you were going to come over and drop that money off you been promisin' me for a week now," Breezy shot back.

Kev smiled, knowing how spoiled he made her. He loved having a woman depend on him like Breezy did. "You know I got you, boo. Why you trippin' like that?"

"C'mon, Kev. You know I have to get something to wear for your little party. You want me to represent you and look better than all those other bitches you gonna have there, don't you?" she whined, stroking his ego.

"You damn right," he said proudly.

"Well then, bring me the money and stop bullshittin'."

"Aight, aight, boo. As soon as I holla at Shug, I'ma breeze through there. And tell your girlfriends they gotta roll because I'm tryna sample that before we go out tonight."

"Boy, you know ain't nobody over here. And what you tryna sample anyway?" she asked.

"You already know," Kev replied, grabbing his dick as he thought about how good her pussy was and how wet she could get.

"You are so nasty, and for the record, once you get a sample of this, you ain't got no choice but to take the rest that come with it—a full course meal. These walls tight, my ass fat, and this pussy stay wet!" she said with a lustful moan.

"That's right. Talk that talk, sexy," he said.

"Bye, boy." Breezy hung up before she got too crazy on the phone.

When Kev ended the call, he zoned out, thinking about how he was going to wear Breezy's sexy ass out tonight. From afar, he heard the sound of dual T5 pipes roaring around, which could only mean someone was riding a Banshee late at night. Nothing about that was surprising; guys rode four-wheelers and dirt-bikes every day, all day throughout the city.

Who would be riding at this time of night and in the rain? Kev thought as he adjusted his seat and leaned back. When the screaming Yamaha drew closer, the hustlers who were bunched together scattered as Ski-Mask emerged from out of nowhere, holding two black .45 caliber Glocks, one in each hand. Both were equipped with extended ladders. Seeing the man dressed in all black with a ski mask, the hustlers tried to flee.

"Oh shitttt!" someone shouted.

Montega wheeled up in an all-black Banshee with quiet stock pipes, holding a fifty-shot Kalashnikov AK-47 and wearing a phantom mask over his face.

Seeing this, the hustlers came to a halt and tried to run for the opening, but Lil' Man popped up on a loud, black and red Banshee with chrome T5 pipes, wearing a stocking cap over his face. Removing the AK strap from around his neck, he aimed the weapon at the group of panicking hustlers. Watching from a short distance, Kev reached for the gear and tried to drive off, but Ski-Mask spotted him and stuck the barrel of the gun inside the window to his head.

"Get out, Dickey, 'fore I blow your damn brains all over your interior."

Not wanting to get popped, Kev did as he was told. He got out with his hands in the air, but Lil' Man grabbed him by the collar and yanked him to the wet ground. Nobody would ever expect to get robbed on the avenue, especially when there were close to fifteen trap stars on the block, plus a lookout who also got snatched up. Kev was waiting for the cops to spin around the block any minute, but no one came. His clothes were soaking wet, and it was pouring non-stop.

"Aight, everybody, stay the fuck on the ground!" Ski-Mask barked. "You talk, you die! You try to run, you die! You be a hero, you die! All me want y'all to do is lay on your bellies, break bread, or play dead!"

Once the guys were all face-down, Montega searched them for anything of value. Ski-Mask removed the book bag he had on and tossed it to Montega, while Lil' Man took guard from a distance just in case someone wanted to be brave. As Montega collected the money, along with the jewelry, weapons, and cell phones, TJ slowly reached for the gun that was tucked by his hip. He was scared, but he knew he had to be the one to represent South Philly. If all went well, he would be the talk of the hood for years to come. Shug would move him up the ranks as one of his brave lieutenants.

As his hand touched the butt of his gun, he heard splashing footsteps closing in on his side. Lil' Man was standing over him with the barrel of the AK pointed at the back of his head. He pulled the trigger without hesitation. A rapid burst caused a line of shells to discharge from the chamber.

The explosive sound had everyone jumping as if they were the ones being shot. Kev and his boys damn near shit themselves when they saw TJ get his brains blown out. Even Montega was looking at Lil' Man like he was crazy.

Lil' Man shrugged. Montega sighed before he turned to Kev and searched his pockets. While doing so, Kev saw the skull head tattoo on his right forearm. It appeared to be gaged by a bandanna and wore a crown over its head.

Across the street, shooters were creeping out of the projects with rain jackets and guns in hand. They took notice of the four-wheelers parked out in the street. A streak of lightning flashed across the sky.

After taking the keys to Kev's car, Montega searched the Infiniti and hit the jackpot when he looked in the armrest and found three bricks of cash. Kev was grateful he put the re-up in his stash spot. The money that Montega found was just penny ante gambling money to Kev. However, Montega also came out with a customized gold-plated tiger stripe .50 caliber Desert Eagle semi-automatic, which he quickly tucked into his waistband. Kev clenched his teeth because that was his favorite gun. He had bought it from a Mexican he met in Cali. The gun had cost him a fortune. Now it was being taken.

Montega quickly handed the backpack to Ski-Mask. By that time, five shooters were lined up on the other side of the street, squatting down with guns ready. One of the shooters peaked up and saw Ski-Mask putting on the book bag. He took a deep breath as the rain dripped from his black hoodie. He peaked again and saw the phantom-masked man and rose to his feet, aimed, and fired. Montega turned and took a straight shot to the chest and fell back onto his ass. He scrambled to his feet in shock just as fast as he fell. Gunshots rained in their direction from across the street. Montega raised the AK and sprayed back at the shooters behind the parked cars. Lil-Man and Ski-Mask joined in.

The drug dealers on the ground covered their heads as shells bounced around them. The cars across the street were decorated with bullets almost simultaneously. Five men quickly subtracted to one. That one ducked behind a mangled parked car with his back to the door. He was breathing heavy. He held his gun to his forehead like a holy cross in prayer.

Montega and Lil' Man continued to fire short bursts as they advanced to their four-wheelers. Montega threw the strap over his shoulder and let his rifle hang from his back. Lil' Man did the same. He kicked on the four-wheeler's 360 engine as more shooters came running out of the projects. Lil' Man let off another round and made them all dive for cover.

Ski-Mask backed him, shooting his way to Montega and his four-wheeler. He climbed on back with one hand holding onto Montega, the other firing at the men hiding.

"That's good lookin' out, Dickey. Blow on y'all tonight!" he teased while Montega popped the clutch and sped off. The hustlers on the ground sprang to their feet to grab their stashed guns, but by the time they got to them, the four-wheelers were long gone.

Chapter Eleven

Broken Promises

"Whoever robbed the projects must have had some big balls."

— DETECTIVE GARY WHITEHEAD

The bright color of red and blue lights painted the damp crime scene of Tasker Street. Police cars and ambulances sat neck and neck. The commissioner and all his men stood around in disgust. The rain had stopped, but death was still in the air. Whitehead and Lucca approached the guy taking photos of the dead bodies for the autopsy report.

"This city if turning into a goddamn war zone, Whitehead," said Lucca. "Three masked men on ATV's robbed the local corner boys, kills two in the process, and injures a third."

"Tell me about it. I've had a word with a few neighbors. They told me that one of the robbers had two handguns. The other two were armed with AK-47s. They rolled right up to the corner boys on four-wheelers."

"That's a goddamn shame. Somebody mind explaining to me how in the hell these punks weren't noticed by any patrol cars?" Lucca asked.

Whitehead shook his head. "I don't know what to tell you, Tony. But hey, let's look at the bright side of things. It could have been worse... a lot worse. Besides, these are just drug dealers we're talking about. It's not like our usual senseless murders over a purse or a wallet."

Whitehead squatted down by the body. He put on a pair of latex gloves, picked up an AK shell casing with a small pair of tongs, inspected it, then pulled out a plastic bag and put the shell inside. A forensic officer stepped up to him.

"Send this to the lab, will ya," he said, handing it to the officer. "Give me a call if anything comes up." He then stood and removed his gloves.

"You're wasting your time with that, ya know. These criminals are getting smarter—"

"No, we're getting lazier," Whitehead replied.

A short distance away, a black Range Rover rode up to the corner. The driver watched the detectives stand around with the rest of the police force. The Range Rover's windows were tinted black, which made it almost impossible for anyone to see the four bodies inside, especially at night.

"Look at this shit here," Gee said from behind the wheel.

Gee was a dark-skinned guy with a low haircut and a goatee. He had eyes as brown as timber and a piglet nose. He kept a toothpick in his mouth and talked slick as oil.

In the passenger's seat was a dread-headed guy dressed in cargo pants, boots, and a leather jacket. He too had a goatee with hazel eyes and brows that looked as if he were always mad. His dreads had gold at the tips, and he went by the name of Maniac.

In the back seat, Shug sat quietly behind Louis Vuitton shades. His big belly rose and fell as he watched the crime scene. His black beard was full and thick, his thick lips pursed with anger. He sat beside his shorty, Tee-Tee—a fine redbone with shiny, long, dark hair highlighted with blue streaks. She had a body one would think was too curvy to be petite, but she was. Her perky breasts complemented a flat stomach and a bubble butt. She crossed her legs that were painted with Fendi thigh-highs, and played in her nails, carefree of what was going on outside.

"Somebody got a lot of balls, pulling some shit like this," Gee said.

"Aye, Shug, I don't think dudes respect your hand out here. You might have to make an example out of one of 'em, cuz." Gee shook his head with a weak smirk. "How the fuck Kev let this go down? All them dudes out there; Chubs, Vito, Homietime. Somebody besides TJ should have been strapped."

"How much Kev have on him?" Maniac asked.

Gee shrugged. "I don't know, like—"

"Pull off, Gee," Shug said calmly.

Gee looked at Maniac then shook his head and pulled off. The reflection of the crime scene flashed off of Shug's sunglasses as the Range Rover sped away quickly.

Later on that night, in the dimly lit bar in West Philadelphia, where all the correctional officers and government officials hung out, it reeked of beer and cigarettes as customers sat around the counter, drinking their troubles away while they listened to the oldies on the digital jukebox. Whitehead and Lucca sat at the far end, watching the 76ers play the New York Knicks. The bartender had just finished pouring them both triple shots of Courvoisier, but by the time she walked away, their glasses were empty.

When Lucca looked over at his partner, who was talking on his cell phone, he saw that something was wrong. After Whitehead got off the phone, he said, "Can you believe this shit? That was Detective Peterson over in South Philly. Tony, I tell ya, these kids are getting really outta hand."

"Did anyone give a full description of the perps?" Lucca asked.

"They said they were wearing masks, remember. They say one in particular, though, had on a mask that looked like a phantom," Whitehead mentioned.

"Wait a minute. You don't think this could be our guy, do you?" Lucca asked.

"I wouldn't put it past him, but to tell you the truth, this guy didn't come off as being a robber, but then again, we are talking about Tasker projects. From the stories we hear daily, whoever robbed the projects must have had some big balls," Whitehead stated.

"Or no brains at all. You know the stories about this Phantom character. He's a stone-cold killer," Lucca added.

When Whitehead looked over at his partner, a pretty woman in her early forties walked into the bar just as Marvin Gaye's "After the Dance" played on the jukebox. Whitehead may have been highly devoted to upholding the law, but even superman had a weakness, and Whitehead was no different. There was no doubt that he loved his wife, but there was just something about sleeping with another woman that always got him excited. Whitehead got up from his stool and fixed himself up. "I think I'm gonna be a little late getting home tonight, Tony. I'm gonna need an alibi," he said before approaching the woman.

"Yeah, yeah, yeah, go ahead and have fun, you lucky son-of-a-bitch. Remember to use a condom this time," Lucca said before sipping his beer. He then mumbled, "It's bad enough you had a baby on your wife and she doesn't know about it."

In the wee hours of the morning when Whitehead got home, it was close to 3 a.m. The first thing he did was take a shower. Once he finished, he walked into his bedroom to see his wife, Maria, sleeping on her side. He then climbed into bed and put his arm around her as if he hadn't just fucked some other woman an hour ago. He might have been forty-eight years old, but he moved like he was twenty-five and believed that he was indestructible.

"Where have you been all day?" his wife asked with a yawn.

"I've been working late on a few homicides," he said.

"You know you were supposed to take Aminah to see about a car this evening. You promised her. Oh, and Shabree called over a hundred times looking for you. It seems like you've been forgetting a lot of things lately," Maria retorted.

"Look. I'm sorry, okay? I'll make it up to them. I've just been swamped with so many cases," Whitehead said with some phony frustration.

"Yeah, well, I hope you don't forget about Aminah's graduation. She worked so hard to please you by becoming a registered nurse instead of a stylist like her big sister, so please don't let her down. She needs all the love and encouragement she can get."

"Look, honey. You don't have to worry about that. There's nothing and nobody that can keep me away from seeing my daughter's greatest achievement—put that on our marriage."

Chapter Twelve

Blood Money

"People tend to live longer when they keep their mouth shut..."

— MONTEGA

The dining room was small and dark from the old chandelier that bore two missing lightbulbs. Lil' Man sat at the table, counting the pile of money in front of him. The guns that were used for the robbery lay as peaceful as they had ever been in front of him. The Dutch burned from the ashtray not too far from Lil' Man's grasp.

Faith sat on the couch in the living room, watching the news. The Mexican cartels were at each other's neck, and the big talk about the election seemed to be on every channel. The sound of giggling came from the table where Montega had Juicy on his lap. He was shirtless and in pain. Juicy stroked is bruise that marked his chest as Ski-Mask walked by, still carrying a gun in his hand.

After counting up the profit, the three robbers ended up with a total of $63,000, seven handguns (including the big and shiny Desert Eagle), a few diamond-face Rolex watches, and an iced-out chain. As Lil' Man divided the money three ways, Montega watched calmly, while Ski-Mask paced the floor behind them with a Glock still clutched in his palm. He was in need of a line of coke but wouldn't snort until he got his cut of the profit. Money came before pleasure.

"That's twenty grand right there, cabrón," Lil' Man said, shoving the money across the table at Montega. "For that type of cash, Juicy should be kissing you where the sun don't shine."

Juicy squinted her eyes and flipped Lil' Man the bird.

Lil' Man ignored her as always. He picked up the Dutch of Wet and pulled the smoke into his lungs. The PCP was stimulating as it was good. He exhaled and said, "Can you believe those fools, keeping all that money on them? I don't know about you, but sixty-three grand is a whole fucking lot of bread for one corner. What you think, Kenny?"

"I don't think it was the hustlers who had all that bread. It was bol in the Infiniti. Main-man was caked up."

"Probably was about to re-up." Lil' Man shook his head. "I know he pissed right about now."

Ski-Mask played with his nose. "Pissed ain't the word. That fool shittin' bricks. See, Dickey, Ski-Mask told y'all. Ski-Mask told y'all this would work." Ski-Mask blocked the view of the TV. "If you want to get money the fast way, you gotta do it..." He placed his shirt collar over his mouth and said, "Ski-Mask-Way!"

"Skeeter, could you move out of my way, boy? I'm trying to watch the news," Faith said.

Ski-Mask looked nothing like his brother or sister, because he was mixed with African American. His complexion was the same as Montega's, only he was taller and thinner with short, curly hair and a goatee. He also had a long neck that was slightly bowed. Unlike Lil' Man, who had no guidance growing up, Ski-Mask was raised by wolves. His father was the best there ever was. He robbed, conned, and killed to bring in money to feed his girl and only son. But it all came to an end one night in an alleyway in the Badlands.

On that night, Ski-Mask witnessed his father being forced to his knees to suck another man's penis right before he was shot in the head. It was the night Skeeter became Ski-Mask.

That night, after a whole lot of fucking and sucking, Montega lay on his back, looking up at the ceiling, with Juicy laying on his chest, exploring his body with her hands.

"Why are you always so quiet?" she asked.

"People tend to live a lot longer when they keep their mouth shut," Montega replied.

"Oh, really?" she asked, lifting her head up and resting her chin on his chest. "You're sure as hell taking a gamble, robbing drug blocks with Beto and Skeeter. You don't seem to care that much about life. You ain't bulletproof, papi."

"Who ever said I was?"

"You don't have to say it. The shit you pulled tonight is living proof. South Philly though? You're taking one hell of a gamble."

"I need money to survive, don't I? This is the hand I was dealt. And since life is a gamble, I gotta play it with a poker face." He touched her soft skin and said, "One thing for sure though; death doesn't scare me. That's the easy part. Life, on the other hand, is a struggle."

Juicy took his hand and kissed it before she laid her head back on his chest.

"If you're not scared of death, then what do you fear?"

"Nothing."

Juicy sucked her teeth. "Yes you do," she said, unconvinced.

"Oh yeah? You must know something I don't."

"I do," she said, lifting her head again. "I know you're afraid of love."

Montega stared at her for a moment then reverted his eyes to the ceiling.

"Yeah, that's right." Juicy nodded. "I hit it right on the mark, didn't I? Look, papi. I'm not asking you to love me. I know I ain't your girl. Besides, you can't love me until you learn to love yourself. And this right here..." Juicy pressed her finger firmly against Montega's bruise. He groaned in pain. "This ain't love."

Montega gripped Juicy up by the wrist. They both sat up. "Fuck is you doing?" he asked, upset. He released her and got out of bed to put on his boxers. "You really trippin', shorty. I ain't got time for—"

"It's your mother, isn't it? That's why you hold back on love."

Montega flashed back to the night he saw his mom getting ready to go out. Juicy's voice broke his thought.

"Her murder still haunts you, doesn't it?"

He then thought of her death and put his head down. "I can't get her out of my head. She was the only woman I ever loved. The only one I've ever cared for. Now look where she is." He brushed his fingers over his waves. "It's *my* fault. I should have been there for her. I should have protected her. I should've…" Montega clenched his fist as a tear rolled down his cheek.

Juicy moved in and wrapped her arms around him from behind. She kissed him on top of the head then rested her face on the back of his neck. Montega put his hand on hers and accepted her warm embrace.

"It's not your fault, papi. You can't keep blaming yourself for something you weren't there to stop. All you can do is be there for the ones who are still around, the ones who love you more than you love yourself."

The next morning, Montega came down to find Lil' Man still seated at the table with his cut waiting for him. It was the most money Montega had ever seen at one time. "I bet you won't have a problem copping four-and-a-half with that, will you?" Lil' Man asked.

"Shit, not only am I coppin' four-and-a-half, but I'm grabbin' a wheel too. I'ma have to put it in my sister's name though."

"Yeah, you could use your own wheels and stop driving your girl's little ass Neon," Lil' Man joked before rolling up another Dutch of wet.

Montega's drug of choice was weed, so when Lil' Man offered, he politely declined then pulled out a Dutch of Haze. That morning, they all got high until the sun came up. A few hours later, J-Rider and Killa drove Montega and Faith to the Gallery Mall downtown so he could get her a few things since Lil' Man and Ski-Mask were too busy.

Faith graduated from high school and was on the waiting list to enroll in the military Special Forces. Montega envied her for having the heart to go overseas and fight for her country. He loved her like a little sister and made sure she was happy whenever he could.

As the two sat in the backseat, Montega asked, "Yo, Faith. Why the hell do you want to enroll in the military anyway?"

For a second, Faith was caught off-guard by the question but allowed herself time to answer. "Because it seems like the only place I can get away from my brothers and do what I want to do," she replied.

"And what do you want to do?"

"Explore. Be part of something that I can be proud of. You know, there's a lot more than Philadelphia, right? There's destiny, and it's out there waiting for us. I know you're smarter than my brothers and everyone else in your crew. Don't spend the rest of your life here, doing the same shit, when you have so much more potential. There comes a time when you have to move on, regardless of what others might think of you. That's what I'm doing—moving on," she explained, looking out the window as they sped down the expressway.

Montega thought back to when they were kids. "Faith, remember when we were young, and you said that when you grew up, you wanted to be like La Femme-Nikita?" he asked, causing her to look at him and smile. "What happened to that?"

"I... guess I grew out of that stage. Now, I just want to be a war hero, I guess."

"Well, promise me that when you're done playing soldier girl, you'll come see me in my castle. By then, I'll be the King of Philly," he said, causing her to laugh.

Faith looked back out the window, murmuring, "That'll be the day."

Chapter Thirteen

A Cursed Black Car

"This was my husband's project before he was killed…"

— OLIVIA HOWARD

After hiding out at Lil' Man's crib for a few days, J-Rider dropped Montega off on Blakemore where J-Black and Razor were chillin' on the Chinese store steps, smoking weed and getting money as always.

The block looked like a drive-thru at McDonald's. Crackheads were coming from every direction. Taliban came out of the alley behind the Chinese store with a handful of dimes. As Montega shut the back door, he saw his sister's white KIA Ultima parked a few inches away from the bullet-riddled mailbox that everyone leaned on in front of the Chinese store. It was the same mailbox that had saved his life a few nights ago.

Breezy sat in the passenger seat, playing in her hair while talking on her Sprint.

In the back seat, Amber and Jasmine spoke amongst themselves until they spotted him. They were still amused by the face he made the day they pulled up beside him and Mike.

"Hey, brother," Jasmine said as J-Rider pulled away.

"Don't hey me," he replied, causing the two to laugh again.

"I heard they scared your ass good," Kia said with a smirk.

Montega gave a weak smile before leaving them and approaching his righthand man. Breezy glanced over at him and looked away quickly. She sucked her teeth with irritation. "Can we go, Kia?"

"Wait, bitch, dag," Kia snapped. "What are you in such a rush for? The mall ain't going nowhere. I need to make sure my brothers are cool."

"Kia, would you quit it," Montega said, taking the Dutch from Razor. "I never thought I'd see the day when my sister starts playing Momma's role."

"Don't get smart, because I can really start playing the momma's role and kick ya ass out here. Let's not forget who's the oldest. You know what?" She started up her car.

"That will get her out of here," Montega mumbled before watching her pull off.

"Yo, you peep shorty in the back seat?" Razor asked, tapping him. "She just moved on the block. They say she be up in them rap videos, shaking her ass. That shit fat too."

"It's fat like that?" Montega asked.

"Dog, that ass dumb fat. A shorty like that be on dudes with heavy bread though. You should already know that from the way Kia roll."

"Yeah, you right. But I ain't feeling that chick Breezy. She pretty and all, but she always looking like she got an attitude—keep giving me the rock like I owe her something."

"She probably like you," J-Black said as a smoker walked up on him to cop.

"She don't like nobody but the almighty dollar," Montega hissed.

"Can you blame her?" Razor asked, plucking the roach to the ground and stepping on it. "Who wants to be with a broke nigga?"

"Who wants to be with a broke bitch?" Montega retorted defensively.

"Shit, I'll take any chick right about now," J-Black said, raising his hand to let a female crackhead know that he was her guy to cop from.

The woman was two pounds away from disappearing. She was tall with a nappy head and dirty, balled-up white sneakers that looked gray.

"You got dimes?" she asked.

"How many?"

Montega's eyes reverted from J-Black to the green Maybach 5'7. It slowed down and pulled into the parking space that Kia once occupied. The car was sparkling with twenty-four-inch rims. Razor was in awe, and so was Black. No one had ever seen a Maybach up close, let alone in the hood.

In the driver's side was a heavy-set guy with a small afro and no facial hair. He wore a Gucci-printed shirt with a diamond chain and watch.

His man in the passenger's seat was bald and a shade lighter than he was. He had a short, scruffy beard and a missing tooth. The driver gritted on Montega from head to toe as if he wasn't worth the ground he stepped on. Taliban came out of the alley and got his attention.

"Young blood," he said.

"Yo, bol, what's good with you, old head?" Taliban greeted.

"Do me a favor," the driver said, going into his pocket. He pulled out a twenty-dollar bill and said, "Grab me a soda. Ginger ale if they have it, and if you hurry, I'll let you keep the change."

Taliban took the money and headed for the Chinese store. Montega watched his brother with disgust. His eyes sharply cut back at the driver. He was looking Black's way. "You seen Mike around!"

"Nah, not this morning," Black told him as Taliban returned. He handed him the soda.

"Good looking out, young blood. Aye, when you see Mike, tell him Fly Ty came through looking for him." He then looked at Montega once more, snorted from an inside joke, and pulled off.

Montega wanted to curse his brother out, but before he could speak, the black Range Rover slowly cruised down the block. Even through the dark tint, he could see the woman inside. She didn't stop, nor did she beep the horn. She just continued on.

"Where you been at anyway?" Razor asked him.

"I was in the Badlands with Lil' Man. You know I had to twist Juicy's back out a couple times," he replied.

"Yeah, I feel you on that one. That's a bad little Spanish broad. You need to pass her off though, and stop handcuffing these hoes. It's too many of 'em out here," Razor stated.

Montega was known for fucking the baddest broads in the hood. He had high standards for his women. His mother once said, "*Women are like watches. You don't borrow them, and you don't lend them out. If she's not what you see yourself having on your arm, then she ain't worth your time. You never know what the future holds. That same girl you have a one-night stand with can end up making me a grandma someday. So therefore, choose who you want. Don't let no woman choose you...*"

Montega took that to heart and applied it to his view of all women. Everyone thought that he was a 'handcuffer' from the way females were so head-over-heels for him. Really, he was just being himself, and females adored the ground he walked on.

"You hit it right on the mark, bro. There is too many women out here, so why are you sweatin' mine? Juicy ain't no pass-off, and can't none of them chicks do what she do and ride like she ride," Montega bragged, taking the weed from him and pulling on it.

"That's understandable," Razor responded. "All these chicks out here be lookin' for a quick come-up. Whatever happened to hard dick and bubble gum?"

"That got played out once dikes, vibrators, and dildos got popular," J-Black joked.

Razor turned to look at his partner. "Man, Mike got us moving bundles now. He told me to let you know, and when you get a chance, call him."

"It ain't 'bout nothin'. You can give bol his bundles back because I got point money. Once I cop, I'll sell you an ounce from it," Montega promised

"Oh yeah?" J-Black asked, listening in on the conversation. "Where you get the money from?"

"I saved my bread, dog... unlike you."

"That's what's up, bol," Razor said. "Yo, we should go to that party at the Penicle. I heard that shit is gonna be bananas. Black said he could get us in. You with it?"

"I don't know, bol. Who all gonna be there?" Montega blew out a cloud of smoke.

"Who gonna be there?" J-Black asked excitedly. "Every bad bitch in the city gonna be there. It's gonna be mad dudes with mad loot, so you know groupies ain't too far behind. I'm tryna rent a 2004 Bentley Flying Spur for the night," J-Black said while sticking his hand in his pockets like a boss.

Montega twisted his lips to the side in doubt and looked at his partner, who had the same expression. They both knew that Black's idea of a Flying Spur, would end up being a Pontiac GT or a Dodge Magnum.

"Yo, we 'bout to hit the mall out in King of Prussia. You rollin' with us?" Razor asked.

"Nah, I'll catch up with y'all. I gotta meet up with somebody. In fact, where is Mike?"

"He chillin' right now," Razor replied. "Whitehead and Lucca ridin' around snatchin' dudes up about the murder that happened out here. They even grabbed Mike and took him to the Round House for questioning. Them thirsty ass dickheads just wanna fuck with somebody. I'm surprised Whitehead don't be gettin' information from his daughter."

"I got some information for him," Montega added, checking his G-Shock watch. "Don't let me play the back seat while you play the front."

As the guys smiled, an orange Dodge Charger pulled up. On the driver's side was a chocolate-brown sista with a crinkly hairstyle, high cheekbones, and thick, glossy lips. She wasn't all that good looking in the face, but the car made her glow with attraction. "I'm looking for Kenny Carter," she said in a sweet voice.

Everyone looked at Montega as he smoothly stepped forward to extend his hand. "That would be me," he said, allowing her to check him out from head-to-toe.

"Nice to meet you. I'm Olivia, the person you spoke with on the phone about the cars. Would you mind riding with me to go see them?"

With no explanation, Montega got into the woman's car, and they pulled off, heading for her house on Old York Road.

It was a large road that started from Broad Street and cut through a vast suburban county called Willow Grove. Olivia pulled off the road, taking a few small streets until she pulled up to a nice-sized house with a five-car garage.

"Here we are," she said before getting out.

Montega opened the door and followed her up the driveway. Olivia hit the key pad. One of the five-garage doors opened. They both stepped inside the spacious area that smelled of gasoline and motor oil. Five cars sat side by side. A red 2004 Corvette sat beside a silver 2004 Mustang GT. There was a yellow 2004 Camaro and a black 2002 Buick Lacrosse. The fifth car beside them had a cover over it.

Juicy's brother, Mario, had hipped Montega to the woman. Somehow, she was able to get cars from a friend who stole them and switched the VIN numbers with cars that were totaled and found in the junkyard. Olivia had a guy friend who worked in a print shop to create VIN numbers for the stolen cars. His job was to make the numbers inside the doors disappear along with the sticker on the windows, which were cut out and removed so that nothing could be traced.

Montega didn't know this, and he didn't need to know. Olivia had been so good at her side hustle that she sold cars to CarMax and could get any vehicle that a person asked for… for the right price. Her second side hustle was with a man who repossessed exotic cars. What he did was repo the car and never mark it down for confiscation. Olivia would be the one to handle the rest of the work and make the sale.

Montega studied each car with admiration. Olivia followed him. "Everything you see here goes for ten grand a piece. The Corvette is fifteen, however, but it's only got a few hundred miles on it."

Montega was quiet as he inspected the red V8. He had nineteen grand in his pocket and was ready to spend it on the 'Vette. He thought about the women that would be on him after seeing him in the driver's seat. He pictured the envious stares he would get from the guys. He could feel the hate as he zoomed by them. He reached into his pocket but stopped when he saw the car under the cover.

"What's that over there?" he asked curiously.

"What? That old thing?" Olivia asked with a frown.

"Yeah. What is it?"

Olivia walked over to the car and grabbed the white cover by its hem. She pulled it off to expose a black, 1996 Chevy Impala SS with a custom Ram Air hood, dual exhaust, and factory rims.

"Damn, now that's off the chain," Montega said, allured.

Olivia was shocked. She glanced at the other car and said, "You like this?"

"Yeah, what's up with it?"

Olivia shrugged as she looked at it. "This was my husband's project before he was killed. Owwww, I hated the attention he paid to this car. I literally fought for his attention. It's funny because I still can't stand the sight of it. It's got low mileage, has over a thousand horsepower. I think he changed the engine to a 430 Hemi. The only problem is the window. They don't roll down. Don't ask me why."

"Damn," was all he could say before looking back at the Corvette. He really wanted to stunt, but then reality hit him. He wasn't a Corvette type of guy, meaning he didn't have the money to back up the status that came with the car. That right there was considered faking, so he turned back to the Impala.

"How much you want for this?"

"You're serious?" she asked. "I would have thought a handsome man like yourself would want the finer things in life."

Montega shook his head with a smirk, saying, "I do want the finer things in life, ma. But right now, I need to be low key for the type of life I live now, or I could risk losing it."

Chapter Fourteen

The Devil's Confessions

"Forgive me, Father, for I have sinned."

— DIAMOND WHITE

The heavy iron hinges squeaked as Bain opened the large, gold ornate doors of the huge Cathedral. A bright ray of sunlight poured inside. He stepped to the side for his boss to enter. Then he closed the doors and stood guard while Diamond walked down the aisle with only the sound of Giuseppe heels tapping the marble floors as she strutted to the confession booth. The cream Hermes ostrich dress she wore was tailored to her curves, complementing the brown color of her shoes and matched her Valentino box bag. Chocolate diamonds flooded her delicious cleavage, matching the five carat studs in her ears and on her bracelet.

Placing her bag down in the front pew, she walked inside and closed the curtains before sitting down, crossing her succulent legs. "Forgive me, Father, for I have sinned," she said while making the cross sign over herself.

Once the priest allowed her to begin her confession, she wasted no time. "Father, I need help. I know that, over the years, I've acted as if I've been dealing with life in a God-fearing way, but truthfully, I'm no better than the Devil himself. I have a lot of skeletons in my closet.

Many of them are because of my past," Diamond confessed as her rage intensified.

She hated to show her emotions, even in the house of God. Whenever she felt like crying, she would counter it with anger. Diamond sniffled but refused to let a tear fall as she thought of her father's death.

"What's a girl to do when she loses almost all of the people who mean so much to her?" Diamond confessed. "JR was my heart, Mercedes my sanity, and my father… He was everything. Without them, I feel alone. And the only way I know how to deal with it is through violence. Lately, I've been getting crazy vibes from my brother and everyone else I work with. It makes me feel as though they're plotting against me. Maybe I'm just delusional, but whatever it is, it's bringing out the demons inside me."

"With that said, I've done something terribly wrong. Yesterday, I hired an assassin to take care of the man responsible for killing my boyfriend. I gave the assassin this son-of-a… guy's address, and he planted a bomb so when he walked in, it would explode. But once again, my plan got botched. See, what happened was the guy was hiding in a house around the corner. I accidentally blew up some nice, old lady's home. Father, I… I feel so bad."

Diamond got quiet, waiting for the priest to clear her of her sins, but he was in a state of questioning. He knew that the streets were dangerous because of all the gang-banging and drug dealing on the south side of L.A., but never did he expect to hear such hideous things from a woman.

"Father?" Diamond repeated.

"Oh, yes?" the priest muttered, snapping back out of his thoughts. "Yes, my child. The Father forgives all who are willing to believe," he said before saying a prayer for her.

Once he finished, Diamond pulled out a fresh stack of hundred-dollar bills and set it beside her. She rose from the wooden bench, adjusted her dress, and headed back up the aisle where her bodyguard stood at the door.

"Let's go, Bain."

The bodyguard nodded before turning to open the door.

Standing with two of his own private henchmen, Justin loitered on the sidewalk by the entrance, puffing on a Newport.

"I see you're still confessing your sins to that crooked-ass priest," Justin lectured. "I would have thought you'd learn your lesson by now with that white boy you trusted in your circle."

"I see you're still minding my damn business. I would have thought a bitch would have finally given you some so you can stay off my ass!" Diamond countered, mocking him as she stopped in front of the men.

Diamond hated Justin's guts. To her, he was sneaky and conniving. Justin wanted to be a white so badly; he'd do or say anything. He was cocky and disrespectful to those who didn't cater to him. For those who did, he pushed them around like they were his personal slaves. Obedience was what he demanded from everyone, including women. Diamond, however, was the only one who wouldn't back down from a verbal war.

Folding her arms over the bust of her chest, she looked up at Justin. "What do you want?"

"I wanna tell you something. You're in the fuckin' way with this attitude bullshit. What you need to do is grow up. You're twenty-fuckin' years old and still throwing temper tantrums. This is a business. No, let me rephrase that. This is a serious business, not a reality show starring you. It's bad enough nobody wants your little ass in the circle as it is, including me. But since you made your bones in the street and somewhat in Cuba, we don't have no choice but to accept it. You can at least have some type of respect for your brother because, truthfully, he's the only one that's keeping you alive."

"Fuck you," Diamond spat.

"Fuck you too, bitch," Justin grunted, causing Bain to step forward, alarmed.

Diamond quickly stopped him when she saw the two henchmen approach. Her eyes cut back at Justin sharply.

"You're not afraid to talk to me like that?" she asked calmly with a smirk.

"Ha! Diamond, you really need to get over yourself. You, of all people, should know you don't put fear in my heart. You do what every other bitch with nice tits and a fat ass does—make my dick hard. You see, you might have these other bustas fooled by the Black Kiss of Death image you put on, but I watched you grow up. I was the one behind the scenes, and I know you like a book. You better get your act together because, God forbid, if Deshawn finds out that nice little view where you hid his brother, then the ball would finally be in my court. You do remember what happened in your bedroom a while back? Next time, you're gonna be beggin' for me to stick my dick in you."

Diamond lurched forward and spat in his face. Justin's men reached for their guns again. Out of nowhere, five of Diamond's armed henchmen appeared with machine guns ready. Three carried HK MP5s, while the other two stood in the back with Ruger SR-556 assault rifles, shit that not even the hood could get their hands on. This time, it was Justin who backed down. He wiped the saliva from his face, put it on his tongue, licked it, and took a step back to laugh. "You even taste sweet."

Diamond's face transformed to a disgusted frown as Justin laughed his way back to his 2003 Cadillac Escalade pickup and pulled off. The only people who knew about her past was A-Z, 4-5, Butch, Bain, and the priest. Since 4-5 and A-Z were dead, Butch was serving time in a federal penitentiary, and Bain was a mute, now realizing who was responsible, she shook her head as she approached the white Rolls Royce Phantom that awaited with her new driver standing outside of it.

Before getting in, she turned and whispered something to her bodyguard as Justin and his boys rode away. Bain nodded his head and pulled out the gold-plated mini Kalashnikov AK-47 from inside his lapel. He turned back to go inside the church once more. Diamond sat inside the vehicle and pulled out her small makeup kit to retouch the highlights in her flawless features. Before she closed the small mirror case, Bain came out of the church, carrying the unconscious priest over his shoulder. The driver popped the trunk. Bain tossed the priest inside, causing a thump, closed the trunk, and got in the car.

Once in the passenger seat, he nodded and grunted.

"Where to, my lady?" the driver asked.

"I need to go to the airport, but first, we have to visit the zoo," Diamond replied with her mind on everything Justin had just said.

"I wasn't aware that the zoo was open today, madam," the driver said.

"Probably not for the public, but for me, they'll always open," Diamond assured him.

The priest opened his eyes to find one arm secured by a large muscular man in a suit and his other arm in the grasp of another. The two henchmen were holding him up off the ground, walking toward a place he did not know. His back was facing their forward stride. He heard something in a distance, something animalish… something big. It roared as the men approached. It was then the priest remembered what had happened. The large bodyguard hand clobbered him in the head with the butt of his gun.

He began to look around frantically. His brown eyes scanned everything. There were cages, empty vending machines, and signs of animals.

"Where am I?" he asked, but the men didn't say a word.

Finally, they came to a stop. As soon as the priest's foot touched the ground, the same seven-foot giant appeared before him and struck him square in the gut. The priest fell to the ground on hands and knees. The roar rumbled again as he clutched his stomach tightly. The priest looked behind him and saw what looked like a pit. It was then he noticed a fine set of legs standing by the edge of the pit. Those legs led up to a cold but attractive woman. She just so happened to be on the phone at the time. She glanced at him but continued her conversation. Slowly, she turned her back to him while toying with the loops in her hair.

The priest looked around for a clear runway to make an escape but noticed five more henchmen standing stiffly in each place he thought of running to. They were holding guns that he'd thought only the government could get their hands on. When the priest finally realized where he was, Diamond hung up the phone and turned to greet him.

"Sorry for keeping you waiting. The pilot says it will take another hour to fuel the jet, so I figured I'd take a little trip to the zoo. Do you like the zoo?" she asked. Before he could answer, she went on to say, "When I was young, all I ever wanted to do was go to the zoo to see the animals. My favorite is the lions, you know."

The priest began to look back at the pit. His eyes widened, putting a bright, attractive smile on Diamond's face. "Oh, no, priest. That isn't what is in there, although I would have loved to feed the big cats tonight. The man who owns this zoo used to let me feed them all the time, but unfortunately, the lions were already fed. However, that doesn't clear you from the water yet. In fact, pick him up. I want him to see what awaits him," she said, snapping her finger at her two henchmen.

"Oh Mary, Mother of God!" the priest said as the two men grabbed him by the arms again. "No, please don't! I don't want to die! Somebody, help!"

The men took him to the edge and held him upside down by his ankles. The priest's brown eyes bulged from his head as he looked down into the pit full of Nile Crocodiles and hippopotamuses.

"The lord is my shepherd!" he shouted in fear as a croc jumped up with a snap. "Ah!"

Diamond signaled for the henchmen to bring him back to safety. The priest fell to his knees, wrapping his arms around the leg of one of the muscular men. His brown skin complexion was now sweaty pale. He looked to be no older than her brother, which brought her suspicion to a head.

"Being as though I've told you many stories about me, you should know I am not a tolerable person. The only reason you are not at the bottom of that pit of water right now is because somewhere behind that stupid suit and that cross you're wearing, you are a man of God. But mark my words, if you lie to me, I will order my men to throw you in and risk facing judgement when my time comes. You know me that well to know that my word is diamond. Now, how long have you known my brother?"

"Since... high school... I think."

"And how long have you been a priest at the catholic church?"

"After I graduated high school," he said nervously, looking at all the men around him. "The cathedral once belonged to my grandfather then was passed down to me."

"And your father?"

The young priest put his hand down. "My father was... He disappeared five years ago. He was a... He did bad things."

Diamond sneered at the man without an ounce of sympathy for him. "Why did you tell Clyde my business? What sort of gain are you looking to reach?"

"Gain? I... I can assure you there is no gain."

Diamond snapped her fingers again. The men snatched him up once more. "I told you not to lie to me."

"Wait, please. I'm telling the truth, on the heavenly Father himself, I have no gain." The men brought him to the edge of the pit once more. "They tortured me. I would have never given in, even in death, but your brother has ways of getting what he wants!" The men went to toss him in, but Diamond stopped them again.

"Wait!" she said, putting up a hand. "What do you mean, my brother has ways of getting what he wants?"

The priest sighed a quick thanks to God and said, "Your brother has ways of making people talk."

Diamond signaled for the men to bring him back away from the edge. They rested him on his knees in front of her.

"And how did they make you talk?"

The priest didn't answer; instead, he began unbuttoning his shirt. The men behind him reached for their weapons, but Diamond irritably flagged them off. She watched as the priest removed his shirt to show his bare chest full of scars, fresh cuts, and burns. Judging from the way the henchmen looked at him from behind, she knew they were on his back as well.

"Your brother has claimed his place with in Satan's shoes. He had those demonic succubi strip me naked and torture me until I did not know whether I had already given you up or I had wished I'd done so."

"And why does my brother want this information so badly?"

"He didn't tell me. In fact, he did no talking; his... hornets did the talking for him. You want to know the worst part of it?" he asked, finding the courage to stand. "He disrespected me in such a way I wouldn't wish on the devil himself." He unbuckled his pants and pulled them down so that Diamond could see.

Diamond did not show an ounce of surprise, even though, inside, her mind thought, *what the fuck!* Whoever tortured him had dismembered his penis. Only his sack hung from a severe wound that had been burned back to a close. "He said that it would save a boy's rectum in the future," the priest cried. "Who would think of such a thing? Dear God, I have nothing left but my faith."

Diamond looked away with an impassive look. "Why didn't you just kill yourself?"

The priest picked up his pants. "That is what the devil wants. Jesus was tested beyond his mortal strength. He did not give in, even while persecuted. I shall not give in either. I may look weak to you, but I have my father's strength in me. He too was strong, I am told, before Clyde had him killed."

Diamond tilted her head to the side curiously. "Who was your father?" she asked, watching him buckle up.

"Why, his name was Sam. I was named after him." The priest shrugged. "Well, minus the 2Guns part that everyone called him."

For the first time, Diamond couldn't hold back her surprise. "2Gun Sam was your father?"

The priest slowly nodded as fear returned to his features. Diamond shook her head then snapped her fingers for the men to grab him once more. The priest knew then that she was all out of questions, and he was soon to be out of time.

Chapter Fifteen

Secret Meetings

"If he thinks he's a Phantom, then make him a ghost."

— SHAREEK 'SHUG' BURMINGTON

The King of Prussia mall was one of the most popular places to shop in Pennsylvania. It was a large mall filled with the top designer stores, just twenty-five minutes away from Philadelphia. Kia and her best friend, Breezy, searched throughout Nordstrom's racks of clothing for something to wear for Kev's party. They had been in the mall for almost two hours, running from store to store. Nordstrom was one of their favorites.

"Ooooh, Kia, now, I like that dress on you. It's cute," Breezy said, complementing the little blue Berluti dress Kia took off the rack. It was hand printed with a zig-zag sweater material and was form fitting when a woman put it on.

Kia held it up to her nice figure. "You think it'll fit? It looks a little too tight."

"So what? The tighter, the better. And in that dress, we might be in competition," Breezy joked while holding up a black Bottega Veneta cocktail dress. It was tight, short, and bore slashes on each side to show off more skin.

Kia smiled then snatched the dress up as Breezy followed her to the register.

"You never told me what you and your brother were talking about last week. You looked like you were upset," Breezy said.

"And I'm not gonna tell you either. Kenny would kill me if I told any of his business. I'm sorry, Bree, but that's between me and him," Kia said.

"Dag, it's like that?" Breezy replied, shifting her weight to one side. "C'mon, Kia, you tell me everything. It can't be that bad. All he does is smoke weed and chill on the block all day."

"Well, this is one thing that I'm not tellin' nobody."

"Shit, you tell me about Taliban all the time. Why don't you ever want to talk about Kenny?" Breezy probed.

"Because this one is nothing like Taliban. All Taliban wants to do is get high on syrup. This one wants a lot more than that—and likes to play with guns," Kia hinted.

"Oh, well, he better chill out with that shit. It's bad enough my dad is on my case about all those murders popping up around the hood like I had something to do with it. Plus, Kev just lost one of his young bols and a few homies last week. Their funerals fell on the same day. Shug was there," Breezy said with a devilish smile, knowing how Shug liked Kia.

"Don't look now, but you just talked his Rick-Ross-lookin' ass up," Kia said, pointed over by the Donna Karan section, where Shug and a group of goons were standing along with his young girl, Tee-Tee. Shug wore dark shades to hide his naturally hooded eyes. His big body looked a bit uncomfortable in the Tom Ford Jean set he wore to go with a pair of white Louie sneakers. He seemed to draw attention wherever he went.

When Breezy saw the girl with him, she rolled her eyes. Neither Kia nor Breezy could stand Tee-Tee. She was conceited, and Kev used to fuck her on the low before she met Shug, who instantly became pussy-whipped and labeled her off-limits.

To the fellas, Tee-Tee had a butter-pecan look about her. Her hair was shiny black and dyed with blue streaks that fell down her back in loops. Breezy didn't care how pretty she was or how cute the white halter sundress she wore around her petite figure went with the tan crocodile skin heels on her feet. It was a territorial thing that she'd dare not admit.

"I hate that bitch. She thinks she's the shit. Shug need to get her a new bag because that Louie is so outdated it's a shame," Breezy said, referring to a bag that came out only two months ago.

"We should go over there and mess with him and make her mad," Kia suggested, knowing Shug had a crush on her.

"No, don't do that. I'm not trying to hear Kevin's mouth if we have to stomp that bitch in here. Besides, I don't want to get into no fight before the party, and I just got my hair done."

"No, you ain't tryna get in no fight because you know Kev will kick your ass," Kia joked.

"Please, Kev too worried about his money to be thinkin' about me like that right now. I wish he was the type of guy that would make enough money then settle down. It seems like that type doesn't exist, you know what I mean? It would be nice to see a brother from the hood make it out once in a while."

Kia looked over at her best friend and saw the emotion that she was holding inside. "You want to marry Kev, don't you?"

"That would be nice, but he doesn't seem like the marrying type." Breezy looked over at Shug, who was now talking on his cell phone.

Standing almost six feet and weighing over three hundred pounds, Shug had a dark-brown complexion with a thick beard and a good grade of hair shaped up and faded out. He wore a different brand of dark shades almost every day and rocked the flyest gear a heavy-set person could wear. As he talked on the phone with his homie, Clyde, Tee-Tee picked out whatever she wanted and gave it to Shug's two goons, Vito and Chubs, to hold until they got to the register. It was their punishment for letting the block get robbed last week. When Shug's enforcer, Maniac, approached, Shug ended the call.

"What's up? I ain't know a wild nigga like you was into shopping," Shug joked with his smooth voice.

"Only shopping I do is for bullets," Maniac responded before giving him some dap.

"Did you find out about the nut that robbed my strip?"

"So far, nobody in South Philly knows anything about that tattoo with the gagged skull wearing a crown, so they must be from somewhere else 'cause when I talked to my man from Uptown, he said that there was a rumor goin' 'round 'bout some creep named the Phantom. They said he was puttin' shit down up in Germantown. So I'ma breeze through there and see if I can get any closer to this cat. He might be the same fool."

"If he ain't the same, kill him anyway, and make the shit public. I want everybody to know that I ain't the one to fuck with. Whoever got that tattoo, murk him as well. If he thinks he's a phantom, make him a ghost. Dudes ain't gonna have shit bad to say about me, because they gonna be too busy reading about my work in the paper. This city is mines, you got that?" Shug asked, poking his index finger at Maniac's chest.

Maniac nodded before glancing over at Tee-Tee, who rolled her eyes back at him with disgust. With a sinister smile, he replied, "I got it, boss."

Shug took notice to the sudden ringtone of his phone. He pulled it out and answered.

"Yeah," he said.

"I need to see you," Diamond replied on the other end. "How fast can you get to New York?"

"I'm only an hour and a half away. What's this about, ma?"

"I'll tell you when you get here. Meet me at the Westside Railyard in Manhattan. There's an old barge terminal there."

Shug locked in the location then placed the phone in his pocket. "There's been a change of plans," he said, giving Tee-Tee the keys to his Range Rover. "I gotta make a run. Maniac, go tell Gee to get his car and bring it around to the front exit."

Maniac got right on it. Without delay, Shug was gone, leaving Tee-Tee to shop alone once again.

The Westside Rail yard in Manhattan seemed calm and abandoned. The sun was slowly fading behind the tall skyscrapers across the Hudson River. The sound of traffic roared in the distance, with the usual horns beeping, engines buzzing, and police sirens howling. Eight vehicles sat in a vacant shipyard by the river. There were cars of those with expensive tastes, all parked in a complete circle. Diamond stood amongst eight powerful men. The Italian boss, John Valentino, stood with his hitman, Frank the Ventriloquist, and Sammy the Bulldozer. Miami George had his lieutenant, Tee, with him and a few other guys from Florida standing curiously in the background. There was Shug, who kept Gee and Maniac with him. The Russian mob boss, Semok Budinov, stood in front of his three shooters. Tommy Gun came alone however, but Wong Lee, the Black Cloud leader, had ten Asians dressed in black suits and shades. His number one, Kim Angeo, stood beside him, staring suspiciously.

In front of them, Bain towered behind Diamond with five additional shooters, along with the priest. She shoved her hands into the pockets of her white linen pants. The breeze rippled across her red silk blouse and tousled her long, lustrous hair. Semok lit a cigar with a silver lighter as she began.

"I called you all out here because there are some things I need to have clarified. As you know, a lot of people don't respect my seat in the Underworld. Some may even see me as unpredictable or childish. I accept the gossip and the idle chatter that I hear. But what I don't accept is a plot to bring about my demise."

The men looked at each other strangely.

"What does this have to do with us?" Don Valentino asked, extending his hands out.

"I called this meeting because I want to know who my enemies are, apart from my friends." Diamond circled while eyeing every man standing in the wide circle.

"Hey," Semok Budinov said. "We're not your enemies, if that's what you're getting at. We were brought in this circle because we were promised a fair share. We don't care what you *do*. As long as we profit, that's all that matters, right?"

"Yeah," Valentino agreed. "If you's paranoid, you might want to keep an eye on that Mexican cocksucker Clyde has for an Underboss. He's the one who has the hard-on for you. He's got every reason to, this fuckin' guy. You threw a dagger at him in front of twenty-eight masterminds." Valentino shrugged before pulling out a cigar. "I'm not saying he didn't have it coming, but you's gotta think a little better than that, doll." Valentino lit a match, burned the tip of his Cuban, pulled, and inhaled the smoke.

"I'm well aware of Chavo's distaste for me. But he's not alone. Trust me. I just want to make sure the people I half-ass respect are not a part of this disaster waiting to happen."

She was looking at Wong Lee this time, who seemed to be quiet and nonchalant. He smirked before saying, "Ms. White, please don't insult my character. If I wanted you dead, I wouldn't say a word. You would already be dead. It was me who trained you, remember? Besides, if you die, who will help me bring the rest of my people here from China?"

Diamond looked at Shug then at Tommy Gun. They seemed to feel the same way. She wasn't a problem to them. In fact, she was a solution. Her product of heroin was making them richer than they could ever imagine. When she was convinced that the men weren't a threat, she looked away and said, "Okay, since we're all on the same page, then I'll say this... Verningo Castor is not someone we want to deal with, and I need you guys to see that."

"What is it with you and this fucking guy?" Valentino asked.

"Isn't it obvious?" Tommy Gun asked. "He killed her father."

"Yes, but this is business," Wong Lee said impassively.

"Business is one thing. Common sense is another," Diamond replied. "Do you really think Castor will actually honor your deal? Let's say he does make a deal with us, and maybe he'll even fall in line for the moment. But make no mistake about it; when he learns everything he needs to know, what do you think he'll do? I'll tell you what he's going to do. He's going to knock us all off and position his own people in our spots."

"What makes you so sure?" Shug asked, leaning on Gee's Maybach.

"Because that is what I would do. I would want business to run my way and my way only. Those that didn't fall in line would fall and die. Let's not be naïve. We're not the only ones out here that can flood cities and states with drugs and whatnot. There are a lot of people that would just love to be in our shoes."

Shug folded his massive arms. "So what do you want from us?"

"Just to keep an open mind about what you're doing before you make the decision to cross over. I got a feeling that my vote won't make a difference sooner or later. But if I have a few good men backing me, then things might just save us from the drama."

"Maybe you," Semok said with a grunt. "Not us. Did you not forget, Ms. White, we still don't have a smuggling ring together?"

"Let me handle that. I'll need time to talk with the cartels," Diamond explained. "I must reason with them and have them see that this war they're fighting is frivolous. They're over there fighting for territory and God-knows what, but in the end, no one profits."

"You're serious about this?" Tommy Gun asked.

"Have you ever known me to play around, Tommy? The Mexicans have unique ways to get out product from point A to point B. You heard Butler. The Underground Kings won't use their resources and risk their business getting hit by some drug sniffing dogs. So this is the only way."

"How long will this take?" Budinov asked curiously.

"Could take months to get in contact with the right people and get them all together. Could even take a year or two," Diamond replied.

"Do we have that time to waste?" Shug asked.

Diamond smirked. "We have plenty of time. Don't let Clyde manipulate you into thinking we don't. That's just one of his many tactics to scare you all into making you guys vote as quickly as possible. Shug and Tommy, you guys know him more than anyone else. For those who are skeptical, what Clyde is doing is seeing the problem down the line before it escalates. Trust me, by the time the South American connection runs out, I'll have the Mexican leaders shaking hands. Unlike our underboss, who's supposed to be affiliated with them," Diamond said, gesturing with her manicured index finger as her sword. "Do me a favor, guys. While this is going on, keep this meeting to yourself. We may sit in a circle as equals, but some of us have ulterior motives that are bad for business in the end."

As the men began to disperse, watching with a pair of binoculars, Deshawn sat in a Dodge Durango with the window down. He had on a pair of earphones with a high-tech sound device aimed in their direction. He heard every word that was said.

Shaking his head, he removed the equipment, saying, "Looks like someone forgot to send the rest of the Underworld an invitation. Let's see what Clyde thinks about this."

Chapter Sixteen

Taking A Chance

"You can't judge a man until you've walked a mile in his shoes..."

— MONTEGA

Later that evening, Montega pulled up in a small neighborhood full of townhouses known as Brickyard. He parked the black car on Ashmead Street where his homie Nino Brown lived. Nino was a Silent King to the core but spent most of his time hooking up stereo systems and putting tint on car windows. Montega waited on the porch of Nino's aunt's house while he put 5 percent tint on the Impala's windows. That's when someone caught his attention. He only got a glimpse of her walking across the intersection down toward Collom Street.

He had to see who the fine shorty was carrying the Nordstrom bags. He trotted up the block toward Wakefield Street and turned a hard left. There, he saw her.

"Damn, shorty, slow down for a second," he urged.

The woman turned to see a familiar face from the past. He was dressed in a blue and red Polo shirt, dark-blue denim jeans, and fresh white, shell-toed Adidas. He approached her at a fast pace, not once losing the swag in his step.

"Oh my God. Not you again. Boy, it is a crime to stalk people; I hope you know that. Who you work for? TMZ?" she asked with a smirk.

"You call it stalking. I call it destiny. Anyway, where you headed?" he asked.

"To my house around the corner. Why? Did you come to help me with these heavy ass bags?" she asked, trying to lug them along.

"Ain't nobody tell you that Nordstrom was going out of business," he joked while taking the bags from her. "You could have left some of this shit behind. You probably ain't even gonna wear half of the clothes you got in here. You just spendin' 'cause a brother payin', I bet."

The girl flushed with a smile at the stranger's comment because he was absolutely right. Montega caught her smile. "Damn, that's my work right there?" he asked.

"What's your work?'

"You glowin' like a muthafucka. I'm used to seeing a lot of rain in a girl's eyes. Never thought I could be the cause of sunshine. What's your name anyway?"

"Tee-Tee," she said as she fingered a strand of hair from her face.

"So Tee-Tee, do you always let strange men carry your bags to your crib when you ain't running them over, or is it just my lucky day?"

"What I look like to you? One of those thirsty-ass chicken heads? I don't talk to people like that, let alone get close to them. You ain't no stranger, boy. I've seen you around here, Mon-te-ga," she said, poppin' her neck from side to side as she said his name. "Ain't that what they call you?"

"Yeah, but you can call me Kenny," Montega replied, admiring her.

Tee-Tee beamed when she saw him staring. Truth be told, ever since she had almost run him over on Ardleigh Street, she had her eyes on him. She found herself riding through Woodlawn just to see if he was out there. She even asked a few people about him and found out what type of guy he was. He wasn't what she expected when she first met him. If anything, she was the one stalking him.

Montega glanced over his shoulder and said, "Look. I'm probably jumpin' out there with this, but what's up with me callin' you later and maybe takin' you out to eat or somethin'?" he asked.

"I can't. I have a dude," she said politely.

"Oh yeah? Well, where he at now? And why he got you walking like this?" Montega wondered.

"Well, for your info, I'm walking by choice. My man doesn't allow me to park in front of my house for security reasons. He also doesn't like to be seen around here. Now, why are you all up in mines?" she asked seductively, rolling her eyes.

"Shit, last chick whose business I was all up in woke up late for work the following morning. Next thing you know, she was tryna run my life."

Tee-Tee sucked her teeth before noticing his devilish grin. "You so nasty," she said.

"No I'm not. I'm an animal. But I know a woman's value, which is why you should give me your number; I can show you how much you're worth, whenever your man be on some bullshit." Montega shrugged. "I ain't tryna take your man's place, because from the looks of it, you straight on the outside," he said before licking his lips. "What I want is what you want, which is probably the reason you keep breezing through my hood every time I'm out there. I just wanna be your nigga; that's all," Montega confessed.

Tee-Tee squinted her eyes to keep from blushing. There was no toying around or playing hard to get with him, because he was too persistent and always a step ahead of her. "How do I know you're not some guy trying to look all big in front of your homies? How do I know this won't get back to my dude?"

"Look. I don't even know your dude, shorty. In fact, I don't even want to know him. All I'm sayin' is that you can't judge a man until you've walked a mile in his shoes or at least walked with him. So walk with me, and take a chance," he said before pulling out a pen and writing down his number on the Auto Zone receipt where he got the tinting done.

Against her better judgment, she snatched the receipt from him and placed it into her Louie bag. After dropping the bags off at Tee-

Tee's house, Montega started for his brother's girlfriend's crib to pick him up so they could get something to wear for the party. Thinking about Tee-Tee as he walked away, he muttered, "Got one."

Tee-Tee watched him stroll off with her number and sighed while thinking to herself, *if he only knew.*

Chapter Seventeen

Go Gettas

"Bitches ain't shit..."
SHUG

As the full moon glowed on the fresh silver paint of the Bentley Flying Spur, Shug maneuvered the vehicle around the sharp curve of Kelly Drive, heading to the club in a four-car motorcade. In the passenger seat, his cousin Mike sat in silence while looking out the window.

Turning the *Becoming* CD down, Shug said, "What's on your mind, cuz?"

"I'm good. Just thinkin' 'bout something," Mike responded.

"Thinkin' 'bout that bitch that ran off with that bread, ain't you?" Shug asked with one hand on the steering wheel, the other clutching his cell phone as if he were waiting for a call. "Fuck that bitch, cuz. That shit's petty. What you need to worry about is how you gonna get the scent of pussy off your gat when you get back to your girl tonight—because you gonna go crazy when you see the shorties that's up in this muthafucka. I talked to Kay Slay, and he bringin' a bunch of those video broads to the club tonight. You know how retarded it gets when shorties see my name on a flyer."

"I ain't trippin' 'bout no broad, and I ain't trippin' 'bout no bread. It's the fact that I put my trust in shorty, and she just bounced on me as soon as I got booked. I can front like I'm good, but inside, that shit hurt. What she did can't be forgiven, nor could it be let go of," Mike reflected.

"Man, bitches ain't shit, and they never will be. That's why you gotta take 'em for what they worth. Just fuck 'em, and send they ass on their way with some La Perla underwear and Louie bags. This should be a lesson to you about trusting a bitch. I would never trust nothing that bleeds once a month. If a bitch cross me, she deadweight. That's on everything I love."

Mike shook his head. "Bol, you cold, cuz. If a shorty only knew the real you before they get involved with your ass—"

"They would still be on my pipe. You got life fucked up, cuz. My money long, even though my temper short. Now, when we get in here, don't be all in your uptown bag. I know you got a rep to uphold, but at least show your big cuz some love."

"Man, don't nobody fuck wit' y'all South Philly dudes like that," Mike joked.

"What? You got me fucked up. I don't just claim South Philly. This whole muthafuckin' state is mine," Shug said as he pulled up to the front of the club on Delaware Avenue where the line was around the corner.

It was an electrifying event in the city of Philadelphia. The club set the tone for Saturday night, and all the playboys on the streets showed their faces. There were so many women, so much jewelry, so many foreign cars, old schools hoopties, and Hollywood spot lights; the parking lot looked like a music video.

Across the street from the club, females in tight designer dresses and high heels approached the line. A black-on-black Chevy Impala pulled into the lot. Montega pulled up and found a parking spot all the way in the back. Accompanying him was his brother, Taliban, and his righthand man, Razor. "Damn, that long-ass line," Razor said, getting out.

Razor drew attention with the diamond chain Montega had given him from the robbery. He had modified the chain by adding an iced-out pendant of the crowned skull with the bandanna gagged in his mouth. Around it read the words, Silent Kings. He had hustled hard to get that pendant and knew it would attract females like a magnet. "Tonight, we gonna make our name known," he said before heading for the line with others following him.

After the hassle of waiting in line, then getting searched, Razor and Taliban paid an extra fee for not having their IDs then walked inside. They headed up the steps where the real party began. Inside, it was off the chain. DJ Diamond Kuts was on the ones and twos, playing Young Jeezy and R. Kelly.

Trap all day, play all night. This is the life of a... (aye) the life of a... go getta... (aye) go getta... (aye) go getta... (aye) go getta (yeaaah!)

In the VIP, Shug and Kev were surrounded by rich gangstas and bad and bourgeois women. The females didn't care how heavyset and dark-skinned Shug was; they loved him, especially the way he rocked his dark Cartier shades like a true winner.

"Aye, Kev, let me holla at you for a second," Shug said, leaning over the balcony.

"What's good?" Kev asked as he joined him.

"Look, homie. What I say to you, don't take to heart," Shug began. "I'm tellin' you this because I fucks with you more than I do anybody else in our circle, but you slippin', man. I meant to get on you the night y'all got robbed, but I didn't because of TJ's death. How you let some thirsty-ass clowns on four-wheelers roll up on y'all like that? Where were your shooters? Matter fact, where was the lookout? I mean, c'mon, man. You smarter than that. This ain't no game. Them fools coulda done you like the others. You my man, cuz. If I lose you, I don't know who to trust, and that's real talk." Shug looked over at his homie.

"And another thing," he continued. "You need to step your game up 'cause fifty bricks a month ain't shit. I got dudes out West Philly buyin' a hunnid, and I'm chargin' them full price. You and Mike the only ones in the city that's getting' them for ten a join, and Mike touching eight to a bean, easy. What I gotta do? Hypnotize you into getting' some of this real paper?"

"You right. I just be tryna take shit slow out here. I ain't tryna end up in the Feds," Kev justified.

"Take it slow, my ass. I know you, cuz. It ain't about the Feds. You just being tight; that's what that is. And don't try to say that broad Breezy is up in your pockets, because you be tight with her fine ass too, got her riding in a Mazda. You kiddin' me? She the type you put in nothing less than a S-class. You better get your mind right before another rich gangsta spark her interest," Shug warned, playfully throwing a right hook to Kev's body, which Kev quickly blocked.

"Oh yeah, one more thing before I forget," Shug mentioned. "Remember that Spanish broad you was hittin' when my cousin got knocked?"

"How can I forget? You're talking about Jennifer. Why? What's up with shorty?" Kev asked.

"I need her info. Mike wants to see her about something," Shug said while running his fingers through his beard.

"But I thought you said he didn't give a fuck about her."

"He *don't* give a shit about her, but shorty took some paper from him, and I need to get it back. So do you have the address, or are you gonna keep asking pointless questions? What? You still bangin' her or something'?"

"Nah," Kev lied, turning back to look down at the bar. "I haven't talked to her in a minute, but I heard she moved across the bridge to Jersey. The address is on my voicemail. I got you," he said as he looked down at Breezy, who was with her girlfriends by the bar.

Shug followed his gaze. "How's that pussy down there?"

"Man, that shit on one thousand, cuz," Kev admitted. "I just can't get enough of her bowlegged ass. She's a super-freak between them sheets."

"Yeah, I bet she is," Shug replied as he checked her out in her mini dress. In the back of his mind, he wondered if he gave her some bread behind Kev's back, would she accept it. Before he could come up with the answer, someone else caught his attention.

"Aye, what's up with her girlfriend Kia?" Shug inquired. "Now, shorty can get it. She look like she got grease between them legs. Look how that ass sittin' in that dress. Goddamn, what she mixed with? Indian?"

"Something like that. Her pop's supposed to be half-Saudi or Afghan, some place overseas. Her mom's Black and Cherokee. Shorty got a good head on her shoulders too. She smart. She work at one of them big-ass buildings downtown, and she's single at the moment," Kev said before looking over at his man with a wry smile.

Montega brushed through a few groups of females who were feeling the handsome thug dressed in Polo from top to bottom. As one of the females grabbed him by the arm, he spotted someone more alluring.

"Excuse me for a quick sec," he told the thick, chocolate shorty he had seen in a *Straight Stuntin'* magazine before walking off.

Razor and Taliban picked up where he left off. Montega followed the pretty redbone in the midnight-blue KIKI Montparnasse designer dress all the way to the back. Before she could enter the restroom, he grabbed her by the arm. Tee-Tee turned, surprised to see him there. "Boy, what the hell are you doing here?" she asked while looking around cautiously.

"It's funny because that's the same thing I was wondering about you," Montega replied.

Tee-Tee quickly pulled him to the side. "I'm here with one of my girlfriends, but my dude is up on the balcony also. I don't want to get you in no shit, because he can get real jealous."

Montega looked up on the terrace, not knowing who was who. There were so many ballers on the balcony, drinking champagne and talking slick to the females around them; he doubted if anyone could be paying them any mind. "So I take it you can't lose him tonight and hangout with me," he said with an attractive smirk.

Looking into his sparkling brown eyes, she couldn't understand why it was so hard to turn him down like she'd done so many others. She didn't want to appear easy either. She placed a hand on his chest and looked him in his brown eyes.

"Slow down, boy. You're speeding real fast," she teased while pinching the collar of his shirt.

"I could be flyin' if I had a copilot to fly with," he replied, moving in closer. "You do like taking flights, don't you?"

Tee-Tee blushed before biting down on her bottom lip. "I don't even know you like that, to be honest."

"That's why it's all the more fun. Don't tell me you don't like to take risks," he said, eyeing her firm, perky breasts as they sat up in her spaghetti-strap dress.

Seeing that she had his full attention boosted her ego. She moved in closer so that her breasts brushed against his chest, took him gently by the nape of his neck, and whispered in his ear, "I'm not the one taking a risk here, Montega. I told you before about dealing with a girl like me. So be careful what you ask for because there's a lot that comes with this right here." She took his hand and let him feel what was up her dress. Her panties were soaked.

Not fully understanding her response, Montega just smirked anyway before she turned and walked off, giving him a show with every sway of her hips. He smelt his hand and enjoyed the cherry scent. *Goddamn,* he thought as the sensation went straight to his dick.

Watching from the bar, Kia and Breezy were shocked at what they just saw. Their mouths were damn near to their collarbones. They slowly looked at each other, wondering if the other saw what just happened.

"Are you serious?" Breezy asked while grabbing her cup of champagne. "She's a fucking whore. Wait 'til I tell Kev this shit."

"That bitch is trouble," Kia retorted. "She better not get my brother into no bullshit if she knows what's best for her."

"I don't know what Shug sees in her."

"Sees in who?" Kev asked as he snuck up on them.

Breezy decided not to inform him about the situation until after they left the club. The last thing she wanted to do was get Montega caught up. "Hey, baby boy," she said, wrapping her arms around Kev's neck. He kissed her on the cheek then stepped back to get a good look at her.

"Damn, Bree, you look good as shit. Umm, I'm 'bout to say fuck this party and roll out with you right now."

Breezy beamed like a pair of headlights. Kev was the only one who could make her flutter. He then stepped forward and kissed her neck. "Stop, boy, 'fore you start something in here," she shyly said, looking around at all the nosy chicks seething with jealousy.

"Why don't y'all come up to the VIP with us? It's plenty of bottles up there. In fact, I'll make some of them move so y'all can sit down," Kev invited.

"Please, Kev, we are not trying to be around all them groupies up there. We fine right where we are," Kia stated as Razor pulled up behind her.

Kia smiled at the sight of her play brother. She had to admit, he looked real good in his outfit. Razor was a vicious, two-piece dickie set, Timberland-boot-wearing kind of guy. Seeing him out of his element—in a pair of PRPS jeans with an Yves Saint Laurent belt and a fresh white Polo V-neck T-shirt with his chain dangling—all he had to do was make a move on her, and all that play brother shit would be out the door.

Kev, however, couldn't believe who was standing a seat away from him. As Razor handed the bartender twenty dollars for a cup of Gray Goose and pineapple juice, Kev noticed the crowned skull pendant that looked to be gagged hanging from his neck. It was the same image as the tattoo that he had seen the night when he got robbed out on the avenue. He had been looking all around South Philly for that so-called gang, and now he was possibly standing right in front of a member. "Baby, I'ma holla at you in a second. I'll be right back," Kev said, gazing up at Razor's chain before stepping off at the same time as Montega showed up.

"Let me get a glass of Goose," Montega said to the bartender.

"What you doin', talkin' to that bitch Tee-Tee?" Breezy demanded to know, causing Montega to turn and frown at her.

"Damn, why you so worried about it? Don't watch me; watch TV," he said, popping fly.

"Ain't nobody watching you. Who is you? I'm just lookin' out for my best friend's brother, but I see you over here feelin' yourself a little too much," Breezy criticized.

"You wanna look out for me?" he asked with his eyebrows raised. "Look out for me when I'm fucked up and in need. Everybody always looking out for shit that don't pertain to them. Look out when a nigga truly falling apart instead of looking down on him. Otherwise, I can look out for myself."

"Excuse me?" Breezy said, snapping her neck back in disbelief. "Aye, Kia, I think you need to getcha brother with his smart-ass mouth before I smack the shit outta him."

Montega chuckled arrogantly. If there was one thing he enjoyed, it was a feisty woman after pushing her buttons. "You ain't scared to talk to me like that?"

"Pussy, fuck you!" Breezy growled.

"You might wanna find somethin' safe to fuck with, sweetheart. Otherwise, I would hate to have to clean this whole bar counter with your pretty ass," he said, giving her a wink and a smile. "Recognize a real G when you see one because there ain't too many in here."

"Whatever. You'd be surprised," Breezy said, before sipping from her cup.

"Would y'all two chill out?" Kia suggested before Breezy snapped. "What's wrong with you two? How did y'all even start arguing when we're supposed to be havin' a good time?"

"He started it when he got smart with me," Breezy protested.

"Nah, you need to mind your business, with ya nosy ass. Let me find out you got a wire on you," Montega fired back.

"I know one thing... You better watch ya mouth. Ain't nobody worried about you and that corny ass bitch. Who the fuck is she to be worried about anyway?" Breezy asked, tossing her Indian-straight, full-length hair back. "You wanna fuck with a whore, go right ahead. I'm over this."

Before Montega could reply, the bartender handed him his drink. "*Bitch*," he mumbled before walking off.

Breezy glared at him with pure evil in her eyes. She was the type who spent her whole life stomping out deception and dirt. Like her father, she was an outstanding investigator, which was evident by how nosy she was. She hated phoniness and dishonesty, which were things she saw in Tee-Tee. Being the overprotective woman that she was, she wanted to warn Montega about her before he got himself in too deep. She knew she could be a little over-the-top at times, but that didn't give him the right to play her like he had. No one had ever talked to her in such a disrespectful manner.

When Kev got to the top of the balcony where Shug was, he sat by his side. "Yo, man, I think one of them dudes that jammed us up is down there by the bar," Kev said, pointing to the light-skinned guy with the sharp, nappy afro. When Shug saw that the guy had Kia blushing, he got hot with jealousy. Kev looked over and saw Shug boiling. "I'ma handle this dude myself," Kev said before rising.

"Wait. Make sure you do it after the party. I don't need you getting caught up behind this shit. Oh, and Kev, when you put that clown down, make it public. You know how I rock. I want everybody to know that no one takes from us and thinks he can live to brag about it," Shug ordered as he leaned back in his seat.

Kev walked off just as Gee started to make it rain over the balcony with twenty-dollar bills. Most of the so-called sophisticated women abandoned their spots to grab some of the cash that showered onto the floor from above. Rent money was on Gee this month. Montega watched from the floor with envy as the guys on the balcony launched stack after stack onto the crowd below. "Damn, them dudes must got crazy money to blow," he mumbled in amazement.

He even saw a few guys scraping up twenties on the low. When he looked a little harder, he couldn't believe that his own brother was on his knees, lunging at bills and shoving women to the side with no shame in his game. Montega quickly moved through the crowd and grabbed him by the arm. “What the fuck you doin’, dickhead?” he asked in disgust. “You’re making an ass out of yourself.”

“Man, money is money, regardless where it comes from. Somebody gotta pay for my get-high this weekend,” Taliban said. His eyes were dilated behind the shades he wore.

“Dog, they’re throwin’ money for the women, not you. Let them get some at least.”

“Man, I don’t care if the money was to help cure cancer; I’m getting’ mine,” Taliban stated before going back down to snatch a few more bills.

Montega shook his head, repulsed, and walked away. He was already pissed from the way Fly-Ty had carried Taliban on the block with the store situation, now this. Although Montega didn’t have much, he still had his pride, and he wore that on his sleeve like a fashion statement.

On the other side of the room, Kev searched the club for Maniac, Shug’s top enforcer. He knew wherever he was, a bunch of whores and hood rats were sure to follow.

When Kev found the dread head, he was on the dance floor with two freaks who worked at Delilah’s strip club. Kev tapped him on the shoulder and pulled him to the side. “What’s up? You good?” Maniac asked.

“Naw, I ain’t good. I got a major problem,” Kev said seriously.

“Where he at?” Maniac snapped to attention, assuming that he had to put somebody down.

Kev motioned for him to calm himself. “Not right now. We gonna get the dude after the party.”

After showing Maniac who the guy was, he abandoned the two Spanish girls and went to keep a close eye on Razor. There was no way he was letting him out of his sight.

Montega sat at the bar, watching Tee-Tee dance to almost every song that came on with a knocking beat. Her movements were magnificent as she gyrated her hips and bounced her bubble-shaped ass to the beat. Tee-Tee knew he was somewhere watching her. Every now and then, she would smile at him and give him a little show to lock in his mind. As he took another sip of Goose, Razor appeared, giving him some dap.

Montega knew what that meant. "Yo, I'm 'bout to fade," Razor said, feeling a little tipsy.

"With who?" Montega asked, looking around.

Razor stood to the side and pointed to the thick chocolate chick who had grabbed Montega's arm earlier and smirked. "The darker the berry—"

"The sweeter the juice," Montega said, finishing the sentence. "She nice, but who is she?"

"I don't know, and I don't really care. In fact, I'm gonna hit. That's all that matters," Razor replied.

"Yeah, but you not gonna do no background on her? She could be tryna set you up or something. You never know, yo."

Razor's excitement quickly started to vanish. He was really getting tired of Montega treating him like a little kid.

"What's up with you, yo?" Razor snapped.

Montega looked into his angry, brown eyes. "What you mean, what's up with me?'

"You know what I mean. Every time I meet a chick, you always got somethin' to say about it. You ain't my fuckin' pops, and you ain't my boss."

"I ain't say I was. I just don't want—"

"You just need to fall the fuck back. That's what you need to do. Just because your ass got kidnapped and tortured by some dumb ass bitches doesn't mean it will happen to me. How you gonna tell me how to move with a broad when you yourself fuck bitches you don't know on the regular? Maybe it ain't the Blood Hornets that got your head messed up. Maybe it's something else. What? You jealous or something?"

"Jealous of what?" Montega asked, sizing him up.

"You don't wanna go there with me. I fucks way more bitches than you ever will. Check my status."

"Man, them busted ass, corner-store-shoppin' bitches easy as shit to fuck. You ain't sayin' nothin' slick," Montega fired back, bruising his homie's ego. "I guarantee I can fuck any of 'em, including shorty. She couldn't touch my bottom-of-the-barrel chick on her best day. Fuck would I be jealous for? You know what? I ain't got shit else to say to you. Go 'head and roll with that slidda."

Montega turned his back on Razor.

Feeling low, Razor shook his head and flagged him. "Fuck you," he said before heading for the exit.

Montega turned and watched him vanish through the crowd then started to feel bad about what he said. Really, he wanted to apologize, but his pride just wouldn't let him.

Chapter Eighteen

The Promise Of Death

"It's like a plant. You just give it a little wetness and watch it grow."

— MONTEGA

When Razor stepped outside of the club, accompanied by the chocolate stallion, a cool gust of night wind greeted them. He had left his jacket in Montega's car. He didn't care about that; all his mind could focus on was how he was going to dive in some pussy. He knew Montega was trying to pull the little redbone shorty and hoped he made out good. He just wished he'd stop being so contradictive. Montega was so worried about everyone else; he failed to take a look at himself.

"Yo, ma, where's your wheels at?" he asked, stuffing his hands in his pocket.

"I parked around the corner," she replied.

"What you park around the corner for? It's a parking lot right by the club," Razor wondered.

"Because people like to break in cars when you park there. I'd rather mine be in a parking garage where it's safe," she explained.

Yeah right. She probably got a piece of shit and don't want anybody to see it. Who she think she foolin'? he thought.

Walking up the street, he glanced over to Delaware Avenue.

As the two cut through the narrow block behind the building, he looked over his shoulder. It seemed like he and the chick were being followed. *Perhaps Montega was right,* he thought before reverting his attention to the chain around his neck and cursed himself for not having a gun on him. He really wanted to tuck his chain down in his shirt but figured the shorty would peep game and try to clown him. He looked behind again but saw no one.

Just then, a white car turned down the one-way street. Razor sighed in relief when he saw a white Lexus—witnesses, just in case anything popped off. As he and the chick walked down the sidewalk, the back window of the Lexus rolled down, and Maniac stuck his head out.

"Aye, man, what does that stand for?" he asked, referring to the chain.

Razor stopped and said, "Silent Kings."

Maniac turned his attention to Kev in the passenger seat. Kev nodded, and Maniac whipped out a HK MP-9 submachine gun with an attached silencer. Razor's eyes looked like two boiled eggs. He froze like ice. His heart felt as if it wanted to burst out of his chest. The suppressed muzzle spit out a hail of bullets. Each slug connected accurately. Razor fell back in a shiver of pain. His back slammed into the wall before his body rolled to the ground. The subsonic lead shower ended just as quickly as it began.

"Hurry up and finish them off so we can bounce," Kev ordered.

Maniac cautiously got out of the car, looking around as both Razor and the chick now fought for their lives. The girl gasped for air, watching the brown-skinned man with dreadlocks stand over her with the machine gun pointed at her skull. Maniac released a silent burst into her skull with no remorse. He pulled the trigger and finished her off. Then he stepped over her body and aimed at Razor.

"No... no," Razor grunted in pain while trying to shield himself. His hands were already bloody. One of the 9mm bullets had already went in and out of his left palm. He had never been as fearful for his life than he was now.

Maniac got a rush out of Razor's fear. With a black heart, he pulled the trigger once more, leaving his body stiff and smoking with hot led. Before rolling out, he snatched the chain from Razor's neck and then got back into the whip. Kev then gave Gee the nod to pull off.

Inside the club, people were starting to make their exits. Montega turned to look at Tee-Tee. She was talking with a dark-skinned, large, big-belly guy with a thick beard and a faded haircut. One thing that stood out on him was his huge arms and his hands, which glistened with diamond jewelry. Judging by the way the two interacted, he concluded that he had to be the dude she was claiming.

"Cock-blockin' ass," he mumbled before finishing his drink.

When Shug and Tee-Tee finished talking, she approached Montega by the counter. Acting as if she was getting something from the bar, she said to him with her back turned, "Give me your car keys and come out in five minutes. My dude thinks I'm stupid. Now he talkin' about going over New Jersey with his homies. I know he goin' with some bitch," she said with an attitude.

Montega slid the keys onto the bar counter then casually walked off. He walked over to his sister. Unintentionally, he bumped into the big fella he suspected of being Tee-Tee's boyfriend. "My fault, big homie," he said as Shug turned to look at him.

Shug quickly sized him up. He didn't see Montega as a threat, so he replied, "You cool, cuz."

When Shug turned his back, Montega headed for the exit with no clue to who the big guy really was. Outside, he noticed that there were a lot of police cars heading up the one-way and turning behind another building. He then approached the black Impala, opened the door, and slid into the leather driver's seat.

The first thing that hit his nostrils was the smell of Tee-Tee's Marc Jacob Daisy Dream perfume. When he shut the door, he looked over to see her smiling at him seductively. Montega didn't say a word; he just started the engine, shifted the gear in drive, and pulled off. The ride was quiet besides the melody of 50 Cent coming from the speakers.

G-Unit... We in here... We gonna get the drama popping, we don't care... It's going down... 'cause I'm around... 50 Cent, you know how I get down. What up, blood... (What!) What up, cuz... (What!) What up, blood... (What!) What up, gang-sta!

They arrived at her house in no time. He parked in front of her door and shut off the engine. Tee-Tee let herself out then looked at him while he sat still in his seat. "Are you comin' in, or are you just gonna sit there and look dumb?"

"I ain't gotta worry about nobody waiting for me behind that door, do I?" he asked. She rolled her eyes then shut the door before walking off. Montego punched in a code on the touch screen of his GPS monitor. The stash spot under his dash board opened. There, the sparkling gold-plated tiger-stripe Desert Eagle rested beside Razor's .357 revolver. He looked at the gun and shook his head, realizing his man was unarmed. He grabbed the Dessy and smoothly tucked the gun behind his waistband and got out.

He cautiously followed her into the house and was relieved to see that he didn't have to shoot anyone.

"Do you feel better now, wit' ya scared ass?" Tee-Tee asked as she shut the door behind them.

"I'm not safe yet. I still gotta keep my eyes on you," he said, taking a seat on her plush tan sofa.

"And why do you have to keep an eye on me?" she asked while walking over to turn on some music.

"Because you was killin' 'em in that little dress and heels tonight, and I'm not ready to go. I don't know why your dude wanna go out when he got something nice right here."

Trying not to blush more than she already had, she replied, "Whatever. You probably just saying that so you can get some pussy tonight."

"I'm serious, shorty. You tight work, *and* you can dance. What more would a man need? And for the record, I ain't gotta say shit to hit that tonight. If you wasn't putting it out there, I wouldn't be here now, would I?" he asked. She slowly walked over to him after putting on the first track of R. Kelly's *TP.2* CD.

"Oh really?" Tee-Tee asked, seductively approaching him. Montega sat on the couch, watching her every move as the melody of the music played. He didn't know whether it was the liquor or just his sexual transmutation, but shorty had him feeling like he'd been dreaming. "Well, I guess there's no point of wasting time then, now is there?"

Montega watched as she stood in front of him with her hands on her hips. He smirked before he unbuckled his belt. "There's always foreplay, you know," he replied.

Tee-Tee looked down at him as he pulled his soft penis out with the cutest smile she had ever seen from a man. "You want me to suck ya dick?" she asked. Her arched eyebrow raised.

"No, but you want to, so stop frontin'."

"Ain't nobody frontin', boy," she said, rolling her eyes at him before pulling loose strands of hair from her face. She found him magnetic. She dropped down to her knees. Holding his softness in her hand, she looked up at him with a smirk. "What am I supposed to do with this little shit?" she joked.

"It's like a plant. You just have to give it a little wetness and watch it grow," Montega coached.

"You have a crazy way with words, you know?" Tee-Tee said as she went down on him.

Montega sat back with both arms sprawled across the back of the sofa, looking up at the white, popcorn ceiling. He grunted as he felt her warm tongue consummating his thickness. "Wait 'til you see what else I have a way with."

Tee-Tee slowly tried to gobble the full length of his shaft. Her neck rolled into half his length then retreated back skillfully. She could feel him grow with every bob of her head, every twist of her tongue, and every constriction of her warm mouth. Before she knew it, he was too large and too much to handle. Popping the head of his member out of her mouth, she paused and took a deep breath while staring at the brown treat glistening before her with her coating of saliva.

Montega was double the size of Shug and had her inner thighs dripping wet. She stood to remove the straps of her dress. Montega stood to help her. Tee-Tee closed her eyes as she felt his wet tongue gently stroke her skin, and his smooth hands pulled the dress down her body until it fell to the floor.

When she opened her eyes, Montega helped her out of her G-string then took his shirt off and pulled his pants down. Tee-Tee pushed him back on the couch and mounted his big, long dick. She sunk to the bottom slowly then stopped to let it marinate inside of her gushy walls. She pulled herself up so that she could concentrate on the length while squeezing her walls in tightly. Montega gripped her small waist and slammed her back down on his lap. Throwing her head back, she moaned, feeling the violent rush of pleasure as he rammed his dick.

"Ssss, ooh, yes, boy, do that again," she moaned while riding him to the beat of the music.

"What's little about this shit now?" Montega asked, palming her firm, apple-shaped ass, matching her movements with long, penetrating strokes; all the while, sucking on her perky, brown nipples. As the sound of her juicy pussy slapped against the base of his shaft, his cell phone rang. It seemed as if the more he forced into her, the louder she moaned. There was no way he would stop in the middle of this intense pleasure. Tee-Tee had a flat, washboard stomach with a diamond piercing right above her navel. Her belly rolled like an exotic dancer. Her pussy was as tight as a vice.

"When you… nut… uhhh… make sure you… you pull out… be… cause… I'm not on… de… po," she warned between strokes.

Montega obliged as he gripped her slim waist and pumped her with force. "Oww! Fuck this. You know what? Fuck me on the table," she demanded with lust.

In one motion, Montega had her in the air. He tripped over his jeans bunched around his ankles and almost stumbled forward. Slowly, he lowered her back on the coffee table. Taking her by the waist, he thrusted forward while pulling her to him. Tee-Tee clawed at his chest and scratched at his tight abs as he plowed her pussy like a maniac and delivered her to the land of ecstasy.

"Kenny! Umm, Kenny! Uhh! I mis… judged… you!" she said, trying to talk between his thunder strokes.

Montega was silent and seemed to be totally focused on what he was doing. The more she tightened her walls around him, the more pressure he felt rising within. When it came time to get his, he started to pull out, but Tee-Tee refused to let his seed go to waste. She found herself curious to what he would look like if he released his seed.

Locking her legs around him, she let him explode inside of her while watching the frenzy in his orgasm contort his face. He dropped forward, catching himself with his hands. He then heaved deeply as beads of sweat formed over his forehead. Tee-Tee smiled, knowing the effect that she had on Shug in the bedroom. But Montega surprised her. He picked her up off the coffee table and walked toward the staircase.

"Boy, where are you taking me?" she asked, wrapping her arms around his neck.

"What you think? It's over? This shit's just the beginning. We gonna take this to the bedroom because that was just a sample. I'm 'bout to go all in now."

Chapter Nineteen

Bad News

"Something tells me that all these murders are tied to that maniac."

— DETECTIVE LUCCA

Moans and grunts came from the bedroom of Detective Whitehead's secret apartment in West Philadelphia. The smell of sex filled the small room, mixed with the aroma of Tommy Hilfiger cologne and Hennessy. On the queen-size mattress, Whitehead's naked, hairy body lay on top of the woman he met at a nearby Wal-Mart. She was a registered nurse that worked at Germantown Hospital. With quick rabbit strokes, he steadily pounded out her insides.

Before he could reach his orgasm, the buzzing of his cell phone distracted him. Whitehead tried to ignore it, thinking it was his wife, but it wouldn't stop ringing. He stopped the fuckfest, sighed, and rolled over to answer it.

"Hello?"

"Gary, where are ya, bud?" his partner asked.

"I'm at the spot, why?"

"I think you need to pull up your pants. We've got another body to deal with, and you won't believe where we found him," Dt. Lucca stated.

"Humor me," Whitehead said dryly.

A half an hour later, Dt. Whitehead got to the scene after hearing that the murder was right around the corner from Delaware Avenue. He saw that the crime scene was flooded with news reporters.

"What we got?" Whitehead asked as he squatted down by a dead girl's body covered with a white sheet.

"Female. African-American in her early 20s, shot multiple times in the chest and once in the head," Lucca explained as his partner pulled back the sheet.

"Any possible motives?" Whitehead asked before placing the sheet back over her head then standing.

"None that I know of. She still has her money in her purse, and his is still in his pocket," the detective said as he walked over to Razor's body to remove the sheet. "Take a look at this though."

Lucca showed his partner the tattoo. "Silent Kings," Whitehead said, thinking back to where he saw that tattoo.

"Do you recognize it? It's the same symbol that Rabeeto Mendez has on his arm. I don't know, Whitehead. Something tells me that all these murders are tied to the same maniac, somehow."

"You know what, Tony? You might be right."

That night, when Whitehead got home, he followed his normal routine before climbing into bed with his wife. Maria didn't say a word this time. She had seen the footage on the news and saw her husband at the crime scene. Turning over to look at him, she frowned when she saw that his back was turned to her. She moved in closer and began kissing him on the back of his neck.

Maria couldn't remember the last time they made love. It had been that long. As she rubbed his hairy chest, Whitehead gently grabbed her wrist and removed her hand.

"Not tonight, honey. It's been a long day, and I've got a lot to do tomorrow," he lied before closing his eyes and drifting off to sleep.

Maria turned back over in disappointment. As she stared at the wall, all she could think about was what he had been up to when she wasn't around. It was obvious that she was losing him fast.

Montega awoke to the sound of his cell phone. The whole room was lit up by the rays of the morning sun. City trucks could be heard chugging along on the streets, and the sound of tree branches being cut overlapped everything else. Looking beside him on the bed, he found Tee-Tee was sleeping peacefully. Slowly, he sat up while the drowsiness of a hangover from last night clouded his vision. He was so drunk he had forgotten he took Tee-Tee home and ended up spending the night.

He remembered having sex with her but thought it may have been just a good dream. Lifting up the covers to see her flawless, naked body, he knew no dream could ever hold so much detail.

Montega reached for his cell phone on the nightstand to answer it as it buzzed with the hustler's anthem. "Yo?" He yawned.

"Oh, thank God you're alright," Kia said with relief. "Where the hell are you, boy?"

"I'm back Brickyard. Why? What's up?" he asked while sitting up, hearing his sister's disturbed voice. Kia didn't answer right away. Her brother could sense that something was clearly wrong with her. "Kia, what's up? Talk to me, sis."

"Kenny... Razor got killed last night," she finally admitted.

The words stabbed Montega in the chest like a stiletto knife. He refused to believe it. He had just seen Razor a few hours earlier. They had had a heated argument that Montega planned on settling over breakfast.

"Kia, stop playing with me, yo."

"I'm serious, boy. Why would I even play like that with you?" Kia snapped.

"Nah, Kia, not my man. I was just with him last night," Montega said, shaking his head. "This can't be happening, yo."

"It's all over the news. They said that he and some chick he was with got killed around the corner from the club. Somebody shot him up real bad. His mother had a hard time identifying the body, so she called you, but you never answered your phone. His sister is too young, so one of your friends ended up doing it."

Montega dropped the phone as reality struck him like lightning. His best friend, his partner, his brother from another mother, was gone.

Chapter Twenty

Ballet Of A Dead Soldier

"I know that kid from somewhere."

— DETECTIVE GARY WHITEHEAD

INSIDE A GIANT CHURCH CALLED IMMACULATE CONCEPTION ON CHELTEN AND ARDLEIGH...

At the funeral, almost the whole Uptown came to pay respects to the young, half-Puerto Rican, half-black soldier. Since the murder made front page, even cats that didn't know Razor showed up. "Delaware Avenue Massacre" was the headline in the Philadelphia Daily Inquirer. The mayor and other city officials were outraged by the homicide. An article inside the newspaper discussed the fact that the city was on pace to set an all-time murder record.

Montega sat in the back of the church by himself, staring at the closed coffin. He felt like crying but couldn't. His eyes just wouldn't allow tears. He had cried himself out when his mother passed. Now his tears were replaced with anger. He looked on with sympathy as he watched Razor's mother try to console her ten-year-old daughter, Carmine, as she cried out for her big brother.

Razor's father was Puerto Rican and had died of an overdose long ago. His mother was left to take care of her two children. The more Montega watched the grieving of Razor's family, the angrier he became. He was at the point where no one could tell him a thing. He would find the man who put his friend in a coffin and sentence him to the same fate; that much, he knew.

A few rows across, Breezy sat with Kia and the rest of the girls. All the way in the back, Dt. Whitehead and Lucca kept watch the whole time. They were assigned to the case and wanted to know as much about the victim as they could. There had been a lot of murders in the city, and they were searching for connections.

Once Razor's coffin was carried out of the church by the pallbearers, Montega gave Razor's mother a big hug to let her know that he felt the same way about her boy.

He didn't know what to say to her to stop her grief. "I'm so sorry, Ms. Dee. I promise you, I'm gonna get to the bottom of this," he said to her as he pulled away from her.

The woman looked in the opposite direction from him. "That's what they all say," she said before taking her daughter's hand and walking off, leaving him standing there.

After the funeral, Montega headed straight for his car parked out on Ardleigh Street. He couldn't control the anger that he felt and had to fade before he snapped.

Suddenly, the two eavesdropping detectives appeared. "Excuse me. I saw you talking to the mother of the victim. Can we speak with you for a minute?" Dt. Lucca asked, trying to play the good cop role.

"Go play in mud, pig. I ain't got nothing to say to you," Montega responded as he continued to walk away.

"Why you little—" Lucca snapped, lunging at Montega. Whitehead stopped him. Together, they watched as he got into the black Impala. "Wise-ass," Lucca muttered.

"You know what? I think I know that kid from somewhere," Whitehead said, eyeing the car suspiciously.

"You might have seen him hanging out with the Puerto Rican nut."

"I don't think so. We all know Rabeeto Mendez rides alone. I couldn't imagine anyone befriending a monster like that."

Montega started up the engine and turned up his *Until the End of*

Time CD by 2Pac. As he pulled off, the track "When Thugs Cry" began.

On hearing that, Montega hit the brake and stopped in the middle of the street where Ardleigh and Price crossed. His heart pounded, and tears were forcing their way down his cheek. He rested his head on the steering wheel, and for the first time in a long time, he cried.

Chapter Twenty-One

The Legacy Of Charles White

"Money is the root of all evil."

— DIAMOND WHITE

The White family mansion was a huge structure taking up over thirty thousand square feet of Hollywood Hills. It was made mostly of white stone with water fountains, marble galleries, spacious entry rooms, and a dual crab claw-like staircase. There were special rooms for exercising, cigars and Brandy, entertaining, even a movie theater. In the basement, beyond the wine cellar lie, the bed of the large aquarium of man-eating sharks took up three floors in height. On the second floor was a total of eight large rooms, which didn't include the master bedroom that once belonged to the late Charles White and his lovely wife, Pearl. That room was off limits.

For a house that used to be well occupied with visitors, now only the maids and a few henchmen wandered around the premises.

Diamond stood at the edge of the Olympic-size indoor swimming pool, dropping her towel to the floor. Samuel, the priest, sat at the opposite end, dressed in his usual black short-sleeved shirt, dress pants and shoes. He made an invisible cross over his forehead and chest and recited a verse when he witnessed what was under the towel.

"Then the rib, which the Lord God had taken from man, he made into a woman, and he brought her to the man. And Adam said, 'This is now bone of my bone and flesh of my flesh; she shall be called woman, because she was taken out of man.'"

Bain, who was standing beside him, grunted in agreement. Diamond was dressed in a white and gold Dior string bikini that left nearly nothing to the imagination. After testing the water with her red-polished, pedicured toes, she was satisfied and dove in for a Monday morning swim. She had just finished target practice at the range. Prior to that, she spent time at the gym, exercising to keep her figure in perfect shape. Her favorite exercise was treadmill sprints, which kept her wind up for her bouts with her personal martial arts trainer—a Black Cloud member who was ranked second under Wong Lee's Underboss. Diamond was scheduled for a one o'clock appointment with her Cuban cartel partner, José Castro, which she knew she would be late to even though she was more than capable of multitasking. She was blessed with an abundance of self-assurance and dignity, while at the same time, harboring a kill-switch she could flick on at any time.

It was just another ordinary day in the life of an Underworld princess, or as they call her, the Snow White Queen. Diamond swam across the pool and back gracefully. When she made it to the wall after her last lap, she came up for air and saw a set of brown, hairy legs. She followed them up to a face and sighed in relief when she saw Clyde smiling. Looking over at Bain and the frightened priest, she caught her bodyguard lowering his gold-plated AK-74. She looked to her right and saw her other henchmen doing the same with their weapons. She then looked back up at her brother.

This afternoon, he wasn't dressed in his usual business attire. He was looking casual in a pair of white Victorinox Khaki shorts and a red and white Zegna polo shirt with sneakers to match.

"No meeting today?" Diamond asked while staying afloat in the water.

"Only one, and it's with you. I figured you wouldn't mind if I left the suit and tie in the closet and came to see you in something a little more casual." He placed his hands behind his back and looked around the area. He frowned when he noticed Samuel there.

"May I ask why you have a priest with you?"

"Priest give exorcisms and extract demons. Perhaps, with him around, mines will continue to stay in the shadows. I think that's best for everyone," she said indirectly.

Clyde picked up her robe and held it out for her. Diamond pulled herself out of the pool and snatched it from him then dried herself off. Once she covered her exquisite assets, her brother headed for the exit. "Come on. Let's go outside. It's a beautiful day." He glanced over at the priest again.

Samuel lowered his head, not wanting a visual confrontation.

Diamond eyed Clyde suspiciously while following him out of the large pool room on the west side of the white brick mansion, where the outdoor pool overlooked a view of the ocean. It was scorching hot out, and the sun seemed angry in a cloudless, blue sky. To block the bright sunlight, Diamond picked up a pair of oval shades off the beach chair, put them on, and laid back on the chair to enjoy the warm California weather. Clyde pulled up a chair and sat next to her. A light breeze ruffled his shirt collar with the marine life scent of the ocean.

"What I want to talk to you about is our last meeting," he said, making her huff and look the other way. "Diamond, I know you don't want to hear this, but we need some kind of muscle in the smuggling business. Okay, we won't deal with Castor, cool, but sooner or later, he's gonna come at us. We're already invading his territory. You know he supplies the whole east coast. And if I know Castor, he's gonna be looking to hit us. Now, if we collaborate with the Agugbo brothers, we'll have a strong connection for drugs and another ally to defend ourselves if Castor wants to go to war."

Diamond whipped her head around to face him with anger. "Save that shit, Clyde. If Castor wanted us dead, we'd already be dead, believe me. No army could stop that. Why he hasn't killed us yet is beyond my comprehension. He doesn't deserve to live, and neither do those stinkin' South Africans. You, of all people, know I can't stand the Agugbo brothers. I've spent years trying to get them," Diamond said, sitting up.

"I understand that, but this is business. We have men sitting in our circle who don't like each other. Look at George and Stoney; better yet, look at you and Chavo. Regardless of feelings, business is never personal. You have to ask yourself, *when am I gonna put my differences aside*? This is money we're talking about. They have the diamond trade on smash; most of the top jewelers buy their diamonds from them.

"Diamonds are the quickest and easiest way to transport drug money. And let's not forget the smuggling methods that the Ape Gang are known for. Let's face it; we need them on our side. Just last week, I made a hell of a deal with an arms dealer who promised to flood us with military weapons if Castor comes at us again. Diamond, this is our father's legacy. He wanted this organization to be on top. We're living it right now. If you don't give a fuck about me, then at least do it for pops; because, from my understanding, he's the reason you are what you are today."

Diamond rolled her eyes, hating when things didn't go her way. If there was anything to get around her stubbornness, it was her father. She would have done anything for him.

"What makes you think that they'll agree to collaborate with us?" she asked sharply.

Clyde gave his sister his signature million-dollar smile. "Just let me handle that. You just have to agree to a cease-fire on Tanetche and his brothers. Is that understood?" he asked, trying to sound like their father.

The truth was that physically, Clyde was the spitting image of the late Charles White. His personality, however, was just the opposite. His father was forgiving; Clyde was vindictive. His father was generous and lenient; Clyde was selfish and impatient. His father was prudent; Clyde was impulsive. One thing that Clyde did share with Charles White, however, was his conniving ways.

Diamond took in a deep breath then exhaled. "Okay, Clyde. You win. I'm calling off all my wolves, but let me tell you something. Yes, this is a big move to accumulate more money and power, but don't for a second let it take your dignity and pride away from you. Money is the root of all evil, and it's not worth dying over."

Clyde smirked but let her words go in one ear and out the other and turned to leave. "If I were you, I'd kill that priest of yours and be done with him. I'd hate if he got in the hands of your enemies."

Diamond watched him stroll away, with squinted eyes. He reminded her of a naïve prince who had no clue about ruling an empire.

He wasn't up to leading the Great White Organization. That spot truly belonged to her.

Chapter Twenty-Two

Trapped In The Closet

"They're like sheep. They can't think for themselves. You gotta think for them."

— SHUG

BRICKYARD...

"*Good evening. I'm Cheryl Williams, and this is Channel 3 News. I'm here in a North Philadelphia neighborhood in front of a bar where, just an hour earlier, two unidentified men walked in and started shooting. Two people were killed in the shooting. The victims were a forty-five-year-old man and a forty-two-year-old woman. Police are withholding the names of the victims at the present time...*"

Montega awoke from the recurring nightmare of watching the news the day his mother was killed by a knocking on the front door downstairs. Tee-Tee jumped out of bed with panic in her eyes.

"What's going on?" Montega asked while quickly looking for his gun.

She looked over at the clock and saw that she overslept.

"Shit, it's my boyfriend. He cannot find you here, Kenny. I swear if he does, we are both dead."

"Well, what the hell you want me to do?" Montega asked, balling his face up.

"You have to hide quickly," she whispered.

"C'mon now. Hide? What I look like?"

"Please, Kenny," she begged, knowing how stubborn he could be. "You don't know him like I do. He'll freak the fuck out. Look. I know you're brave and all, think you have to take on the world with a challenging attitude. I get all that, but if you really care for me, you'll do what I say. Just hide in the closet until he leaves." She put on a robe and walked out of the room.

"Fuck you think I am? R. Kelly?" he spat as he got out of bed. He then irritably got dressed, walked into the closet, and hid behind her rack of clothes. He pulled out his cell phone and shut it off just in case someone decided to call.

When Tee-Tee opened the door, Shug came barging in. "What the fuck is up, bitch!" His voice boomed. "What took you so long to answer the damn door!"

"Shug, relax. I just woke up, okay? Why do you have to act so paranoid all the damn time?" Tee-Tee responded, rubbing her eyes as three of Shug's goons stepped in.

"You better watch ya damn mouth when you talkin' to me, bitch, 'fore I smack the shit out of you," he said, pointing his index finger in her face. "Now go get washed and dressed. We goin' out today." He flopped down on her sofa and extended his thick arms in a wide stretch.

Tee-Tee rolled her eyes as she looked at the guys who were standing around in her living room and walked upstairs to do what she was told. Shug looked around the room then picked up the remote and turned on the TV. The first thing that popped up was ESPN. He frowned as he watched the NBA highlights. He didn't take Tee-Tee as one who watched sports. His eyes reverted to the staircase with suspicion.

As she got in the shower, Montega stood in the closet in disbelief. First the nightmare of his mother, now this. Today was definitely starting off bad, not to mention, sneaking around with spoken-for women wasn't as exciting as he thought. He pondered on that until he heard footsteps approaching.

Looking through the gaps in the door, he saw a husky, dark-skinned guy walking into the room. *Trapped in a goddamn closet,* he thought. He gripped the hem of his shirt slowly and lifted it, pulling out the tiger-striped, gold-plated Desert Eagle. His heart pounded because he knew there was no talking his way out of this one. Shug searched through the dresser then made his way toward the bed. When he saw how messy it was, he looked toward the closet door. Montega exhaled with disbelief and frustration. Shug walked toward it. Montega backed to the wall, lifting the heavy .50 caliber face high, aiming at the door. He just knew he was going to catch a body early in the morning. His heartbeats increased. This was it. As Shug grabbed the handle to the closet door, Tee-Tee came in the room.

"Shareek, what are you doing?" she asked, causing him to spin around. She was wrapped in a towel, her skin was damp, and her hair was wrapped in a shower cap.

He opened his mouth but didn't have anything to say. His dumbfounded look turned serious again. "Would you hurry up and get dressed!" he barked, then walked out of the room. "I ain't got all day."

Montega respired in relief. Sweat beaded down his head, and his T-shirt was damp, sticking to his chest. Tee-Tee opened the closet to catch him tucking his gun back in his pants. She smirked and said, "You ain't no gangsta, boy, you fakin'."

"And you ain't no real girlfriend," he retorted with sarcasm.

She rolled her eyes and sucked her teeth while pushing him to the side to pick out an outfit for the day. She put together a D&G pencil skirt with a white Alexander Wang blouse, a large belt, and a pair of Chanel shoes.

"Don't forget to lock up when you leave," she whispered before kissing him on the cheek.

"You better not kiss him with those lips," Montega warned with a smirk. Tee-Tee squinted at him before slamming the closet back in his face.

After she got dressed and left with her man and his entourage, Montega came out of the closet, feeling like a cold sucka. If it were up to him, he would have walked right past her boyfriend and out the door, but out of respect for her, he obeyed her wishes. He then locked up her house and headed out to his car while turning on his cell phone. Instantly, it started to ring. He ignored it with his mind on what had just transpired.

He was tired of sneaking around. Tee-Tee acted as if her dude were royalty in the streets. He never asked her who he was, because he didn't care. He felt as though he could take on anybody, anytime. He had lost his pop, his mother, and now his best friend. Even though he had a loyal, vicious crew, he still felt alone in the world.

He stepped down the concrete steps while answering his cell phone. "Yo."

"What are you doing?" Kia asked.

"I'm on my way out. Why?" he asked, approaching his car.

"Nothing, just checkin' on you. That's all," she lied. Montega could sense the lie coming off her tongue.

"Yeah, aight, Kia. Only time you call to check up on me is when you want something. Now what's really good?"

Kia sucked her teeth. Then the truth eased out. "I need to hold your car," she professed. "Me and Breezy 'bout to go to the mall."

"Man, why that bitch can't drive her own car? I'm sure she got one."

"Boy, don't be callin' my friend no bitch. She ain't do nothin' to you. You don't see me going around disrespecting your friends, do you? So don't disrespect mine."

"Damn, why you getting all sentimental with me? You act like you don't call her a bitch all the time," Montega replied.

"That's my girlfriend. I can call her anything I want, and she knows it don't mean shit, but you seem to be rising up on her shit list. Now, her cousin, Crystal, has her car, and mine is in the shop, so I need yours. You ain't doing nothing anyway but hustling like you always do."

Montega huffed, knowing he couldn't deny her even if he wanted to. "Aight, shorty, just give me a few minutes, and I'll be over there. I gotta stop down 7th and Huntington to pick up some tree. I need to wake up."

"You need to stop smoking. That's why you so retarded now."

It ain't the weed that got me like this. It's these niggas.

After getting off the phone, he jumped in the Impala and peeled out.

As Shug drove around the city in a brand-new, white, 2005 Rolls Royce Phantom, followed by his entourage of young gunners in the black Range Rover Sport, his intention was to stop at a restaurant downtown, but instead, he ended up riding through South Philly to show off his prized possession. On the passenger side, Tee-Tee sat in boredom, twirling her finger around in her hair. She was tired of the same old shit every time she got with Shug. There were never any exciting trips out of the country, no surprises, no compliments on her attire, not even roses like he used to send to her. Now it was simple—ride around to show her off, fuck her, and drop her off.

Before she could say anything, Shug turned down the T.I. *Urban Legend* album. "Let me ask you a question while I got you here," he said, deep in thought.

"Who was that dude you was talkin' to that night in the club a few weeks back?"

Tee-Tee's heart began to thud. "What are you talking about?" she asked, trying to buy herself time to think.

"You know what I'm talkin' 'bout. Kev said his shorty seen you rappin' with some dude, and Gee said the same thing. Gee said he never seen dude before. Now you gonna sit here and lie to me? Who was he?" Shug demanded as his volume went up.

"Shareek, it's not that serious. It was just some guy tryna talk to me. I told him that I had a dude. He respected it and walked off. If your friends are so concerned about what I do, then maybe they should make their presence known instead of hiding in the shadows all the time. I'm sure they would see that there's nothing going on."

Shug backslapped her in the face with his free hand, causing the Phantom to swerve a bit on the road. Tee-Tee's head bounced off the window. Shug shouted, "Bitch, stop fuckin' lying!"

"I'm not lying, Shug!" Tee-Tee shouted back with tears.

He grabbed her hair and yanked her head toward him. "You fuckin' whore. You think I'm fuckin' stupid? Gee said y'all was talking for a minute, and you was givin' cuz some rhythm. Now, who the fuck was he?" he asked again as he pulled up to the block where Kev was flagging them down. Shug mugged Tee-Tee in the head. "I'll deal with your ass later," he said, stopping when he got to Kev.

Tee-Tee had to use every ounce of strength inside her not to cry, even though the tears were there. She felt so embarrassed. This was the fourth time Shug had put his hands on her. She instantly knew that she and Montega had to cut their relationship short before shit got ugly. Shug was nobody to play with. As she tried to fix herself up, Shug rolled down his window.

"What's up?" he asked with a mean mug. Kev saw that he wasn't wearing his glasses, which he almost always did. His lazy eye looked even heavier than before, and his eyes were red.

"Yo, we got problems. Dumb ass Homie-Time got booked last night with the same gun we used to smoke that Silent King dude at the club," Kev informed him.

Shug looked over his shoulder at Tee-Tee, making sure she wasn't being nosy, before turning back to his man. "How the fuck did he get booked, cuz? I just seen his ass at the Crab House last night."

"The dickhead was tryna sell the jawn out in New York; now he's at Riker's Island, bitchin'. It's only a matter of time before those ballistics get back and match the gun to the shooting," Kev said, putting his hands in his pockets.

"Well, he gotta take the case. That's on him. Ain't nobody tell him to go sell no gun. Fuck's wrong with him? We got the crash dummies to do that. What he worried about selling a gun for with as much money as he making? You see what I mean about these dumb ass dudes? This is why you gotta be hard on 'em. This is why you got to put a leash around they fucking necks and walk 'em. They're like sheep. They can't think for themselves, so you gotta think for 'em."

He glanced over at Tee-Tee again and said, "Bitches too."

"Oh yeah, I almost forgot." Kev added. "I got that address you were looking for. I talked to her a few hours ago. She still over in Jersey."

Shug rubbed his thick beard as he pondered his next move. Looking over at Tee-Tee again, he said, "We gonna have to do this another time, shorty. Business comes first. Kev, have one of your young bols drop this bitch off at her crib, and come with me." He unlocked his door to let her out of the Phantom.

Tee-Tee rolled her eyes then got out. Her light-skinned complexion bore a thick, red handprint from where Shug had hit her. Eyes from all around her watched with a shocked look. People began to whisper. Some even snickered under their breaths, knowing that Shug had put his foot down again. She really lost a lot of love for him after that. Although she couldn't choose a side, she decided that some payback would make her feel better. One thing for sure, and two things for certain; there was nothing worse than a woman scorned. And Shug would realize that.

Chapter Twenty-Three

Payback

"First I'm gonna get my money's worth out of her..."

— MILLION-DOLLAR MIKE

INSIDE THE CHEVY IMPALA SS...

Breezy and Kia drove across the Benjamin Franklin Bridge in Montega's tinted-out car, swerving in and out of traffic. They had just dropped him off on Blakemore Street and were trying to beat the five-o'clock rush hour.

"This car is fast as shit," Breezy said, admiring the black leather interior while jerking the steering wheel from left-to-right. The suspension bounced from side-to-side and the engine vibrated the interior. "Where did your brother get it from?"

"Girl, slow the hell down 'fore you get us both killed. It's bad enough I'm lettin' you drive his car. If he knew it was you behind the wheel, he'd have a fucking fit," Kia said.

"Fuck him, with his smart-ass mouth. He gets on my damn nerves with that nonchalant attitude of his, like he that bol. He ain't nobody. I would hate to see him with some real money—gonna call me out my name like I did something to him. He better worry about that whore he sleepin' with."

"You two always at it. If I didn't know any better, I'd think y'all liked each other," Kia said, suspiciously eyeing her girlfriend.

"Ha! Imagine that. I wish I would mess with someone from around topside. Besides, your brother ain't my type," Breezy acknowledged.

"And what's not your type?" Kia asked, a little offended.

"You know, guys that are in a rush to die or get locked up. Don't tell me that's not where he's headed if he don't cut his bullshit out. Oh, and did I mention he likes to fuck whores?"

Kia ignored Breezy's insult. "Anyway, where are we going?"

"To that bitch's house. Where else?" Breezy asked while switching lanes. "I followed Kevin a few days ago, and I think it was to her house. That's why I needed to use a different car."

"Who is she? That Spanish chick you was about to beat up a while back?"

"Yup," Breezy admitted while applying more pressure to the gas pedal with her foot.

Kia curled up her lip.

"This time, there ain't gonna be nobody to save her ass," Breezy said. "I'ma teach this hoe to keep her hands to herself and find her own man. God, it's hot as hell in here with all this black leather. Why the fuck! Don't these windows roll down?"

"I don't know, but why don't you just turn the air conditioner on? That's the smart thing to do," Kia replied, punching different buttons on the middle panel.

Once they arrived in Cherry Hill where the woman lived, Breezy parked across the street. It was a nice, quiet setting with modest houses and large front lawns split in half by concrete pathways that led from the sidewalk to the front porch. The girl that she was looking for had an indoor-porch. Breezy grabbed her mace and started to get out. "Wait, Bree, look," Kia said, pointing to the Rolls Royce Phantom Drophead that pulled up across the street from where they were parked.

When Shug and Kev got out, she quickly ducked. "Kia get down, girl, before they see us," Breezy whispered.

"Bitch, these windows are tinted black. Superman couldn't see through 'em, so stop panickin'. Now what the hell are they doin'?"

"I don't know," Breezy said, whipping out her phone. "But I'm gonna call Kevin and see—"

Kia snatched the phone from her and set it between the seats. "Are you crazy? Think about what you're about to do. You're not supposed to be here. Now, you brought me out to this girl's house. Let's see what they're up to."

When Kev started to walk up the steps, Shug followed with his hands in the pockets of his hoodie. "You sure this the spot?" Shug asked, looking around for any witnesses. The neighborhood was quiet. Cars were parked up and down the block, but there was no sign of anyone.

"Positive," Kev said before stepping up to knock. "I told you I drove out here before. Look. When I knock on the door, stay to the side until she opens it up because shorty be on some paranoid shit after we let her keep that bread." Kev knocked.

A minute later, the door opened. Jennifer stood in the doorway, smiling. Before she could say a word, Shug came out of nowhere and landed a hard right hook to her jaw and almost took her head off.

"Oh my God?" Kia said with her hand over her wide-open mouth.

"What happened? I missed it," Breezy said, cursing herself for trying to reach for her cell phone. Before Kia could respond, tires screeched to a halt as Mike pulled up in his Benz. He double parked next to the black Range Rover and quickly got out. The goons in the Rover did the same. Together, they all headed for the house.

Inside, Shug dragged a screaming Jennifer into the living room, pulling out a custom Taurus 1911 semi-automatic .45. It was a chrome pistol with a pearl white handle and gold trigger. Shug saw none of its beauty as he smacked her over the head several times with it. The loud cracks to her skull were so powerful that Kev turned his head away in discomfort.

"You think you can steal from my family and get away with it, you grimy bitch? Huh?" Shug growled.

Just then, Mike walked through the front door. When he saw

Jennifer lying on the floor, he felt no sense of remorse. Shug grabbed her by her hair and made her get on her knees to face Mike.

"Look at him!" he said coldly to the Dominican chick.

"Mike, please. I have your money. I never spent a dime. Please, Michael—"

"Shut up, bitch!" Shug snapped, smacking her to the floor with a backhand.

Jennifer cried hysterically. She was totally confused. When Mike went to jail, Shug was the one who told her that Mike never wanted to see her again because he wasn't coming home. It was his way of getting into her head and into her panties as well. Afterward, he introduced her to Kev. Even though she believed him, she still kept Mike's money in a safe place just in case he did get out. Shug, on the other hand, had no idea Mike really loved the broad. He surely didn't want his cousin to know he busted her ass a little after he got locked up. He had to make his anger look real in the eyes of his cousin, so he continued to pistol whip her. This time, she blacked out.

"What you want to do, Mike?" Shug asked. "I can have my shooter kill this snake right now if you want."

"Not yet. First, I'm gonna get my money's worth out of her..." Mike said, unbuttoning his pants. Instantly, he started pissing on her. Warm golden urine splashed Jennifer's bruised face, washing some of the blood from her battered skin.

Shug looked at Kev with a crooked smile. Kev shook his head in disbelief, while Shug turned back to look at his cousin. "Payback makes my dick hard, cuz," he said. "I'm after you."

After waiting in the car for almost an hour, Kia and Breezy watched as Kev was the first to come out of the house. Then came Mike, Shug, and the rest of the guys, all of them cautiously checking their surroundings before getting into their vehicles and speeding off. When Kia saw the smoke coming from the house, her eyes bulged. "Oh my God, Bree, we shouldn't have come here," she said as reality set in.

"What? Kia..."

"We should not have come here," Kia said again. "The house is on fire, and nobody else came out. We gotta get outta here, bitch. Drive! Drive off now!" she shouted.

"Okay, okay, I'm going. Relax." Breezy quickly started up the engine and peeled out just in time to see the house go up in flames in the rear-view mirror. Although neither wanted to admit it, they had just been witnesses to a murder. And if this was the way Shug and his people operated, then her brother was in serious trouble.

Chapter Twenty-Four

The Battery Pack

"Never turn a hoe into a housewife."

— MANIAC

The next morning, Montega lay in the bed, exhausted from another long episode of mind-blowing sex. As Tee-Tee tried to regain her breath, she sat up and braced herself, knowing that what she was about to tell him would change his life for the worst.

"Damn, Tee-Tee, what was that all about?" he asked, amazed by her sudden sex drive.

"Kenny, we have to talk," she said, fidgeting with her fingers. "There's something I have to tell you, and you might not like what you hear, but I can assure you, it's the truth."

Montega sat up with his elbows pressed to the bed, frowning. "What's up?" he asked.

"Look. I know I should have told you this last night, but I couldn't find the words to say it. Well, here it goes. I know who killed your best friend," she said, watching his face turn to ice.

"What!" he snapped.

"Yesterday, when I was with my boyfriend, I overheard Kev from South Philly telling my dude that he killed someone outside the club. He described him as a Silent King guy," she revealed, looking at the tattoo on his arm.

"Kev?" Montega replied, trying to figure out where he heard that name from.

"Yeah, Kevin. You know, Breezy's boyfriend. He said that your friend robbed him on Tasker one night. That's all I know."

"What!" Montega jumped out of bed. "Kev killed Razor? He killed my homie? Oh fuck no. I can't let that ride. He got life fucked up if he think this is over."

"Kenny, how do you expect to get close to him? You know he has an army of young bols out there. You gotta be smart about it."

Montega thought about this and dismissed it quickly.

"Check this out, shorty. I got close to him once; I can get close to him again. He ain't the pope or the president, just a regular nigga like me. Besides, he don't know me. He won't even know what hit 'em," Montega promised as he headed out of her bedroom.

"Kenny, wait!"

"What?" he asked, staring at her on the bed.

"Look. After today we can't see each other anymore. It's too dangerous for the both of us. Shug will kill us if he found out that we've been foolin' around like this."

"Shug?" Montega asked, remembering the name.

This was the first time Tee-Tee ever mentioned her dude's street name to him. Now that he knew who he was, Montega saw why she was so cautious. "So what? This is it?" he asked, a little calmer.

Tee-Tee nodded. She knew that after Montega did what he did, Shug would certainly retaliate and kill him, and she didn't want to get caught in the mix. All she wanted was to put a battery in Montega's back to ensure that he got the job done. Kev had been the reason she had the bruise on the side of her face, and he would pay for it. She knew how much Shug loved him like a brother. This would devastate him. And if she had to kill two birds with one stone by using a man that she had caught feelings for, then so be it.

Better him than me, she thought. "I'm sorry, Kenny, but it has to be this way... at least for now," she said, frowning.

Montega nodded as his feelings for her started to fade. One thing his mother told him: *never allow yourself to fall for a woman too quickly, because she might break your heart in the end. Then you'd be stuck in love with an enemy.*

As he walked away, Tee-Tee said, "Wait, Montega, before you go..."

When Montega turned around, she said softly, "You take care of yourself."

He didn't respond. He just headed out the door and hit his remote to start the car. The Hemi engine came to life instantly. Sitting four cars away in a silver Nissan Titan, Maniac watched as the brown-skinned bol with the wavy hair and dark shades got into his black Impala and pulled off.

Maniac chuckled to himself. "I told Shug we shoulda tag teamed that bitch, but, no, 'she a good girl'. Fuck outta here with that shit. You can't turn a hoe into a housewife, and you damn sure can't trust 'em no further than you can throw 'em."

He dialed Shug's number. When he answered, Maniac said, "Yeah, boss, your suspicions were right. Your little shorty been creepin', and she got herself a little thug too," he joked, watching the black car disappear around the corner.

As Montega headed south, he pondered on a way to get Kev without getting killed. He couldn't believe Razor got murdered over something he and Lil' Man did. Guilt washed over him. Twenty-thousand dollars may have been the most money he had ever collected at once, but it wasn't worth the life of his homie. Revenge would never bring him back. However, it would have to ease his pain a bit.

Thinking of a plan was harder than he thought. He knew nothing about Kev or how he could get to him without getting in a big shootout. He didn't want to make a scene, using a bunch of shells. All he needed was one shot. Before he got too frustrated, he heard the ringing of a cell phone.

He knew the phone didn't belong to him, because Destiny's Child was singing "Cater to You." Montega reached between the seat and the armrest and retrieved Breezy's phone that she left when she and Kia supposedly went to the mall.

Looking at the caller ID, he saw the name 'Kev' on the phone's screen. "Get the fuck outta here. What a coincidence," he muttered, holding up the phone.

Suddenly, a vicious plan came to mind. It was farfetched, but if everything fell into place, he could get his revenge without getting himself killed. He decided that the Phantom would play a part in this. Instead of heading south, he made a U-turn and sped north with Styles P *Phantom* mixtape blasting out of the speakers. It was music that inspired him. He turned up the factory 6-by-9s and let "The Ghost" put him in the proper mood.

Chapter Twenty-Five

Snatch-N-Grab

"He better be prepared to use that machine gun."

— DETECTIVE LUCCA

Breezy spent the day at the Chameleon Creation Beauty Salon on 5th and Chew Avenue, doing a client's hair. After yesterday's events, she didn't know what to think of her boyfriend. There were a thousand questions floating in her head, but the main one was unavoidable. *Did he really kill that girl?*

She had seen the news footage last night and almost freaked out, but she couldn't tell Kev about it, due to the fact she wasn't supposed to be there in the first place. She then started to think about herself. *Would he kill me if we ever fell out?* The thought of it really scared her. It was because of this she couldn't talk to him right now.

"Did y'all see Jovana at the mall the other day?" Crystal asked. "She looked a hot mess with all that pink on, like some fucking Barbie doll."

The girls in the shop burst out with laughter. "Girl, the things that come outta your mouth," Breezy said as she bumped someone's hair.

"I'm serious, Bree. Sometimes people need some pointers on how to dress. Fashion sense is a must for women. If you don't have it, then you're screwed. Take Shug for example. If Shug couldn't dress, wouldn't nobody want his fat, arrogant, nasty ass."

"Please," Gi-Gi said from the far side of the room. "Fashion ain't got nothing to do with Shug. That nigga paid. Bitches gonna want him regardless. And all these guys out here are scared of him. I can't understand that. Men are way different than women. How can you be scared of just one person? You know what I'm talkin' about, Bree?"

Breezy nodded and faked a smile. Really, she was still shaken up by what she and her girlfriend Kia had seen yesterday in Jersey, and if the rest of them were with her, they would understand why guys were so scared of Shug.

"Remember when we were all in Cancun? Did y'all peep when Shug smacked the bol Vito in the face because he didn't give him the correct phone number he asked for? Vito just stood there like a lame in front of everybody. I wish a nigga would put his hands on me," Crystal said.

"You know who I wouldn't mind smacking?" Gi-Gi asked from her station next to Breezy's.

"Who?" they all asked.

"That bitch Tee-Tee."

Instantly, comments flew around the shop from stylist to customers. "Now, that's a conceited bitch," Breezy said as a red flag went up. "I swear, if she wasn't Shug's main squeeze, I woulda been beat that ass. You know she and Kia's brother be on the low with it."

"What?" Gi-Gi said with a thirst for some good gossip.

"Not Taliban." Crystal frowned.

"Nope, the other one."

"Ohhh, you talkin' 'bout the quiet one. I like him. He's got a cute-ass smile. Plus, he laid back, and he fine."

"Puh-lease, bol ain't laid-back," Breezy said, rolling her eyes at the compliment.

After Montega got smart with her at the night club, he had made an enemy. She couldn't tolerate his smart mouth. No one had ever popped fly with her like he did and got away with it.

Her younger sister, Aminah, walked into the shop. They were about the same complexion with a similar beauty and physique, only Aminah was much smaller than her sister and had an innocent look to her appearance. She had long hair pulled back into a ponytail and looked to be troubled by something. Breezy could see the attitude on her pretty, golden face.

"Girl, what's wrong with you now?" she asked.

"Daddy is really pissing me off with his bullshit. He was supposed to go with me to look at some hospitals today after he got off, but like always, something came up. I'm tired of this shit, Bree," Aminah said, jostling her sister to the side while taking the bumpers from her to finish up on her client. "I'm beginning to think he really doesn't care."

Breezy didn't stop her. She knew that if there was anybody who was as talented as she was with hair, it had to be her protégé. "Don't get discouraged Minah, You know how Gary is. He be so busy telling us to stay off the streets but be in them 24-7. I think he cheatin' on Mommy too, but don't say nothin', because I'm not sure."

"Oh, y'all got some real family issues over there," Crystal said. "Who Uncle Gary cheating on my aunt with?"

While Gi-Gi and her employees gossiped about the latest new in the streets, Breezy had her sister finish up on her client so she could make a run.

"Where you off to?" Crystal asked.

"I'm about to go to Quizno's and get something to eat. I'm so hungry it ain't funny."

"Get me something too," Gi-Gi said, going to retrieve her wallet.

"Yeah, grab me a meatball sub," Crystal seconded, and before Breezy knew it, she was taking down orders for everyone. "What you cooking for Thanksgiving anyway?" Crystal asked her.

Breezy shrugged. "I don't know, probably some chicken, stuffing, mac and cheese—the works," she said.

"I know where to go next week then," Gi-Gi said.

"Bitch, you better bring something with you, with your tight ass," Breezy said, turning to leave.

Once she walked outside, she headed down the street to where her Mazda was parked. She dug in her purse for her car keys. It was a typical Gucci bag full of a woman's necessities—make up kit, a hair-brush full of stringy hair, a wallet, some tampons, perfume, and a bunch of receipts and folded-up bills.

Before she had a chance to hit her alarm button, a black sack was thrown over her head. Breezy screamed and tried to fight, but she was helpless in the grips of her abductor. Before she knew it, the person overpowered her. He was strong and fast. Her hands were taped behind her back before she could defend herself.

She was thrown into the back seat of a car, screaming at the top of her lungs, but no one heard her. She tried kicking and punching, but he used his weight to hold her down. He taped her hands behind her back then taped her ankles and slammed the door. She was still able to scream, and that she did well. But still, no one could hear her through the thick, dark-tinted, bullet-proof glass of the SS Chevy Impala.

Montega took of his Phantom mask and turned up his *Styles* mixtape again for a song that he felt was made to define his demented thoughts. It was his rider music. Turning up the volume so it drowned out Breezy's screams, he headed to South Philly, singing, "S Dot P dot Ghost. Get lit like the weed I smoke. Get dumped like the gut of the dutch. Street chuffed, do you love it or what? I get high until the day me and my brother get up…"

Dt. Lucca maneuvered the Grand Marquis through the Badlands of North Philly in search of Lil' Man. He was wanted for the murder of T.J., who was killed on Tasker. The fingerprints on the empty 7.62 mm shell casing came back from the lab with his name all over them. It was Dt. Lucca's first big break in his campaign to bring the crazy Puerto Rican down.

Since his partner, Whitehead, was on vacation, he had to go on this mission alone. As he pulled up at Lil' Man's mother's house, he got out and headed for the front door. After five hard knocks, Faith answered from behind it.

"Who is it?"

"Detective Lucca. Open up!" he demanded.

When Faith opened the door, Lucca didn't say a word. He just brushed right by her and walked in. "What are you doing?" she asked.

"I know that son of a bitch is in here. Now, where's he hiding?" Dt. Lucca trashed the living room.

"Excuse me, but you don't just come bargin' in here like that without a warrant. Who the hell do you think you are?" She folded her arms over her chest with anger.

A warrant had been issued, but Lucca was so revved up he forgot to pick it up at the office. However, he wouldn't let her know that. "I advise you to sit down before I call immigration and have your ass shipped back to your bean-eating country," he racistly warned.

"For your information. I'm Puerto Rican, not Mexican. My country is your country, if you didn't notice."

He didn't respond.

Faith snapped her head back with her mouth wide open. "That's it. I'm calling the police," she said, walking over to the phone.

"You better sit your ass down," he demanded, pointing to the couch.

Faith stopped in her tracks as the detective headed for the door. "Now, if you see that pile of shit, be sure to inform him that he has twenty-four hours to turn himself in, or he better be prepared to use that machine gun of his once more."

On his way out, he turned over a lampstand, causing it to shatter all over the wooden floor. Faith watched with rage as Lucca walked out of her house, leaving the door wide open. She quickly slammed it shut behind him, flopping down on the couch with tears flowing down her cheeks. Burying her face in her palms, she cried, wondering, *what has my brother done now?*

Chapter Twenty-Six

Face-Off

"I gotcha, shorty…"

— MONTEGA

Montega pulled up on Tasker Street, a block away from where Kev was posted with his workers. Turning the music down, he sat back to observe. Breezy had cried herself numb and was now silent. She had come to the conclusion that whoever had taken her was out to get at her boyfriend. Maybe it had something to do with money. She hoped she played her cards right so she would be released. She had always heard of people getting kidnapped and held for ransom, but she didn't think it could happen to her. She was wrong.

Montega speed-dialed Kev's number from Breezy's cell phone. He watched as Kev pulled out his phone, looked at the screen, then answered. "What's up, baby? I been callin' you all morning. Where you at?"

"Oh, you were expecting ya bitch, right?" Montega asked arrogantly.

Kev's whole demeanor changed. "Who the fuck is this?" he challenged.

Breezy listened closely to the smooth voice but couldn't tell who it was. "Yo, we gonna stop all the games. I gotcha shorty, and you won't see her again unless you do as I say."

On hearing that, Breezy then started shouting once more. "Kevin, please help me. He has me tie—"

"Shut the hell up, bitch!" Montega shouted.

Kev's eyes widened. This was most certainly real. *Not again,* he thought.

He quickly grew humble. "Aight, man, you got it. Just don't hurt her."

Montega smiled. His plan was working. Breezy was actually valuable to Kev. Not only did she know a lot about his stash spots, but the whole city would be in an uproar if something happened to her. Detective Gary Whitehead would make sure of that.

Montega considered all this the moment he found Breezy's phone in his car. He had no intention of harming her. Although he didn't like her, she was still his sister's best friend, and for that, she got a pass. That didn't mean he wouldn't use her to get what he wanted.

"How much do you want, cuz?" Kev asked.

Montega was stuck for a second. His plan had nothing to do with money. He was seeking revenge—a life for a life. Now two things were in his favor. "I want $100,000, and I want it brought to the end of Champlost where the dead-end meets the train tracks. There, you'll find me with your shorty, and I'm telling you now, if you try anything stupid, I'll splatter her ass all over the tracks, feel me?"

"Yeah cuz, I feel you," Kev replied as he flagged down his young bol, Spade, who was coming down the block in a green Dodge Magnum on twenty-two-inch chrome rims.

"You got until eight o'clock tonight," Montega said before hanging up.

When Kev got into the passenger side of the Magnum, he directed Spade to the stash house he and Shug had on 16th Street. Montega followed behind from a distance to make sure he wasn't trying to pull a move. Every time the Magnum stopped, he pulled over and jotted down the addresses Kev entered. Every house he walked into, he came back out with a back pack.

As Montega followed the car to the next spot, his cell phone vibrated. He turned the music up a bit, so Breezy couldn't hear his voice when he answered. "What's up?" he said.

"Damn, what's all that noise in the background?" Tasha asked.

"I'm in a bar right now," he lied.

"At this time of day? Boy, you are a drunk."

Montega didn't respond.

"Sorry about your friend," she said, speaking of Razor, trying to sound sympathetic.

"How's ATL?" Montega said, missing her condolence.

"It's alright, but it would be even better if you were here with me. I miss you, boo. I'm sorry we broke up. I realize that now. I showed my sorority sister your picture, and they said I'm an ass for letting you go," she said.

Montega chuckled at that. "Your sorority sisters sound like my type of girls. You showed them my picture though?"

"Hi, Kenny!" a voice hollered in the background.

Montega watched the Magnum head for the next location. "Who was that?" he asked.

"Some girl name Samorah. She just trying to be smart. She know I don't mess with her like that. I'll be glad when she graduates. Dag! Anyway, are you coming down here for Thanksgiving or not? I miss you," she whined.

"Look, I'll call you back and let you know," he said as he made a detour to a quicker route to Broad Street.

Kev got on the phone and called Maniac. "Yizzo, what's good?" Maniac answered.

"Yo, I need you."

"Where you at?" Maniac asked.

"Breezy got snatched. Main-man want a small bean for her. I'm supposed to meet him at the dead-end of Champlost where them apartments at uptown."

"You talkin' 'bout the dead-end down the street from the 35th district, right?"

"That's right. How fast can you get there?" Kev asked.

"Fifteen minutes," Maniac replied before mashing down on the gas pedal.

"Oh yeah, and Maniac… I got fifty stacks for you if you don't tell Shug about this."

"I got you, my nigga. I got you," he said before hanging up.

Kev had taken a big loss already and refused to take another, even if his girl's life was involved. He brought the money just in case, but there was no way he would let this guy walk away.

When Spade pulled into the parking lot of the apartment complex, Kev looked around to see if he saw Maniac's Titan anywhere. "Where the fuck is he?" he asked himself, checking his watch.

"Maybe we should wait for him?" Spade suggested.

"Nah, nah. I'm supposed to be there on time."

It was now 7:58 p.m.

He knew he had to do something, and he had to do it now. "You gotcha gun on you?" he asked Spade.

Spade reached under the seat and handed him his HK-P7 9mm handgun. Kev tucked the compact hand gun in his waistband, then grabbed the bag. "If Maniac don't get here and something happens, you ain't got no choice but to call Shug. Other than that, this stays between me, you, and Maniac," he instructed before getting out and heading through the bushes and up to the hill of the Regional Rail train tracks.

A minute later, the Titan pulled up and parked next to the Magnum. Maniac jumped out with a Sig Sauer P226. It was a stainless steel and black .40 caliber with a black laminated grip. He walked up to the car. Spade rolled the window down and directed him to where Kev had gone.

When Kev got to the top of the tracks, he saw a man dressed in all black and wearing a phantom mask. Breezy was on her knees, bound and duct-taped. Her head was still covered with a black sack, and her arms were aching with pain. "I got the money. Let her go," Kev said, holding up the bag.

Breezy's heart skipped a beat when she heard his deep voice. He really did care for her. She wanted to scream out to him but knew it wouldn't be wise. The only thing that would save her life now would be the money.

"Throw it over!" Montega shouted.

Damn, I know that voice. Where have I heard it before? Breezy asked herself.

Maniac rushed up the hill and through the bushes toward the tracks.

"So you were the one, right? The one I was supposed to kill that night after the club," Kev said, trying to stall. "That's crazy you let your man take the bullet for you. This could have all been avoided had you found a different neighborhood to stick up. Now you're a dead man."

Montega aimed the gold-plated tiger-stripe .50 caliber that once belonged to Kev and removed the mask from his face so Kev could see him. Kev stopped in his tracks and thought, *What sort of man would show his face to the one he's robbin'... unless...*

"You should have left Razor alone, Kev. He ain't have nothing to do with it. It you wanted me that bad, all you had to do was ask around. I'm not hard to find. Now you just pissed me off," Montega said. "Let me ask *you* a question, Kev," Montega went on to say. "You ever dance with the devil in the pale moonlight?"

Kev frowned in confusion at Montega's impersonation of the Joker. The comment was made to do just that. Once Kev was thrown off-track, Montega aimed.

Breezy's eyes widened, she now knew who her captor was. Kev tried to reach for his gun, but it was pointless. Montega pulled the trigger, and the gun exploded. The kick was tremendous against his slim arm, thrusting upward as a .50 caliber bullet slammed into Kev's forehead and damn near took half his head off. Blood, bone, and brain matter painted the tracks like pig slop.

"Nooo!" Breezy shouted.

After putting the mask back on, Montega rushed over to pick up the bag of money. He then put the strap over his shoulder and untaped Breezy's wrist.

That was when he heard footsteps coming from the bushes. He

looked up and saw the man with the dreads emerge. He then quickly aimed and fired the huge tiger-stripe beast three times more. His arm jerked and slammed into his shoulder.

Boom! Boom! Boom!

Maniac ducked down, nearly tripping over the rails, and fired back at the masked man, who was now running across the tracks and into the woods. Maniac squeezed off four shots but missed. Montega ran into the dense forest quickly. He dodged thorny bushes and brushed against sticky balls that clung to his pant legs. Maniac left Breezy where she was and ran after him. When he came out on the other end of the woods, he saw his target running down the hill with a bag in one hand, gun in the other. Maniac clutched the SIG with both hands and fired another two shots. He then stopped with surprise.

What caught Maniac's attention was the car the masked man was running to. It was the same black car he saw leaving Tee-Tee's house earlier. The shooter wore the same clothes as the man he had seen leave. Maniac couldn't believe who the kidnapper was. He took aim and squeezed until his gun went empty. Montega crouched and ducked his head as angry bullets whizzed by. Once he was in his car on Franklin Street, he stepped on the gas and peeled off.

Meanwhile, on the other side of the tracks, after hearing the gunshots, Spade came running to the scene. When he arrived, he found Breezy hysterically crying over Kev's dead body. He hurried over and finished un-taping her.

"C'mon!" Maniac barked as he walked by. "We gotta get the fuck outta here."

"What about cuz?" Spade asked. "Did you get him?"

"Nah. The lucky muthafucka got away."

Spade escorted Breezy to his wheels. She was still in shock, not just because she saw her boyfriend dead with the top of his head missing, but because she knew exactly who to blame.

Chapter Twenty-Seven

Stakes Are High

"An eye for an eye..."

— MONTEGA

JULY 14TH, 2005
EIGHT MONTHS LATER...

It was a breezy Sunday morning in July. The streets were quiet, and most of the neighbors were in their homes, watching TV or cooking Sunday dinner. Others were at church, receiving the good word. A couple of kids played out in front of their houses, enjoying the beautiful day. Everything seemed normal until the air was filled with the sounds of a Yamaha Banshee screaming as it zoomed from block to block.

Lil' Man rode hard on the four-wheeler with one intention. With the strap slung across his neck and the AK on his back, he swerved onto Belfield Avenue with a tunnel vision for blood. He had been on the run for eight months since the police came to his house with a warrant, but on this day, he would run no more.

Inside the large church on the corner of Broad and Courtland Street, Anthony Lucca, his wife, and his kids were exiting the church with everyone else. "That was a good service, wasn't it?" he asked his wife.

"It sure was, honey."

"Daddy, can we get some ice cream?" his two little girls begged. "Please. Oh, please!"

"No, no. Ice cream is bad for your teeth. Eat some fruit instead," he replied, bringing frowns.

"Tony!" his wife said with her hands on her hips.

"What? I'm tellin' the truth."

"No, you're being cheap. Now get these girls some ice cream. Besides, I wouldn't mind a hot fudge sundae myself," his wife ordered as they walked down the sidewalk.

"Oh, alright," he replied, giving in.

"Yaaay!" the girls cheered.

Suddenly, the sound of a four-wheeler approached while people paused to watch. Lucca heard the sound as well. He looked around to see what the fuss was about. He saw, standing about fifty feet away, a short Puerto Rican with an AK-47 pointed right at him.

"Lucca!" Lil' Man shouted. "You want me! Well, here I am, puta!"

Lucca's eyes widened. "Get down!" he shouted while trying to push his family to the ground just as Lil' Man began to unleash a barrage of bullets in their direction.

The assault rifle vibrated like a jackhammer in Lil' Man's hand as he chopped down everything in his path, including Tony, who spun like a top before hitting the ground. Screams of horror could be heard from afar. Panic came in a wave of madness. As Tony's hand twitched, Lil' Man slowly approached him while he was lying on his back, struggling to breath. He, as well as his wife and one of his two daughters, had been hit.

Lil' Man stood over Tony and looked him dead in the eyes, waiting for him to die. Tony, however, was strong. In Lil' Man's mind, there was no glory in shooting a man then leaving him to die. But to shoot him and watch him die was what fueled his desire for revenge. Lucca wouldn't give him that satisfaction though. He tried his best of hold onto his life until the paramedics got there.

Impatient, Lil' Man pointed the gun at Lucca's head and said, "You picked the wrong Puerto Rican to fuck with. Now I'll be the last thing you ever see." Then he squeezed the trigger. "Hell is low," Lil' Man said before making his getaway.

Montega walked up Woodlawn so he could meet with Nino, who wanted to buy a quarter ounce of hard from him. The sun was beaming down, and the weather was starting to heat up. A gust of wind blew some hot air every now and then, and perspiration built up within his T-shirt. He saw some of the corner boys hustling in front of the Chinese store. The effect of the Purple Haze for what was supposed to be his birthday was nothing more than a regular day. He didn't want to celebrate. He had nothing to celebrate for. He just wanted to hustle, and the smoke had him on cloud nine.

When the hustlers on Blakemore Street saw him approaching, they all cautiously crossed over to the other side of the block to make sales. It had been almost eight months since Montega killed Kev on the train tracks, and now Shug had adopted Kev's beef. Montega became a wanted man with a $150,000 price tag on his head. The bounty attracted a slew of cheap assassins willing to take a chance at cashing in.

Every now and then, Montega found himself in a shootout with a hungry wolf he didn't know—either on foot or on the move. He had nearly lost his life on two occasions. But no matter how bad the odds, he always kept something to back a killer down and a bulletproof vest to protect himself. Because of his will to survive, and with the unwanted help of gossip, his reputation grew overnight.

As he waited for Nino, his mind was going in circles. Tasha had been in touch, constantly begging him to come down to Atlanta to be with her for a while, but Montega was too busy on the lookout for an opportunity to make big money. His ambition was relentless. It didn't matter that he was up a hundred grand in the game. Everyone was too paranoid to deal with him. What he needed was a connect. Mike had distanced himself from him as well. And to make matters worse, he wouldn't sell him anything over nine ounces. Montega knew there was something strange about that because Mike sold Reek a half a bird every other week.

As Montega leaned on the wall of the Chinese store, he observed everything moving around him. There were hustlers across the street, counting money out in the open, young bols walking around, looking for weed, cars slowly cruising down the block with fancy rims and loud enhanced stereo systems, and little kids running in and out of the store with popsicles in their hands.

Nino rode up to the block in a burgundy 2001 Buick Lasabre. The car pulled over to the corner before he got out. His dark skin glistened as if he had been covered in oil, and he was a bit taller than Montega with a very slim built. "What's good, bol," Nino said, giving Montega some dap.

Montega exchanged the quarter with a handshake. He then watched as Nino placed the drugs in his pocket.

Suddenly, Montega's whole demeanor changed when he saw Breezy pull up in her Mazda. "Awwl, man. Here come this bitch," he said, now irritated.

When she saw Montega, she scowled and looked the other way, mumbling something under her breath.

"Damn, who dat?" Nino asked with interest.

"You don't even want to know," Montega stated.

After Kev's death, Breezy found it hard to move on without him. Her world as she knew it was destroyed, and it was all Montega's fault. She hated his guts, and had it not been for Kia being her best friend, she would have sicked Maniac on his ass.

Maniac had been searching for the so-called 'Phantom' ever since the day they shot at each other. Maniac blamed himself for not getting to the scene in time. He felt that Kev could still be alive if he hadn't been trying to trick around. What made the situation even worse was that Montega had shot back at him. No one had ever done anything like that and lived to tell about it. He swore that whenever the two met up again, it would go down like Young Joc's video. He didn't care if he was at the district, reporting a stolen vehicle; guns would be drawn, and someone's life would be lost.

Nino watched as Breezy parked her car and got out.

"Goddamn. Look at the body on her. Yo, I gots to try my hand with—"

Montega tapped him hard in the gut as an unmarked cop car shot up the one-way street. The hustlers on the other side tried to break and run, but regular squad patrol cars blocked their escape. The entire city was on fire from the incident that transpired in front of the church. Cops were everywhere, looking for a single suspect.

"Oh shit!" Montega said as he tried to walk off with Nino undetected.

He started to use Breezy as a distraction but wouldn't dare, based on the look she gave him when she walked into the store. He had already used her enough.

"Get up on the wall!" a big, black officer ordered as he approached Montega and Nino.

Nino looked like a deer caught in the headlights. He froze, not knowing what to do. "Yo," Montega whispered. "Run, man. You dirty." But Nino had nowhere to go.

High as a kite, Montega knew he was going to jail. He had not one but two chrome Taurus 9mm's tucked in his waistband. As an officer searched Nino, the black cop grabbed Montega and shoved him against the wall. He kicked Montega's legs apart so that he could spread 'em, and a woman's voice said, "I got him, Jankens. Get the others."

"Well, well, well, look what we have here," one cop sad, holding up the plastic bag with the quarter inside. Nino put his head down in shame as the officer handcuffed him and led him to the back of the cop car.

When the big ape walked off with Nino, Montega felt the small hands of a woman probe his body, starting with the chest. She then worked her way down and around his waist where her palms ran across the two guns that were tucked away. To Montega's surprise, the woman kept searching him. "He's clean," she said just as Breezy walked out of the store, alarmed to see so many cops.

When Montega turned around to see Olivia, he cracked a smirk. "Don't let me catch you out here on this corner again," she warned, trying to put on a front for her coworkers. "You hear me?"

Montega nodded respectfully then appreciatively walked down the block. Seeing him stroll away with his cool, apathetic swag, Breezy peeped game as she got into her car. If there was one thing she was good at, it was figuring people out. If she didn't know any better, she would have thought that those two were fucking on the calm. This was news she knew she had to run by her best friend.

As Montega walked down the block, Mike pulled up in a silver Dodge Ram 1500, motioning with his hand for him to get in. Montega crossed the street as Breezy was coming down the block. Seeing him strolling across, she stepped on the gas. The car picked up speed, and Breezy gripped the steering wheel tightly.

When Montega heard the roar of the V-6 engine, he dove to the other side of the street like Max Payne, dodging bullets just as the Mazda flew by. Breezy chuckled at his quick agility. She looked in her rearview and saw him tumbling to the other side of the street just before swerving around the corner. She hadn't laughed that hard since Kev was alive.

When Montega got up and dusted himself off, he saw Mike cracking up as well. "Crazy bitch!" he shouted.

"Damn, bol, you looked like Neo in *The Matrix* just now," Mike joked as Montega slid into the passenger seat. "I didn't know you were that quick on your feet. It's no wonder your ass ain't dead yet."

"Can you believe that shit, yo? First, my man get booked up the block; now, this bitch just tried to kill me," Montega exclaimed, studying the cherries on his kneecaps.

"How you expect shorty to feel? You gotta realize, dog, you rocked her dude. Bol was her bread and butter, and you took that away from her. You lucky she ain't tell her cop ass father," Mike said, trying to reason with him

"Her dude killed my homie. What was I supposed to do? Sit there and let that shit ride? Fuck that. An eye for an eye. Right or wrong?"

Mike nodded in agreement. Truthfully, he didn't care about Shug wanting Montega killed, which was why Montega was still breathing. Mike hadn't told Shug anything about Montega. All he cared about was his money. "Yo, I wanted you to know that my case in the state got picked up by the Feds."

"What?" Montega said in disbelief.

"Yeah, man, I'm lookin' at forty-six months. I gotta turn myself in tomorrow," Mike said sadly. "But as far as business goes, I'm gonna hand it back over to Reek. Stay loyal to him, and he'll lookout for you."

Yeah right, like he did the last time, Montega thought as Mike continued.

"As far as this beef with Shug is concerned, you need to find a way to squash it because if you ain't gotcha money right, and I mean multi-millions right, then you ain't gonna win. Trust me. A single knight can't mate a king alone. Shug got hundreds of goons at his disposal. It's some major people backing him as well. I'm talking international. You think you getting' swarmed now; wait until he gets fed up and sends the real hit squad at you."

Montega sucked his teeth and ignored this advice. He was already pissed that Mike was once again giving Reek some power. He knew that Reek was the type of guy who you gave an inch, but he took a mile. He abused his authority and thought he was John Gotti. Besides that. Nino had gotten booked, trying to cop work off him. The first thing Montega wanted to do was get him a lawyer. Nino was already on probation for a drug case he copped out to before. He knew Nino's PO would drop a detainer on him now. Before he could speak on it, his phone vibrated. Montega gave Mike some dap then got out to answer it. "Yo, what's good?" he said, shutting the door behind him.

"Kenny, my brother just got locked up," Faith said hysterically.

"What? What the hell happened?" he asked.

"The detectives kicked in my mother's door and beat him up so bad. There's blood all over my carpet. Then they dragged him out to the car and took him to jail. Kenny, they said he killed a detective along with his wife. His two daughters were the only ones to survive. It's all over the news. I'm so scared for him. I hope they don't kill him."

"Damn, yo. Look, Faith, I'll call you back. Matta fact, call me when your brother gets in touch with you. They're going to take him down to the Roundhouse then process him. When he gets to the county, call me, and let me know what his situation is, you hear me?" he commanded.

"Yes, Kenny, I hear you," she said before hanging up.

Ever since that day when Lucca punched holes in the tires of Lil-Man's four-wheeler, he made a dangerous enemy. Lil' Man knew exactly who the cop was. Montega wasn't surprised about Lil' Man one bit. Lil' Man hated a certain detective. It was all he ever talked about. He had discussed countless times of a way to kill the racist detective, and now he finally did it. This bit of news really made Montega unsettled. If Lil' Man fell, it could be for life, if not Death Row. As Montega sadly headed for his car, his phone rang again. "What?" he said, frustrated.

"Uh-oh, somebody's upset. Maybe it's not a good time to tell you that you owe me a drink tonight," Olivia said, bringing a relieved smirk to his face.

"I owe you a lot more than that, but yo, can you do anything for my homie?"

"Sorry, boo, I can't. It was either check him or check you, and quite frankly, I don't know him. But I do know you owe me a drink tonight."

"I guess I can sip a few shots with you. It *is* my birthday."

"Ohh, boy, why ain't you say something earlier? Happy Birthday."

"Thanks, but truthfully, I don't feel all that happy," he replied. "But be ready by eight," he said before ending the call. He sighed dryly. He needed something to clear his mind. Anything was better than worrying about both his homies. Then he thought about what he and Lil' Man had done together and wondered if he could hold water. The streets were different than being locked behind bars, and the talk of football numbers could make even the most dangerous criminals change sides. Smoke was a prime example. It was then Montega realized how serious the situation was, and paranoia set in.

Chapter Twenty-Eight

Hunting Season

"I'm huntin' a nigga that's hard to kill."

— MANIAC

Maniac pulled off Sansom Street and headed north on Broad Street. He had just finished enjoying a wonderful blowjob from one of the Chinese girls at a massage parlor in center city, and now it was back to business. When he got uptown, he pulled into a gas station on Broad and Godfrey that he knew all too well. He parked by the back exit.

Shutting off the engine, he got out and went around to the front to meet with Mujahid. Mujahid was the Pakistani owner of the gas station. Maniac met him through Kev a while back when Shug first started taking over the city. When Mujahid saw him walk in, he had one of his employees take over the register while he went to greet him. "As-Salamu Alaikum," he said, coming from behind the thick, bullet-proof glass door.

"Walaikum Salam. What's good, Ocky?" Maniac replied, shaking the tan-skinned, white-bearded man's hand.

"I don't know, my brother. You tell me. I have a feeling you didn't come to fill up your tank, no?" he asked in his thick accent.

"Nah, I came to fill up my ego. I need some big shit. It's for huntin' a cufar that's hard to kill, and I'm afraid them AK bullets you sold me a while back are too small for the prey I got now."

"What?" Mujahid said, looking around to see if anyone was eavesdropping on their conversation. "Since when is 7.62 bullets too small for a man? You have to learn how to aim; that's all, my brother. You people are always shooting and wasting ammo. One shot is all you need. Otherwise, don't shoot at all. Come. I have just the thing for you, my friend."

Maniac followed the man down into the dense cellar of the gas station. There, the room looked as if Mujahid was planning a holy war. There were machine guns everywhere, along with all types of military-base weapons and ammunition. He even had a .50 caliber Gatling gun that looked as if it could have been attached to the side of a helicopter. Everything sat side-by-side, crowding the walls. It was no wonder Mujahid was Shug's main gun supplier outside of the Underworld. He could get the team anything.

"Over here. Take a look at this, Ocky," he said, picking up a rocket-propelled grenade launcher.

"Goddamn! This the shit they be usin' over in Iraq," Maniac said, holding it up.

"Yes, my friend, it's an RPG. You see how many Americans it takes out. This, I can assure you, will do the job. Trust me, Ocky. Once he sees one of these coming his way, he'll never know what hit him until it's too late."

He handed the weapon to Maniac and stepped back. Maniac placed it over his shoulder and looked through the crosshairs then smiled.

"How much for this?"

"I give to you for $3,500, and I include rockets, but please, don't get caught with that. If they catch you, they think you terrorist. Then things will get very, very bad for you," he advised.

Maniac held the weapon of mass destruction in his hands firmly. It was at that moment that he felt invincible. Then he thought of the look Montega would have on his face when he saw a rocket coming for him and said, "Aight, I'll take it."

Chapter Twenty-Nine

Tragedy

"The streets is one big chess board..."

— MONTEGA

As the night blanketed the city, Montega and Olivia relaxed and had a couple of drinks at Scooters, a laid-back bar in West Philly. Montega hadn't been in too many bars, but for some reason, he liked this one. It was the only spot where he could almost be anonymous. As the two sipped on Gray Goose and pineapple juice, they talked and got to know each other better. The jukebox had been playing nonstop with requested songs. The music was so loud that Montega had to raise his voice.

"So what made you want to be a cop in the first place?" Montega asked, placing his cup down on the counter.

"Well, my father was a dedicated police officer, for one. He taught me how to shoot. I got so good at it, before I knew it, I started going to competitions. Eventually, I became a marksman," Olivia answered.

"A marksman?" he asked, intrigued.

"Yes. Are you surprised? Don't let my pretty face and unlawful ways fool you. I'm a two-time champion. Maybe I'll take you to the range sometime, when you're not too busy, and teach you a thing or two. You don't have a record, do you?" she asked.

"Nah, my record's clean, ma. And now it's gonna stay that way, thanks to you."

Olivia smiled as she placed her cup down to look at him. "You're a very handsome and intelligent guy, Kenny. I can see that in you. You could have been anything you wanted to be. How did you end up being a drug dealer?" she asked seriously.

"I have a problem with authority, and I like fast cash, I guess," he replied. "It wasn't always like that though. I used to work at a lot of fast food restaurants, even worked at a WaWa's. I was a good kid once upon a time. But when my mom lost her job, I lost my patience. I remember nights when all we had was just a roof over our head and a kerosene heater. I would run errands for the neighbors just so I could make enough money to buy a chicken wing platter with fried rice. I'd take a wing and some rice and give my mom the rest.

"I came a long way since then. Living every week off of a check wasn't enough either, so I stole cigarettes and sold them for the low. Sort of like what you do with cars, only I was careless. I got caught and fired. Then I told myself that I didn't need a job or a boss to tell me what to do or look down on me like he was better than I was, so I looked to the streets for help."

"And what did you find?" she asked, sipping her drink.

"Dead dreams and living nightmares, I guess," he said, shrugging his shoulders. "Money comes fast on the streets. There's no complaints about that, but it's still the same as when I was working. I'm still under somebody, whether I'm buying or getting fronted. I know what the streets are made of. The streets is one big chess board full of kings, queens, bishops, knights, castles, and pawns. I'm no pawn, Olivia. I want to get that straight, right here, right now." He sighed before taking another sip of liquor. "For real, for real, sometimes, I don't know who I am anymore."

"Well, what do you need two guns for if that's the case?"

"Because dudes rather see me die than to see me rise. Seems like all I know is trouble. With me, trouble is my sidekick. It follows me no matter where I go or what I do."

"Um, well, I can fix that."

"Nah, shorty. I'm not that type of guy. I handle my own affairs and live by the sayin': If you want something done right, do it yourself."

Olivia smiled as she studied him. She would never have known he was twenty-three from the way he carried himself. He was always so relaxed and confident when he spoke. She could tell he had been forced to become a man before his time.

They were interrupted by a text message. To Montega, it seemed odd since he hadn't texted anyone. Looking at his phone, he saw the message was from Tee-Tee. He hadn't spoken to her since the day she told him that they couldn't see each other anymore. He couldn't deny the fact that it felt good seeing her name on the screen of his phone but wouldn't give Olivia the satisfaction of seeing it.

"Is there something wrong?" she asked.

"Yeah. I gotta get goin'. My sister needs my help with something important," he lied while saving the message to read later.

"Damn, and here I was, having a good time with you," Olivia said with a pouting face. "God willingly, there will always be another."

On the way to drop Olivia off, Montega's mind was elsewhere. He couldn't wait to read what Tee-Tee had to say. Last he heard, she had been hiding out from Shug. Montega figured she missed him just as much as he missed fucking her. During the ride, Olivia stared at him with admiration. Montega hadn't noticed but, it was killing her to be polite.

When he pulled up to her house, she reached over and put her hand on his leg. At first, he paid it no mind because his mind was elsewhere—until her hand migrated to the bulge in his pants, and she began to massage it. The feeling sent blood flowing between his legs. He looked at her and saw the desire in her eyes. Olivia licked her lips like a hungry predator.

Before Montega could speak, his dick was being devoured by Olivia's warm, wet mouth.

"Uh, shit, ma. Damn, you good," he gasped out as her head bobbed up and down in his lap.

Olivia sucked with hunger. She jerked and squeezed and slurped at the base and moved her head faster. He gripped the back of her head and eased it down. He sucked in as much air as he could before deflating quickly to the sensation of her tongue.

The slurps and gags of her deepthroat game had him floating. Her tongue twirled around his head like a lollipop until he exploded in her tonsils. Olivia continued until she had him throwing his back against the headrest.

When she finally popped it out of her mouth, she purred, "Don't be a stranger." Then she got out of the car.

Montega sat there, exhausted, as if he'd just run a marathon.

Once he was able to recover, he took another deep breath, shifted the car's transmission in drive, and pulled off. While heading north, he checked the text message that Tee-Tee had sent him.

Meet me at the house. We have 2 talk. It's important.

It wasn't what he was expecting, but still, she did want to see him. He made a quick detour and headed for Brickyard. The weed and liquor fogged his brain. All he could seem to think of was Tee-Tee—her pretty face, her sexy, petite body, her perfect ass, and her good pussy—all in which made him drive a little faster.

Within minutes, he pulled up to the block and parked around the corner. Punching in a code on the touch screen of his navigation system, one of his stash spots slid open underneath the dashboard. Montega grabbed his black 9mm Beretta and tucked it in his waistband. It was close to midnight, and none of the neighbors were awake. When he got to the porch, he saw that the lights were off throughout the house. The first thing he did was knock.

There was no answer.

He looked around from the porch and saw no one then tried the knob, and the door opened. He walked inside slowly then headed upstairs. On his way, he noticed that the door to the master bedroom was cracked, and the TV was on. As he approached through the hallway, he pulled out his Beretta because something didn't feel right. Tee-Tee's house seemed way too quiet.

When he opened the door, there she was, lying naked on the bed. Her eyes were wide open, and the smell of death was in the air. Her skin was pale, her lips as blue as the streaks in her hair. Montega flicked on the light and walked toward the bed. Inspecting the discoloration around her neck, it didn't take a forensic scientist to figure out she had been strangled.

He put his head down with sadness.

"Damn, Tee-Tee," he muttered with disappointment and grief while touching her cold cheek.

His phone rang.

Montega answered his cell phone hesitantly. "Hello?" His voice was scratchy.

"Kenny, where the hell are you right now?" Kia asked, sounding the same way she did the day she informed him of Razor's murder.

"I... I'm... I'm at Tee-Tee's crib," he mumbled.

"Boy, get the hell out of there now. I just got off the phone with my girlfriend, Amber, and she said some guy name Maniac just came from around Blakemore lookin' for you!" Kia shouted.

"Yeah, so?"

"Kenny, Breezy said he's Shug's number one shooter. He doesn't go looking for people to talk. He's looking to kill you."

As soon as she finished that sentence, Montega heard the sound of a car trunk close outside of the house. "Hang on, sis," he said, walking to the window. He peeked out the blinds. His eyes burst open with surprise. It was the same shooter with the dreads he got into a shootout with on the train tracks. This time, he was carrying something much larger than a handgun.

That can't be real, he thought.

In fact, it looked like something that belonged to the real Taliban, and not his brother.

Maniac propped the RPG on his shoulder and aimed at the shadowy figure in the window. Montega jumped back. "Oh shit!" he gasped as he turned to run.

Maniac pulled the trigger. Just as Montega made it out of the room, the rocket streaked up to the second-floor window and detonated inside, bringing a big ball of fire that tore the master bedroom to pieces.

The impact of the blast sent Montega's body flying into the

hallway as bits and pieces of sheetrock showered down on top of him. The explosion almost knocked the life out of him. A door was taken off the hinges and fell on top of him with the rest of the debris.

Maniac smiled as he witnessed the damage he had caused. The whole master bedroom looked as if it had been struck dead-on by an F5 tornado.

It's no way that coward survived that, Maniac thought as he hopped back into the tan Chevy Camaro and drove down to South Philly to give Shug the good news personally.

Inside the damaged row home, the sound of burning wood crackled through the hallway. Miraculously, Montega slowly pushed the door off himself and sat up, coughing from the dust and smoke. When he got to his feet, he was still dazed. His ears were ringing, and his face was as black as tar from the sulfur in the air. He couldn't hear a thing, and everything around him seemed grayish. Looking behind him to where the master bedroom once was, he saw nothing but rubble and smoke and could feel a strong gust of wind as if he were outside.

A second earlier, and that could have been him. It now dawned on him that this was no game. He was too busy running the streets, smoking weed, and drinking liquor to see it coming. He then thought about the jewel Mike had given him earlier. Shug wanted him dead, which meant war had been declared. But he wasn't in any position to go against the Pennsylvania black don. If he stayed in the city, he probably wouldn't live to see another day. Leaving was his only option. Sometimes a person had to leave in order to make a strong comeback.

Chapter Thirty

When A Woman's Fed Up

"The only thing you care about is yourself…"

— MARIA WHITEHEAD

After a tiresome night of filling out paperwork and dodging reporters, Dt. Whitehead entered his suburban home on the outskirts of Cedarbrook and was surprised to see his wife sitting at the living room table with a cup of coffee in her hand. Maria appeared to be daydreaming, but as he drew closer, she turned to look at him with red eyes. Whitehead knew she was pissed about him not showing up to his daughter's graduation. He tried to explain. "Baby, I'm sorry, bu—"

"You're sorry?" Maria repeated mockingly, slamming her cup down. "That's all you can say? You're sorry? It's because of you Aminah doesn't want to be a nurse anymore. Did you know that? She doesn't even want to stay in this house. How could you miss her graduation, Gary? How could you?"

"Maria, there was a tragedy. My partner—"

"Were you and your partner fucking, Gary?" Maria asked a little calmer.

"Maria! For God sake, no."

"Do you have kids with him?" she questioned.

"No, we don't, bu—"

"Then why the hell were you there and not with your family on the most important day of your daughter's life? I'll answer that for you. Because that damn job is more important than your own goddamn family. This is why our oldest child left this house at such a young age. Now Aminah. The only thing you care about is your-fucking-self and those streets!"

"That's not true," Whitehead replied, shaking his head.

"You're right. That's not true, because you do love something else. Or should I say someone else?" she exclaimed as she went into her robe pocket and pulled out a piece of paper. "I did a little detective work of my own while you were away."

Slamming it down on the table, she shouted, "What about the child you had with this other woman! You might as well tell me now, because I had a huge conversation with her!"

"Maria, you can't believe everything you—"

"Hear?" she asked, finishing his sentence for him. "You're right. That's why I went over there to see your mystery daughter myself. Isn't it funny how she looks just like you, how she resembles Shabree and Aminah? I also took a drive to your little secret apartment. Yeah, she told me about that too, and I can't believe what I found there."

Calming herself down so that she wouldn't break down, she asked, "How long have you been cheating on me, Gary?"

Detective Whitehead saw the hurt and pain in her eyes and found himself speechless. "Honey, I..."

"Did you think I would be such a fool to not notice the different soap scents on your body or the smells of perfume coming from your clothes? Is that what you took me for? A dumb wife?"

"Honey, please, let me expl—"

"I want a divorce," she said as her emotions burst into words.

"Maria, please, don't—"

"Go to hell, Gary. Since you're so obsessed with those goddamn thugs and whores out there that you'd neglect your own family, you can be with them... full-time. Now, get out of this house! I want you gone!"

Whitehead looked at the woman he had been married to for over twenty-seven years. He tried to find words to save his marriage—words that might make her understand—but there were none. All he could do was sigh then turn around and walk out of the house.

Chapter Thirty-One

"You people think money can change the way we feel?"

— TANETCHE AGUGBO

The living-room inside the White's family mansion took up 1,500 square feet of space. It was sectioned between the west gallery and the entry hall, just across from the entertainment room. In the very center was an Italian wraparound, white, leather sofa with a crystal coffee table in the middle. A giant crystal chandelier hung overhead. The large, open windows draped with silk white curtains, letting the Los Angeles sunrays poor in from the hills. Clyde, his cousin Justin, and his sister, Diamond, sat on the Italian sectional across from the most-feared individuals in South Africa—the Agugbo brothers. Standing behind them were ten of their best henchmen.

The White family also had wolves backing them, including Bain, who was holding the gold-plated AK-47 that once belonged to Tanetche before he was almost electrocuted by Diamond. This alone was a slap in the face. Since the street wars in L.A., the Agugbo brothers became the most-dominating force up north.

Whenever their names were mentioned, two things were likely involved—drugs and diamonds. They were the top diamond smugglers in the country. The head of the family was Hillary Agugbo. He was the brains and dealt with most of the financial issues. Hillary was a rather tall man with a nappy afro, strong jawline, and wide nose. He had brown eyes and wore prescription glasses to see better. The second was Simon, who was doing time in a federal prison. He was in charge of the heroin distribution. Then there was Tanetche, who was in charge of the diamond trade, accompanied by all the lieutenants. His only problem was sitting across the coffee table from him.

Tanetche almost matched his brother's height. He was stockier and had strong facial features. His eyes were dark, angry, and convictive. His nose was shaped like a squash. He had thick lips and a narrow face. Being a man who relied on instincts instead of what was in his head, he was known for lashing out in a rage without regards for anyone else. Quite frankly, he didn't give a damn about what everyone else thought of him. He would destroy himself before he let Diamond do it for him. After the death of his wife, Shelly, he lost touch with his soft side. With a hot-tempered man like him at a meeting, trouble was likely if words weren't properly chosen.

Diamond looked over to her right where the priest stood nervously. From all the confessions he'd heard from her, he knew these men were extremely dangerous. He made the sign of a cross over his head and chest and said a silent prayer for her.

As both sides eyed each other, Hillary broke the ice. "Okay, we're all here, Clyde. What is it you have to say?"

Clyde rubbed his sweaty palms together and extended his hands. "Hillary, Tanetche, how long has there been tension between us? Too long, right? This war between you and my sister is pointless. A lot of people have died behind it. A lot of senseless murders have occurred. For what? Neither one of you have been harmed behind it, only the people around you. Now, to avoid any more bloodshed, we've come up with a solution. Why not end this beef and collaborate? I guess what I'm trying to say is, why not have the Agugbo brothers and the Ape Gang share a spot at the table with us in the Underworld?"

The room remained silent for a while. The butler suddenly walked in, rattling a silver coffee pot. Seeing this, Hillary spoke with caution. "Clyde, let me be forward with you. We have no problem with you or your organization, but her..." he said, pointing at Diamond before continuing. "The poison that she brings threatens all of us. Now, you speak of a collaboration. I'm willing to consider this great honor... but the only way we accept... is if she is six-feet under."

Diamond listened but wasn't fazed by his threat. In fact, she smirked as if it were a compliment. She never wanted to collaborate with them and knew they wouldn't collaborate with her. She just went along with it so that her brother could see for himself. Clyde looked at his sister then back at Hillary. "Come on, gentlemen. We're all businessmen and women. Surely there's some way we can resolve this."

"Yes, there is a way," Tanetche snarled. "You can cut off her damn head. Give it to me so that I can burn it while the rest of her poisonous body twitches. Isn't that what you do to serpents?"

"Tanetc—" Clyde said.

"Spare me your speech, Clyde. I do not wish to hear it. You people think money can change the way we feel! You think money can bring back my wife! How many bodyguards must I replace from being used as a human shield? How many drivers must I lose from car bombs that were intended for me? How many houses must I repair because of her dirty work? How many, Clyde! Tell me!"

With fire in his eyes, Tanetche sat back. "You don't know what it's like to live in darkness. Where no one survives. I've come too far to let a bitch get one up on me, so no. There can never be peace between us until that bitch is dead. She killed my wife!"

Diamond tracked a devilish grin then said, "I can assure you, Mr. Agugbo, it wasn't intentional." Her gaze fell to her nails, which she examined, saying, "But look on the bright side. You should be proud of her. At least she took one for the team."

On hearing that, Tanetche jumped out of his seat, but Hillary quickly grabbed him by the arm before he got to her. His hand was extremely close to her grasp. The others helped keep the angry South African at bay. Tanetche wanted so badly to strangle the life out of her. What burned him up the most was her arrogance. They began to pull him toward the exit. "You will meet your end soon enough," Tanetche promised as his men escorted him out of the room, followed by his brother.

"I'm sure I will. Too bad it won't be by the hands of you," Diamond replied, tossing her wavy, long hair over her right shoulder. She then looked at her brother and rose from her seat to fix her black Versace dress. "That certainly went well," she said charismatically.

She walked off, leaving Clyde with his head in his hands. He badly needed to talk to Butler before the organization was plundered. He was convinced that before he let that happen, something had to be done about his sister.

That night, Shug lay on his California king-size bed with a sleeping dime-piece on each side of his large frame. He flicked through the channels of the fifty-two-inch plasma TV in search of something to watch. When he stopped on *Action News 6,* he saw the damage that Maniac had done to Tee-Tee's house in Brickyard. He turned up the volume.

"A local row house was leveled last night in the Germantown section of Philadelphia. Police are on the lookout for a man driving a tan-colored Chevy Camaro. Although no one was able to get a positive ID of the suspect, neighbors said they heard a hissing sound followed by a loud explosion. The FBI Counter Terrorist Unit and other government officials have been brought out tonight to find out exactly what that hissing sound was. Police believe that the front of the house could have possibly been struck by a small, rocket-propelled grenade."

"Goddamn!" Shug chuckled in amusement. "That Maniac is one crazy muthafucka."

"Police found the body of a twenty-four-year-old woman, whose name is being withheld at this time. If you have any information about the tragic incident, you are encouraged to call the police hotline at 1-800-5..."

Shug frowned in confusion. "Wait a minute. What about the male that was supposed to be there too? What the fuck happened to Montega?" he spoke to the reporter as if she could hear him through the television. He immediately jumped on the phone and called Maniac.

"Yizzo," Maniac answered on the second ring.

"Are you watchin' the news?" Shug asked dryly.

Maniac turned on the TV. The incident was on every station. When the reporter only mentioned the female, he snapped. "What the fuck! Naw, man, that can't be right. How the fuck did he survive that? I looked dead at him before I pulled the—"

"I don't know, but I do know one thing... You better fix it," Shug growled out before hanging up on him.

Chapter Thirty-Two

"This is where the real ballers play..."

— RODNEY

Atlanta, Georgia

When Montega arrived in the beautiful city of Atlanta, it was like being in a different world. Atlanta was nothing like he had imagined. Unlike the mean streets of Philly, where all he heard in the ghetto were police sirens and gunshots, Atlanta was much more peaceful, and almost everyone showed that good old southern hospitality.

He spent his first week there with Tasha inside her sorority house. He had never seen so many pretty women all living under one roof. Every morning, while going to use the bathroom, he would run into Samorah, who played the shower at the same time. It got to the point Montega knew what time she got up and did her thing.

He made it part of his routine to see the mixed redbone with the nice, wet body. She was by far the best-looking female in the house. She had an exotic Spanish-White look to her. She had long hair that touched the small of her back. She was naturally dark haired but dyed it a golden blonde. It framed her beautiful, U-shaped features—dreamy, hazel eyes; a short, thin nose that remained small at the nostrils; puckered, red Jessica Rabbit lips; high cheekbones; and soft, French-vanilla skin.

She was a few inches shorter than Tasha and was thick in all the right places.

As Montega took a piss, Samorah, as usual, got out of the shower butt-naked. She had no shame in her nudity. And why would she? Every part of her body was perfect, which was why she was the most envied in the house. Her vagina was bald like a swimsuit model's, and her breasts bounced like two water balloons. Even her nipples were red with small areolas. She had a flat stomach that showed how much she exercised in the gym, wide hips, and a beautiful, round backside that made the others jealous enough to spread rumors that it wasn't real.

When she looked at Montega, she gave him a sneaky smirk before grabbing her towel to dry off. She was pretty and even sexier when she smiled. Not a word was spoken. Each knew the other's thoughts; they just never acted on them.

Everyone knew that he was Tasha's, and no one tried anything. Nevertheless, they still did what they could to get his attention because they all loved a fine man from out-of-town. Montega watched as Samorah wrapped herself with a towel, folding it above her breasts before walking out. *Damn, that is one bad bitch,* he thought as he flushed the toilet and got ready to go out for the day.

After getting washed and dressed, he headed for his cousin's house in Gwinnett County. Rodney was Montega's cousin, originally from Chicago, but he moved to Atlanta with his grandparents because his mother abandoned him at an early age to be a hooker. When Rodney got old enough, he started his own escort service, and by the time he turned twenty-four, he purchased his first BMW. Now he was twenty-six and up in the game at a high level. He had a stable of bad bitches and a nice house with three expensive cars out front.

When Montega met up with him, the first thing they did was tour the city. Rodney introduced his younger cousin to everyone, mainly females. Montega couldn't believe that mostly all southern girls had bodies like video dancers, and most of them were financially secure.

Later that night, Rodney took him to a club named 112, where

Montega got to see Atlanta at its best. Usher and Lil' Jon's "Yeah" thundered from the speakers.

While men did their latest two-steps to a down-south beat, the women seductively clapped their asses and got down and dirty on the dancefloor.

"This is where the real ballers play, cousin. Remember when Biggie said Room 112 is where the players dwell? Well, this is it, shawty," Rodney said over the music as the two made their way upstairs to the VIP.

Being from the mean streets of Philly, Montega was star-struck by the amount of entertainers, sports figures, video vixens, and ballers that flew in town for the weekend to pop bottles and fuck big-bootie women.

As soon as he and his cousin sat at their table, Rodney gave the bouncer a head nod. Within the wave of a hand, they were surrounded by Atlanta's finest. A pretty, caramel waitress with blonde hair pushed through the mob of sack chasers to take their order.

Montega was mesmerized by the variety of sistas in the club. Their asses were unreal. It was like a candy store with all his favorite flavors. He didn't know which one to pick.

"What would you like, baby?" the waitress asked.

"Lemme get a shot of Gray Goose and—"

"Let us get two bottles, shawty," Rodney, said cutting in.

The girl smiled, looked at Montega, and asked, "You ain't from 'round here, are ya?"

Montega shook his head. "Nah, I'm from Philly."

"Oooh, a Philly boy," she flirted as her face lit up.

She turned and went to get the bottles for them. Rodney put his arm around his cousin's shoulders. "Ya see, shawty, ya cousin ain't no small-time cat 'round here. We don't buy no drinks from the bar. We pop bottles like y'all Northerners pop guns."

The bartender placed the two bottles of Gray Goose on the table. "That'll be five hundred even," she said, still eyeing Montega.

Before Rodney could go into his pockets, Montega pulled out a huge rack of hundreds, peeled off six, then handed them to the woman. He then took a bottle, peeled off the cellophane, and popped it open. Rodney, who had no idea his cousin was getting it like that, said, "Aye, shawty, I thought you said you was just a small-time hustler?"

"I am. Don't let this money fool you, dog. It's just for show. I came up on a lick a little while ago. Almost cost me my life in the end. You see the little cuts on my face, don't you? Anyway, I got a long way to go, and I'm far from where I need to be," Montega explained.

"And where do you need to be?"

"On top. I need to be one of the top five gangstas in the country. I'm not just talking 'cause I have lips either. I don't have the gift of gab like my brother. I have a drive that can't be stopped. All I need is the line to get me started, and it's on from there."

Rodney nodded his head while deep in thought. "Okay, well, I might be able to assist you with that. I know somebody, a Colombian. Good dude too. He just moved to Atlanta on business. I gotta pull a few strings, but I'm sure everything will go smoothly. That's crazy. The other day, he was just asking if I knew anyone that I could vouch for. If you ask me, you couldn't have come to the "A" at a better time."

The DJ threw on Lil' Jon with the Ying Yang Twins called "Salt Shaker." The atmosphere got electrical, and so did the woman. As Montega took a sip of his Goose, Rodney tapped him and pointed to someone just a table away.

Montega turned to see a fat Mexican draped in diamond-studded platinum chains with a watch so iced out it was impossible to tell the time. He too was surrounded by beautiful half-dressed women. He gestured to Montega with two bottles of Patrón Platinum as if to say, 'game recognize game.' Montega responded by raising his bottle of Gray Goose, acknowledging the fat Mexican, which received a puzzled look.

"No, no de lincuete!" he shouted over the music at him.

Montega frowned. "What you say?"

"You big time like me!" He directed his hand at the women, bottles, and jewels he had on. "You drink like me! Come! Sit with me!"

Montega was feeling the fat Mexican's style. He looked back at

Rodney with a grin. "I'll be right back, cuz. Let me rap with this guy for a sec."

"You sure about dude?" Rodney asked.

Montega looked back at the fat guy. "Yeah, he looks official. Probably works with the cartels. I'll be back. Just keep my seat warm."

"Shit. All these women around us. I'll get one of them to do that for you."

Montega scooted out the booth as the girls sitting next to him made way. He got up and walked to the fat guy's table. His women got up to let him sit beside him. The two shook hands.

"I'm Montega."

The fat man nodded and said, "Sergio, but call me Meat Ball. You from ATL, amigo?"

"Nah, Philly."

"Philly, huh? What Philly Montega drink?"

"Gray Goose," Montega replied.

The Mexican snapped his finger for the waitress and had her get them more bottles. While they waited, the two men began feeling each other out. Montega had pegged him wrong, assuming he was a high-ranking drug cartel member. He was surprised to find out Meat Ball made his fortune in human trafficking. He went on to tell him he smuggled women, children, fugitives, and prostitutes in and out of the United States at $10,000 a head. The only people he wouldn't deal with were terrorist.

"Why?" Montega asked.

"Because they will blow up all this beautiful cha-cha!" He bursted into a loud laughter while grabbing the asses of the two nearest females.

Meat Ball schooled Montega on the ins and outs of human trafficking. He sensed the Mexican was trying to recruit him. Although it sounded lucrative, Montega let it be known it wasn't his twist. Even still, before the night was over, they exchanged numbers. Meat Ball let him know that his number never changed.

Moments later, Montega excused himself to go take a piss. On his way back, someone grabbed his hand and said, "Hey, handsome."

He turned to see the goddess with hazel eyes standing in front of him.

Samorah was dressed in a skimpy, red Chanel dress with gold Joan & David pumps. "You wanna dance?" she asked, whispering in his ear before stepping back to do a little twist of her hips and drop down a bit.

"I don't dance," Montega stated, but she took his hand anyway and led him over to the vacant corner so he could lean on the wall while she did her thing. "What are you doing?" he asked as she turned her back to him and brushed her ass against his crotch. She wiggled her hips and bounced her butt up and down in perfect rhythm, throwing her golden hair over her shoulder so she could see what she was doing. Montega kept the bottle to his lips, tilting it back every now and then, watching Samorah give him all ass while dancing to the beat. She jiggled her ass until her dress rose above her ass cheeks. She then grabbed the hem and pulled it back down while continuing to bounce to the beat.

♫ Shake it like a salt shaker. Shake it like a salt shaker...

Her rhythm reminded him of Tee-Tee back at the nightclub. He put one hand on her slim waist with the other cocking the bottle of Goose. He nearly choked when Samorah dropped it low, bent over, and twerked like a video vixen. An erotic feeling overcame him. He was aroused but not aroused. It felt weird.

After the song, Nelly's "Flap Your Wings," Montega took the dancefloor by surprise and did a mean two-step. Before they knew it, they had a little audience.

After the song was over, Montega held her hand and pulled her close. He was a little out of breath, but was enjoying himself. Life had been so serious for him at times that he had almost forgotten what it was like to have fun.

"I thought you couldn't dance," she said.

"I can't. I just know how to move my feet. But fuck all that. What's good with you?" he asked.

Samorah smiled. "What do you mean by that?"

"You already know what I mean. Let's start from the sorority house. Every morning, you take a shower at the same time I come down. I know you see me watching you."

"Watching me? Why would you be watching me? Aren't you Tasha's man?"

"I was once told that the only way to claim a man is to marry him. And right now, you don't see no ring on my finger. Me and Tasha split up when she came back to college. We just get it in whenever we can," he confessed. "Right now, I ain't thinking about Tasha. I'm thinking about how far I can get with a beautiful girl like you."

Samorah smiled. Her glossy lips sparkled, along with the small diamond-studded nose ring she had. That reminded him of Juicy. She was gorgeous. Montega couldn't help but stare at her. After a minute of silence, she asked, "Is there a reason why you're staring at me like that without saying something?"

"Yeah, I'm standin' here, sayin' to myself, 'Damn, she can't be this pretty. Something has to be wrong with her.' Even diamonds are flawed, you know?"

Samorah blushed while he continued. "I don't think we've been properly introduced. I'm Kenny," he said, holding out his hand.

"Samorah," she replied, taking his hand in hers and shaking it. "Nice to meet you, Kenny."

Samorah and Montega danced and drank the whole night until last call, which was called at six in the morning. As the two got ready to leave, Samorah asked, "Do you want to go get some breakfast?"

"Hell yeah, I'm starvin'. Let me go tell my cousin I'm out."

When Montega saw Rodney, he let him know where he was headed and informed him that he would meet him later. Once he got outside, Samorah was waiting for him in a gold Lexus GS450.

"Damn, I guess even the women in Atlanta get at a dollar too," he said, closing the passenger side door after getting in. "This is nice."

"Thanks, but I'm not from Atlanta. I'm from Miami," she corrected him, starting up the car.

"Oh yeah? What part?" he asked as if he had been there before.

"North Miami Beach. Have you ever been there?"

"Nah, not me. Now that I think about it, I don't think I've ever left my city until now."

"Oh my God, Kenny, you should see it. It's so beautiful—the palm trees, the golden beaches of sand, and blue water. It's all so spectacular. Why don't you come visit me down there some time? I'm sure you would love it."

"You know what? That don't sound like a bad idea."

"I think I should warn you though. You might not want to leave."

"I can believe that, especially if half the women are as appealing as you are," he replied.

Samorah glowed. "I see I may have to put my guard up on you. You are quite the charmer, not to mention, you're cute. Those are pluses that can get you far with me."

Once the two arrived at the Flying Biscuit for breakfast, they seated themselves. Montega was far from home. He was still cautious, so they sat by the window. After the episode with the grenade launcher, he made sure he looked at every face that came in the restaurant. If a person didn't look right, he would flip into war mode.

"So what are you takin' up in college?" he asked.

"Business. I want to own my own club someday when I get a chance to settle down after my modeling career."

"Oh yeah? You're a model?" Montega asked, surprised.

"Well, not exactly. I'm actually goin' to school for that. I have taken pictures and been in magazines like *King* and *Smooth Girls*, but I don't want to be one of those ghetto models with just a big ass. I want to go for the big labels like Victoria's Secret or Cover Girl. What do you think?" she asked.

"I think the sky's the limit for an angel. Besides, one of my sister's girlfriends, Amber Paschel, she models for those magazines. Do you know her?"

"I've heard of her. She's very popular in the industry too. But I want more than that. I want the world."

Montega smirked and replied, "So do I."

After their meal, Samorah took him to her getaway spot at the W on 14th Street. Montega worried about her 16th-floor suite. For one, she was a college student driving a Lexus, and two; she had credit cards up the ass. Now, he was standing in the largest hotel suite he had ever seen, and it was just her *getaway spot*? He made a mental note to do more research about this woman; there was something she just wasn't telling him.

Chapter Thirty-Three

The Warning

"Watch your back..."

— BUTCH

"Please take a seat, miss. Your visit will start in a few minutes," the black female officer at the visiting room desk said before attending to the next person in line.

Diamond headed through a room filled with inmates and their visitors and took a seat by the snack machine. A few sets of eyes were locked onto her voluptuous backside as she strutted along in a pair of tight, black, leather leggings and black, high-heeled platforms.

Once she found a seat, she decided to grab some snacks from the vending machine. When she returned, her cousin Butch was approaching her from the back. Butch was related to Diamond on her father's side of the family. He used to run with her a few years back when she was trying to make a name for herself out on the streets of Los Angeles as the Black Kiss of Death.

He got arrested on gun charges and had been incarcerated in a federal prison ever since. During that time, Butch had gotten some unexpected visits from models and legendary mobsters; none, however, were as important or spellbinding as the Snow White Queen, Diamond.

Once he handed the guard his card, he headed through the

receiving room to the other side, swaggering like he owned the place because, truthfully, he did. Butch had most of the jail in his pocket. Even the warden catered to him at times.

When Diamond saw the husky Ving Rhames lookalike, she couldn't help but crack a big smile. "I see you're eating well in here," she said, giving him a big hug before they sat.

"I'm maintaining; that's all. But look at you. I swear you get prettier every time I see you. You staying outta trouble out there? I don't want to hear that you had to put another boyfriend down because he was trippin'."

Diamond smiled. Seeing her cousin brought back memories, some good and some sadly depressing. "So what's up with you in here? I thought you were coming home soon. What changed?" she asked, brushing a loose strand of hair behind her ear.

The look on Butch's face told her something wasn't right. He then looked away.

"Butch, what's the problem?"

"Look, Dee. I'm just gonna tell you like this. Sometimes, you just can't duck no rec in here. Even if you try your hardest. Long story short, I caught a new charge. So I won't be coming home anytime soon. But don't sweat it. I'm good in here. You might as well say this is my jail. I got C.O.s bringing shit in for me. I get a little pussy every now and then, so I don't sweat it."

"Well, I certainly hope it's not her," Diamond said, pointing at the dark, nasty woman sitting at the desk. Butch burst out laughing. "You gotta be kiddin' me if you think I'm sticking my dick in that. Anyway, what's goin' on with you? Who's the new big-time boyfriend?"

Embarrassment swept over Diamond before she could look away. "I don't have a boyfriend," she mumbled.

"Get outta here! You don't got no man? Wait a minute. Don't tell me you switched over to—"

"Do you want to die in this visiting room? Don't come at me like that."

"Well then, what's the problem?"

Diamond tried to find an answer to his question but came up

empty. "I don't know. I guess I haven't found the right one yet. I don't want to end up with another Hector or Stephon. I want this one to be different than the others I've fallen in love with before."

"Dee, c'mon, cuz. Ya trippin'. Here you are, twenty-four-years-old, waiting for the right guy to step forward. Ya young, baby girl. Live ya life. You can't get nowhere like that. Ya got to take chances and make mistakes. You might think you a princess, but you might not be able to find Prince Charming. So I guess you may have to settle for the knight or even a pawn and be happy."

"You mean as in a small-timer?" Diamond asked as if he'd just soiled her shoes. "What I need is someone well established, who doesn't feel intimidated by me—someone who is confident in himself and can think for the both of us when I need him to. I need a boss, Butch, not a soldier," Diamond explained.

"Shit, those be the ones, Dee. You need to stop being so stubborn and give a real nigga a chance, regardless of what that fool makes. Everything ain't always about money. But I ain't here to beat your head in. What I want to tell you about has nothing to do with your love life. It's about your brother. That mark is a snake, Diamond. He and his organization. A lotta fools been talkin' 'bout him and those marks and how they used to work for the Great Whites. Then, when something happens, Clyde turns his back on them completely and even puts out a hit on them in jail to keep them from retaliating. I didn't believe the shit until somebody put a hit out on me. Since I'm alive to tell you this, you can guess why I caught the new charge and won't be comin' home no time soon, right? No matter what, he wins, and I lose."

Diamond looked confused. "But why would Clyde put a hit out on you? I don't understand. You don't work for him. You work for me," she said.

"I don't know, Dee. I really don't. All I know is I got an attempted murder charge over a guard your brother sent at me. I'll tell you this; that circle you surrounded by ain't right, cuz. So you need to reconsider the team you're on because your brother don't care about nothin' but money, so watch your back."

After the brief visit, Diamond got into the back seat of her Maybach with Sam and sighed. Bain, who was seated in the passenger, grunted for the driver to pull off. The priest, whose head was in the Bible, looked over at her.

"Is something wrong, Madam?" he asked while putting a book marker in the crease and closing it, but all he got was silence and the back of her head.

Chapter Thirty-Four

Anti-Diamond

"You'll have your revenge..."

— CLYDE WHITE

Clyde White held a meeting with his Great White committee on the spacious terrace of the Viceroy Hotel that overlooked the spectacular Santa Monica Beach. The only three members that weren't present for the meeting were Carlos, Tommy Gun, and Diamond. Everyone knew Tommy Gun couldn't make it because he wanted to be there for his girlfriend, Beauty, who was graduating from college.

As for Carlos Morin, no one could get in contact with him. His phones, accounts, and address had been changed, making him a hard man to find. Diamond was absent because she knew nothing about the meeting. She wasn't invited; the meeting was about her.

"What did the Agugbo brothers say when you spoke about collaborating?" Chavo asked.

Clyde sighed. "Well, the Agugbo brothers were very interested in our proposal, but there were certain conditions that we could not meet at the time," he said, choosing his words wisely.

"And what are those circumstances, may I ask?" Semok Budinov questioned.

Clyde looked at his cousin, whose expression said, *The ball is in your court now.*

"The demise of my sister," he said.

"And you denied that proposal?" Chavo wondered, grabbing everyone's attention.

"Mr. Garcia!" Semok shot. "Are you out of your mind? This is Diamond we're talking about. She's contributed to this organization more than any of us."

"I don't know, Mr. Budinov," Wong Lee stated. "You know that without the Agugbo brothers, we're vulnerable. Our empire could crumble. You said it yourself: the connection in South America is closing. Soon, we must find another source. Even with the contribution that Ms. White put it in, it doesn't matter if we have no way of transporting the merchandise."

"He's right," Chavo agreed. "I think we should take a vote whether or not Diamond should be—"

"That's enough!" Shug snapped, causing everyone to shut their mouths. "We ain't killing Diamond. That's over my dead body. You guys should hear yourselves. Sounds like you're letting this money we getting go to your heads. It's clouding your judgement. Now, she's an important part of this organization, like Semok said."

"If that's the case, why not settle our differences with Castor?" Tony Wright suggested. "He has everything we're looking for. What has Diamond offered us? Nothing but a bunch of outbursts. Forget your sister. It's business, never personal."

Clyde considered this. His thoughts were more on the people who were defending his sister. "This is not something we can just agree to right away. This must be carefully thought out," Clyde said. "Maybe we should warn Diamond about her actions before we take such drastic measures." Clyde studied the faces around the table. The last thing he wanted was for one of Diamond's allies getting a whiff of his plan and running back to tell her. He had talked with Deshawn and wasn't happy with what he'd heard.

Chavo leaned forward, folding his hands. He took a deep breath and said, "Well, let's not wait too long, because sooner or later, Castor will be looking for us."

The group went silent as everyone looked at each other with concern.

After the meeting, as the members of the Great White packed their things and left, Clyde called Shug back. His whole time there, he noticed the distance in Shug.

"Shug, is everything straight with you?" Clyde asked, patting him on the back. He thought that maybe Shug was upset about the things that were said about Diamond.

"Yeah, I'm cool, cuz. Just in my bag over my homie, Kev. It's kinda hard for me since we grew up together from yea-high," Shug said.

"Kev was a good guy. I remember when you used to bring him out west," Clyde said.

"Remember our clubbing days? When he went into his pocket and asked the waiters how much for the bottles? I think we bought like fifty Magnum bottles that night." Clyde put his arm around his long-time friend. "Have you found the guy who did this yet?"

"Nah, not yet. It's like he disappeared or something. Nobody seen dude," Shug replied, sounding frustrated.

"Well, keep looking. If he's just some small-time mark, then his money will eventually run out, and he'll pop right back up to the surface. Then you'll have your revenge."

Chapter Thirty-Five

Betrayal

"The next time we bump heads, you're gonna wish you never met me..."

— TASHA

Montega and Samorah laughed all the way to the condo that she was renting. They had just come from the Mike Epps stand-up comedy show and had been laughing about the event the entire ride home. For the past two weeks, Samorah took her new boo everywhere. The two spent so much time together that Montega didn't have time to see Tasha on campus anymore. He even went to Samorah's graduation.

Montega didn't have this much fun with a woman he hadn't had sex with since he and Tasha first started kicking it. As they sat on the sofa, Samorah got up and went to the mini-bar to get them a drink. "What would you like?" she asked while pouring herself a glass of Belvedere.

"Gray Goose is good for me," he replied before turning on the TV. A Breaking News report was on the screen, and a bunch of Coast Guard officials were raiding a large ship. The bottom of the screen read: ***1 METRIC TON HEROIN BUST OFF THE COAST OF THE CARIBBEAN.*** Montega quickly lost interest and asked, "Since we met, you never spoke of your family. What's up with that?"

"That's because you never asked. But if you must know, my father was Columbian, and my mother was French. They were killed when I was just a baby in a car accident in Florida. My only family left is my brother. Ever since my parents died, he has been taking care of me. Of course, I met guys who had potential, but they either turned out to be jerks, or I just got bored with them."

"So how do you explain all of this?" he asked as she handed him his drink.

Samorah shrugged and smiled. "Do you always ask so many questions?"

Montega set the drink down and stood. "I'm very cautious, especially when it comes to a very pretty girl."

"Do you find me that pretty that I can only date men that can take care of me?" she asked as she stood to face him.

"I find you extremely pretty, but you didn't answer my question."

Samorah didn't respond. She was staring at him openly. He was standing before her in a black and red striped Polo shirt with black YSL jeans and black, red, and white Nikes. She reached out and played with the collar of his shirt, running her soft, French-manicured fingers across the cotton fabric. The smell of his Blue Label cologne caused her to close her eyes and step forward.

She rose on her tippy toes and pressed her lips against his while locking her hands behind his neck to kiss him hard. Her hands were cold but soft. He kissed her back, inviting her cool tongue into his warm mouth against his own. Her breath smelled fresh. Her tongue was very quick and slick, constricting around his own. She tasted of mint and lip gloss. Her perfume rose from the pores of her soft, French-vanilla skin and long, golden hair.

Montega enjoyed the feel of her breasts resting against this chest. He held her lower back with one hand and her upper back with the other, traveling up to the nape of her neck and back down again.

He felt as if he were about to suffocate. That's when she stopped and pulled away. Both were so out of breath that they had to take two more steps away from each other just to avoid another magnetic pull.

Samorah eyed him for a moment, biting her bottom lip to hold from saying something she might regret. He was everything she could ever want and more. In that one kiss, she planned her entire life with him while standing there. The thought of his body caused her to fan herself and walk away.

"It's so sticky in here. I need to get in the shower," she said, trying to avoid him for a moment.

Montega kept his eyes on her ass bulging out of her Tory Burch jeans all the way to the bathroom. She knew he was watching her, so she put an extra twist in her hips. Stopping at the bathroom door, she turned around to catch him gawking. But Montega was not a man who hid his intentions from women.

Just knowing he wanted her made her extremely moist between her legs. "Why are you staring like you want to join me or something?" she asked with a sultry voice before walking into the bathroom.

Montega gulped the rest of his drink, set it down on the coffee table, and headed after her. He got there just as she was bending over to pull down her jeans. The view of her hairless pussy and heart-shaped ass was enough to make his mouth water, and in no time, he was out of his clothes and following her into the steaming overhead shower.

Samorah turned around to gaze at him as the water cascaded down their bodies. He was nude and extremely muscular for a slim guy. The top of her head came to his chin. He towered over her. Looking down at his erection, she was shocked by the size. Montega placed his arms around her waist as she wrapped hers around his neck. He moved his hands behind her, squeezed her soft ass, and then propped her up against the cold walls. Samara invited him between her thighs, guiding his hardness into her wet slot. A moan of delight escaped from her soft, pink lips. Montega filled her insides until pelvis bone met pelvis bone.

"Ummmh!" he said with an unsuspected burst of appreciation for good pussy.

She was just the right fit and very light. He slowly slid in and out of her, enjoying the way her forehead rested against his own. Her pillowy boobs sat on his chiseled chest like two overfilled water balloons, and her ass sat in his palms like two balls of cotton candy. Samara kissed his lips again before she threw her head back and moaned with pleasure as he drove his lustful sword through her, deep enough for the hilt of his waist to touch hers over and over again. His chest smothered her breasts to the point she could feel his heart thundering with excitement.

"Oh, Ken-ney, uhhh!" she moaned, while stroking the nape of his neck. Her body thumped against the wall, making a whole-note sound of base. Montega grimaced as he picked up the pace, pounding her pussy like an oilrig drill. The feeling sent Samorah into a lustful frenzy.

She arched her back more, perking up her chest to squeeze both her breasts together, and fed him like an infant. Montega licked her pink nipples, enjoying her alluring rack and the wet taste of her skin.

"Ummm, that feels so good. You feel so good in me," she whispered as her body began to tremble.

"I like the way you takin' this dick, but I'm 'bout to stop with the teasing."

"Do what you have to do, handsome."

Montega pulled out and turned her around. Samorah pressed her hands against the wall as if she were good for a pat-down. Wrapping his palms around her wrists, he guided her hands higher. He then took her by the waist, pulled her back so that she bent over, and entered her again. This time, he launched his shaft in and out of her like a torpedo. Her ass waved to the impact of penetration, clapping against his thighs. Everything had happened so quickly, and his excitement shot to the roof. Looking down at the way her soft body responded to his thrust, he felt himself ready to release his seed. He pulled out and tried to stop himself from getting too excited, squeezing the base of his shaft while trying to control his breathing. Samorah turned to see what the problem was and grinned. "Who's teasing who?" she asked.

Montega took a deep breath as he looked her in the eyes. Watching the way her ass clapped had almost brought him to an early climax. He wasn't ready to tap out, not when he was just getting started.

"Why don't we take this someplace else?" he asked before scooping her up into his arms and carrying her wet body to the bedroom.

Once they got there, he laid her on the bed. The cold, crisp sheets became damp instantly. He then spread her legs and put his face between her thighs, licking her throbbing clitoris. Samorah moved her body in a snake-like dance as she oozed with flavor. Montega had her right where he wanted her.

She wiggled and whined and clawed at his head while enjoying his magical tongue. She then opened her eyes and looked down at him to find him watching her reaction to his touch. His tongue trailed her smooth pelvis up to her breasts. He cuffed and squeezed them firmly. His arms, cut and swollen, crawled forward like an alligator over top of her. He teased her breasts and watched her facial expression again. She tightened her jaw against the cries that wanted to escape her. They echoed throughout her mind like an empty hallway.

His fingertips trailed to the back of her knees, causing them to rise and bend. Chills climbed her thighs, forcing anticipation in her gut, along with the throbbing pulsation growing between her legs. His gaze and domination pose made her body tremble. His eyes were so dark but so beautiful. He was admiring the color of her pupils and how it complemented her damp skin. Her smile brought him back to reality. *She's definitely the one for me,* he thought.

When he entered her again, Samorah wrapped her arms around him, sliding her hands up and down his back as he delivered himself deep into her abyss. She moaned softly each time. He put both of her legs on his shoulders and continued thrusting.

"Oh God, boy, you're in my stomach!" she moaned. "Uhh! Oh shit, I'm cummin'!" Her legs began to quiver.

Grabbing her ankles and compressing her legs to her breasts, he drilled her with every inch of himself. Stroke after stroke, he felt the intensity grow until he was out of breath. His face twisted up as he released all that was built up inside of him. Her insides had never felt so warm as he filled her with seeds then laid on top of her, out of breath. Neither wanted to move and mess up the bond that they had just shared. Samorah was more shocked than tired. No one had ever brought her to such a climax before. It had all felt unreal.

Every guy she dealt with had flaws when it came to sex; they either couldn't get up because of intimidation, or they went out too fast from anticipation. She had a sex drive that could shame the most energetic men. Montega, however, was different. She realized this, but her instincts troubled her. Samorah knew that she had to be careful with him, because her feelings were getting too intense, way too fast. Not only was he handsome and fun to be with, but he could also fuck like a sex god. The last thing she wanted was to end up with a broken heart. She rested her head on his chest. He placed his arm around her, which really surprised her. Before she knew it, she was fast asleep.

The next morning, Montega awoke to the sound of his cell phone. He reached over on the nightstand and picked it up.

"Yo," he said, sitting up in bed.

"Aye, shawty, where you at?" Rodney asked.

"I'm out. Why? Something wrong?"

"Yeah, something's wrong. You ain't here. Remember that guy I was tellin' you about? Well, he on his way over, so you better get yo' ass here before you miss out on the opportunity of a lifetime."

When Montega hung up with his cousin, he took a long stretch before yawning. Samorah sat up slowly on the bed just as his phone started to buzz again. "Somebody's got a hotline," she teased while holding the sheets over her breasts.

"Yo," he answered again.

"What's up?" Tasha replied with a hint of hostility.

Montega looked over at Samorah and shushed her with his index finger. "Damn, Tasha, why you sound like that?"

Samorah smiled devilishly then rose to her knees. Her covers fell from her naked body. She moved in close and began kissing his neck. "What do you mean, why do I sound like this? Why haven't you been to see me lately? I know you haven't left Atlanta yet," she complained.

"Chill," Montega whispered to Samorah, who was licking his chest.

"Don't tell me to chill," Tasha snapped. "Where have you been?"

"I been chillin' with Rodney. Damn, why you buggin'?" he asked, trying to stop Samorah from tantalizing him.

Samorah decided to take her fun to the next level. She grabbed his hand and placed one of his fingers into her wet pussy. The feeling of her spongy insides sent his rocket to the moon. Montega saw that she was getting a kick out of all of this and shoved his finger deep inside of her. Samorah made an incredible sex face. She pushed the covers from over his lap and went down on him. Bringing him back to reality, Tasha shouted, "Boy, you are a fucking liar because I called Rodney, and he said that you were out. What? You think I'm stupid?"

"Yesss," he said, with pink, warm lips and a wicked tongue caressing his erect penis.

"What!"

"I mean… no," he corrected himself as Samorah worked him over. It was extremely hard to get a word out with the head he was getting.

"Boy, are you listening?" Tasha pressed him

"Tasha, you gotta calm down," he said, almost moaning out the words.

"You know what, Kenny? You ain't shit. I was tryna give you the benefit of the doubt. Had you been a man about it and just told me you were fucking Samorah, I wouldn't be so mad."

"Aight, I'm fuckin' Samorah. You happy now?" he said, watching Samorah deepthroat him while he played with her pussy.

"Ohh, it's like that! You know what? The next time we bump heads, you're gonna wish you never met me. I swear," she said before slamming the phone down in his ear.

Montega paid her no mind. He lay back on the bed, feeling like a king. His eyes were rolling in the back of his head as he erupted like a volcano down Samorah's throat.

Chapter Thirty-Six

The Plug

"Today can be your lucky day… or your worst nightmare…"

— CARLOS MORIN

An hour later, Montega was out of Samorah's condo. He got in his car and drove to Rodney's house, exhausted. Samorah was definitely a handful, and if he wasn't careful, she could possibly steal his heart like a thief in the night. Not only was she paid, but she was also a stone-cold freak. The entire night was a rather erotic experience he had not anticipated. She did things with him that he'd only seen in pornography magazines because in the public eye, they were just downright nasty. But for some dark, odd reason, it made him like her even more.

Once Montega opened the door, he spotted Rodney seated on the couch across from a Spanish guy with oily, jet-black, shoulder-length hair. He was conservatively dressed in a pair of tan slacks, brown Salvatore Ferragamo shoes, and a short-sleeved button-up. The man rose to match his size as he walked in.

"Carlos, this is my cousin, Montega. This is the guy that I've been trying to get to come down here for so long. Montega, this is Carlos Morin. He's from Miami."

Montega shook his hand. "Nice to meet you, Mr. Morin," he said.

"Likewise. Your cousin here has told me much about you. He also tells me that you're looking for a line. Why don't we take a little ride so we can talk in private?" Carlos said, tossing Montega the keys. "You drive."

When Montega got outside, he and Carlos walked to the blue Mercedes Benz CL550.

"Nice wheels you got here," Montega said, deactivating the alarm before getting in.

"What? This piece of shit? It's only a rental," Carlos said modestly, getting into the passenger side.

Carlos directed him down to Simpson Road, which was the hood for real. As Montega drove down a block, Carlos had him pull over in front of a deli on the corner. Across the street was a small crowd of dope boys gambling on the steps. Montega noticed one with an iced-out chain that had the initials 'TG' hanging from his neck.

Even from a distance, he could tell he was the one running things. "You see that guy right there?" Carlos asked, pointing to the man with the tattoo under his left eye and the shining chain. "That's Tommy Gun. Have you heard of him?"

"Rodney said something about him running Atlanta. What is he doin' out here in the open like he one of the dope boys?" Montega asked, watching the man fondle his girlfriend in broad daylight. There were four guys that looked like stiffs around him. The girl, however, was nice looking and had the signature down-south booty.

He recalled seeing her somewhere but hadn't the faintest idea where. There were so many alluring women in the city; it was hard to pinpoint where he saw her before. "Rodney said that he was considered untouchable," he went on to say.

"And does he look untouchable?"

Montega scanned the area and saw how easy it was for stick-up boys to run down on the guy.

"Put it this way," he said. "If this was Philly, he wouldn't even make the menu. He'd just be a snack."

Carlos gave him a weak smile then told him to pull off. He had Montega drive all the way to Buckhead this time, where Carlos's nice, five-bedroom home was located.

When the two walked inside, the first thing Montega noticed was its darkness. It had a scent of a familiar fragrance. The place was spacious but cozy with a living room of white and blue furniture that appeared outside the foyer. A ninety-inch flat-screen TV sat on a stand facing a recliner the same color as the other furnishings. There were no pictures hanging around anywhere, no certificates, no diplomas, no nothing. Montega figured this couldn't have been a house where Carlos rested his head. He also noticed the kitchen light was on, so he assumed someone else was home.

"It's about time my sister remembered this address," Carlos said. "I haven't seen her in a while. I thought maybe she might've already headed back home."

Montega listened to Carlos speak of his sister. Before he could ask her name, she began to descend down the staircase. When she got to the bottom, she stopped in her tracks and looked as if she had seen a ghost.

"You think you could come home once in a while to check on your brother?" Carlos said in Spanish, but she didn't respond. She was too busy looking at the guy beside him. "Samorah, this is a friend of mines. He goes by the name, Montega."

"That's funny. I thought his name was Kenny," Samorah replied, causing Carlos to look at them both.

Her eyes never left Montega's, and she didn't look happy.

"Oh, I see. You two know each other."

"It's a small world," she said with irritation.

Carlos patted Montega on his back. "You really do get around, don't you? I'm surprised. My sister hates everyone she comes in contact with. I like you already. Come. Take a seat over here. Samorah, why don't you get me and your friend here something to drink? I'll have a shot of Louis the 13th, and what will you have, Mr. Montega?"

Samorah answered for him. "Gray Goose and pineapple juice, right?" she asked. She was definitely unhappy about seeing him there.

Once the two men were on the sofa, Carlos got right down to business. "Montega, your cousin tells me that you are a very ambitious man who knows a lot about moving cocaine. He says that you're very popular in Philadelphia, and that people are influenced by your ambition. He also tells me that you're not afraid to get your hands dirty."

Looking over at Samorah as she fixed the drinks, Montega replied, "That sounds about right."

"Yes, well, I have a lot of people who can move cocaine around here. That's not what I'm looking for, however. What I'm looking for is a person that can get his hands dirty. From my understanding, you're a loyal man with a heart of stone. I need people like that in my circle, Montega," he said as Samorah handed the two men their drinks.

She then gave Montega another look that indicated she wasn't feeling this at all. Samorah didn't want to admit it, but for the past few weeks, she had developed strong feelings for Montega. And even though she suspected he was a dope boy, she still looked the other way. She had no idea that he knew her brother. That right there scared the living shit out of her. Carlos wasn't one to play around with, nor did he usually do business in a place where he rested his head. The fact that Montega was there told her that he trusted him, and trust was bad. One fuck up, and Montega would be a memory.

"How much cocaine have you handled at one time?" Carlos asked.

"Uh, I would say nine ounces," Montega said.

When Carlos heard that, he burst out laughing. Montega frowned, wondering what was so funny. When Carlos caught his vibe, he apologized. "I'm sorry, my friend, but I haven't seen something that small in a long time. It's no wonder the bottom turns men into wolves when you should be considered lions. Montega, today could go two ways for you. It could either be your lucky day or your worst nightmare. Let me ask you something else; can you handle one hundred kilograms of pure-white Columbian cocaine?"

Montega almost lost his breath. "One... hundred... k-keys?" he repeated hesitantly.

"That's right. I'll have a shipment delivered to you as soon as you get back to Philly. Of course, there's a heavy price to pay before you get that first shipment. Don't you think I'm being generous? There are heavy strings attached. There are no such things as 'favor for a favor' in business. Everything costs. What do you think about that? Are you interested?" Carlos asked.

"As a shark is to blood," Montega responded excitedly.

"Great. Now, before we can do business, you must pass the test."

"A test? What kind of test?"

"Remember the guy I showed you earlier? Well, he's a member of a rival organization, and someone wants him… disposed of. This is the test and the price you have to pay for the consignment of hundred keys. In fact, I'll even throw in twenty bricks of heroin."

Montega got out of his seat. "Is that all you want?" he asked as if the task was nothing.

With admiration, Carlos gave him the keys to his car. "That's all I need," he said.

In a flash, Montega was out the door. There was nothing else to discuss. He was signing the contract with the blood of another man—a hundred keys and twenty bricks of dope for the price of some guy he didn't give a shit about. He was about to find out how untouchable this Tommy Gun really was. Like KK used to say: If his heart didn't pump concrete and his skin wasn't made of Teflon, his blood would quench the ground's thirst.

As the door shut, Carlos smiled wickedly. He then turned to look at his sister. Samorah folded her arms across her chest with an attitude. "What?" Carlos asked.

"It's not fair. I saw him first, and you know it," she complained.

Carlos shrugged. "What do you want me to do? The man made his decision. Money talks, sweetheart. Besides, you should be happy. At least he's not a weak guy. Fuck it. If you love him that much, pay for his casket if he fails."

When Montega got back to his cousin's house, he switched vehicles from the Benz to the black Impala. He then headed for Simpson Road with two things on his mind. Money and murder. He truly had a heart of stone. But little did he know, the odds might have been stacked against him from the start. What he planned to face could possibly be the death of him.

Chapter Thirty-Seven

The Snow White Committee

"They say a diamond's value grows the older it gets."

— JOSE CASTRO

Diamond sat next to Bain in her private jet as it slowly touched down on a dirt road in Cuba not too far from her grandfather's estate. It was a bright morning and very warm despite the gray clouds that covered the sky. Awaiting her arrival were five armored SUVs filled with Cuban paramilitary soldiers. Diamond stepped out of the G-500 and into the extremely warm weather, dressed in cream linen and croc-skin pumps, courtesy of Oscar de la Renta.

The warm breeze tousled her long hair like a silk cape. She wore dark shades while lugging a brown, leather Hermés bag. The priest followed, wiry of his surroundings. This was his first visit to Cuba, and with the thought of the embargo law on the land, he knew they weren't supposed to be sneaking in like that. Diamond stepped to the bottom and allowed him to go first. Her bodyguards took the lead, carrying Armalite AR-10A4 machine guns.

Samuel followed, making an invisible cross as he always did and mumbled, *"In the lord, I must trust. How can you say to my soul, flee as a bird to the mountain? For look! The wicked bend their bows. They make ready their arrows on the string that they may shoot secretly at—"*

"Enough, priest," Diamond hissed irritably. "You've been reciting scriptures ever since you got on the plane. Is there nothing you don't fear?"

"What's not to fear when there are over a million ways to die in this world?" he asked as he looked at the soldier awaiting them. "I may appear a coward in your eyes, Madam White, but when I recite a scripture from the Bible, it gives me joy, and that joy sometimes makes me forget to be afraid."

Diamond had no response. She didn't really know why she kept the priest around. She told herself she was doing this for 2 Gun Sam, who was nothing but loyal to her father, but really, this was for her own understanding. Priest Samuel was her own personal experiment that she hadn't a clue what to do with.

"Senora Blanca," the men said respectfully in Spanish, which meant Ms. White.

Diamond returned the greeting before getting inside one of the vehicles and being escorted to her grandfather's fortress. Twice a year, Diamond had been secretly taking trips back and forth to Cuba behind her brother's back. Smuggling pure-white heroin into the United States wasn't the issue. The Underworld knew full-well that Diamond had inherited her grandfather's business at a young age. It was the only reason she was brought to the table. But what they didn't know was that Jose had helped her put together her own little commission to ensure her reign as queen—the Snow White Committee, which incorporated some of the most lucrative organizations around the world.

The hacienda seemed to amaze her every time she pulled up to the steel gates. It was an old mansion that sat on nearly 640 acres of poppy fields and occupied 32,000 square feet. Built in 1928, the mansion was designed with three stories of tan stucco topped with brown terra-cotta roof tiles. Balconies and terraces hugged the upper windows, and the paramilitary were positioned everywhere.

When her entourage pulled through the gate of the large mansion, José waited for her at the door.

"Diamond. Well… it is good to see you," he greeted with a broad smile. José was a tall man with a cappuccino skin tone, salt and pepper hair, a light beard, and wore glasses. His smile was always polite and welcoming, making her feel as if she was in the company of an actual relative.

The two embraced. The man, who was no older than Diamond's mother, kissed her on both cheeks then said, "They say a diamond's value grows the older it gets, and you, my queen, are a prime example of radiant beauty."

"José, please. Stop trying to butter me up. I'm not that mad about the four-ton deal you secretly set up with the Jamaicans. It was a good idea to try and take the Caribbean. Too bad the ship got intercepted by the U.S. Coast Guards," Diamond reassured him.

José's smile suddenly vanished. "You heard about that?" he asked.

"*Drug dealers of the Caribbean?* Heard about it? It was all over CNN, José. The Government is making a big deal about it. How could I not? Now, have my guests arrived yet?" They headed down the pale marble gallery full of antiques, oil paintings, and silver, lobster-plated statue knights that stood guard every ten paces.

"They're down the hall, awaiting your arrival," José responded.

Diamond nodded and headed to the meeting. The mansion was like an old museum with the smell of oak, timber, and stone. The meeting room was on the second floor. It was freakishly large with a giant fireplace on the opposite side of the balcony window. Diamond walked in and blessed the men with a whiff of her Givenchy perfume. Amongst the men in expensive suits was Japan's organized crime syndicate, the Six Yamaguchi-gumi, run by a short, stocky man named Yochi. Along with him was the head of the Albanian mafia, the Mexican Juarez cartel boss, Jesus "EL Chango" Vargas and the Rizzuto crime family boss from Canada. The United Kingdom was represented by the A-Team. Translators were also present to help with communications. All were almost twice Diamond's age, yet she saw them as equals, which they saw her as an alluring profit.

Once she was comfortably seated, she and the men discussed business. It was sort of like being at the UN; each translator would relay each message to his boss. The boss would think on it then relay their message back in return.

"I've got a problem. Well, actually, two problems," Diamond began. "I am in a tight situation, so I'm reaching out to you all. I have four targets I need eliminated. I'm willing to pay $5 million for each individual. One of them, however, is incarcerated. Two are in America, and one is in Columbia."

Yochi spoke in Japanese. Next, his translator asked, "Who are these men?"

"Three of them are from South Africa. The Agugbo brothers. The other is Verningo Castor."

After the translations, the men had stern looks on their faces. "There's no way we can bring that type of heat on us," the Albanian mob boss said. "Especially with Castor. He's way too powerful in Columbia."

"The minute you set foot in Columbia, he'll know, and you'll be dead. I'm not risking good assassins for a suicide mission," Yochi's translator stated.

"I don't think you've heard about the Agugbo brothers lately," the Rizzuto family boss warned.

"Enlighten me," Diamond challenged, crossing her legs, her hands folded over her knee.

"The Agugbo brothers are the top diamond smugglers in the world, meaning they have a lot of dangerous allies. You fuck with them, and you'll have a swarm of killer bees stinging you. You can pay me $100 million; I still won't do it. A war with them is bad for business. My advice to you is to back off them before they back you down."

"Speaking of killer bees," Yochi went on to say. "I hear Castor has a wide variety of torturing assassins he calls Blood Hornets. The things they do to a man will make your skin crawl. These vile killers are positioned in hives all over the world. All he has to do is make a call."

Then why hasn't he already? What is he waiting for? Diamond thought, displaying her poker face, but inside, she was crushed. She had lost a lot of good people to both the Agugbo brothers and Castor. So she didn't blame the men in her group for running scared, but she did lose a lot of respect for them. They were supposed to be the most dangerous syndicates in the world. *How could they back down from four men?*

After the meeting, Diamond stood on the balcony, staring down as the men, one by one, got into their cars. Once the last man entered his vehicle, Diamond turned to look at the commander of her small, Cuban paramilitary army. She whispered something in his ear. He nodded then quickly rushed off while Sam joined her and Bain on the rail.

"I guess this meeting was a waste of time and jet fuel. Bain, Priest Samuel, let's go. We need to get to Atlanta," Diamond said, sounding upset.

"You're leaving already?" José asked.

"Yes, my business is finished here for now. Be sure to give me a call when you are ready to send out the next shipment this time."

"Ms. White, have you forgotten that I run the business until you are ready to step up?" José reminded her.

"Yes, but Mr. Castro, it's clear to see this business would be ruined without me. All you do is sit here in this mansion. You need to get out and see what's going on around you before you end up an antique like the rest of the stuff in this place. Now, we'll be in touch."

"Absolutely," José said, somewhat embarrassed.

Diamond turned and headed for the SUVs. She was angry and consumed by rage. José watched her as she made her exit. Shaking his head, he knew she was still too young to run the business, which was the reason she didn't value the lives of others.

Inside her vehicle, she looked over at Sam and said, "Pray, Priest. I am in need of a prayer."

"On what occasion, Madam White?" the priest asked.

"Pray for the dead because, in a few minutes, twelve of the living will soon join them."

As the men from Diamond's international organization pulled up to their private jets at the small airstrip designed for smugglers, they got out of their vehicles and approached their planes. But before they could board them, Diamond's Cuban paramilitaries emerged from the woods with Cobra M-11s. The sound of fully automatic choppers cried out copper tears. The Canadian boss was the first to catch the led storm. Blood splattered everywhere.

As bodies fell like buzz-sawed trees, Yochi, who was already hit five times, tried to take a few more steps toward his plane. Three more bullets hit him, sending his blood flying. He fell dead to the ground with the others. Every last one of them had been snuffed out because they had shown weakness. All except the Mexican leader of the Juarez cartel. Jesus "EL Chango" Vargas looked around at all the dead bodies. He looked down at himself to see he was unharmed and took it as a sign. He then stepped over them and got on his jet. This was a message that Diamond wanted to send to the cartels in Mexico. Weak men and weakness was something that Diamond White refused to tolerate.

TWO DAYS EARLIER...

In Washington, D.C., inside the White House situation room, the President of the United States sat with the directors of Homeland Security, the FBI, U.S. Border Patrol, the CIA, the DEA, and the United States Coast Guard about a very big problem. Throwing a newspaper down on the table, he said, "One metric ton of pure-white heroin was found a few weeks ago aboard a ship coming from Cuba.

One Metric Ton. Does anyone have any idea where these drugs were going?"

The U.S. Coast Guard director spoke up. "Well, Mr. President, my agents apprehended a few of the men on the ship, but before they could interrogate them, they swallowed cyanide and forever held their peace."

"What about this bandit from Columbia, the drug lord Castor?" the FBI director asked.

"No, it's not Castor's style to smuggle heroin on a ship like that. This was a rush job. And Castor's heroin usually isn't pure and white," the DEA director added.

"What about the Chinese?" the President asked.

"It could be. Or it could be that Cuban guy. What's his name? Elcano?" The FBI chief speculated.

"No, it can't be. Diego Elcano died a few years ago," the DEA director countered.

"That doesn't mean his business died with him. Someone always steps up to bat," the FBI director replied.

"Which is why I am signing this document here," the President interjected.

"What document, sir?" the FBI director asked.

"I'm putting together an anti-drug task force. I want three of the best men from each of your agencies for this position. I also need a chairman to run the task force. I want this task force up and running before the next election. So you have a year to pull it together. The first target is Miami, Florida. Now, are there any suggestions on who we can recruit to run this operation? Anyone at all?"

Everyone got quiet and looked around at each other. The FBI director raised his hand and said, "Sir, I think I have someone in the makings, someone who has a passion for this kind of operation."

"Okay, well, who is he?"

Chapter Thirty-Eight

Cold-Blooded

"Diamond is on her way down here..."

— CLYDE WHITE

Seated in a hole in the wall bar, drunk on Courvoisier and Coronas, Gary Whitehead was drowning in his misery. Not only had he lost his partner, but his wife also left him, and his youngest daughter hated his guts. To add insult to injury, the person responsible for his partner's death was now in custody, taking responsibility for every homicide in the city and calling himself the Phantom while the real killer roamed free. He knew that Lil' Man couldn't possibly be responsible for all those bodies. There was somebody he was hiding. But who?

As the bartender poured him another double shot, the police commissioner walked in and took a seat beside him.

Commissioner Allen was a large, white man, with a giant head full of gray hair, beady, blue eyes, and a nose like a cow. He wore a gray and black plaid suit with a white shirt and black tie. He signaled for a bartender and looked over at his detective.

"Why do you look so down, Whitehead? You just captured the man responsible for the death of your partner, along with seventeen men, women, and children. You should be celebrating."

"Commissioner, we all know that Mendez couldn't possibly be

responsible for even half those murders. Some of the fingerprints found at the scene of some of those crimes don't even match his," Whitehead stated.

"I know, but if it makes the mayor of this city look good—along with me and the police force; that includes you—then I don't give a shit who takes the blame. And you shouldn't either."

"Yeah, well, sorry I'm not jumping for joy. I've got a lot of things on my mind."

The commissioner looked over at Whitehead and immediately realized something. He had seen this situation before. Whitehead resembled himself at one time. "What can I get you, sir?" the bartender asked.

"I'll have a shot of Brandy. In fact, make it a double. And get my friend here whatever he's drinking."

"Hennessy," Whitehead replied.

"Coming right up," the woman said before walking off.

The Commissioner looked back at his detective and said, "It's the wife, huh?"

"We're getting a divorce," Whitehead blurted.

The commissioner exhaled. "Women… They just don't understand the stress of this job. If it's worth anything, I have something that might cheer you up," he said, going into his pocket, pulling out an envelope, and then handing it to him.

"What's this?" Whitehead asked as the bartender returned with their alcohol.

"It's a promotion," the commissioner said, paying the tab. "A few days ago, a guy named Stanley Robinson was appointed head of an anti-drug committee. Turns out that after the case with Rabeeto Mendez, the FBI checked your file when you were on our task force and had it sent to the DEA. They want you to be a part of this special program they have. It's a task force that they're pulling together in Miami. If all goes well, this could be big."

"That sounds good, but my life is here in Philadelphia," the detective said.

"Look. You won't have to pay for anything. You can stay in a five-star hotel if you want. And did I mention you'll be getting paid triple what you're getting now? I tell you what. Think it over because, believe me, there's eight hundred men out there that wish they were in your shoes right about now. And to be honest, I'm one of them."

"**D**amn, baby, you been chillin' out here with ya boy all morning," Tommy Gun stated. "You must want something."

"No, I just want you, boy, so don't even go there," Beauty replied, wrapping her arms around his neck to hug him.

Most of the guys at the dice game had cleared out except for a few of his henchmen. Tommy Gun loved his hood and refused to abandon it, no matter how paid he was. His reputation was so heavy in ATL that he felt he didn't need an army of bodyguards. His homeboys were tough enough. If Shug could do it, so could he.

"Boo, I'm about to get something from the store. Do you want anything?" she asked.

"Nah, I'm cool. Go 'head and hurry up with that pretty ass of yours," he replied, tapping her butt. "Oh, and before you go, I never got to tell you how proud I am of you for graduating. Your parents would have been proud as well."

Beauty beamed before turning to leave. He watched her sway her hips all the way across the street. Tommy then pulled out his cell phone to call Clyde.

"What's up, cuz?" Clyde answered.

"Aye, shawty, you still comin' down?" Tommy asked. "I'm throwing a big party at 112."

"Nah, I can't make it. I have a few things I need to take care of, but Diamond is on her way down there. This could be good for her," Clyde said.

"How long ago did she leave?"

"Her jet should have landed at Fulton County Airport by now. I'm sure she's in a limo on her way to you as we speak if she's not at Lenox Mall already."

Tommy nodded just as a black car with tinted windows pulled up on the block. He was standing with his back to the car. "Aight, I'll let you know when she gets here."

"Don't bother. I'm sure she'll be there soon," Clyde said before hanging up.

Montega grabbed the two Taurus 9mms out of the stash spot then opened the door. As Beauty came out of the store with a Mystic iced tea and a bag of Cool Ranch Doritos, she placed her wallet bag in her bag but stopped when she saw a man get out of a black car across the street from her boyfriend.

Beauty had recalled seeing the guy at her graduation with Samorah. If she wasn't mistaken, his name was Montega.

What's he doing here? she thought.

As he approached Tommy with his hands behind his back, the two big stiffs were the first to intercept. Montega whipped out the two guns from behind his back and blasted them in the chest. Each took two slugs to get the job done. Their corpses thudded to the ground faster than the shells of the pistols.

Tommy got low and tried to make a run for it. Montega chopped on him with a hunger to see him fall. Before Tommy could get a chance to pull out his weapon, he caught a slug in his back and one in his leg. He then collapsed in the middle of the street. Two more shooters came out of the house with Mossberg shotguns.

Click-clack-boom!

"Oh shit!" Montega hollered, ducking as the second shot went off.

The bullet just missed his head and slammed into Tommy's red 600 Benz. Before the shooter could rack another slug in the chamber, Montega stood, aimed, and put three in his chest. The shooter went down in a blaze of failure.

The second gunman was on point. He let his shotty roar. The bullet struck Montega square in the chest, awaking his solar plex, causing him to swerve out into the street like a toy action figure. When the gunman saw that he hit his mark, he quickly rushed over to tend to his boss.

As soon as he hit the street, Montega was no longer on the ground. Before the henchman knew what hit him, his brains exploded out the side of his head. Montega held his chest in pain. Even though the slug didn't penetrate his vest, it thumped him good and damn near knocked the wind out of him. Six inches higher, and he wouldn't have a neck.

Beauty was in shock when she saw Montega rise from the ground. She dropped the bottle she had in her hand, and it shattered in front of her feet. The gamblers on the steps all took off as Montega approached Tommy in the street. He watched as Tommy crawled on his belly toward the middle of the intersection. Montega walked up to him, aimed the gun, and put a bullet in the back of his head without hesitation.

He turned him over, snatched the chain off his neck, then headed back to the car. Beauty quickly ran to her man's side as the black car sped off. A hail of bullets came from henchmen who got to the scene too late. They heard bullets hit the car's outer shell but got no effect. All they saw was the red taillights shrinking in the distance.

"No, Tommy, nooo!" Beauty cried, but there was no saving him. Tommy was already gone.

By the time Diamond's driver pulled up to Tommy's block, there were police cars everywhere, along with the homicide unit talking to Beauty. The news vans were posted at the corner of the block, and the whole neighborhood was full of spectators. Diamond spotted one of Tommy's lieutenants standing on the corner. She lowered the window of the rented 600 Benz.

"What happened?"

"Some guy hopped out of a black '96 Impala SS and started spraying. He killed Tommy. Blew his brains out all over the street. I just got here, but his shorty seen the whole thing. I'm waiting for the cops to skate so I can find out who the killer was. I doubt if she'll tell them anything. She's got a little street smart in her."

Diamond arched her eyebrows in shock. She knew Tommy had been waiting for her. He was almost like a brother to her, and now he was gone. She rolled the window back up and had her driver take her to her hideaway so she could vent. Her day was not going the way she planned.

Chapter Thirty-Nine

Ambition Of A Killer

"Who sent you?"

— DIAMOND WHITE

ONE WEEK LATER...

Montega felt like a king as he lounged in the backseat of the silver Rolls Royce Phantom on his way to the beauty salon in search of Samorah. Carlos had checked him into a five-star hotel called the Intercontinental, which provided its own transportation service. Since Montega didn't know too much about Atlanta, he decided to park the Impala and see how it felt to travel like royalty.

He had plans on hitting the strip club that night, but first, he wanted to kick it with the woman he had become so fond of—Samorah. She had been giving him the cold shoulder ever since she found out he did business with her brother. Montega may have been a rolling stone, but that still didn't negate the fact that he had feelings for her. Maybe it was just the good sex, or maybe he dug her personality. Whatever it was, it had drawn him in, which always happened when females got too close.

Montega went into his pocket and pulled out a jar of Sour Diesel.

He screwed off the top and caught the strong stench of its contents. Instantly, he started coughing.

"Ah shit!" He grunted as he clutched the right side of his chest where the twelve-gauge slug had slammed into his bulletproof vest.

He then lifted his shirt to see the red bruise and clenched his teeth at the thought of the man who shot him. "Muthafucka!" he growled out to no one in particular.

The Rolls Royce pulled up to the beauty salon, and Montega got out, dressed in Gucci. He was hiding his brown eyes behind a pair of Chrome Hearts shades. His watch said one thing; time is money. He strolled into the salon where all the stylists were busy. This was the place where most of the well-known sistas came to get their hair tossed. The endless waiting line of clients inspired Montega to one day open a salon of his own. His presence, however, was unescapable. Eyes began to aim in his direction and the whispers like, *"Who is that?"* began.

His smile was infectious. He attracted most of the women around him.

Samorah was seated in a salon chair with an apron on. She noticed him the moment he stepped inside. He approached her calmly. She cursed under her breath because usually she had a chance to escape, but not now.

"What are you doing here?" she asked dryly.

"I'm here to see you, of course," Montega replied while removing his shades.

"Oh, really. What? My brother doesn't have anything else for you to do? Now you decide to come bother me."

"Behave, shorty. Only bosses give orders. I'm no soldier, and I don't listen to nobody but the man in the mirror. Money, however, is a different story. Sorry I wasn't born fortunate enough to have a large condo as a hideaway or a 2005 Lex or a platinum card with endless credit. I come from the bottom of the barrel. Just another crab trying to make it out, or more like a mercenary or an opportunist. Nonetheless, none of it has anything to do with me being here."

The woman doing Samorah's hair smiled as she got a front-row seat to view the little love affair that was going on.

Not even Samorah could stay angry with the handsome man standing before her, which was why she tried so hard not to box herself in like this. She knew, sooner or later, he would compel her into his good graces again. He was just too charming. Crossing her legs, she asked, "Mr. Opportunist, like I said before, what are you doin' here?"

"I'm taking you out. What you think I'm doing here?"

"And what makes you think I want to go anywhere with you?"

"'Cause you miss me like I miss you."

"I don't miss you," Samorah said, wickedly rolling her eyes away from him.

"You're not a good liar, baby girl. I advise you to quit acting too. I like you better when you say things more realistic," Montega replied.

"Oh yeah?" Samorah said, trying her hardest not to blush. "Well, I have to go to the car wash first."

"We can do that too. I'ma just tell my driver to pull off," Montega said before turning back.

"Who is he? He's cute," the stylist whispered.

"His name is Montega, and he's from Philadelphia," Samorah said, blushing.

"What is he? A rapper or something?"

"No," Samorah replied while thinking, *he's a killer.*

After getting her hair and nails done, Samorah took Montega to the car wash on Piedmont. It was a popular hand-wash joint called Cactus. He was so astounded to see so many expensive cars waiting to get washed. It almost reminded him of a club. When they got out of the car, he went to pay for the wash. He then ran into a few strippers who handed him a flyer of the club they would be dancing at that night.

Montega pocketed the flyer then headed back to where he saw Samorah talking with a guy who looked to be in his late thirties or early forties. Seeing this didn't make him the jealous type at all, so he went to grab some snacks. When he came back, the car was sparkling clean, and Samorah was waiting for him. "What took you so long?" she inquired.

"I went to grab a Snickers? Besides, I saw you havin' a conversation with bol. I ain't want to interrupt or nothin'."

"Oh, that was some guy name Clark Bey. He's from Baltimore. He wants to do some business with my brother."

"Oh yeah? He look like he already doin' business," Montega replied, checking out the cherry-red Maserati.

Samorah shook her head and smiled, ignoring his comment. "So what did you have in mind, Mr. Opportunist?"

"There's this nice bowling alley that Rodney said is aight. It's called Ten Pin. You tryna go?"

"Well, I don't see why not," Samorah answered.

When they got to the bowling alley, Montega paid eighty dollars for the first game and got a private lane away from the others, which had an odd-looking bookshelf inside. A DJ played one of Lil' Wayne's latest hits while the waitress brought them drinks.

Samorah watched as Montega rolled back to back strikes. "You seem to be good at this," she said, sipping on Don Julio and ginger ale.

"Me and my homie Razor used to go to this bowling alley in Philly called Lucky Strikes every Saturday." Montega reminisced about the fun times he had with his best friend. "I miss my homie, man."

"I wish I could bowl like you." Samorah pouted.

"C'mon. I'll teach you," he said as he took her drink out of her hand and helped her to her feet.

"Wow, an expert in bowling. I'm impressed."

"Don't patronize me, shorty," Montega said as he wrapped one arm around her waist from behind. He enjoyed the feel of her soft butt pressed against his print and the fruity smell of her hair mixed with the scent of her perfume. There was nothing like the smell of a woman to make a man feel like a man. "Now grab the pink ball. It's lighter."

Samorah reluctantly complied. Montega placed his hand on her wrist and went through the motion with her as if they were one. He took a step forward with her, pulled her arm back, and moved it forward.

Once Samorah let the ball go, it went straight to the side and into the gutter. "Well, Mr. Opportunist, it seems that you're not such a professional after all, now does it?"

"You just some shit. I hope that doesn't rub off on me," Montega replied, finally getting her to laugh.

"Am I that bad?" Samorah asked.

"You bad, aight, but having skills in bowling ain't got nothin' to do with it." Montega brushed a strand of her golden hair to the side as he stroked her cheek with his thumb.

Just then, the bookshelf mysteriously opened, exposing a secret room. A couple emerged. They closed it and giggled as they walked off. "Oh yeahhhh? That's how they do it here?" Montega said. "I wonder what's back there."

"Let's go find out," Samorah suggested with a devilish smirk.

Montega moved the bookshelf to the side and closed it behind them. Samorah faced him and pushed him up against the wall. She then unbuckled his jeans and squatted down.

"What you doing, shorty?" he asked.

"I'm taking a lunch break," she replied, reaching in his boxers.

Montega watched as she pulled his shaft out and made it disappear in her mouth. He hissed breathlessly while sliding his fingers through her hair. The warm feeling got him fully aroused in seconds. He hadn't touched another woman since he met Samorah. She seemed to please him in every way possible. He never thought he would ever find a woman to make him think only of her.

With one hand behind her head, Montega slowly pumped in and out of her mouth until she cleared her tonsils and let him go deeper. Pulling back, she watched as a string of saliva connected from the head of his member to the bottom of her lip. She looked at it then sucked on the head like a popsicle. It was all too thrilling for her victim, and before she knew it, he exploded in her mouth with a thick, warm ooze that she continued to devour until the very end.

When Montega snuck out of the secret room, he felt weak. He was exhausted and sweating constantly. “So what do you want to do now?” she asked as she followed him.

“I’m hungry,” was Montega’s response as he flopped down in a chair. Samorah placed her hand on her hip and thought, *just like a nigga.* She looked at Montega and asked, “Have you ever had a fried lobster?”

That night after coming from the Fish Market, Montega dropped Samorah off at her brother’s crib then headed for the strip club on Marietta Boulevard called D.O.A.

In Atlanta, most of the strippers danced at different clubs every night. Tonight was D.O.A., and the club was doing numbers. Montega sat in a booth by himself with a bottle of Don P, watching how the strippers in the ‘A’ got down. As he sipped on champagne, he noticed a crowd of guys at the booth opposite of him. They seemed to be enjoying themselves. Their smiles were golden from the caps they had on their teeth. They looked to be from B-More. That’s when he spotted the guy from the car wash—Clark Bey. He was the center of attention. Montega watched as they threw money around as if it were on fire. He didn’t realize it, but he had a smile on his face. He knew that one day, he could be the bigshot in the booth if he played his hand right. One day, he could be larger than him. That was if Shug didn’t kill him first.

In an upscale neighborhood thirty minutes north of Atlanta called Alpharetta, Diamond ran on the treadmill inside the exercise room of a swank mansion while Bain flicked through the TV channels. When the news came on about Tommy Gun's murder, Diamond huffed over the humming of the treadmill's motor.

"Do you mind turnin' to something else, Bain?" she complained.

She was still coping with the fact that Tommy was dead. Everything had happened so fast that it was hard to investigate. She had no idea why he was killed, but she was determined to find out who was responsible. She would start off by rounding up all of Tommy's men. Once she collected some facts, she would have them all executed for failing to protect him.

As she soaked her spandex tights and sports bra with sweat, Diamond picked up the pace.

Outside, in the dark and quiet neighborhood, two black minivans pulled up to the front. The sliding doors opened, and several men and women wearing all black got out. They were armed with high-tech machine guns. Besides the silver collars around their necks, they all wore ski mask with eyes that had seen death on plenty of occasions.

"Remember what the Colombian said. She's worth more alive. So be light on the trigger," one of the masked women instructed her team before chucking a burning cigarette butt.

The assailants were experts at picking locks and scrambling alarm systems. Their specialty was kidnapping and contract killings. The first thing they did was take out the security, who were surrounding the perimeter, using a sniper from the roof top of another home across the street. The rest of the group moved in for the kill.

After Diamond finished her run, she grabbed a towel and headed for the exit. "I'm gonna run some bath water," she said before walking out of the room.

On her way down the dimly lit hall to the bathroom, she stopped for a second and frowned. Thinking she was tripping, she continued down the hall. When she walked into the bathroom, she started the shower and got ready to remove her clothes. The sound of running water muffled other noises as two assassins quietly crept up the steps and toward the bathroom.

Slowly, as their heels pressed onto the marble floor, one got on his hand mic and whispered, "She's upstairs. I think she's in the bathroom." The second, who was a female, followed behind.

When they crept down the hallway, they stayed close to the wall. The first stepped out the bathroom door and signaled for his partner to go in. His partner tightly clutched his Heckler & Koch MP5 SD6 and slowly walked inside; the other one followed while armed with the same weapon. It was a silencer submachine gun with thirty standard 9mm parabellums. The suppressed barrel was accessorized with thirty holes for the gas to escape, reducing muzzle velocity to a subsonic speed. The victim wouldn't even know what hit her. Neither would the neighbors.

When they were both inside the bathroom, Diamond, who had both her hands and feet planted against the small, confined, four-cornered wall above the door, jumped down onto the last assassin's back. She reached for his Bowie knife in his breast pocket, shoved the blade against the skin of his neck, and quickly slit his throat. The sound of gurgling came afterward.

Diamond knew she wasn't hallucinating when she smelled the scent of cigarettes that fumed from his clothes. As blood shot out to the white floors, Diamond moved in on her next victim. The masked woman quickly spun around with her gun leveled. Diamond swatted the barrel left but slipped under her arm with her hand clutched on the gun. She grabbed the assailant's left hand as well and twisted up her arms before kneeing her in the gut and jamming the knife into her rib cage. The woman let out a roaring scream as she bent over. Diamond never released her left hand. She twisted her wrist then flipped her onto her back and plunged the knife through her chest and into her heart. "Sleep tight, bitch," she whispered.

When her assailant's body lay still, she turned around and was staring down the barrel of an assault rifle. "Don't move," the masked man warned her.

Diamond slowly dropped the knife and put her hands up. She had no more tricks up her sleeves. The man took a step forward into the bathroom. Out of the darkness of the hallway, Bain came from behind and bashed him in the back of his neck. The assailant stumbled forward, dropping the weapon right before Bain wrapped around him like a python with a chokehold. The assassin was no match for Bain's massive arms.

Within two minutes, he too was a corpse. Bain dropped his body and picked up the Cobra M-11, checking the thirty-two-round clip to make sure it was fully loaded. He then turned for the door, peeked out of the bathroom, and then gave Diamond the nod to follow him. Suddenly, all the lights went out in the mansion. Diamond picked up the MP-5 and followed her bodyguard.

Both crouched low along the dark hallway. They hugged the walls tightly and headed for the steps. Diamond thought of Samuel down in the guestroom. If they found her, then most likely he was already dead. As soon as Bain saw the red laser beams aimed at them, he fired. The rifle blasts flared up orange and yellow in the darkness. Out of nowhere, more of Diamond's henchmen appeared like trained soldiers with assault rifles.

Diamond stood on the wing and fired at will into the darkness. Before she could react, one of the assassins grabbed her from behind. She slammed the back of her head into his nose and broke free of his grip. He stumbled back. Diamond twisted her body and elbowed him in the nose again before plowing the rifle butt into his scrotum. The man folded up like a hundred-dollar bill.

As Bain gunned down the last of the intruders downstairs, Diamond put her assailant in a headlock, threatening to break his neck if he didn't talk. The rest of the henchmen began to gather around, including Bain. It was then she saw the priest balled up in a corner, covering his head from any stray bullets. The only reason he hadn't been spotted was because of the black dress suit he wore. When he saw that she had regained her control of the fort, he slowly rose to his feet. Embarrassed, he fixed his suit jacket and approached with his eyes on Diamond's captive.

"Who sent you?" Diamond demanded while tightening the hold she had on him. The man gasped in pain.

"Some… some Columbian guy," he moaned as he struggled for breath. "He said… he said if we kidnapped you, there… there would be a million-dollar reward."

"And if you kill me?" Diamond shouted, twisting his neck a little more.

"We… ah… we would only get half."

Diamond then released him. He toppled face-first to the floor.

"Okay, here's how this is going to go," Diamond said, aiming the gun at him. "What's this guy's name? Tell me, you live. Don't tell me, you die. It's that simple."

"Okay, okay," the assassin said, putting his hands up. "His name is Carlos."

When Diamond heard that, she frowned.

What beef does Carlos have with me? She thought. "I'm only letting you walk because I want you to deliver a message to Carlos. You tell him Diamond White lives. And if he wants to kill me, he better send the fucking Navy Seals next time. Now get out."

The man quickly fixed his collar and made his way to freedom as Bain looked at his boss like she was crazy. "What are you doing?" Samuel asked. "You're just going to let him leave?"

She shrugged and said, "What? Am I not compassionate?"

"Forgive me if I may speak harshly, Madam White, but these men." He pointed at the fleeing assailant. "Him. They are the Blood Hornets. The same Blood Hornets that tortured me in that dungeon."

"Relax, Priest. These men are mercenaries. They are not sworn to one man."

"And who told you this? Because I was told that they are all loyal to the one who put their collars on."

"Collars?" Diamond repeated, looking down at the dead assailants lying on her floor. They all wore collars around their necks. She had seen these exact collars before when Clyde hired a group of men to abduct her a couple years back. *Was Clyde involved in this too? If so, why would he want to abduct her again?*

"Pack your things after you guys clean up this mess," Diamond said before walking away. "We're going back to Cali."

Chapter Forty

Sacrifice

"Would you accept my offer?"

— SAMORAH MORIN

That night, after a session of lovemaking in the hot tub, Montega and Samorah dried off and lay comfortably on the bed, looking up at the ceiling. Samorah couldn't believe the two thunderous orgasms she had fifteen minutes apart. It was something that she would really miss when she left for Miami. However, the short time they did spend together would never be forgotten.

"Kenny, why haven't you ever spoken about your parents? You told me about your brother, sister, and Rodney, but never your mother or father," she said as she lay on her side, propping up her head with her hand.

Montega continued to lie on his back and stare at the ceiling. He never really liked to talk about his parents, but because Samorah was basically in the same boat as he was, he felt like they shared a bond.

Taking a deep breath, he said, "They're both dead. My father committed suicide when I was only a few years old."

"Oh my God, that's terrible," Samorah gasped out.

"Yeah, I know. But then, a few years ago, my mother got killed in a crossfire. On top of that, my godmother, Stacy, told me I have another brother I've never seen in my life. He's floating around somewhere. I feel like every day I wake up is the day that draws me closer to meeting him," Montega said, deep in thought.

"I guess all that makes you feel alone, huh?" Samorah asked.

"How can I be alone when I got you?" he asked, kissing her on her forehead. "Truthfully, if my father was alive, I would probably have more confidence, more discipline. A mother can't keep you in line the way your father can, you know? You need a man to teach you about manhood. Me, I found manhood on my own."

Samorah turned over on her back. As much as she wanted a relationship with this man, she knew that his type wouldn't last, especially dealing with people like her brother. She thought, *if this guy were just a small-time hustler, maybe I could turn his life around.*

Growing up under the same roof with Carlos, she learned more about the drug business than any girl her age. The main thing that stuck with her was the saying, 'Get rich, or die trying.' Even with odds like that, there was no guarantee. Few people were able to dodge the chains of bondage or the barrel of a gun. She just couldn't sit around and wait to see the outcome with him.

"Kenny, you know that I leave tomorrow, right?" she asked.

"Yeah, I know," Montega replied. "You're going back to Florida."

"That's right… I just want you to know the time we shared together was fantastic. You showed me more than what I deserved for backstabbing Tasha. I'm not gonna lie; at first, I thought you were just going to be a one-time thing, then I would get over you. You fooled me. You even compelled me to fall in love with you…" she admitted, then paused.

Montega turned to look at her. "Why do I sense a *but* at the end of that sentence?"

Samorah took a deep breath. "If I asked you to leave everything and come live with me in Miami with no worries about money, clothing, or transportation, would you accept my offer?"

Montega looked over at the beautiful woman beside him and sighed with disappointment. "Look, Samorah. As tempting as that offer is, I can't accept it. If I do that, then I would be abandoning all I stand for. My goals in life would never be accomplished. My dreams and hopes would never be fulfilled, and the people that are depending on me will lose faith in me. I would be lying to myself if I told you yes."

Samorah knew this would happen. She cursed herself for making him choose between her and the life of a drug dealer. Her eyes started to tear. She wanted to cry but just wouldn't allow herself to be embarrassed any more than she already was. "So you're sayin' you don't want to be rich?"

"No, I'm saying I don't want to be rich in that way. I want to be proud of myself at the end of the day because I earned my success, not because it was given to me. That's cheating. It's just like school in a way. When you smarten up, the money you earn ends up being like a report card. I've been getting F's all my life. It's time to start earning some A's for once."

"And if you don't earn it? If somebody just so happens to kill you along the way?" Samorah said.

"Then I'll just die trying. Look. I fucks with you heavy, shorty. I'll even admit I have strong feelings for you, but I also have dignity and pride, and most importantly, a destiny. And that destiny is in Philly, not in Miami," he replied as he softly raked his fingers through her silky hair.

As much as Samorah disliked his decision, she respected it and didn't speak about it anymore.

The next morning, Montega drove Samorah to the airport. Carrying her two suitcases, he followed her through the crowded terminal. It was a sad day for them both. Neither knew the next time they would ever see each other again. Samorah made it even harder for him in their last moments together. Watching her ass bounce in the blue Donna Karen sundress made it even more tempting to just say 'fuck it' and roll out to Miami with her and never look back, but he wasn't a quitter, nor did he care for a handout. He was used to suffering before he could earn anything, and suffering built character.

As the two made it to the check-in counter, Samorah turned back to look at him. He could see the sadness she was trying to hide behind her sunglasses as he leaned forward to give her a kiss. At first, it was just a peck, then it turned into a burst of passion that felt like an eternity. Their tongues danced one last time before the announcement was made.

"Attention, passengers. Southwest Flight 157 to Miami will be boarding in five minutes." On hearing that, the two slowly released each other, panting for air.

"I guess nothing lasts forever, huh?" she said, bringing a smile to his face.

Montega reached at and brushed a strand of hair from her face and touched her cheek. "Only our names and the destiny we fulfill," he replied, stroking her cheek and pinching her chin.

She fixed his shirt collar for him and said, "If you somehow reach it to the top of that barrel and you find yourself alone up there, don't look down. I'll be up there with you somewhere, so don't be a stranger. Look me up."

Montega watched as a tear trickled down her cheek. She quickly wiped it before turning and walking away. Just like that, she was gone. Montega sighed. He could have avoided the drama altogether by just getting on that flight with her and living happily ever after, but he knew he had important things to do. He then headed for the escalator. The thought made his chest harden.

When he got to the ground floor, he noticed a huge, muscular man in a gray, tailored suit, leading at least five men in his direction. One looked to be a black priest. The whole ordeal looked weird. A priest, five dangerous-looking men, and a giant. Montega thought the guy was a wrestler from his size and the way people gawked at him and the others. Then he saw the woman they were protecting. He slowed his pace as the guys approached.

He wanted to get a better look at the cocoa butter beauty with long, dark hair that flowed in swirls down her back. She had a fascinating figure smothered in a blue Roberto Cavalli dress with a matching belt wrapped around her waist. Her blue five-inch Christian Louboutin heels displayed perfectly pedicured toes, and judging by her hourglass shape, he knew her ass had to be fabulous. He made eye contact with her for the moment and noticed the long, curled length of her lashes and the caramel color of her eyes.

Damn, she is super bad, he thought.

Ummm, he is so cute, Diamond said to herself as she strutted by the handsome, almond-brown-skinned brother, who stood out in a green and white striped Lacoste shirt. Both looked back at the other as they passed, but neither spoke.

After coming from the airport, Montega prepared himself for the long ride back to Philadelphia. Before his departure, he did a little shopping at Phipps Plaza across the street from the Lenox Mall. He bought a few outfits and some footwear and then called it a day. He had seen enough. Atlanta was a beautiful place with a lot of space and opportunity, but like Dorothy said in 'The Wiz', *There is no place like home.*

It was time he got back and began planning his takeover, which meant he would have to face Shug. After spending close to $10,000 of Kev's money on clothes, he headed for his final stop in the city to see Carlos. Montega wasn't the only one leaving ATL. Carlos was also preparing to head back to his hometown in Florida. Thanks to his new lieutenant, his mission was complete.

Castor now had control of Georgia again. Montega shook Carlos's hand. "Thanks for everything," he said.

"No. Thank you. You make sure you call me as soon as you enter Pennsylvania. I will send the shipment through FedEx and UPS. Just make sure you find that address I gave you. And remember what I said. Always be ready because there will be a time when I call on you again; only it will be for someone more powerful than myself," Carlos promised.

"I need to ask you something," Montega said seriously. "I'm lookin' for a gun connect. Do you know anyone I can deal with that's close to home? I've got a little problem in Philly that I must face, and he goes by the name of Shug."

That name sent chills through Carlos. Rodney had spoken of Montega getting into trouble with Shug, who was actually another target on Castor's list. Carlos failed to mention this for the simple fact that if Montega was as smart as he thought, then all would go well. If not, then maybe he wasn't as good as he made himself out to be.

"Can you get access to an eighteen-wheeler when you get back?"

"I should be able to," Montega replied. "I know a smoker who owns a semi. Maybe he'll let me rent it out."

"Okay, then when you get back to Philly, there's an import/export dock by Delaware Avenue. Are you familiar with that dock?"

Montega nodded his head as Carlos dug into his pocket for his keys.

"Find the crate with the number 358 on it. I keep one available in every major city. It will have everything you desire and more."

He searched his key ring and pulled off a master key then handed it to Montega.

"This particular crate once belonged to a friend of mine. He used to run the Gulf cartel in Mexico, so some of the things you'll find in there are probably worth more than the life you plan to take. However, it should keep you busy for a while. We'll be in touch," Carlos said, letting him go on his way.

Montega got back into his Impala and headed for I-95 North. He had already learned to become a man. Now it was time to show his strength. It was time to go back to Philly to face the rest of the wolves.

Chapter Forty-One

Afterlife

"Welcome back from the dead..."

— SKI-MASK

The clicks and clacks of Diamond's tan, patent-leather Gucci shoes echoed throughout the gallery of the White family's L.A. mansion as she headed for Clyde's office. Pushing open the French doors, she walked in, dressed in a white, cotton, sleeveless, collared blouse with a sheer scarf tied in a bow and a red umbrella skirt that stopped just above her calves.

Bain followed not too far behind with Samuel. Clyde was on his stomach with just a towel covering his rear, with a topless Brazilian chick, who wore nothing but a G-string, sitting on his back, massaging him. She paused the moment Diamond entered. The priest turned his head from sight as Clyde looked up.

Clyde could practically smell her perfume and said, "Don't you ever knock? And why the fuck is that priest still alive? For God's sake, Diamond. I told you to get rid of him."

"Why? Because your Blood Hornets have no more use for him?" she asked. "Or is it you who has no more use? Is that why you sent them to kill me in Atlanta?"

"What the hell are you talking about? I did no such thing. Don't go putting words in my mouth, Diamond."

"Then explain why a fucking mob of assassins that you had abduct me before raid my hideout and try to abduct me again?"

"Do you hear yourself? I had you abducted before because I didn't know the Black Kiss of Death was my own fucking sister. Why the hell would I want to abduct you now? Can you answer that for me since you're so fucking smart? For your info, the Blood Hornets are mercenaries. Anyone could have hired them."

Diamond folded her arms but had nothing to say. Clyde shook his head before resting his face back down. He was disappointed she came back from her vacation so soon. Diamond watched as the woman returned to her work.

"Funny. If I didn't know any better, I would think you didn't even care about what happened to Tommy yesterday," she said, folding her arms over her chest.

"Diamond, Tommy was my best friend. Of course, I feel some way about his death, but make no mistake about it, just because I don't show my emotion doesn't mean anything. I'm not you," he shot back as the girl continued.

"Ouch, that hurts," she said sarcastically.

"Look. You see I'm busy here? Why don't you and your dickless preacher or priest go find a man or something? How long has it been, huh?" he asked with a smirk.

Diamond caught on to his sarcasm and tensed up.

"That's none of your business."

"Well, why don't you tend to yours and let me finish mines? I'm sure you're tired of buying batteries every other week."

"Fuck you!" she spat.

Clyde chuckled at his own joke.

Diamond rolled her eyes, moved her hands down to her waist, and shifted her weight to one side.

"You picked a fine time to joke around. This atrocity is far from funny. Besides Tommy's death, you want to know what those Blood Hornets said to me last night? Your former Great White member—Carlos—was the one who sent them to abduct me. God knows what the hell he had in store had he succeeded."

"And why would Carlos do something like that?" Clyde asked in disbelief.

"How the hell am I supposed to know? I never did anything to him. In fact, I want to know how he even knew where I was. What we need to do is find out what's going on, just like we need to find out who killed Tommy," Diamond snapped.

"Alright, alright," Clyde said, sitting up on his elbows. "Did you get a name or anything about the man who killed Tommy?"

"From what his girlfriend said, the guy's name is Montega, and he drives a black SS Impala. He was dealing with a girl that went to college with her. Her name's Samorah. Now she's gone, and God knows where he is." Diamond sat on the edge of the desk, rubbing her hands down the wool fabric of her skirt.

"Was the car a new model?" Clyde asked while enjoying his massage.

"No, it's a '95 or '96."

"And he just jumped outta the car and started shooting without sayin' anything?"

"Damn right he did. There were shells all over the place. I saw at least three body bags. This guy's got heart, I'll give him that. You think it was a hit from Castor?" she asked.

"It's not like him to be so sloppy with a hit. Then again..." He looked at his sister.

Diamond looked away from him. "Please don't bring that shit up," she said, referring to the incident with her father at the after-hour. She couldn't bear to hear the tragedy a second time. It made her think of the funeral, which turned out to be a nightmare.

"This shit doesn't look good. Did anybody get the license plate number of the vehicle?"

"No, but they were Pennsylvania plates. Maybe this Montega is from Philadelphia. That would be something, right? I'm supposed to take a little trip down there next year once it gets warm. You know how I hate the cold weather. I've always wanted to visit the city where my father was killed," she said, getting up and walking out.

"For what?" Clyde asked.

"I don't know," Diamond replied. "It's just something about the City of Brotherly Love that makes me feel like there's a connection there with my father."

"The City of Brotherly Love. Yeah, right. Their murder rate is fifth in the country. Where's the love in that?" Clyde said.

Diamond stopped at the door and slowly spun around. Her long, dark hair followed and whipped over her shoulder. "You act as if you and Shug aren't playing a major part in that murder rate, so don't be so contradictive."

"That may be true, lil' sis, and until we find out who put Tommy down, the murder rate won't stop rising. I'll have Shug make sure of that. Oh, and before you go, I want to ask, why Philly? Pennsylvania's a big state. Why can't the killer be from Pittsburgh or Harrisburg or any other city?"

Diamond rolled her eyes and shook her head as if the answer was so obvious. "You said it yourself, Clyde—the murder rate. The city practically breeds killers."

When Montega arrived in Philly, he called Carlos and had him send the shipment through the mail; it would get there in a week and a half. Meanwhile, he found a truck driver who was willing to help him move the cargo crate at the import/export for a small fee.

Once the crate was strapped on the eighteen-wheeler, they headed uptown.

Taliban was on Blakemore Street, hustling up money from fiend-to-fiend. He had put his syrup drinking aside for the moment to get his cash flow going again. He was a born hustler who could out-hustle almost anyone. He knew he had to get his money up because his brother was in danger. Taliban wouldn't just sit around while killers constantly rode through the hood, looking for Montega. As he sat on the steps of the Chinese store, counting money, Breezy and his sister, Kia, pulled up and parked in front of him.

When they got out in their freak 'em girl dresses and four-inch stilettos, he automatically knew they were going out. The two were practically party animals. Anyone who threw a major event in the city knew to expect Kia and her sexy friends.

"What club y'all hittin' up tonight?" he asked dryly.

"Shug's havin' a little something at Onyx," Breezy replied.

"What! Why y'all goin' to bol party, knowin' he tryna kill my brother?" Taliban snapped.

Breezy started to say *Fuck your brother,* but her girlfriend beat her to it.

"We're not going for him," Kia explained. "I couldn't care less whose party it was. We just tryna have a good time; that's all. We've been through a lot this past year. The least we can do is have a few drinks, dag."

"Y'all ain't been through nothing but a carwash," Taliban ridiculed. "Stop fakin'. Shit real out here. It's way more serious issues going on besides the nail salon and where to get a fucking outfit."

Before Kia could cuss him out, a huge eighteen-wheeler pulled up on the block. The sound of the brakes hissed like steam as it came to a complete stop. The truck took up the entire width of the one-way street. Montega hopped out the passenger side and came around to where the three were, surprising them.

"Boy, where the hell have you been hidin'?" Kia questioned. "I've been calling all over for you." She was relieved to see that he wasn't harmed, contrary to hood gossip. Word on the street was Montega had been vaporized by an RPG. Kia, however, knew that couldn't be true if shooters were still driving through the neighborhood, looking for him.

"It's good to see you too, sis. But let's get something straight. Me? Hiding? Never. I just needed to get my head straight and my mind right," he replied, glancing at Breezy lustfully. Her tight party dress had her hips looking wide and curvy. Her breasts were puffy and round, and her legs were glossy and thick. Even her feet looked good in peek-a-boo pumps.

"What's the truck for, bro?" Taliban asked as he gave his brother a hug.

"I got some things I gotta unload at my crib. I need you to take a ride with me. It's up the street. Come on."

"Crib?" Kia repeated. "Where did you get a crib from?"

"Two words: power moves," was all Montega said before heading back around the truck.

"Hold up, bro. I gotta finish knocking off this work. It's poppin' out here," Taliban said, ready to make another sale.

Montega stopped and doubled back. "Man, fuck that shit, bol. I got us. Believe me. In two weeks, you'll never have to do another hand-to-hand transaction again. Now come on, will you?"

When Taliban heard that, he got up and followed his brother to the truck, leaving Kia and Breezy curious about what he meant by that statement.

Awbury Park was a secluded area of dense trees and wooded land. It was only a few blocks away from Summerville. Ardleigh Street split the forest in half. On one side was a tennis court with its own playground and swimming pool sitting by an old middle school that rested up at the very top of the hill. On the other side was dense trees and a trail that lead through the forest.

The truck pulled into a dark maze-like pathway that cut through the woods into a small confined area that surrounded a large, old, Victorian-style home with a beat-up porch. The entire house looked abandoned yet sturdy. A three-car garage leaned against the left side of the single house.

"What the hell we doin' here?" Taliban asked.

"A friend of mine gave me this crib."

Taliban looked out the window again at the old-fashioned, Victorian-style home. "All I see is a old-ass crib."

Montega smiled and got out. Outside the boarded-up house, the white paint had chipped off and cluttered the porch. The front door had a lock around the knob.

Montega unlocked the door and opened it. They stepped inside. Taliban damn near got woozy when he saw the well-furnished interior filled with wall-to-wall, plush, black carpeting. The house smelled brand new. The sofa and table were all new and imported, as well as the kitchen appliances.

If Taliban thought that was amazing, he almost lost it when he saw what he was helping his brother unload off the truck. The crate was filled with artillery and ammunition, brand-new handguns, and military assault rifles. What made these weapons so unique was that half of the guns were custom-made; some were even gold-plated. There were also full-body armor suits with face masks and other things Montega could have fun with. By the time the two finished unloading the truck, it was close to 11:30 p.m.

Montega paid the truck driver for looking out, then he and his brother got in the Impala and headed for the Badlands. They had some unfinished business to take care of, and they needed someone crazy enough to ride with them.

MONTEGA

The Mendez house in the Badlands was a lot quieter since Lil' Man went to jail. All that could be heard now was deafening silence. Ski-Mask snorted a long line of dope he had cut up on the glass table. Once the drug reached his bloodstream, he stood with his head held back, feeling good.

"Ahhh yeah," he whispered while wiping his nose with the back of his hand.

He glanced at himself in the mirror, and then quickly did a double-take as if he saw a guy he was beefing with.

"Fuck you lookin' at, Dickey?" he asked, pointing at his reflection.

"Me?" he then replied, rocking back and forth, stabbing himself in the chest with his index finger. "You talkin' to Ski-Mask? Oh yeah? Ski-Mask got you, Dickey. You think Ski-Mask sweet? You think Ski-Mask a bitch?"

Ski-Mask reached in his waistband and pulled out his Glock 17 and aimed it at his reflection. Seeing a guy in the mirror pulling out a gun caused him to get low and hide behind a desk. "You wanna pull out guns on Ski-Mask? Well, fuck you, Dickey, 'cause Ski-Mask ain't afraid to die. If Ski-Mask gotta go, then so do you, muthafucka!"

He rose from his hiding space, and before he could pull the trigger, the phone rang. Ski-Mask wiped his powdered nose before going to answer it. "Ski-Mask deal with you later," he said before picking up the phone. "Hello?"

"You still fuckin' with that white girl?" a familiar voice asked.

"Shit, is the pope a Catholic? Who the hell is this?"

"Who else would be crazy enough to call ya ass?"

"Montega?" Ski-Mask whispered as if someone else was there.

"In the flesh."

"Damn, Dickey! Welcome back from the dead!" Ski-Mask went to do another line. "They told Ski-Mask you got hit with a grenade launcher. Ski-Mask just knew you was dead."

"Thanks for the lack of emotion. I feel a lot better now. Anyway, what's up with Lil' Man?" Montega asked, ignoring his comment. "How did he make out?"

Ski-Mask snorted a line, held his head back, and said, "He's fine, Dickey. He pleaded out to those murders he committed. Not only that, but he's takin' bodies for a stack a piece up on Death Row. They're askin' for death penalty. He don't give a fuck. Ski-Mask little bro going out like a cold G," Ski-Mask glorified as he enjoyed the effects of his high.

"Damn," Montega said sadly. "What about Faith? How's she takin' it?"

"Man, that bitch done went off somewhere. Ski-Mask think it was army because some green vehicles came and picked her up. What the hell was she thinkin'?"

Montega smiled, remembering their last conversation. *She finally got what she wanted.* "Well, what about you? You still at it?"

"Shit, can cars fly?" Ski-Mask replied with excitement.

Montega frowned. "Nah, bol. I ain't seen no cars fly yet."

"Oh well, you know what Ski-Mask talkin' 'bout," Ski-Mask said, reflecting on the Jetsons.

Ten minutes later, the black Impala pulled up to the house. Montega beeped the horn, and Ski-Mask came out. As soon as he got in, Montega introduced him to his brother.

"Ski-Mask, this is my brother, Taliban. Taliban, meet Lil' Man brother, Ski-Mask."

"Taliban, huh? Ski-Mask like him already," Ski-Mask stated.

"They don't call me that for nothing," Taliban said, going into his green duffle bag and handing him a nickel-plated, fifty-shot Uzi, which was the prettiest gun Ski-Mask had ever seen.

"What are you gonna do tonight, Dickey? Take down another block?" Ski-Mask held up the machine gun to admire its beauty. He pulled the fifty-round magazine out, checked to see if it was loaded, then shoved it back inside and cocked back the slide to put one in the head.

"We definitely gonna take a block down," Montega replied. "That and set off some fireworks. They hit me with an RPG; well, I got some shit for them." He handed his brother a few blocks of C-4, fuses, and the detonator. "I hope you know how to use that, bol."

"It's nothin'. I seen dudes do it in the movies all the time. Don't worry," Taliban stated. "All you gotta do is stick the fuse inside, cut the switch on, and press this button."

Ski-Mask pushed himself forward, wedging himself between the two front-seat chairs to see what Taliban had. His eyes showed too much white.

"That shit gonna have every federal agent slipping out the woodworks to find out who's responsible if you let that off, Dickey."

"I hope it attracts more attention than that," Montega responded as he tossed Ski-Mask a familiar disguise. "Truthfully, I wanna send a message to someone in particular." He chuckled and shook his head. "Wait 'til he finds out I'm back."

Chapter Forty-Two

The Definition Of Trouble

"I know that Kenny is your brother, but I hate him."

— BREEZY

Shug lounged in Club Onyx with a bottle of Rosé in his hand, observing the crowd in boredom. Although it was his birthday and almost half the city came out to celebrate with him, it felt like another night at the strip club. He had already gotten the news about Tommy, and that really ruined his mood. Tommy meant just as much to him as Kev. It was hard to believe that the same guy was responsible, but the evidence was as clear as day. As he looked over to his right, his lieutenants were getting table dances from some hot broads, and to his left, Maniac was practically begging the shorty with a tight, green, see-through dress to leave with him for the night.

"I'm surrounded by dickheads, literally," Shug mumbled.

As Shug cocked the bottle and drank, he noticed Kia and Breezy approaching the bar. Shug almost choked on champagne when he got a glimpse of their asses. For one, he was infatuated with Kia but could never find the time to get at her. And two, he had a thing for Breezy as well and wondered if she was hip to his intentions. He got up out of his seat and swaggered toward them. He refused to let two bad bitches like that get away from him again. Anything was better than sitting around, reminiscing about the past.

When the two women arrived at the bar, Kia noticed something had been bothering her best friend all day. In fact, she saw it the minute her brother returned to the city. "You alright, Bree?" she asked.

"No, I'm not. Kia, I know that Kenny is your brother, but I hate him. I wish he would have just stayed dead or whatever. He took away my boyfriend, Kia. Not only that, but he used me to do it. That shit is cruel. Don't get me wrong; I don't wish death on anyone, but I do wish that he could stop for a second and realize what he's done," Breezy said as her eyes welled up.

Shug then popped up on them, causing Breezy to quickly regain her composure. "What are y'all doin' over here at the bar? Why don't y'all come join me and the homies over at my table?"

"We cool," Kia replied dryly. "We just tryna build."

"Well, before y'all engage in y'all little girl talk, I wanna know if I can take you out to breakfast in the morning? You know, one day with me, and you'll be considered the queen of PA." He was talking to Kia, but his eyes were peering at Breezy.

"I gotta work," Kia lied. She too looked at her best friend, who was now smiling. Kia gave her a look as if to say, *if this bol only knew.*

On Tasker Street, the walking dead swarmed the hustlers from every angle in search of a good high. Spade and all his homies were out, collecting as much money as they could before going to Shug's party. As Spade went to make a sale to a fiend across the street by the Chinese store, he noticed a black car creeping down the block with no headlights on.

"Aye, heads up, y'all," he said, trying to alert the others.

As the streetlight shone on the hood of the car where a man wearing a Phantom mask laid on the windshield, everyone broke out in a panic. The tires screeched, the engine roared, and the gunman fired the machine gun at the fleeing hustlers. Spade looked on in horror before diving for cover behind a parked car as one of his workers got hit in the face. The clattering sound of an Uzi pierced the quiet night. The hustlers on the corner scattered as hot lead came spiraling by them. Taliban stepped on the gas and whipped around the corner then came to a stop. When Ski-Mask got back in the car, he was charged up.

"Did you see them coward, Dickey! They looked like rodents when lights get cut on."

"The correct phrase is 'roaches when the lights come on,' not rodents when the lights get cut on," Montega corrected.

"You know what Ski-Mask mean." Ski-Mask shrugged.

"Where to now?" Taliban asked.

Montega pulled out his pad and gave his brother the address to one of the stash houses he once saw Kev go into. He just hoped it was still operating.

Kia saw that Shug wouldn't take no for an answer, nor would he go away, so she handed Breezy her purse and said, "I have to use the bathroom. Watch my stuff for me."

"Damn, you gonna roll out on me like that, huh?" Shug asked, watching as she walked off. "Guess she ain't tryna get rich no time soon."

"I guess not," Breezy replied before sipping on her cup of champagne.

"What about you?" he asked, causing her to damn near break her neck to look at him. "I know you all about the money. What you say we get up outta here tonight and go do us?"

Breezy's surprised look turned to a frown. "Shug, I used to date Kev. We would still be together if it wasn't for—"

"What? You gonna hold on to Kev's ghost? That's my man and all, but he's dead. You gotta move on. It took me a while, but I did. So what you need? I got a dime for you. Ten bands will get you something nice."

"Shug, I don't know who you think you're talking to, but I'm not one of these strippers in here. I don't—"

"What you want? A car?" he asked with persistence. "What? A 750? A-8? S-500? What?"

Breezy took a deep breath to keep herself from spitting in his face. As if God could hear her prayers, Shug's cell phone vibrated in his pocket. "This better be good," he said as Kia returned.

He placed the phone to his ear and listened.

"Yo, Shug, some dude in a black car with a Phantom mask just did a drive-by on Tasker, man. I think it was the bol, Montega," Spade explained.

"What!" he said, alerting everyone around him.

"Yeah, man. Couple dudes got hit. Now it's cops and ambulances all over the fuckin' place, just like last time. This shit is crazy, and it's fucking up money."

Kia could see the irked expression on Shug's face. For some reason, her brother came to mind. Shug listened to Spade explain as his other line beeped. He saw that it was Chino from the stash house.

"I'ma call you back, Spade," he said before clicking over. "What?"

"Aye, Shug, you won't believe what just jumped off. We got hit by some dude with a Phantom mask in a black SS Impala. I think it was cuz that killed Kev, man!"

"What the fuck is goin' on out there? Y'all let one chump overpower y'all!" Shug snapped.

"It wasn't just one. It was three, and they just came in blastin'. They didn't ask no questions either. I was lucky enough to get out the back door because dudes were droppin' like flies. Them dudes had choppas with ladders like a fire-engine," Chino explained.

Shug clenched his teeth. "Did they take the money?" he asked as his blood pressure soared.

Chino sighed. "Jack said they took half the bread and set the other half on fire."

Shug shook his head with disappointment. *He's taunting me. A fucking nobody wants to beef with me? He wants to make me look like a fool?* "Well, where the hell is Jack right now?" Shug snapped.

"They're puttin' him in the ambulance as we—"

Ba-boom!

Shug heard the sound of an explosion just before the phone got disconnected.

"Hello? Hello?"

As his phone buzzed once more, he flagged Maniac over as he answered. "Who is this?"

"It's Monte, Papi. We got a problem."

Shug took the phone from his ear and pressed the end call button. When Maniac approached, Shug whispered something into his ear right before the two made their way for the exit. Kia looked over at Breezy, who was shaking her head with a serious attitude. Kia suspected what Shug's departure was about.

Who would leave his own birthday party unless it was an emergency? And all emergencies meant trouble.

And, for some reason, in Kia's mind, trouble spelled M-O-N-T-E-G-A.

Chapter Forty-Three

Connecting The Dots

"The bol is a problem…"

— SHUG

"Are you sure about this, cuz?" Clyde asked on the phone.

"Hell yeah, I'm sure," Shug said. "You said it yourself. Cuz hopped out a black SS '96 Impala and rocked Tommy to sleep. The car had Pennsylvania plates. Why was that same wheel seen comin' down one of my strips, firin' nickel-plated 'uwops at my soldiers, then blew up three of my stash houses? It's not a coincidence, Clyde. This Montega cat is the same muthafucka who killed my homie on the tracks. Now he's back, and he's trying to taunt me. He's taunting us all. The bol is a problem."

Clyde looked at his sister, who was sitting by the window with her legs crossed. Her giant bodyguard, Bain, stood near her with the gold-plated mini AK slung over his shoulder. The priest held the Bible up, reciting a scripture to her as if she were listening.

"Shug, you're gonna have to handle this mark on your own. He's pennies compared to what we have on our plate. Right now, we're backed up, tryna purchase a legitimate building for the Underworld in New York."

"That goes without saying, cuz. I've already sent the wolves to sniff cuz out. He cost me a lot of money, but I'll find him, and when I do, he's gonna—"

"Not over the phone, Shug," Clyde said, cutting him off.

"My fault, cuz. My fault. I'll rap with you later," he said before ending the call.

Clyde sighed then began to massage his temple.

"What happened?" Diamond asked, silencing the priest.

"Shug said that Montega was spotted in Philly, just as you predicted. He even believes this is the same guy who killed his homie, Kev," Clyde said as he tried to relax a bit.

"Wow. The rising lone wolf strikes again. This guy really gets around," Diamond said, standing. "Well, what is Shug prepared to do?"

"He'll handle it. If there's one thing he's good at besides making money, it's getting rid of a pest. I've seen Shug and his men put in work. They are good at what they do. This mark—Montega—won't stand a second in the ring with him. Trust me."

Diamond looked her brother in the eye seriously. She wanted to say something but decided to look away and leave it alone. Then the urge came again.

"If you ask me, I don't think this is a pest, and honestly, he deserves more credit than what you gave him. I mean, think about it. How does he kill Shug's best friend then end up in Atlanta and kill Tommy? Seems awfully strange," Diamond said.

"What are you gettin' at?" Clyde asked suspiciously.

"I don't know. I just got a funny feeling about what's happening underneath our noses. First, Tommy gets whacked; then there was an attempt on my life by a former Great White. What's next? We hear that this Montega's wreaking havoc in Underworld territory. Maybe when I fly over to Pennsylvania to meet with Wong Lee next summer, I can help Shug finish this."

"C'mon, Diamond. Don't flatter yourself. First of all, Shug doesn't need any help finding this man. Have you forgotten that all of PA is under his command? All he has to do is find the black car this mark drives, and the rest will be easy. Yeah, he killed one or two major guys, but you know what they say. 'Ain't no fun when the rabbit got the gun.'"

"Now, you, on the other hand, don't know a thing about Philly. It's not like he'll just fall right into your lap out of the clear, blue sky. Shit don't work like that, sweetheart. Besides, there's no way he can take anything that belongs to us. For one, he doesn't have the manpower. And two, you have to have money to buy a strong army. Now, stop worrying yourself about some smell fish and relax," Clyde said, getting up to leave.

"It's funny you said that," Diamond replied. "Because you can have all the money in the world to buy soldiers, but what good are they if they have no heart or brains? It's not the big fish you need to worry about, Clyde. It's the hungry ones. You wanna know why? Because they have everything to gain and nothing to lose."

Chapter Forty-Four

The Plan

"Silent kings for life!"

The hideout in Awbury Park was a two-story structure with five bedrooms and two bathrooms. The dining room and the kitchen were joined, separated by a kitchen bar counter, and the living room was sectioned off with a sunroom that had floor-to-ceiling tinted glass. The area surrounding the house was equipped with cameras and monitors that extended throughout the woods toward the entrance. The walls, carpet, and furniture were all black.

Montega sat on one of the leather sofas, dumbfounded by the hundred bricks of cocaine that were stacked in the middle of the floor. What really had him delusional was the additional twenty bricks of heroin. With him was his brother, Taliban, and his homies, Ski-Mask, J-Rider, Killa, Mook, FatBoy, Lil' Luchiano, Gutter, Tank and the first lady, Juicy. Everyone had the same look of amazement as Montega. "You really outdid yourself this time, my nigga," Tank said, rubbing his hands together. "So… what's the plan?"

"It's like this." Montega carefully looked at the work and took a deep breath. He exhaled, saying, "I don't care how many of these joints y'all take from this circle or what you do with 'em, but you gotta bring back fifteen grand for the coke and ninety off the dope."

"Word?" Killa asked excitedly. "That's it? Just as simple as that?"

"Yeah, that's it," Montega replied. He rubbed his hands over his blue denim Black Label jeans. "Look, y'all. This ain't no game no more," he told them with his eyes on the product. "We ain't no cheap hustlers or no small-time, hand-to-hand bols. That went out the door the moment I set foot back in the city. We deserve success, and this proves it. We earned our keep. This is our business now. These drugs are essential to the growth of the Silent Kings. We are the foundation."

"Now, I wouldn't have called you here if I didn't think y'all could handle this. I would have just done the shit on my own. So if you have a vice that will sidetrack your success—drugs, gamblin', women, or disloyalty—then don't touch this work. The last thing I want to do is put down someone I love, but I will. And to tell you the truth, I hope you'd do the same to me if I ever betray the Silent Kings." He scanned all of the serious faces.

He then got up from the couch and took a seat in the recliner chair, allowing Juicy to sit on his lap. Rubbing her leg, he went on to explain. "Like I said, we a team, and a team sticks together through thick and thin. If we see one of our homies fallin' off, we help them. If they don't wanna be helped, we let 'em drift. It's just that simple. If anyone gets in our way, we run and gun 'em down. We all equal in this room, believe it or not. Now, me, personally, I believe that I'm a born leader. I like to give orders sometimes because I survive by following my heart and my instincts, but I'm also a good soldier. We should all feel the same way because this is how I've survived this long. This is how I've gotten to this point in my life."

"There's no other way to go now but up the ladder. The only way down is if we slip and fall. And if we fall, we get back up and climb again. But let me warn y'all. There will be people out there that will make it their job to see us fall. And if you're too high up, it's a chance that fall might break you. And broken niggas say, *the end*. With that said, create a circle within your own circle and choose the people you deal with wisely. You may not get a second chance at it."

Montega stuck his fist out. "Silent Kings for life," he proclaimed, and everyone else saluted and did the same.

"Silent Kings for life!"

Chapter Forty-Five

What's Beef

"Actions speak louder than words..."

— MONTEGA

AFTER THE FIRST SHIPMENT...

The following year was a nightmare for Shug and his organization. The Silent Kings flooded the streets with 98 percent Columbian white cocaine and 79 percent heroin. Both came wrapped in clear plastic with a red devil logo stamped on it. The deals they gave out caused a fiend frenzy. Dope fiends and crackheads from all over were rushing to cop the devil-stamped bags.

The Silent Kings started uptown, bullying major strips like Chew and Chelten, Forest Avenue, Haines Street and Limekiln Pike, and Brickyard and Happy Hollow. From there, they worked their way through small blocks in North Philly, the Northeast, and West Philly, knocking aside some of Shug's product with cheaper prices. Shug may have had quality work, but it was hard to move with the prices the SK's were giving out.

What made their rise something to talk about was the fact that Montega really didn't have to use much violence. He figured that if Shug sold bricks of coke for thirty-two grand, then he would charge twenty-two. It was an easy come-up. Everything moved faster than he had anticipated. He got his shipment for only ten grand on every brick just as long as he purchased a hundred or more.

He made a $5,000 profit off his own circle, not to mention what he made off out-of-towners, young up-and-coming trap stars, and crack houses. Even Juicy had parts in the circle. Since she learned accounting in high school and took another course in college, Montega appointed her the organization's accountant, secretary, and treasurer. She collected the money from the lieutenants, counted it, and stored it in a big safe sitting in the basement of the Awbury Park hideout, which they called the Vault.

Montega did some serious renovating to the place. He had the whole basement constructed to look like a cave, with a hot water jacuzzi built amongst rocks in the ground. The place had a secret tunnel that led to a carport where the getaway cars were parked. Guns were mounted all over the house for both decoration and protection. It was the only place where he rested his head and could feel safe. He added more security cameras throughout the perimeter as well.

He was now twenty-four years old, making more money than anyone his age, and no one knew who he was. In the next two months, almost half the city was questioning the wealth and the sudden rise of the Silent Kings. When Carlos saw how fast Montega came back for a re-up, he upped the delivery quantity to a thousand bricks of coke a month and increased the heroin to fifty bricks. Not long after, the Silent Kings' product was heavy in the streets, along with an army of hustlers schooled by Killa and J-Rider.

On the legal side of things, Montega started his own construction company, using ex-offenders who just got out of prison and were willing to work. He also started a real estate agency called Heaven on Earth, ran by his sister, along with the Unisex salon, Gi-Gi's, which was owned and operated by Breezy's cousin, Gi-Gi. Although they were a legitimate business, he used them also to wash some of his dirty money.

He kept everyone guessing from the way he presented himself. No one really knew how much money he was actually making, being as though the only car he drove was the SS Impala. It was hard to believe that he was the leader of the rising syndicate—and even harder to believe that he was still breathing.

Once Shug realized what was really going on, all hell broke loose, and a street war was initiated.

The entire dealership seemed to be silent as Shug stood in front of a foreign car with his hands behind his back. The henchmen stood behind him, along with his underboss, Gee, watching the large man in a gray suit make a decision. Even his new girlfriend looked a bit impatient, standing by the registration desk.

Shug was finding a hard time picking from the new black Rolls Royce Phantom and the Maybach 62s. They were both luxurious cars, fit for a street king, yet Shug couldn't seem to choose which one he wanted to be seen in first. For him, shopping for cars was worse than women picking out clothes at the mall. Undecided, he turned to the dealer. A white woman in a business suit approached Shug and said, "I'll take 'em both."

"I'll get the papers right away," she said before walking off.

Shug nodded while standing next to Gee, watching her, and said, "Twenty-two stacks a joint. That's what this muthafucka's charging for his work. Twenty-two fuckin' thousand. He keep this shit up, and I'm going to be selling cars instead of buying them."

Gee snorted a laugh. "You kiddin' me? As long as your money is? You shouldn't be so worried about a lil' nigga. He probably robbed some plug for his work. That's why he's selling em' for so cheap. It's so he can get rid of 'em fast. But mark my words, cuz. He won't be around with those prices for long. There's no way he has a plug, selling work for that cheap. And he got people moving too? He ain't making no money."

"He shouldn't be making shit," Shug hissed. "He should be somewhere stinkin', hadn't it been for Maniac. What the hell did he need a rocket launcher for anyway? The Feds are still trying to figure out what happened that night. All Maniac had to do was have some shooters hidden so when Montega went in the house, it was guaranteed he wouldn't be coming out. Now he has the streets talking. You know the worst thing about all of this? He doesn't even show his face.

I've had undercover spies positioned in bars, gyms, restaurants, and clubs, and no one's seen him. Cuz making drug money, and not a single luxurious car has popped up with him inside. It's like he's a ghost… a real-live fucking ghost."

Gee looked at his homie and shook his head. Shug may have seemed calm, but Gee knew he was pissed about the whole ordeal. Shug wasn't in the category of anyone in the city. He ran the entire state. Most of the guys and girls whose names were at the top for moving coke and heroin got their supply from him. They recognized him as the top of the food chain, and to receive a challenge from some nobody was a slap in the face.

After the paperwork was signed and the titles were changed over, Shug climbed into the back seat of the Maybach. Gee got into the back seat of the Rolls Royce. His henchmen filled in the rest, along with the other vehicle they had, and rolled out.

Shug sat in the back seat, relaxed in the soft leather interior. He looked over at his shorty. She was a far cry away from being Tee-Tee, but she did nasty things to him that he enjoyed, which made him overlook her beauty. As he adjusted the curtains, his cell phone rang. He looked over at his girlfriend just in time to catch her trying to open a bottle of Rosé.

"Chill, shorty," he said, pulling out his cell phone. "It's too early for that."

He placed the phone to his ear and answered. "Speak."

"Action speaks louder than words," a voice replied from the other end.

Shug took the phone from his ear to see a distant number starting with 787. Placing the phone back to his ear, he said, "Puerto Rico, huh? I don't have anybody in Puerto Rico, so who playing games on my line?"

"This ain't no game, main-man, nor is this one of your clients. You know what you get when you got a death collector that you can't see?"

"Nah, what's that?"

"A phantom."

Shug froze for a brief moment then exhaled calmly. "How'd you get my number?"

"I don't know. Could be one of your old clients or perhaps some chick who you got tired of and dissed. Or it could be the chick you're dealing with now."

Shug glanced over at the woman who didn't have a care in the world and said, "What is it you want? Tired of my wolves sniffing that ass out? Is that the reason you're hiding in PR? What? Are you calling me for a truce?"

"I'm not hiding. I'm enjoying a little sunlight with a friend. I just wanted to call you and let you know that it's still on with me for killing my homie and Tee-Tee. I'm coming for you, you fat fuck."

Shug chuckled. "Phone gangsters. Well, if you're coming, then bring the money with you."

"What money?" Montega asked.

"The money for your fucking casket 'cause that's the only outcome if we ever meet. I'ma bury yo' ass."

"I hear you talking, big man. But hear me."

"Fuck I want to listen to a dead man talking for?"

"Well, you better stop listening to yourself then." Montega hung up.

As Shug took the phone from his ear, the driver hit the brakes and made a hard right as gun shots went off in the middle of the intersection. Shug got low as his brand-new car was riddled with bullets. The driver stepped on the gas along with the other vehicles. When they got to the next intersection, another SUV blocked them off.

Shooters with AK's jumped out. "Turn left!" Shug shouted.

The driver did as told as more bullets showered through the carbon fiber. Shug's shorty was riddled from the side and back. The Maybach broke away from Gee and the other vehicles. Up ahead, another SUV blocked off the street. The driver turned right down a darker block and skidded to a halt. It was a dead end.

"What the fuck are you doing! Back up!" Shug barked as he looked over at his dead girlfriend slumped in the back seat.

The driver put the car in reverse. Suddenly, another SUV blocked them off. Shug's eyes got wide as men hopped out with AK's. The passenger and driver jumped out to defend their boss, but they were quickly torn to shreds. They reloaded, prepared to finish Shug off. He was trapped in the vehicle with no place to go. He climbed over the seat to the front just as a wave of chopper bullets tore holes into the $300,000 car.

They reloaded again as they walked forward toward the car. Four more men came from around the SUV to assist. Shug looked around for anything he could use to help him. He saw nothing. He could see the two men drawing near. His eyes reverted to the gear. He shifted to reverse then stepped on the gas. The Maybach shot backward, hitting both men so hard they went airborne.

The remaining four raised their weapons to fire but couldn't get out of the way. The Maybach slammed into them then into the SUV, causing it to tail whip into the street. Shug put the sedan in drive then peeled off down the block with gunshots echoing in the distance. Shug looked down at himself and saw that his suit was ruined with sweat and blood. Thankfully, it wasn't his blood. He looked in the back seat at the dead body and grinded his teeth together. The beef was definitely on and popping now.

Chapter Forty-Six

Letter To Breezy

"This is the letter I'll never send..."

— MONTEGA

Maniac pulled up on Blakemore Street in front of Reek and the rest of the hustlers who were standing in front of the Chinese store. After rolling down his window, he signaled for Reek to get into his cranberry Lincoln MKL. Reek got in and shut the door before Maniac pulled off.

"What's up with you?" Maniac greeted.

"Ain't shit. What's the problem?" Reek asked, looking over at him.

"There's been some changes in the streets. Shug don't want to do business with y'all no more. He thinks y'all harboring cuz with the black car."

"What!" Reek frowned with his lip curled. "I already told Shug we ain't got nothing to do with Montega. He don't even come around the hood like that anymore."

"Oh well, Reek. It is what it is. You know how Shug gets down. Y'all lettin' this dude mess up y'all money. You don't fuck with dude like that, prove it. Whenever he come around, hit my phone up and keep him here. That's all you gotta do. If you can handle that, I'll talk to Shug and let him know that y'all truly ridin' with us."

Reek considered Maniac's plan. He knew he had to play his part.

He would be a fool to let the connect slip out of his hand. Mike would not appreciate it one bit. Once Maniac dropped Reek off, the first thing Reek did was call Mike's phone. Mike had a cell phone that one of the prison guards had smuggled into jail for him. It was direct contact to the outside world. He could talk as long as he wanted.

On the third ring, Mike picked up. "Yo," he answered.

"What's up, big homie? We got a problem… a big problem."

"**K**ia, what the hell is in there?" Breezy asked as Kia pulled into the jungle-like setting of Awbury Park. Thick, white snowflakes fell from the sky, covering the entire property. "This place looks like no one's lived here in years. It's no wonder the hood is so infested with racoons."

"Both of y'all gotta promise not to say anything," Kia said seriously. "I gotta pick up some papers from Kenny's house. He doesn't want anyone to know where he lives, so y'all two bitches better keep y'all mouth shut." Kia was referring to both Breezy and Crystal, who was in the backseat. "Especially you, Bree."

"Please, if I wanted something to happen to your brother, he would be dead already," Breezy replied. "I'm over him." She looked out the window again with amazement. "Dag, this is one hell of a hideout, though. I had no idea there were houses back here. Your brother is so secretive, like he getting it at an all-time high. He still driving around in the same car he started out with."

"Bitch, don't be talking about my boo like that," Crystal joked. "He might not be getting it like Shug, but at least he putting his money to good use, right, Kia?"

Kia didn't respond. She just smirked as she advanced through the snow toward the house. They followed the trail and pulled into the driveway of a large, old, Victorian house that was boarded up on the outside. "Damn, for somebody that's supposed to be gettin' at a dollar, this is a real fucked-up way to live," Breezy stated, getting out the car with a sour look.

"Come on," Kia said, brushing by them to walk around the side where the garage was.

"Where is baby boy anyway?" Crystal asked as she got out.

"Probably over one of his little whore's house," Breezy suggested sarcastically.

"You ain't never lied," Kia replied.

They approached the mini carport. Once Kia punched in a code on the digital keypad, the first garage door was opened. Their eyes zoomed in on the black Lamborghini Murciélago LP-640. It was tinted with black rims and sat beside a black 2007 Dodge Charger SRT-8. They were the only cars inside the carport.

"Oh my God," Breezy said, stunned, as she looked at the Lambo.

"I've never seen him drive this," Crystal said, amazed, touching the fresh paint.

"That's 'cause he doesn't. He's too scared to drive it in the city," Kia explained.

"Shit, I would be too," Breezy said. "That's a $350,000 car, bitch. I don't think no one in Philly owns one of these. Not even Shug."

"Imagine Shug fat ass in one of them," Crystal said with a sarcastic laugh.

Kia looked from the car to the other side of the room where the Charger sat. Beside it, there was a set of steps leading down to a door. She and her girlfriends headed that way. She opened it and walked inside. The girls tore their gaze from the Lambo and walked through a tunnel and into the basement where they encountered a jacuzzi waterfall inside some kind of concocted cave.

"Oh my God, is that a hot tub?" Crystal asked while looking down at the bubbling water.

"Come on, will y'all? Now y'all wanna be on his dick. Just a few moments ago, y'all was trying to play him," Kia said, heading up the staircase to the first floor, which also blew their minds. The whole place looked as if it belonged in a museum. It was dark and gloomy but cool and smelled of oil and spices. The place was well organized and clean. The walls were decorated with guns like a gun store. The furnishings were comfortable and welcoming. Even Breezy was impressed.

"Where did he get so many gold guns from? Are they even real?" Crystal asked as she touched one that was mounted by the computer.

"I don't know, and I don't wanna find out," Breezy answered as she followed Kia to Montega's office across from the living room. There was a desk and a leather chair by the wall. There, they saw more guns, and a pile of money just sitting on the white and black pool table. It was then Breezy realized, the streets didn't have a clue what they were talking about. Montega was getting it at an all-time high, under their noses.

Since the drive-by in South Philly, no one had seen Montega, but everyone knew he was still in action because the streets stayed talking about the Silent Kings. The truth was, while the squad took Philly, Montega was out of town, taking other spots down. As Kia searched for the information she needed to do her income taxes for her legitimate business, Breezy noticed a piece of paper that had her name written on it.

Breaking away from the two, she nervously picked the paper up and began to read it.

A LETTER TO BREEZY

I'm writing U a letter I know I can never send.
The things I've done 2 U are unforgivable.
U probably hate me, U probably wish 4 my demise.

Just 2 see U cry makes me wish I would die.
What I took from U I could never give back.
It was the thing that made you happy, the thing that made U laugh.
The thing that made you smile, the thing that made me bad.
I never meant to hurt U, but life doesn't offer gems.
I'm sorry I killed your lover, I'm sorry I killed your friend.
I fear 4 the future because hurting people never ends.
Now you'll always hate me, because this is the letter I'll never send.
Montega.

Breezy carefully placed the letter back where she found it just as Kia found the paperwork. "What's wrong with you?" she asked, seeing the sudden emotion in Breezy's face.

Breezy shook her head and tried not to cry. "Nothing. Are you ready to go?"

"Yeah, let's get outta here before this boy come back."

When they made it back to the car, no one said a word about what they had seen inside the house. Breezy suddenly had a different view of Montega. Besides his wealth, she now saw something he may have hidden deep inside—a heart.

Chapter Forty-Seven

Party 2 Death

"You're gonna either have the feds on your ass or the wolves..."

— MONTEGA

♫ I can feel it in the air...

— BEANIE SIGEL

Montega awoke from a pleasant dream of a foursome with three exotic females—one Ethiopian/Asian, a Brazilian, and the other Caucasian. It was, by far, one of the best dreams he'd ever had. Lying on his back, he wiped his eyes and looked up at the ceiling, one he hadn't recalled seeing before. He sat up quickly and noticed his dream wasn't a dream at all. Scattered across the bed were three beautiful, exotic, naked females sleeping that he'd picked up from Delilah's the night before. The empty bottle of Gray Goose on the nightstand told a story in itself. Montega looked at his rose-gold, diamond-faced Cartier watch and saw that it was 9:05 p.m. He reached over the Brazilian girl's small breasts and picked up the ringing phone.

"Hello," he answered in a groggy voice.

"Hey, papi," Juicy said, changing his reaction. "You still coming to my party?"

"Shit, I forgot your party was tonight," Montega said, wiping his tired face. "Where is it gonna be?"

Juicy sucked her teeth. "Plush. I told you that like a hundred times already, nigga. Wake up."

"How is it that you are allowed to throw parties anyway? You ain't even twenty-one yet."

"Don't get cute. I'm twenty-three, for your information, *and* I got clout on the internet. I'm practically a star, so don't hate. Now make sure your butt show up. Oh yeah, Gutter called me too. He said Nino just got out of jail yesterday. He's not coming to the party though, for some reason, but Gutter will be there. I remember you said you was looking for him. He said he's coming."

"Oh really?" Montega asked dryly. "Well, in that case, I'll see you there."

"You better," Juicy said before ending the call.

Montega stretched before climbing out of bed and into the shower. He realized he was in the Borgata Hotel from the monogrammed towels. He showered, dressed, and left the women behind. He couldn't believe he had been partying for a day and a half with those strippers. The first thing he did was drive back to Philly to one of his stash spots. Walking down into the basement, he whipped out his phone and called one of his clients.

On the first ring, he answered. "Yo, where you been? I've been calling you all day," the guy said.

"Be easy, homie," Montega replied as he opened the old washing machine and pulled out a brick of cocaine. "I lost track of time, and I apologize for that. In fact, I'll throw you a little extra on the lookout."

"Say no more," the guy said before hanging up.

Montega brought the coke upstairs and set it on the counter by the stove. Grabbing a pot from the cabinet, he poured water into it and set it over the fire. He weighed each portion to 250 grams, dropped it in the boiling water and cooked up a fourth kilo of raw, straight to the oils. After dropping the ice and drying the coke off, he broke them up into single, onion-shaped ounces and weighed them again on a digital scale.

Montega carefully bagged up each ounce, threw them in a bag, then headed back to the car. It was a cold night in the city. An old blanket of snow on the ground had turned to ice. Those who didn't have to drive were advised not to, extra-duty police included. Montega took advantage of it by making deliveries to his workers who were hustling in the crack houses he had around the city.

He pulled up around the corner from College Wall to find his young bol Jay hustling hand-to-hand on the corner. Montega had a soft spot for the young shooter. He met him through his brother, Taliban. As soon as he saw him, he beeped the horn to get his attention. The slim, brown-skinned guy with the light beard and unibrow stopped what he was doing and approached the black Impala.

He got into the passenger side and spoke in a normal seventeen-year-old voice.

"What's good, dog."

"You wanna make a quick nickel?" Montega asked.

"Hell yeah. What you need me to do?"

"Just ride with me across the bridge. In fact, call your homies and tell them to come on with you."

Jay got his homies, Mac and Jackpot, to join them. Together, they drove across the Ben Franklin Bridge into Camden territory. They pulled in a driveway behind a 7-Eleven and got out. Montega went to the trunk of his car and opened the stash spot in the floor. A small arsenal appeared. He handed Jay an AK-74, Mac an HK-MP-5, and Jackpot a Bushmaster AR-15. They got back in the Impala and headed for the block where the client awaited.

Montega pulled over and spotted Stormin' Norman posted with his people. He got out the Impala along with his young bols. When the guys saw the guns they were armed with, they turned to Norman nervously. Norm smiled as he ignored the threatening pose and crossed the street with two of his people with him. He carried a duffle bag full of cash. He handed it to him and followed Norm over to the car.

"You want me to count this in front of you," Norm asked.

"How much is it?" Montega asked.

"A hunnid grand."

Montega took the bag. *Yeah right?* "Nah, I trust you. I'll have the work sent to you in a few days," he said before heading back to the car where his young shooters were posted.

He placed the money in the stash spot then got in the driver's side. Once he was safely inside, the young goons got in as well. Montega hit off all his players and crack houses throughout Philly then dropped his youngins off.

Afterward, he headed for the club. He drove into the parking lot of Plush nightclub. There, he spotted his homie Gutter's sky-blue Maserati three cars away. Gutter had been way too flamboyant since he started his rise with Silent Kings. There wasn't a problem with his re-up. In fact, Gutter was one of the fastest on the team when it came to moving heroin. It was just his flashy style that bothered Montega.

For one, he partied every weekend, and when he did, he made sure he was seen. His jewelry was outrageous. The iced-out Silent Kings chain that he had made on Jeweler's Row was damn near the size of a toaster. He came in the club with different chinchillas on every week and threw twenty to thirty thousand around at females like it was Monopoly money. Montega knew if the Feds didn't bring him down, the goons who prayed on ballers like him would.

The club was packed, and the line was out the door. Juicy was hosting one of the biggest afterparties of the century. She started off doing cabarets for an older crowd, then she hooked up with some friends in community college that specialized in web design. They hooked up her website and brought a lot of traffic to it, using photos from her cabarets. From there, she started doing promotions inside the clubs. Using her good looks and flawless assets, she started meeting very important people.

Tonight, she had a few entertainers making special guest appearances, entertainers that nobody would have guessed would come. Montega avoided the long line that stretched around the corner and approached the front. He watched as some of the women began to stir when they saw the rapper Pitbull get out of a limo with his friends and security to head inside.

Montega slowed his pace when he saw two beautiful women step up on the curb. One was apple-butter-brown with long, brass-shaded, crinkly hair. She wore a tight, caramel Prada mini dress that barely covered her voluptuous ass. Black Tory Burch heels told him that shorty was about money. The other was Italian with long, dark hair. She was shorter than her girlfriend and wore a black Valentino Garavani dress and Stuart Weitzman croc-skin sandals. She looked a tad bit innocent, compared to her companion, and had a slim body with bulging breasts and a small, round ass.

As soon as they spotted him, the Italian one spoke first. "You're Kia's brother, aren't you?" she asked, getting her friend Amber's attention.

"Yup," Montega replied. "Aren't you a little too young to be up in here?"

Ebo smiled bashfully and replied. "I could be."

Montega's eyes went from her eyes to Amber's. "What's up, pretty girl," he greeted.

Amber smiled and waved at him.

"Y'all trying to get in?"

"Can you get us in?" Amber asked him

"I don't know. I might have a little pull in here. Let me see."

Montega turned to the bouncers who were patting everyone down one by one. They were big and wore black shirts that said *security* printed across their chests in white.

One of the Italian bouncers saw him approaching and frowned. "What do you want?" he asked.

"I want you to call Misty, and tell her the guy name Montega is out front."

When the bouncer heard that, his hard face slowly vanished as he whipped out his phone and dialed a number. The people waiting in line tried their hardest to listen in on the conversation. Even Amber and Ebo were curious to know what was going on. A few seconds after the bouncer got off the phone, an Italian woman with blonde hair, dressed in a cream suit and heels, came out to greet him. She looked to be in her mid-thirties.

"Kenny!" she greeted him with a hug. "How's everything going with you? Juicy told me you weren't coming."

"I know, but there's someone I gotta talk to in here."

"Well, come on in. What are you waiting for?"

"Oh, these are my friends," Montega said. "They're with me."

The owner took a look at the two quickly and said, "Caramel and vanilla. What a combination. Wait a second. Do I know you?" She was studying Ebo.

"No," Montega quickly said, taking the owner by the small of her back and guiding her inside. He looked over his shoulder at Ebo and gave her a wink.

As the four entered the club through the side door, the loud siren tune of Meek Mill, T.I., and Rick Ross's "Rosé Red" had the ballers and divas bouncing their heads. Montega hadn't been to a club since Atlanta. He found himself too busy lately, trying to make moves. Everything seemed so distant to him now. He had felt like Bin Laden hiding in a cave and had lost track of time about what was hip and what was not. It was a good thing he had a sister who stayed on point with the times.

He noticed a few guys who were getting some major paper in the city doing it big over in the VIP. Gutter was amongst them.

"You got a nice little spot here," he told Misty.

"Thanks, baby. I pride myself in keeping her well stocked." She looked over at Juicy, who was seated at a booth with some of her girlfriends. "Looks like your girl is in for one hell of a night."

"Yeah," Montega said with a smile before spotting his sister and her girlfriends. Amber and Ebo walked toward their booth with Montega eyeing them the entire way.

Misty tapped him on the chest and said, "I'll be in my office. Stick around for a sec and stop by, kay?"

Montega nodded as he watched curious eyes glance up at him.

When Amber and Ebo got to the table, Breezy looked up and nudged Kia to get her attention. Kia looked up to see her two beautiful girlfriends.

"Okay, divas," Kia said with her familiar signature smile. "I'm glad y'all could make it. It took y'all long enough. Where's Jazz?"

"Mike won't let her out the house," Amber said, tossing her hair over her shoulder.

"That sucks. I didn't think they would let y'all in, as crowded as it is in here," Crystal said.

"Yeah and how much did y'all pay to get Ebo in here?" Breezy asked. "You know she underage."

"Shit, Kia brother got us in," Ebo said, grabbing an empty glass.

"What brother are you talking about?" Kia asked, looking around.

Amber pointed to Montega, who was talking to the bouncer from earlier.

"What is he doing in here?" Breezy asked suspiciously.

"I don't know," Crystal said. "But he's coming this way."

Montega glanced at Gutter and shook his head as he approached him. He made it halfway across before bumping into someone. "Damn," a light-brown-skinned guy said as he looked him in the face.

"My fault, homie," Montega replied before continuing to walk toward Gutter. The guy's eyes lit up. His heart skipped a beat. He couldn't believe who he just ran into. As Montega came within a foot of Gutter, he felt someone grab hold of his arm. He turned to see a booth full of glowing faces. The first person who caught his eye was Breezy. For some reason, she was sparkling.

"Damn," Montega said with surprise, looking at all the faces. "And here I thought all the pretty girls in Philly were overrated. How y'all doing tonight?" he asked.

"We would be doing even better if we could get some drinks over here. It seems like these waitresses are only catering to the VIP," Gi-Gi said, checking him out. "But forget all that. How you doing tonight?"

"No, fuck that. Why don't you come see me no more?" Kia asked. "You getting too much money for family? Why I gotta sneak in your house and find out what you been up to?"

"You got a house?" Crystal asked, glancing at Breezy as if to play it off. "Where you live?"

"You should know," Montega said before revealing his secret. "You and Breezy were there yesterday with my sister. So who you foolin'?"

"How do you know all that?" Kia asked in shock.

"C'mon, now. I got eyes everywhere, sis. The streets ain't the only thing that's watchin', shorty. Twenty thousand dollars of surveillance works even better. Plus, I noticed more than one set of footprints in the snow. You should try covering your tracks a little better than that. And I never put my money before my family, especially my only sister. Now, give me some sugah." He wrapped his arms around her to give her a kiss on the cheek.

"Stop, boy, you gonna mess up my makeup," she said while her friends smiled with envy.

Even Breezy couldn't help but feel a little warmth when she saw the attention Kia got from her brother.

"So what sort of relationship do you have with the owner?" Ebo asked, catching him off guard. "I remember her. She knows my father; that's why she recognized me outside."

Montega froze, speechless. It was true. He and the owner had been banging pelvises, but he wasn't about to tell them that.

"Probably fucking her," Amber blurted out.

Montega looked over at Gutter and decided now was the time to make his escape.

"Excuse me," he said, walking off while the girls ridiculed him.

"I was just joking, damn. Talk about no sense of humor," Amber said.

Breezy couldn't stop staring. Even though she despised him, she still admired his charm. She wasn't the only one in the group. When she looked at Amber, she saw the same effect he had on her.

"Your brother is so sweet," Crystal said to Kia, but Breezy rolled her eyes. She thought to herself, *he wasn't so sweet when he kidnapped me and killed my boyfriend. That's all for show. Ain't nobody buyin' his act.*

She then looked at her friends, who were practically gawking at him. *Well, he ain't fooling me,* she thought.

When Gutter saw Montega approach, he extended his arms like he owned the place. "Yo, what's the deal, bol? What you doin' up in here?"

He turned to all the other ballers. "Everybody, listen up. We got a real hood billionaire in this—"

"I need to rap with you for a second."

Gutter caught Montega's serious tone. He looked around at all his entourage, nodded, and followed him through the crowd and into the bathroom. "What's up?" he asked.

"What's up?" Montega repeated as if Gutter didn't know. "What's up is you, yo. You and all this flamboyant shit," he said, lifting Gutter's iced-out chain and letting the symbol of the crowned, gagged skull plop back on his chest. "You drawlin', dog. You hangin' 'round with these leeches. These dudes is lames. They want your blood, and they'll suck you dry if they could. You act like you ain't tryna make enough to get out the hood and expand. You just want to get by and have a bunch of nothin' ass bitches speak highly of you and trick you out your money."

Montega spat on the floor and said, "Keep it up. You gonna either have the feds on your ass of the wolves on your head. Out here, throwin' bread to these pigeons like this shit a walk in the park, like it's legal. The ones that act like they interested in you will leave you quicker than you can say 'I'm broke.' I'm not telling you this 'cause I'm hatin' or anything. I'm telling you because you family, and I got love for you. You got to be smarter than this, bol."

Gutter hung his head. "My bad, yo. I know I *have* been drawlin'. It's just this life, dog. You don't understand. You don't know what it's like to be the dirtiest nigga on the street, to be looked at like trash and, then, one day, overcoming all that. Ain't nobody give a damn about Gutter then. Now all I hear is my name wherever I go. I guess I let it get to my head," he said.

"Nah, pick ya head up, yo. You ain't gotta be ashamed around me. You forgettin' I was in the same boat. Dudes ain't care about me when I was broke. You see the bol Fly-Ty out there? I remember when bol looked at me like I didn't deserve to be stepped on. What he doing now? Copping off a nigga I'm servin'. You're right. It's a good feeling, but you don't give into them. Let 'em carry it like they been carrying it. We family, and ain't no man in this family bigger than the next. We just need to tighten up, homie," Montega said, sticking out his hand.

Gutter nodded before taking it and giving him a brotherly hug. He said, "Since you here, you can at least stay for a little while and have a couple drinks. I know Juicy probably looking for you right now. She's gonna be pissed if she found out you came and ain't say nothing to her. Don't be like Nino burnt-out ass."

"What's up with Nino anyway? Why he ain't come to the party?"

"Man, that nigga done went upstate and came back Muslim."

"Oh yeaaahhhh?" Montega said, rubbing his thick, curly beard. "Well, what's wrong with that?"

"What's wrong with it? Nothing's wrong with it. It's just when you come home, telling me that I'm sinning, and I need to fear Allah, or whoever he worships, now that's problem. The nigga think he the prophet Muhammad himself."

Montega smiled, not grasping the seriousness of the situation.

"So you staying or what?" Gutter asked.

Montega thought about that and sighed. "Yeah, I guess you're right, but first, let me grab these flyers for Gi-Gi's Unisex. I want to surprise her with 'em."

"Here, give me the keys. I'll get 'em," Gutter said, thinking Montega was trying to pull a spin move on him. "Besides, I gotta grab some more money out my car anyway. Those hoes be breakin' me, bol."

Montega started to say something but stopped. He then gave him the keys. "The flyers are in the trunk," he said before walking out and heading over to the bartender. "How many bottles of Spade you got back there?" he asked the girl with the curly hair.

"Well, with all the guys in the VIP buying them out, I'll say—"

"No," Montega responded, stopping her. "I mean the magnum bottles."

"Oh," the girl said. "We have about seventy-five bottles."

"Load 'em all up and bring them out."

Over at Kia's table, the girls were in suspense as they listened to Crystal talk about Montega's crib and the Lamborghini he had in the carport. Suddenly, the waitress came out with sparkling flare candles and giant bottles of Spades. Everyone turned to see where the bottles were going. Montega sat with Juicy as the bottles stopped in front of their booth. He started having the bouncers that once stopped him at the door distribute the bottles to those around him.

A waitress brought Kia and her girlfriend's five magnum bottles of Ace of Spades. "We didn't order these," Kia said.

"The cutie over there asked that these be brought over," the waitress said, pointing to her brother.

Kia shook her head before looking at all the gold bottles.

When Gutter got outside in the parking lot, he headed for the black SS Impala first so he could grab the flyers for Montega. It was a cold night, but he couldn't feel it, because he was somewhat drunk. He pressed the button on the keypad, opening the trunk.

Gutter stuck his head inside to retrieve the flyers. He didn't hear someone creep up on him. When Maniac got within a foot of his target, who was wearing a chinchilla hood over his head, he cocked his Mossberg twelve-gauge riot pump.

Click-clack!

Before Gutter could get his head out of the trunk, Maniac pulled the trigger.

Boom!

Once Gutter's brains splattered in the trunk of the Impala, his body went limp. Maniac then sprinted away, hoping no one saw him. He got into the passenger side of the Lincoln and ordered Spade to drive off.

"Did you get him?" Spade asked anxiously.

"What do you think?" Maniac sighed with relief. "Hell yeah. I caught him right while he was goin' in the trunk of his car," he said with a laugh. "Dumb muthafucka had a big ass chinchilla on. He couldn't even hear me comin'."

"*A chinchilla?*" Spade repeated with a frown, thinking about the flashy guy he saw in the club.

"Yeah, he had on a black and white chinchilla, right?"

Spade put his head down.

"*Right!*" Maniac repeated.

"No, man. He ain't have on no goddamn chinchilla. He had on a black leather Gucci jacket," Spade stated.

"Fuckkkkkk!" Maniac said, pounding his fist on the dashboard. He had shot the wrong guy, and he couldn't go back, because the cops would be everywhere.

Montega looked at his watch and saw that thirty minutes had passed, and there was still no sign of Gutter. Placing his bottle down, he excused himself from the table of women then made his way toward the exit. When he got outside and saw the blue and red lights flashing throughout the parking lot, he immediately sensed what had happened. His heart was in his stomach as he approached the lot.

He wanted to get close, but the cops wouldn't allow it. However, what he saw from a distance was gruesome. It quickly dawned on him then. The body hanging out of the trunk of his car was supposed to be him.

Chapter Forty-Eight

Friend Or Foe

"Don't trust bol..."

— J-BLACK

The death of Gutter hit the team hard. His funeral was memorable and very dramatic. However, that still didn't stop the Kings from their endless paper chase and bloodshed, nor did it stop the war between Montega and Shug. Since the cops took his car for evidence, Montega was forced to drive his black Dodge Charger SRT-8. Like the Impala, the windows were tinted, and the entire body was covered in a bullet-proof shell.

With the vision of Gutter's dead body fresh in his mind, he vowed to find the guy responsible and lay him to rest. Gutter had been his homie for years, and now he was gone. Just knowing that hurt Montega like an aching tooth. Montega pulled up in front of the Masjid of Germantown Avenue. He saw Nino waiting out front and beeped his horn. Nino approached, wearing a white Muslim thobe and a white kufi. Upstate had transformed him from the dark-skinned goon to a husky black man, with a thick beard.

He opened the door, letting out Jim Jones' "Emotions" as he got in.

"Subhenallah!" he said, closing the door and turning the music down.

Montega looked at him like he was crazy. "What the hell is wrong with you, bol? Why you turn that down?"

"Because you got this fitness playing in front of the masjid," Nino said. "Matter fact, just pull off. *Aluh-du-belah-hemanal-shaytan-near-rah-jen!"*

"Fitnah? What the fuck is you talking about, Nino?"

"My name is not *Nino*. My attribute is Abdulallah."

Montega shook his head as he pulled off and out of the parking space. "Yo, bol, what the hell did jail do to you? You was only gone for eighteen months. How the hell did you end up so... holy?"

"Jail didn't do anything to me. Allah did this. He put me in a place where I would remember him the most, and that I did. I found myself through Islam. I took shahada, started making my five salats, and began studying. The more I started studying, the more I came to realize that what I was doing was wrong. The Dunya wanted me."

"The what?"

"Dunya—this wicked system of things."

"Look, yo. I ain't really trying to hear all that bullshit you talking unless any of it got something to do with moving these birds I got floodin' in every month."

"So the stories are true, huh?" Abdulallah asked before chuckling to himself. "You have become Shaytan's advocate, poisoning the people with his white jinn."

Montega sighed with irritation. Nino, or should he say Abdulallah, was never this way. He used to be a wild killer who slept with any woman that would put out, and he liked to fix cars and do tint jobs. He even did the tint to his black SS Impala a few years back. Now he was portraying to be this holy fighter of God. It was really starting to freak Montega out.

"So you saying you don't want to make no money?" Montega asked, looking over his shoulder at his homie. "You just going to let Allah provide some dough for you?"

"I never said that, ocky. Allah is the most merciful all knower and the best of planners, but I still have to tie my camel."

Montega was confused, but before he could question him, Abdulallah pulled out a bottle with a blue substance in it.

"What the fuck is that?" Montega asked. "Some kind of syrup?"

"No, it's oil. It's how I make my living. Here, try. Put some on. I sell this for ten dollars. It's called Blue Nile." Nino went to grab his hand to put a dab of oil on it.

"Man, I don't want none of that cheap shit," Montega said, snatching his hand back. "Are you fucking kidding me, Nino? You selling oils? Is this what it all boils down to?" He dug in his pocket while shaking his head. He pulled out a wad of hundreds. "Man, here. Take this, yo. You don't have to—"

"I don't want your haram currency," Abdulallah said, swatting the money away. "I don't want your poisonous drugs either."

"Well, what the fuck are you here for if you don't want shit then? Why the hell are you sitting in the passenger's side if you're too holy for everyone else?"

Abdulallah looked away from Montega and out the window and said, "I'm here to save you from the Dunya."

Montega wrapped both hands around the steering wheel tightly, took a deep breath, and sighed a laugh. "And how do you expect to do that, homie?"

"The Quran said that Allah tells us to call upon those who do wrong and guide them to the light. I love you like a brother, Kenny, and I will die before I let the Dunya take you. Inshallah, one day, you and the others will see me in a different light and follow in the footsteps of the prophet Muhammad. I hope that one day, you will open your heart and embrace Islam."

"Yeah, well, I hope you're prepared for a long ride because that ain't happening no time soon," Montega replied as he turned up Ardleigh Street.

He rode across Woodlawn, looked up the block, and saw some people out in front of the Chinese store. He drove by and circled around and came up Blakemore Street.

When he and Abdulallah pulled up to the corner, he spotted Reek and Black talking to Breezy and her cousin Jasmine by the corner house where everyone hung out. Montega parked and calmly stepped out of the car, looking irritated. He was happy Nino didn't get out with him. He didn't think he could take a few more minutes of his mouth. He spat to the ground, trying to control his irritation, while he walked into the store with Reek's eyes following him the whole time.

Once he grabbed a vanilla Dutch, he headed back out to approach the four of them. Reek was on Jasmine's phone at the time.

"Hey, brother," Jasmine said, beaming when she saw Montega walking her way. She always referred to him as her brother because she and Kia were like sisters.

"What's up, Jazz? Long time, no see," he greeted before glancing at Breezy, who quickly looked away.

"Yeah, here he go right here," Reek said before handing the phone to Montega.

When he put the phone to his ear, Reek stepped off to make another call. "Yo," Montega said, knowing exactly who was on the other end.

"What's up?" Mike replied, not sounding like himself.

Montega frowned. "What's up with you? Why you sound like that?"

"Because, yo, you fuckin' up shit for us; that's why," Mike shot back.

"What you talkin' 'bout?"

"You know what I'm talkin' 'bout. I'm talkin' 'bout the foolishness you bringing on me. By you beefin' with Shug, it's stopping the block from doin' business. Now they're holding out on us. I told ya dumb ass to fall the fuck back."

"So what I'm supposed to do, huh? Just let the bol kill me because you worried about him supplying you?" Montega reasoned.

"I ain't say that. Don't start putting words in my mouth. What I'm sayin' is you gotta roll and stop coming around there. Your beef is affecting my bread."

"What?" Montega twisted up his face. "Man, you got me fucked up all the way around the board if you think I'm gonna do that! I come around here because this is where I'm from! I got family around here!

This is where I was born and raised! I don't come around here, steppin' on y'all toes either! I don't need Summerville! I got my own strips and houses for that, no thanks to you! Now you gonna come at me, talkin' 'bout I gotta roll out and stop comin' around! Fuck you and whoever else think I'm sweet!" he shouted, clicking the phone off and handing it back to Jazz.

He leaned on the wall and began to empty the contents out of the Dutch. It was how he got by when he was stressed. Getting high was the only way he knew how to make the pain go away. Breezy looked at him and could see his rage. She couldn't believe he had just cursed Mike out like that.

Suddenly, the dark-tinted backseat window rolled down from his Charger, and Abdulallah leaned back from the passenger's seat. "Still smoking that green devil," Abdulallah said, shaking his head.

"Not right now, yo," Montega said with clenched teeth.

Abdulallah got his drift and rolled the window back up.

"Let me smoke with you," J-Black said, watching him dump out a jar of Haze. As the two shared the Dutch, Reek crossed Woodlawn and called Jasmine over as Breezy got into her car to wait for Amber to come up the street.

"Yo, don't trust bol. He's a fuckin' snake," Black said.

"Who?" Montega asked, glancing at Abdulallah.

"Reek," Black replied. "The other day, I seen him ridin' with one of Shug's hitmen."

Montega's eyes went dark. "His *hitman?* What bol look like?"

"Brown skin, 'bout your height with dreads..."

That was all Montega needed to hear, not just because he'd seen him before but because the man who J-Black just described was now getting out of a Lincoln with a Mac-11, holding it by its suppressed muzzle. "What the fuck! Black, get down!" Montega shouted as Maniac aimed the gun in his direction.

Black hit the deck while Montega tripped. But before he touched the concrete, he caught his fall, injuring his finger.

"Ahh, fuck, man!" he shouted as glass shattered over his head from the parked car he hid behind. The muzzle did no justice when it came to silencing. Maniac had a full fifty-shot clip of hollows. The copper shower from the machine gun splattered into the wall behind them, digging chunks out of the red brick of the Chinese store.

"Oh my God!" Jazz screamed in a panic as she rushed to get into Breezy's car.

Car windows shattered as bullets trailed Montega, who was sprinting to get away. He had him in plain sight. There was nowhere Montega could escape now. His time had finally come. "Allah-who-ackbar!" someone else shouted before a gun started firing.

Maniac ducked after hearing three big quakes coming from Abdulallah's P-89 Ruger. Seeing this, Maniac dipped and scrambled low and ran back to the car to shield his head. As he started his engine, Taliban appeared, jumping on the hood of the Lincoln with two Glock 40s firing at the windshield. Bullet after bullet smashed inside at the driver.

"Ahhh!" Maniac squealed as he got hit in the side.

To avoid getting hit a second time, he dipped low under the dash and stepped on the gas pedal. The car bolted forward as the tires ate up the street.

Eeeeeeerrrrrbbb!

Taliban tumbled over the roof top and rolled to the ground as the Lincoln sped down the street. When he got back to his feet, he fired a few more rounds until the car was clearly out of sight. Montega looked up to see Abdulallah's hand offering to help him up. He took it.

When Montega got up from between two parked cars, Jasmine and Breezy were gone, and so were Reek and J-Black. The only person still outside besides Abdulallah was his brother, who was approaching him with two smoking guns.

"Y'all two aight?" Taliban asked.

"Mashallah," Abdulallah said. "All praises due to Allah, the most merciful."

"Naw, I ain't aight, man. I fuckin' broke my finger," Montega complained with his arm around Abdulallah's shoulder.

"Let me see," Taliban replied, taking his brother's hand.

"Man, I swear I'ma kill bol when I catch him," Montega said with anger, watching his brother inspect his hand. "That's probably the muthafucka that pushed Gutter's shit back that night at the club. Damn, this shit hurts. How the fuck am I gonna shoot now."

"Calm down, yo. Your finger ain't broke. You just jammed it. All you need is some ice."

"You see?" Abdulallah said, stroking his thick beard. "Allah is the best of planners. That was a sign."

"It was a sign, alright," Montega said, brushing by him. "It means for me to smarten up. This war ain't over. So come on and let's get the hell out of here."

The three got into the Charger and drove off with another enemy added to their list: Reek.

Chapter Forty-Nine

Chinatown

"It will make us all billionaires..."

— MASTER WONG LEE

When Diamond's private G-600 landed in the Northeast Philadelphia Airport, a maroon, stretch Range Rover awaited at a nearby hanger. Philadelphia weather was the polar opposite from the West Coast this time of year. It was windy and cold, and the skies looked gray, threatening more snow.

Diamond wore a leopard-print Valentino dress. It was wool and rippled around the edges and rose halfway up her thighs. She matched it with a gold, silk, long-sleeve blouse, peek-a-boo toe Versace heels, and a leopard fur overcoat. Her hair was pulled straight back in a ponytail and reached down the small of her back. Fancy, intense, butterscotch, pear-shaped diamonds sparkled in her ears and around her neck.

As the hatchet extracted, Diamond picked up the custom Taurus off the seat beside her. It was a .380 ACP with a pink body and black stainless-steel slide. She placed it into her Tory Burch bag, stood, and then headed for the exit of the plane.

When Samuel stood, she stopped him. "No, Priest. I want you to stay here with the pilot. This city needs more than a prayer to save it," she said.

The priest nodded. "As you wish, Madam White."

The driver of the stretch Range Rover got out and opened the back door for her and the bodyguard, Bain, while the others got into a rented Suburban. Inside of the luxurious vehicle sat Shug dressed in a tailor-made black Brioni suit with a white collared shirt and a black, red, and white, hand-printed tie. He was accompanied by his underboss, Gee, who was just as stylish. Both observed Diamond as she sat across from them. The whole limousine blossomed with the scent of her perfume.

As she fixed her dress and crossed her succulent, tanned thighs, Shug peered at her then scanned her legs down to her pretty feet that captured his attention. He imagined tasting those feet, along with other hidden body parts that he knew he couldn't have. Even Gee found it hard not to stare at her. She barely wore makeup, yet her face shined as if she had been drowned in the fountain of youth.

Once Bain placed the luggage into the trunk, he got in with his boss. "Planning on stayin' a while?" Shug asked.

"Clyde suggested I take a vacation, which is bullshit. He just wants me out of his hairs," she replied dryly.

"Well, you can stay at my condo at the Murano. No one barely goes there," Shug said, hoping she would accept the invitation.

In your dreams, Diamond thought as she smiled ever so politely. "No thanks. I'll be residing at the Phoenix. My father still owns a penthouse suite there," she said, shutting him down.

Shug nodded fraudulently and said, "Well… the Phoenix it is." He then had the driver pull out of the airport and head for Center City, Philadelphia. Diamond marveled at the boathouses on the Schuylkil River as they turned off the expressway and into the land of the skyscrapers. Once she passed the art museum, she made a mental note to do a little sightseeing while she was in town and maybe even meet a nice guy.

Yeah right, she thought.

"How's Wong Lee holding up in Chinatown?" Diamond asked.

"I've never seen anything like it. Wong Lee brought his entire gang to Philly, and just like that, they were able to pull out the weeds and blossom. They didn't even have to use force. Wong Lee's Black Cloud has long been feared. Stories from China have been traveling over the ocean. Now that they are finally here, people have just fell in line. It's not just in Philly either. We're talking New York, L.A., Miami and other major cities."

Diamond nodded as she observed City Hall. "That's interesting," she said.

Crouched and coiled on the shoulder of Center City like a bad influence was Chinatown.

When they got to 10th and Cherry Street in Chinatown, the vehicle stopped in front of a line of restaurants tattooed with Chinese symbols. Diamond and her companions stepped out of the limo and frowned. The environment smelled extremely weird to them. The area looked confusing, unusual and alternately exotic but ugly. Aside from the steam coming out of the street grates, it was surprisingly quiet. Diamond looked down the street toward the Gallery then back at the place she was supposed to meet Master Wong Lee. Everything was so close together, it reminded her of Manhattan, New York.

"He wants to meet here? It looks like a hole in the wall," she said irritably, crossing the one-way street.

Shug ignored her and headed for the front door. Diamond looked up at the sign that read 'PENANG' and headed for the entrance.

When two of her henchmen opened the two doors for her, she walked inside and saw that the place was beautiful with its Chinese essentials and accents. The whole place made her feel as if she weren't even in America.

"A hole in a wall, huh?" Shug asked with sarcasm before following the waiter to the back.

Diamond followed Shug and Gee back to where Wong Lee and his underboss, Kim Angeo, were sitting, sipping tea.

Wong Lee was an average-size man with flaky, tan skin, a pie face, and straight, shoulder-length, dark hair. He wore a black Hermés suit, a white, button-up shirt, and a blue tie. His slanted eyes were black and cold but not as cold as his beautiful underboss. She was extremely young, perhaps three years younger than Diamond. She had soft, high-yellow skin, high cheekbones, and dark, beautiful Asian eyes. Her hair was long, straight, dark, and shiny. She, too, wore a suit much more fitted than her boss. She had Black Cloud foot soldiers surrounding her.

Diamond bowed her head respectfully and took a seat with the others. Bain and the henchmen stood nearby as Shug and Gee joined her at the booth. "Would you like to order something?" Wong Lee asked after shaking everyone's hand.

"I'll eat later," Diamond responded. "Right now, I want to get down to business. It was brought to my attention that you wanted to speak with me. So here I am."

Master Lee looked across the table at his beautiful but deadly underboss then back at Diamond. "I've known you since you were a teenager and long enough to know when you're in way over your head. Everyone knows that was your ship that got busted a year and a half ago, and soon, the Feds will close in on us all. That's not how business is supposed to operate. Yes, you brought us into the Underworld, but you are trying to destroy it for your own selfish reasons. I've admired your willfulness and your passion to learn, but lashing out every meeting is not the way of the Ninja. By showing your anger, you dishonor everything you were taught and stand for, including yourself. And if this continues, I'm pulling out, and so is the Black Cloud."

Diamond looked at the man across the booth from her, contemplating whether or not he was fast enough to catch a flying knife intended for his throat. She knew from experience that he was. He had once beaten her with his hands tied behind his back. She could still remember her tainted ego, and sighed.

"You know, it's funny how you can point out all of my faults, Master Lee, but then go behind our back and schedule a meeting with Verningo Castor," Diamond said with a poker face.

"What are you talking about? I've done no such thing," Master Lee retorted, looking back at Kim for verification.

"Is that so?" Diamond asked, reaching into her bag and pulling out photos of him in Miami on Castor's three-hundred-foot yacht.

Master Lee looked at the pictures and knew he could no longer continue to lie. Shaking his head, he sighed before explaining. "Okay, Castor invited me and a few other men on his yacht. He claimed he had been working on a new drug that is processed into a pill. Says it will make us all billionaires. Of course, I didn't believe him at first. That is until we saw first-hand what the drug does."

"What kind of pill are we talking about?" Shug asked.

"I don't know for certain. All I know is that it is manufactured with a combination of drugs like cocaine, heroin, PCP, and a whole lot of other ingredients, forming one black pill. It gives a high like no other."

"It's impossible to interlace all those drugs," Diamond stated emphatically.

Master Lee placed his hands on the table and folded them. "Do you remember when you first came to me as a young student? You told me you were one of the favored few who didn't have any enemies. Do you remember what I said?"

"Yes," Diamond responded, glancing at Shug. "How can I forget? You said that the devil's greatest trick was convincing the world that he did not exist."

"This is no different," Wong Lee explained. "Castor gave us a demonstration. Turns out that there's a genetic chemical that balances every compound. With it, the pill is extremely effective. It's not just a high; it gives a person amazing awareness and energy… energy that can be dangerous if placed in the wrong hands or used with the wrong mindset."

Diamond considered this startling piece of news. "Is this drug ready for the market by any chance?" she asked.

"No, not yet," Master Lee vindicated.

"And how do you know this?" Shug asked.

"Because if it was, I would be the first to buy," he confessed.

Diamond looked around the table at the men seated then back to Wong Lee. "Okay, so Castor is inventing a new drug," Diamond said, trying to figure this out. "What I don't get is why he invited *you* to come check it out. Doesn't he know you already manufacture your own designer drugs in China? Why would he want to mingle with the competition?"

"Castor wants to use my labs to create this drug."

"But if that's the case, won't *you* have the ingredients?" Shug asked. "Who's to say you won't just steal it and make the drug yourself?"

"This was the reason I went to Miami. I had to see for myself if, perhaps, it was that easy, but I found out that Castor isn't as foolish as he looks. He's only using my resources for manufacturing, not manpower. His chemist and his soldiers will be present to watch over the operation. He wants my people to distribute his product throughout China."

"What makes this drug better than Molly?" Diamond asked.

"Because of what it does to the brain cells. It enhances them to a higher level than I've ever seen. You think I'm crazy? Try watching one of the weakest members in your organization take down ten of your strongest. This drug isn't just some get-high; it's a super drug."

Hearing the words come out of Wong Lee's own mouth caused silence and trepidation within the group. Diamond looked away as she thought of what Verningo Castor was planning. If he was really creating a new drug that was worth billions of dollars, then their whole organization was clearly at risk.

Chapter Fifty

Fatal Attraction

"If it's destined for us to meet again…"

— DIAMOND

Montega, Abdullah, and Taliban pulled up to the front of the Phoenix and shut off the engine. A valet stood by the front, waiting to park their car. "You can leave it running. I'll only be a minute," Taliban told him as he followed his brother inside. Montega had just come from the doctor's office. He sprained his finger and now had to wear a soft cast.

"I still can't believe Reek set you up. Don't he know that we're gonna kill his bitch-ass?" Taliban asked as they walked into the lobby. "He's not gonna make any more money in the 'Ville. He's history. Now the blocks gonna be wide open, just waiting for us to take it."

He was staring at Abdullah and the ridiculous attire he had on. He really did look like a Muslim. "You know, for someone so holy, you sure did have my back, back there," he said.

Montega didn't respond to his brother's remarks toward Abdullah. His eyes were scanning the lobby as they advanced to the front.

"All praises are due to the Most High and most merciful," Abdulallah said calmly while carefully scrutinizing the scene.

There were only a few people waiting to talk to the woman at the front desk. He had already gotten the key from Misty, who was out on vacation, but he needed to talk to the clerk anyway to see if they offered twenty-four-hour concierge and room service.

Out front, the Range Rover limousine pulled up to the entrance. Diamond sat across from Shug, pondering the information she had gotten from Wong Lee. She looked at the entrance and watched the valet approach.

"I heard you have a problem here in Philly," she pointed out.

"There's no problem here. Everything's under control," Shug stated.

"That's not what I heard. The sooner you admit to it rather than soak in denial, we can handle the situation properly. This Montega has killed twice already. There's no telling what he's up to or who he will target next." She looked Shug in the eye. "Actually, we know who he's coming after. He's still here in the city, and no one's made a move on him yet. That seems like a big problem to me."

Shug could feel his anger beginning to rise. He had a sour taste for authority and even more so for women who showed it.

"I said I'll handle it. I don't need your help."

"Yes you do."

"No I don't," he said firmly. "Let's be straight up for a moment. I've been doing this shit since you were trying to find a date to the prom. When you were at the mall, looking for an outfit to wear with your little girlfriends, I was looking for a spot to ditch a dead body. Don't think for a second that you know more about the streets than I do. Yeah, Montega is here in the city, but he's hiding. The moment he shows his face will be the moment it gets blown off. Now you have a nice day and enjoy your stay in *my* city."

The door opened. Diamond forced a smile at Shug then stepped out. Bain and four other men surrounded her with her luggage. Shug didn't wait to see if she made it safely inside. He just ordered his driver to pull off.

After Montega spoke with the clerk, he turned to speak with his brother and Abdulallah.

"Yo, I'ma need you to take care of a few things. The bol Stormin' Norman waiting for a delivery in Jersey. I need you to take it to him. He already paid for the work upfront."

"How much do you want me to take to him?" Taliban asked.

"Five chickens."

"Damn, Norm coppin' 'em like that?"

"Yeah, but you know what's funny though? Norm was once under the bol Fly-Ty. Remember when he came looking for Mike a few years back, and he had you get him a soda from out of the Chinese store?"

"Nah, I don't remember that," Taliban lied as he looked away with embarrassment.

"Yeah, well, Norm was the guy in the passenger side. My point is, he was Fly-Ty's lieutenant; now he's serving Fly-Ty and all the rest of them dudes from Jersey. See how fast the tables turn?"

Taliban didn't hear his brother. His eyes gazed upon the woman who had just walked into the building.

"Damn, bro. Look at shorty right there."

Abdulallah was the first to observe what was amongst them. His eyes bulged more than he dared to admit. "Sub-hena-allah," he gasped.

Montega turned for a glance that ended up becoming a stare. His mouth opened slightly, but nothing came out.

"Shaytan has done it again," Abdulallah said while finding it hard to look away. "He has placed before us the jinn of all jinns."

Montega ignored his righteous homie and continued to enjoy his view of the woman in leopard print. He recognized her from Atlanta. She had the same group of stiffs with her, including the seven-footer. He didn't see the priest however.

The woman's eyes scanned the lobby and fell upon his. She stopped unexpectedly. The big guy with her did the same. He noticed the look on her face then reached into his lapel for his gun.

Abdulallah began to rise so he could reach for his first.

Diamond quickly stopped her bodyguard. "No, Bain... it's... it's nothing."

Bain looked at the three frozen men then back at his boss. He released the handle, nodded, and led the way to the elevator. Montega and Taliban couldn't seem to move. Abdualallah, on the other hand, lowered his gaze. "Kafrs," he said with disgust. "A -ou-tho-bela-hemanal-shaytan-neer-ra-jeen!"

Diamond glanced at them again but continued on the elevator.

"What was that all about?" Taliban asked.

"I don't know. Maybe that was her man."

"That was one jealous muthafucka. You know what? I'm not gonna stick around here too long. This ain't even my type of environment. It's too snobby for hood-rich niggas like us. Right, Nino?"

"My attribute is Abdulallah, and I'm not rich nor a nigga. I'm a Muslim. But I agree with you. These devils need to fear Allah and repent."

"Whatever *he* said, so I'll get at you, bro." Taliban gave his brother some dap then turned for the exit.

"Assalamu Alaikum," Abdulallah said before following him out.

When Montega arrived at Misty's suite, he immediately fell in love with the amount of space he had. He walked to the window and frowned. The view wasn't exactly what he expected. The buildings across the street blocked most of the scenery. The suite wasn't high enough to see the city like he wanted to, which disappointed him. After showering, he took a nap, which felt like a full eight hours.

He awoke to find the room dark. He checked his watch and saw that it was only 9:30 p.m. From there, he got out of bed and dressed himself in a black and white polo with black trousers and a pair of black leather Salvatore Ferragamo sneakers. He then brushed his hair and teeth, sprayed some Chanel Allure cologne on, and then headed down to the bar. The Phoenix had a mini-club down on the first floor. There was a small crowd of individuals surrounded by blue lights and glass counters.

Eurythmics "Sweet Dreams" played from the system while some of the people talked and drank. Montega spotted a few stiffs that didn't belong. That was when he saw her sitting at the counter. He smirked before approaching her. She just so happened to be babysitting a Bloody Mary. She looked up and shook the tresses of her hair from her face. Her eyes were glued to his even before he took a seat beside her.

"Hi," he said.

Diamond smiled shyly but didn't speak. She wasn't sure what to do. It had been so long since she'd spoken with someone outside of business. This didn't bother Montega one bit. He took notice of her attire. She no longer wore the leopard-printed skirt with the gold blouse. Now she looked more casual.

"Can I get you something, sir?" the barmaid asked.

Montega fought to rip his eyes away from the woman beside him and said, "I'll have a triple shot of Gray Goose and pineapple juice, please." He then looked over at Diamond again as if he were afraid she would disappear. "Can I offer you a drink?"

"No, thank you," she said, causing the barmaid to retreat and prepare his order. "I'm not much of a drinker, as you can see."

"That's good. You don't take me as a woman who drowns her sorrow in alcohol when things get stressful. What is your secret? Yoga?"

Diamond smirked and entertained this question.

"Tai Chi," she replied.

Montega's eyebrows raised. "Wow. I'm impressed. I strongly admire a woman who takes care of her body," he said, sticking his hand out. "I'm Kenny."

Diamond grabbed her bag from the counter and replied, "And I'm leaving."

"What's the rush? It's only a little after ten. Why don't you just have one drink with me?"

Diamond stood then looked at Montega. She wasn't sure about him. Her instincts usually played an important role in her decision making, but nothing seemed to work right. When that happened, she was liable to make mistakes. She'd done it before, and the results were never good. She looked at her watch and then at him.

"Why do you want me to have a drink with you so badly? And be honest."

Montega smiled with an infectious grin. "Because I got this feeling about you. It's weird, but I feel like I know you from somewhere. I think I've seen you before, and when I saw you in Atlanta, I thought to myself, '*How did I let her get away from me?*' Then I let it happen a second time when the big guy went to draw on me and my boys. Now I see you here, there's no way in hell I'm gonna let you get away from me again."

"That's sweet," Diamond said, bemused. "But unfortunately, I do have to go." Diamond studied his face for deception. If there was any, she hadn't noticed.

"Why, when we have so much chemistry at the moment?"

"What do you know about chemistry?" Diamond grinned.

Montega glanced around and said, "I know a thing or two that will blow your mind." The barmaid brought his drink. "But seriously, I would really like to get to know you. You seem like a nice girl and all. So why don't you stay for a while and have that drink?"

Diamond studied the handsome man in front of her. She really wanted to take him up on his offer, but something just didn't sit well with her.

"Let me ask you something. Do you believe in fate?" she asked.

"No, but I believe in destiny."

"Good, because if it's destined for us to bump heads again, then maybe I might have that drink with you. Right now, I'm going through something, and I don't think I need any company with it." She slung the strap to her bag over her shoulder and said, "Enjoy your night, handsome."

Montega watched as she walked off, shifting her hips and round ass like the confident woman she was. Her backside was lovely and couldn't be missed. Her walk made him feel as if no other woman existed. From each side of the bar, the stiffs began to rise and follow her out.

Montega took down the liquor with a new profound desire. He wanted her. If she was an angel, then she was heaven sent, but if she was truly the devil's spawn like Nino thought, then he would just have to be hell bound. One way or another, he would travel far and wide and would not stop until he captured that woman's heart, stolen like a thief in the night… the same way she did his.

Chapter Fifty-One

Sleeping With The Enemy

"Kenny, what do you truly want from me?"

— DIAMOND

After a tremendous workout at the Phoenix's gym, Montega strolled to the indoor swimming pool where he could get a couple of good laps in. Ever since the recent attempt on his life, his paranoia wouldn't allow him to leave the building. He loved Misty's condo. It was a much safer atmosphere, one that he was getting comfortable with.

When he walked into the large room with the Olympic-size pool, he was surprised to see the same four stiffs posted on each side of the pool. They were watching the female swim. Montega slowed his pace to observe. Her endurance impressed him as she swam lap for lap. He sat in one of the white beach chairs and opened the Philadelphia Inquirer and read the headline: **WAR IN THE STREETS**. He knew his team was making a lot of noise lately throughout the city. Their reputation was slowly spreading from hood to hood like a virus.

Bain sat across the pool, watching him like a hawk. He rarely forgot a face. This was the same guy he saw when they were checking in, which left him suspicious.

When Diamond finished her laps, she pulled herself out of the warm pool. Water cascaded down her body. She shook out her hair but stopped when something caught her attention. An odd look of disbelief crept across her face as she walked over to the gentleman with the blue Polo swim trunks and wife-beater, who was sitting on her towel. Recognizing him from the bar, she tried to suppress her grin.

"Excuse me, but you're sitting on my towel," she said, trying to keep a straight face.

When Montega put the paper down and looked up, he slowly slid the towel from under him and handed it to her. His eyes lustfully scanned up her smooth calves and juicy, elongated thighs that created a gap between her legs. There, he could see her ass cheeks from the front. She was blessed with curvaceous hips, a washboard stomach, and bulging breasts. Diamond took the towel and began to dry her hair first.

"I'm sorry, Miss, but I just got this feeling I know you from somewhere," Montega said with a smirk.

Diamond couldn't help but play along with his little game. "That's funny, because I was just thinking the same about you." She turned to see Bain's hand in his lapel and quickly shook her head no. The rest of the men also understood the gesture and stood down.

Montega couldn't help but stare. The bikini she wore left little to the imagination.

He rose to his feet and stuck his hand out. "I'm Kenny," he said for a second time.

She looked at his hand for a moment, sighed, and took it.

"I'm... Dee," she replied.

"Are you a resident here, Dee?"

"No, I'm just visiting the city."

Montega brought her hand to his lips and kissed the back of it. She flushed shyly. She hadn't done that in years. She had almost forgotten what it felt like.

"Well, Dee, it's a pleasure to finally meet you. I guess destiny works in mysterious ways, right?"

Diamond shrugged bashfully. "What makes you think this is destiny?" she questioned.

"What makes you think it isn't?"

"I asked you first."

Montega studied her face, ignoring her question. "You mind telling me your nationality?" he asked.

Diamond looked away to fight the urge of entertaining his question, but somehow, she gave in.

Turning to look back at him, she said, "My mother is Italian and Cuban. My father was Black."

"That's interesting," Montega said, stroking his beard.

"Why is that?"

"Because I can tell a lot about you already just from the three races."

"Oh, really?" she asked folding her arms. "Please, continue. I'd love to hear your assessment of me."

"Well, Cuban tells me that you have rebellion in your blood, along with survival. Italian means you're smart, short-tempered, and well organized, and Black… well, let's just say, Black dominates them all. It's like an enhancement pill, for instance. It intensifies all those great qualities you have, inside and out, making you a beautiful hybrid."

Chewing on her bottom lip, Diamond broke her gaze and looked away. He was too charming for her not to continue flushing with interest. His body looked ripped and wide at the shoulders. He had well-formed traps, a deliciously carved chest, sharp abs, and strong legs. For a man who was barely over 180 pounds, he was perfect. Her eyes wandered down to where his print bulged from his shorts. Montega caught her staring before she looked away. He then tried to act as if he didn't notice. Secretly, his confidence shot to the roof.

"So are you stayin' for a while?" he asked. "If you want, I'd be happy to show you around the city. You can consider me your personal tour guide."

"How can I say no to that when you advertise so well?" she asked innocently.

Montega continued sizing her up, figuring she had to be a tease. "An enemy of the moon," he blurted out.

"Excuse me?" Diamond asked, trying to comprehend what he just said.

"I'm sorry. I was just thinking out loud."

"You said something about the moon's enemy."

Montega nodded.

Curious, Diamond asked, "What did you mean by that?"

"You. You're the enemy of the moon. Only a star as bright as you could steal its shine."

"So what does that make you?" she asked with a curious expression.

Montega shrugged, took a chance, and reached out to touch her cheek. She allowed it. "I guess that might make me your biggest fan ever."

Diamond laughed at his sense of humor then looked deeply into his eyes. She had never been so attracted to someone like this before in her life. This was beyond scary. It was magnetic. *He does look familiar,* she thought, but there was no way she could have met him before. He was from Philly, and she, from L.A. Perhaps even two different worlds. *In-Yo*, she thought, which meant yin and yang in Japanese.

Montega showed no inhibition. He was forward, direct, and breezing right through her like the wind. When he saw that he had her full attention, he made a suggestion. "You know what? Why don't you come to my place, and we can have that drink we were *destined* for?"

"No, that won't be necessary," Diamond replied, pulling back while letting her rejection marinate. "But you can come up to *my* place if you want."

Montega displayed a suave smile. "You got some shit with you, Miss Dee. However, it's crazy because it's like I've met you before in another life."

"Can you please stop with the sweettalking? You're not that good at it," Diamond lied as she wrapped herself in a towel and headed for the exit.

Montega followed her out of the room. One at a time, the henchmen did the same.

When the two got up to the top floor, Montega was mesmerized as he entered the penthouse. The place was an enormous 3,900 square feet. It featured a large living room and three bedrooms. Diamond made her guards stay in the lounging area. She figured she could handle one man on her own, so she headed for the bathroom.

"I'm gonna take a shower to rinse off. The bar's over there if you want something to drink. The remote to the TV is here. Be careful… It's universal and controls everything in the condo. Make yourself at home," she said, disappearing beyond the foyer.

Montega walked to the bar and poured himself a glass of Patrón to loosen up. His mind asked questions like, *who was this woman, and why did she need so much security?* When he heard the shower turning, he decided to have a look around the extravagant suite. His curiosity was getting the best of him. For a woman that needed five bodyguards with her must have meant she was royalty. The fact that she chose him to kick it with had Montega feeling himself.

The condo was just too big for one woman. It had a spectacular view of the Benjamin Franklin Parkway. The Art Museum loomed in the distance, and the lights from the city shined brighter than a Christmas tree at night. After looking through the first two bedrooms, he bugged out. The master bedroom was huge. It had a sitting room and its own terrace with sliding doors.

As Montega walked to open it, his eyes focused on the weapon sitting on the enormous king-size bed, next to a cap of black lipstick. Taking a few steps forward, he saw it was a gold-plated mini AK-74, almost exactly like the one he had mounted on his wall in the cave.

Kalashnikov, he thought as he picked it up. He knew it held 7.62x39mm bullets inside a fifty-round banana clip. He raised it toward a full-length mirror, closed one eye to check the sighting, and aimed at his reflection.

"What are you doing?" a voice said behind him, causing him to drop the gun back on the bed.

Diamond had a towel wrapped around her body from her breasts down to her thighs. Her feet were bare, her hair damp and pulled back.

"I was, ah... just makin' myself at home, so I took a tour around the place. It's pretty nice, I must say."

Diamond stared at him suspiciously for a moment. But when he smiled, there was something that fought her anger away. "Look. When I said make yourself at home, I didn't mean come into my bedroom and invade my privacy," she said, walking by him with the smell of Dove body soap fuming from her pores. She picked up the gun and set it on the nightstand.

"My fault, shorty. Truth is, I'm just cautious when it comes to meeting new people. Maybe I'm just paranoid like that. I'll tell you what. I'ma step out an—"

"No," Diamond said, stopping him. "You're here now." She grabbed the blow dryer from her dresser. "You might as well stay. You want to ask me a question, ask. I have nothing to hide."

Montega studied her demeanor for a moment before walking toward the door and shutting it. She didn't have to tell him twice. "What's the choppa for?" he asked before sitting down on the bed next to her.

"It's not mine. It belongs to one of my bodyguards."

"Your *bodyguards?* What are you? A superstar or somethin'? What you need a bunch of stiffs to pose as bodyguards for?"

Diamond smiled at his sense of humor. "I'm a very important woman, Kenny—one that needs protection," she replied curtly, placing the gun and the lipstick on the nightstand.

"So you're royalty. That explains it. In fact... where are your bodyguards now?" he asked while tilting his head to the side and taking a chance by putting his hand on her smooth, moist leg.

"You really don't know who you're dealing with, do you?" she asked, looking down at his hand, expecting him to move it.

She could break his arm quicker than he could blink, but she was so turned on by his directness that violence was the last thing on her mind. She tried to act casual by crossing her legs. Seeing that she didn't remove his hand, Montega slowly inched it up her towel. Diamond gasped softly as her eyes slowly closed.

"No, wait." She sighed before placing her hand on top of his to stop him.

"What's wrong?"

Diamond dropped her head. "I shouldn't be doing this. I mean, I hardly know you. For all I know, you could be here to kill me," she said modestly.

Montega twisted his lips as he looked into her eyes. *Is she serious?* He thought. *I'm not the one armed with a gold-plated machine gun. She must be crazy.*

"What do you feel when I touch you?" he asked before licking his lips with hooded eyes.

"I don't know," she lied.

"I think you do. I think you feel the same way as I do. You just don't want to admit it. I was never good at the cat and mouse games, Dee. Besides, we have all the time in the world to get to know each other, but right now, let's not waste any more of it with doubts when we both know this is everything we've ever wanted from the start."

Diamond looked down at where she stopped his hand. Slowly, she released it. No man had ever had that much puissance over her so quickly. This was different. This was scary. This was magnetic. This was destiny.

His gaze shifted to her face even as his fingers continued to follow their seductive path. He eased between places where not a single grain of hair existed. She closed her eyes and uncrossed her moist thighs as his fingers traced her pink pearl. She gasped harshly.

He pressed a soft kiss on the tip of her shoulder then began his gentle assault on her neck. Diamond tilted her head to the side, letting her hair swing out of his way. Slow, biting kisses invoked desire within her. Her breathing became erratic. Her breasts rose and fell quickly to his touch. His fingers were soaked with her juices. She now had both her hands pressed to the bed behind her to hold herself up. He tugged on her towel. The soft, damp fabric slid from across her breasts and stomach, teasing her skin as it slowly peeled away to expose her to the room's temperature.

Her breasts were swollen and appealing. With his free hand,

Montega squeezed the closest one to him and smothered his face with it. His tongue swirled around her hard, brown nipple, causing her body to tense from such a thrill. His hand came from between her thighs, dripping wet. His face moved from her breasts to her ear. She felt helpless when she looked into the darkness of his beautiful eyes. He was now talking calmly. Even his words felt like intercourse.

"Lay back for me, sexy, and let me take care of you the right way," he whispered.

Instantly, he got a perfect view of her heavenly body.

As he moved between her legs, he could feel the tension in her gaze. It was like she was a virgin. He stared at her first before he entered her.

Diamond reached for his face and brought him directly in front of her. *Why am I doing this?* she thought.

"Kenny, what do you really want from me?" she whispered passionately while looking into his brown, lustful eyes.

Montega admired her intimidating beauty and said, "Truthfully, I just want to fuck you… to the point you'll always remember this day. Now lay back and close your eyes."

Diamond did as he said.

Montega moved back down so she could feel his warm breath touching her skin as he made his way between her legs. There, he began to feast on her inner flesh.

Oh my God, Diamond said in her head. *This is unbelievable.* "Ummm, don't stop!" She gasped as she rubbed her fingers through his wavy hair while grinding her delicious treasure into his face.

Montega sucked and concentrated on her hard, pink pearl until his tongue got numb and the back of his head started to ache. Diamond squirmed in the middle of the bed, looking up at the ceiling fan as it slowly spun around and around. She didn't realize the fan wasn't even on. It was her own mind that was spinning. Montega was divine with his tongue. He worked his way from her love box down to her feet then up her thighs to her breasts, tasting every inch of her body. He then returned to her wet crotch.

"Kenny, please… stop. I can't… take it any… moreeee," she

whined out.

Montega tore his face away from her the way a lion did when feasting. He stood on his knees and began removing his clothes. His eyes never left the magnificent body lying in front of him on the bed.

When he removed all of his clothes, Diamond didn't realize her mouth was wide open when she saw what he was packing. He climbed on the bed. She sat up to kiss him. His thick-lip kisses put her on her back once more as he moved his waist between her legs. Their kisses were devouring with passion. Her legs wedged the outside of his hips. Her arms wrapped around his neck. She raised her hips as he entered her then caught her breath before he impatiently slammed into her in a desperate quest for union. The feeling of glory, ecstasy, and magic appeared within every stroke.

He listened to her harsh breaths every time he slid inside of her.

His body sealed itself to hers while their lustful embrace took them to another world. She had known pleasure before, but not like this. What he did to her destroyed the protective walls that surrounded her emotions, leaving it as naked and vulnerable as her body. It was as if he were claiming her soul, which was something she was truly afraid of.

He came back down into her arms once again. Diamond enjoyed the connection of their skin. She wrapped her arms around him and felt the ripples along his back. She then raised her forehead and moaned as she felt him deep inside of her. He sucked on her smooth chin, kissing her jaw line as her mouth opened and shut with every thrust he delivered. She rocked with each form of penetration, milking him for every inch he gave her until it became too unbearable to continue. Her legs quivered with ecstasy.

Montega swam her tight channel in the middle of the bed, bringing her to a full climax. He didn't care who she'd been with in the past or whom she saw herself with in the future. He was determined to change the way she viewed sex and, most importantly, the way she viewed a man from the streets. He was going all out. He made his dick dig deep inside of her, venturing the places even she didn't know existed. When she shouted out a passionate moan, he paused for a brief moment to look at the lustful frown in her arched eyebrows. Diamond was as intense as she was beautiful. He wanted her to absorb his fullness. Raising up on his arms, he rolled his hips out of her then back inside her again. Every stroke was a touch of ecstasy that needed to be savored.

She placed both hands on his face as he spoke to her softly.

"You take me as a woman who likes to give orders. Well, tell me you want me to fuck you from the back," he said between his slow rhythms.

Diamond's hands trembled. She slid her fingers across his face and down to his thick lips and said, "I want you to fuck me any way you see fit; just don't stop when you do. No matter how much I tell you it hurts, no matter how loud I scream, just fuck me senseless. That's an order," she purred.

Montega kissed her hard on the lips then turned her around on her stomach and positioned himself behind her. Grabbing her slim waist, he brought her ass up in the air and entered her tight pussy. He splashed deep within, colliding his skin against hers. Her heart-shaped ass was incredible, soft, and warm. Her breasts were extra juicy yet firm, and her nipples were like two three-carat diamonds. He bought her backside to his pelvis with gruesome force. True to her word, Diamond screamed and moaned and clawed at the sheets. The sound of applause came from their rapid connection. Montega's excitement began to weaken. Watching the show before him brought him to a peak.

He stopped to catch his breath, but Diamond wouldn't let him off the hook. Thrusting her ass back at him, he watched as she swallowed every inch of his erection before spitting it back out. He joined her once more, pounding deeper and deeper. Her skin slapping against his pelvis continued to fill the room.

Stretching her arms out, she gripped the sheets and arched her back. Montega slowly plunged inside of her then pulled back out to see a slick coating on his dick. He then hit it harder until his thrust sounded like gunshots. Tears rolled down Diamond's face from his long strokes. His hand cupped her breasts, and his fingers wedged her erect nipples between each other. The sensation caused her to stuff her face into the pillow and cry with joy.

Before she could do anything, he rolled her over onto her back, looked into her eyes, and stuffed it back inside of her. Her mascara was ruined, running down her cheek. Out of breath, Diamond brought his lips to hers and kissed him softly. Their bodies grinded in the middle of the bed. It blew her mind to feel the definition of his rock-hard frame that glistened with sweat as he gave her the greatest sex she had ever felt.

She closed her eyes and clawed at his scarred back as she climaxed again. She wrapped her arms and legs around him and rolled them over until she was on top. Montega's fingers slipped through her long, dark hair, causing her to buck as she rode his dick with persistence.

Her juices burst out of her like a broken water pipe, soaking him and the sheets they lay on. Montega's hands gripped her wide hips and pulled her to him, making more clapping noises. Her breasts bounced on impact. Her moans filled the room.

He loved how she grinded her hips against his. She watched his face writhe with beads of sweat dripping into his eyes.

Just when she thought it was over, he reversed her blissful toucher and maneuvered her onto her back again. "Nooo," she whined, certain she had had enough, but Montega had her pinned down.

Hooking her under the armpits and locking onto her shoulders for more leverage, he gave her the platinum fuck of her life. Diamond clenched her teeth and growled as she made herself take his thrust. She dug her nails into his back, drawing blood this time until he exploded inside of her. He had never moaned like he'd done at that moment. It was as if the life inside of him was being sucked out.

When it was over, he flopped down on her chest, exhausted. His back looked like Kunta Kinte's after being beaten with a whip. He didn't say a word, but Diamond, who was also breathing heavily, surprised him with, "That was really, really, good." She displayed a satisfied smile then looked at him and said, "Let's do it again."

Montega matched her grin and kissed her on the cheek.

"I thought you'd never ask," he replied before rolling over on to his back. Diamond didn't have to be told what to do. She leaned over his manhood, her hair blocking the view as her mouth sank down onto his lap.

Never had she experienced such pleasure in her life. *This man can't be human,* she thought. He just had to be some type of sex god sent down to her. He knew what to do and where to maneuver his shaft without her directing him.

Once she had him stiff again, she threw her arms around him, kissed his forehead, and smiled before his lips met hers, followed by his tongue. She then mounted him once more. It was blissful all over again.

Chapter Fifty-Two

The Man Behind The Mask

"Please tell me you have a picture of Montega..."

— DIAMOND

Diamond's moans filled the spacious bathroom of the Franklin Institute Museum. Montega had her back against the wall of a toilet stall.

"Shhh, you too loud," he grunted out as their bodies moved as one against the wall.

"Well, stop fuckin' me like this."

"For what? You know you love this dick," Montega whispered before pecking her on the lips.

"I dooo, sss, love it. Ummm, do you feel that!" Diamond asked before biting down on her bottom lip while closing her eyes.

For the past two weeks, Montega and Diamond had been like peanut butter and jelly. He took her everywhere—to see the Liberty Bell, historical museums, and all the usual tourist attractions in Philadelphia. They went out to jog Kelly Drive then went back to the penthouse with some of the best Philly cheesesteaks in town. On one particular night, they went to the Walnut Street Theatre to see a play then afterward to Penn's Landing to sit and talk.

Then the following morning, Montega took her to a basketball game on Wister Street where they received nothing but curious eyes.

Montega hadn't seen anyone he associated with there, so he took her to Blakemore Street and brought her and her bodyguard a chicken wing platter with shrimp-fried rice.

Normally, Diamond wouldn't dare try something like that, but for him, she did, and she liked it. She never knew Chinese food was so good, especially from the slums.

No matter where they ventured, they always managed to get a spontaneous quickie in. Crammed into a restroom, Diamond kept her arms and legs wrapped around him tightly as she climaxed. Montega clenched his jaw while thrusting faster. He let out a sharp gasp, getting his as well.

"Damn, this pussy is the best," he confessed.

He pulled out of her and fixed himself up. Diamond went in her bag and pulled out baby wipes and cleaned them both off.

She had never done anything so spontaneous. If her girlfriend Mercades were still alive, Diamond wondered what she would have thought if she knew she was getting fucked in a toilet stall. She caught Montega staring at her and smiled bashfully.

"You ready?" he asked calmly, taking her hand.

She nodded while clipping a strand of hair behind her ear. When the two stepped out of the stall, an old lady who was washing her hands stared at them convictingly. Diamond patted Montega on the dick and whispered in his ear, "What's she lookin' at?"

"I don't know, with her old dried-up pussy," he joked.

He followed Diamond out of the bathroom, trying to keep from laughing while shaking his head. Bain waited by the door quietly with the others. When the two emerged, they were escorted to the black Rolls Royce Phantom double parked out front.

Montega looked over at the seven-foot block of granite and asked, "Does bol ever say anything?"

"Only when he doesn't get paid," she joked.

"Now, I feel that," he replied as the two got into the back seat of the sedan.

"So, handsome, what are you doin' later on?" she asked while playing in his wavy hair.

Montega froze in a daze. He began to look around as if experiencing a dose of déjà vu.

"Are you alright?" Diamond asked with concern.

"Yeah, I'm… I'm straight," he replied, shaking off his foolish imagination. "I gotta go pick up my car in a few, but after that, my schedule is empty. Why? What you wanna do?" he asked, brushing a strand of Diamond's hair behind her ear to stroke her cheek with his thumb.

She put a hand on his and held it there.

"Well, I was hoping we could go eat at this restaurant I read about in the paper. It's on 1338 Chestnut street."

"I think I know which one you're talkin' about. We can do that. You just make sure your fine ass is there," Montega said, intertwining his fingers with hers and kissing the back of her hand.

"Oh, if your sexy ass will be there, then so will I. And…" She leaned in to kiss him and whispered, "I won't be wearing any panties either. So you know what's for dessert."

Montega looked into Diamond's beautiful eyes with a look of pure desire. *Either she's the one, or I'm caught in the Matrix,* he thought, quoting Jay-Z.

Diamond had her driver take Montega to the police impound lot so he could get his car. He had already explained to her half the truth about his homie getting killed at a club and his car being held as evidence. Diamond thought nothing of it until they pulled up to the gate. Her attention was on the black car that was waiting out front. The car had a custom ram air hood with a low bumper and side skirts like a huge race car.

"There go my baby," Montega said, pointing to the car with the silver Chevy emblem on the grill.

Diamond hid her suspicion well. "What kind of car is that?" she asked as her heart started to thud.

"Oh, that? That's a '96 Impala SS. Probably the fastest ever built," he bragged before stealing a kiss on her cheek and getting out.

Diamond's whole world seemed to turn upside down in that instant. *It can't possibly be him,* she told herself while pondering the coincidence. She then got on the phone and called Shug. On the first ring, he picked up.

"If you called to ridicule—"

"No, it's nothing like that," she said, cutting him off.

"Then what seems to be the problem?" he asked smoothly.

Diamond took a deep breath and said, "Please tell me you have a picture of this guy, Montega."

Chapter Fifty-Three

Family Ties

"She's his sister…"

— GEE

"Did y'all see the news yesterday?" Breezy asked her girlfriends, Kia and Tee-Tee, and her cousin, Gi-Gi. "Man-Man from Bloomsburg got killed in his apartment the night before. They said some guys ran up in there and killed him. It was like close to a hundred grand on the table, and they ain't take none of it. That was my dog too. It's fucked up how a person could be talking to you one day then gone the next."

"That's crazy. These dudes out here is the worst. They don't even want money anymore; they just wanna kill. I heard Stormin' Norman's homie Fly-Ty got killed last week in a big shootout with Spade and all them guys from South Philly. They said Two-Face Tone killed him. His mom was so messed up over his death; she had a nervous breakdown," Kia replied.

Gi-Gi shook her head. "Wasn't he with the Silent Kings?"

"Shit, Gi, ever since my brother started getting money, damn near half the city is connected with the Silent Kings. They got T-shirts with those gagged skull heads wearing crowns, hats, jewelry, and bumper stickers. I even seen the bol Fresh, you know, the DJ who be at Chrome. I seen him drivin' an Expedition with that Silent King logo painted all over it. I guess they got a rap group out now. The only one that seems to be out of the loop is their homie Nino. He look like he on his deep hard."

"Tell me about it," Amber said. "He gonna come up to me and say 'Sista, you Muslim, ain't you?' I was like 'yeah, so?' He gonna say, 'Subhenna allah. You need to guard your Chasity and that I got all these brothers sinning with their eyes. I started to check his ass, but I couldn't even get mad at him. I just walked away."

Just then, Amber spotted a group of females she didn't like. When she saw who they were flirting with, she brought it to Kia's attention. "Unh-unh, look who your brother talkin' to over there. Ain't that Sakeena, with her whore ass? I'm 'bout to go say somethin'," she said, ready to start a fight in the mall.

When Taliban spotted them, he quickly jotted down the number that Sakeena's girlfriend Jovanna gave him. His two favorite young bols, Jay and Mac, were with him. They were the first to notice Taliban's sister and tapped their old head.

Kia placed her hand on her hip as her brother strolled toward them. He thought he was killing 'em in a pair of black Ralph Lauren jeans, a LRG vest over a long sleeve Polo shirt that matched his hat, tan butters, and Cartier sunglasses.

"This asshole here, man," Kia said, disgusted.

"Yo," he said, giving Breezy a hug first like he hadn't seen her in months. He then hugged Amber and tried to grab her butt. She pushed him away quickly, leaving him to hug his sister. As he went to extend his arms, Kia stepped back.

"Don't try to hug me. I told you about goin' against the grain. You and Kenny keep on fuckin' with these whores. Watch, they gonna end up cuttin' ya dick right off, Rafeek." Kia sneered.

"Yo, man, why you spillin' out my government like that? Fuck is wrong with you, girl? See, that's what I'm talkin' 'bout, man. You always trippin' when you get around your girlfriends. You worse than these hoes."

"Don't compare me to none of your dirty ass bitches. What I look like? By the way, you were supposed to do something for Gi-Gi, weren't you?" Kia reminded him. "And what happened to the money you were supposed to bring five days ago when I told your dumbass I was trying to pay the mortgage on my house? What was it you said when I was gonna have my dude Larry do it for me? 'Naw, fuck that. My sister ain't gotta ask no man for money. I got this.' It's because of you I woulda missed my payment if it hadn't been for Larry."

Taliban was caught, dead-to-rights. "You see, what happened was, I got caught up in some—"

"Oh, yeah? Fo'real, Rafeek?" Breezy broke in, interrupting his lame excuse. "That's corny. You can give all these nothing ass bitches money but can't even lookout for your own peoples. You wrong."

"What! Aye, Bree, why don't you find something safe to play with, because ain't no dildos over here," he said, grabbing his package. "This real dick. Y'all all up in my square like you the Feds or something. I see why half y'all can't keep a man. Back to you, Gi-Gi. You need some money? Huh?"

He went into his pocket and pulled out a wad of Ben Franklins that got caught in the mouth of his pocket. He yanked it out and started counting hundreds.

"Rafeek, I don't want cha money. Y'all eatin' too much for me. The way you act, you probably got the Feds watchin' you, for real. The last thing I need is for them to take my shop and everything I worked for," Gi-Gi joked.

Taliban animatedly looked around to see if there really was someone watching him. He quickly stuffed the money back in his pocket and fixed his shades over his bloodshot eyes. He was high as the north star.

"Where is your brother? He another one who don't call nobody any more to let them know he alright. What's up with him?" Gi-Gi asked.

"Man, he coolin'. He be in the Cave, planning his next move. He antisocial, nahmean?"

"The Cave?" Breezy said, curling her top lip with her neck thrusted back. "Who he think he is? Bin Laden? Y'all are too much for me. He feelin' himself; you feelin' yourself. Y'all need to sit down somewhere before y'all get killed. It's real out in them streets, boy. People are really dying, and y'all walkin' 'round with a hundred bags of clothes and sneakers like y'all can't be touched. I'm tellin' you, Shug ain't the type of dude to sleep on."

"Man, fuck Shug! Bol don't put no fear in my heart, gang. He bleed and breathe just like us. Watch, his end is comin'. That's on Stacy," Taliban exclaimed, swearing on his mother.

"Yeah, his end definitely comin' because my brother, Tooky, on his way home. And he ain't tryna hear no bullshit. He gonna take back what belong to him," Gi-Gi boasted, causing everyone to turn and stare at her with frowns.

Gi-Gi had been claiming that her older brother was coming home for over a decade now, and still, he hadn't shown his face. Everyone knew that Tooky had life without parole. It had been so long since he and his team ruled the streets of Philly; three generations had come and gone. Everything had changed now, and no one gave a damn who he was or what he would do if he ever got out.

"First off, Gi-Gi, let's get something straight," Taliban proclaimed. "A nigga ain't gonna take a damn thing from me unless he takin' a headshot. Second, your brother is as washed-up as a wet food stamp. Get over it. He ain't comin' home. Even if he did, all his squad is either dead or booked for life, just like him. This a new day, baby girl. Dudes gettin' money over here. And if you ain't running toward it, you better run from it because we runnin' niggas over—point, blank, period."

Before anyone could respond, his phone buzzed with Montega's name displayed across the screen. "I gotta take this. Enjoy y'all day. And tell Tamie over at Gucci's that everything is on me today. I'm showin' love," he bragged before walking off with the phone held up to his ear.

As Kia watched him, Breezy leaned over her best friend's shoulder. "You know, Kia, as much as I can't stand Kenny, I'm glad he's the head of the Silent Kings because it would be a cold day in hell if Taliban ever had any real power."

Kia nodded in agreement. "You ain't never lied."

Shug sat in the restaurant on the first floor of the Marriot Hotel downtown, eating brunch by himself. With the *Inquirer* on one side and the *Daily News* on the other, he didn't know which to read first. Both would have information he was already aware of. In fact, he was behind half of it. Shug took a deep breath and sighed.

It had already been over two years since Kev's death, and still, he hadn't gotten his hands on Montega. Not only that, but he was also losing money in the street due to the war. As Shug sliced into his soft buttermilk pancakes, Gee headed toward him.

"Whoever this Montega is dealing with got top-notch product, cannon. He must be just givin' the shit away because when we ran up in Fly-Ty's crib, dude had ten bricks of pure coke with an alligator stamped on it," Gee stated.

"Alligator stamp," Shug repeated, trying to recall where he saw it before.

"Yeah, but, yo, I got the picture you asked for from that nightclub."

Gee went into his pocket and handed Shug the photos from when Gutter was mistakenly killed. Shug wiped his mouth and hands then looked through the pictures.

"Which one is him?" he asked.

Gee pointed to the man in the black leather Gucci jacket so that Shug could study his enemy. When he turned to the next photo, his thick neck snapped back in shock when he saw Montega's arm around Kia, and his lips pressed to her cheek. “He know Kia?” Shug asked as he glowered.

Gee smiled sinisterly.

“Do he know Kia? She’s his sister.”

Shug did a doubletake at the picture and immediately noticed the family ties. “You gotta be shittin’ me. All this time.” He shook his head with disappointment.

Chapter Fifty-Four

M.I.A

"So who the chick you sprung over?"

— JAZZ

After the horrendous day of shopping, Taliban sat on the block with E, J-Black, and a few other hustlers. The wind was biting under a cold, gray sky. December was slowly coming to an end, yet the beef seemed to continue, taking them into the year 2008. Finding out about Reek's betrayal, Taliban set out to kill him, only to find out that Reek had mysteriously disappeared. He stopped serving the hustlers from around the way, leaving Mike stranded. J-Black called his man E and had him relocate from Chew and Locust to Topside. E had his own plug. And whenever J-Black ran out of work, he would cop something small from him. Now E had the block to himself.

Taliban went into the passenger side of his car to get his ounce of yellow. As he dug into the glove compartment, Jazz pulled up alongside him in her sky-blue Audi A-5. She beeped the horn. Taliban was so frightened by the sudden sound that he fumbled with the jar and spilled it all over his clothes.

"What the fuck, gang!" he shouted in surprise.

Jazz, Amber, and Gi-Gi burst out laughing. "What the fuck is y'all beepin' the horn for like that? I could've shot one of y'all. You know what? Y'all gotta keep it movin'. This ain't no hangout spot here," he complained.

"Oh, whatever, boy," Jazz said. "You get some paper, now you think you Sosa. This ain't even your block." Gi-Gi giggled with amusement.

"Aye, Gi-Gi, I know you ain't over there laughin'. Don't make me put you out there."

"Fuck you, Rafeek. Ain't nobody scared of you," Gi-Gi spat.

"Boy, you are scattered," Jazz said before looking around. "Where is my brother?"

"Man, bol probably still with that rich broad he met downtown," Taliban replied.

"What? Montega got a rich chick?" Gi-Gi asked in shock. Her antennas were up, and the laughter was over.

"Do he," Taliban added, not seeing his brother's black car pull up. "She got him open too. In fact—"

Taliban stopped when he saw Jazz's eyes peering behind him. Turning around to see Montega there with Nino, he said, "Brotha!"

"Fuck outta here. I heard what you said," Montega replied as he walked past him to give Jazz a hug.

"Hey, boo," Jazz said. "Look at you, growing a beard now. Let me find out."

"What's up, Amber?" he greeted while lustfully eyeing what he could see of her sexy curves.

"Hi, Kenny," Amber replied seductively in return. Even her voice was alluring.

Montega leaned on the driver side window. "Let me hold somethin'," he said.

"Shit, you got all the money," Amber replied. "You need to put my little brothers on though."

"They cool already. This Mike block, remember," he said, glancing at Jazz. "I guess he got E running things now. I can talk to E for you if you want. He'll get 'em. Anyway, I was watching videos yesterday and seen you in that Rick Ross video. You was looking like millions, real rap. That's all you back there?"

Amber smirked devilishly before responding, "You wanna find out?"

"Okay," Jazz said, interfering. "Don't be tryna fuck my friends, Kenny. I do not need to hear them stressing when they find out you ain't tryna settle down because you chasing someone else. Now, who the chick you all sprung over?"

Montega jerked his neck back with a frown. He then looked at his brother as if he were going to kill him. Instead, he defended himself. "I ain't sprung. Don't listen to that drug addict. He just jealous he ain't see her first."

"Taliban? Jealous? Picture that wit' a Kodak. Only man I'm jealous of is a nigga with two dicks, nahmean?" Taliban said. "I know he fucking twice as much as me, ain't that right, Nino?"

"Allah knows best," Abdulallah sighed before walking off to try and sell a jar of oil.

"Yeah, whatever. Talk that shit. Anyway, where y'all headed?" Montega asked, ignoring his brother and Abdulallah.

"We going over Breezy's crib to mess with her," Gi-Gi said, causing him to hiss at the name. "Unh-unh, don't act like that toward my cousin. You fucked her around, remember? You need to be tryna get with her instead of hissin' at her. I mean, she ain't tell her pops, nor did she tell Shug about what you did, so she gotta like somethin' about you."

Amber then rolled her eyes at that.

"Yeah, she like something about me, aight. She'd like to see me six-feet under," Montega mumbled, causing Amber to snort out a laugh. "Look. Tell her I'm sorry and I would like to maybe take her out someday—when hell freezes over and—"

"Oh, God, bye, boy," Jazz replied before pulling off and leaving Montega in the rearview mirror.

Once they got to Breezy's house, they walked right in. Breezy was too busy looking through her bedroom closet to hear their footsteps. "What you doing!" Jazz said, making her jump with surprise.

"Bitch, you gonna stop scaring me before you give me a freakin' heart attack," Breezy said, shaken up.

Amber and Gi-Gi burst out laughing.

Jazz looked around at all the bags of clothes and shoes that were everywhere and was about to ask what Gi-Gi blurted out before she could.

"What is all this?"

"I have a date," Breezy said, beaming.

Jazz, Gi-Gi, and Amber rejoiced. They knew she hadn't been with anyone since Kev's death, and seeing her back to normal reassured them. "Well, are you going to tell us who this lucky guy is, or do we have to beat it out of you?" Amber asked.

"Y'all don't know him, sluts. He works at a bank downtown, and he is so cute, so fine, and so paid."

"Oh shit, do that, girl," Jazz said as Breezy smiled.

"We're supposed to meet up at this nice restaurant called the Capital Grill for dinner, then who knows," she said devilishly.

"My cousin is definitely back," Gi-Gi said.

"Back? Bitch, I ain't never left. Now, which one of y'all gonna give me a ride?" Breezy asked, holding up a black Yves Saint Laurent dress. It was see-through with flowered designs to cover her goods.

Amber raised her eyebrows and said, "Damn, Bree. Now, that dress is perfect."

♫ What's beef? Beef is when you need two gats to go to

sleep. Beef is when ya moms ain't safe up in the streets. Beef is when I see you, guaranteed to be in ICU...

Ski-Mask dumped almost four and a half ounces of cocaine on the glass table inside of his Cherry Hill apartment. With the sound of Biggie influencing him in the background, a lump of cash in his pocket, thirty-one shots in the magazine of an Uzi lying on the speaker, and a naked white broad with blonde hair and blue eyes sleeping on the sofa behind him, he felt like life couldn't get any better than it was now. He was finally winning and loved every second of fame.

Using a razor, he stretched the coke all the way across the table, forming a miniature football field. Grabbing a straw, he sang, "Are you ready for some footballllll!"

"What the hell are you doin', gang?" a voice said behind him, causing him to snatch up the machine gun and point it in that direction.

Taliban quickly dipped behind his brother. "Yo, gang. It's me. Now put that slammer away 'fore you do something stupid, dickhead. And what the hell is wrong wit' you? You singing the old Monday night football anthem like you... What the... Bro, look at this," Taliban said, walking up to the table.

"Hey, what you think Ski Mask doin', Dickey? Game is about to start," Ski-Mask said with the gun in one hand, straw in the other.

Abdulallah looked down at the table with disappointment. "Typical. This swine-eating kafr's about to murder himself in his own home. First, you have the filthy kafr bint' who probably hasn't made extenga in her life, then you got the white shaytan here, waiting to take you on a first-class trip to the hellfire."

Montega looked over on the couch at the sexy white chick with the nice-size breasts. She was out cold with no panties or bra on. He shook his head. "I know you wasn't about to snort all this, was you? Who the hell do you think you are? Boston George? You supposed to be my main enforcer, and you over here tryna check out already," he said as Abdulallah destroyed Ski-Mask's cocaine creation with a quick wave of the hand.

The coke blew about like baby powder.

"Hey! What da fuck, Dickey. Ski-Mask was about to drag that. You muthafuckas mess up wet dream, you know that? Look what you've done!" Ski-Mask protested with his arms spread wide.

"Man, get ready. We 'bout to roll upstate to see your brother. I know he's probably going through it right now. Nobody has been to see him yet."

"What about the range?"

"Olivia ain't there. She got some kind of promotion out in Florida, so I guess the firing range is a done deal, and so is the exotic car thing we had going. Now, c'mon, bol. We ain't got all day. You want me to wake your shorty up and tell her to bounce while you at it?"

"Naw, she cool," Ski-mask said, wiping his nose. "She gonna wait for Ski-Mask to come back and put her ass back to sleep again. Ski-Mask got dope dick that make 'em drowsy." Ski-Mask grabbed his crotch.

"Man, ya ass gonna overdose for real if you don't stop getting' high on your own supply," Taliban lectured before picking up the machine gun to inspect it. "It ain't a day that goes by that you ain't high."

Abdulallah leaned over Montega's shoulder and said, "Look who's talkin'."

Chapter Fifty-Five

Dead Man Walking

"Cuz still talkin'. He still breathin'..."

— SHUG

In a maximum-security prison upstate, Lil' Man was escorted down the corridor in chains with four guards surrounding him. When he got into the visiting booth, the guards uncuffed him then locked the door behind him. Sitting down, he recognized the friendly face across the glass and smiled. They both grabbed the phone on each side of the glass.

"What's up, bol?" Montega asked.

"Ta bien, just another day in hell, waitin' to meet Satan at the end of the road," Lil' Man replied.

Montega sadly nodded. He felt bad that it had to end like this, but they both knew where Lil' Man was headed to begin with. "Did you get the bread I sent you?"

"Every month. Looks like you really living up to your name now, but yo, stop sendin' it. It ain't no use for me to be rich on death row. I'm deadweight. Save that bread for that castle you always talked about. You know, the one with the underground parking lot with all the fancy cars."

Montega smiled. It was obvious that Lil' Man had been listening to him talk to Faith about his dreams.

"So what's poppin' out there? Did you get at fat ass yet?"

Montega shook his head no. "Well, what are you waiting for? That puta shoulda been dead. C'mon, Montega. You supposed to be smarter than that. And from what I hear, Shug is dangerous. You keep stallin', and he's gonna get the upper hand on you like he did with the others. It don't take long for someone to find out about a family member, so I advise you to go at him with everything you got—unless you getting soft on me because you got a little dough now."

Montega snorted with a smile. "Never that, bol. You heard what 'Pac said. *They say money bring bitches, and bitches tell lies. It's more niggas jealous—"*

"Then muthafuckas die," Lil' Man said, nodding his head to his favorite song. "Just make sure you handle your business because what happened to Gutter was fucked up. I lost two close friends. I'm not tryna lose another, so be careful, homie. I hear that dude got some major ties to some people that's really doing numbers. You ever heard of the Great White Family?"

"Naw," Montega said, oblivious to the name.

"Well, they live in Cali, and they don't play around. There's this guy name Clyde; he runs the organization with this bitch name Diamond. That's his sister. From what I hear, she's the coldest, even colder than us. I heard she kills her enemy with just a kiss. It sounds crazy, but it's true. They damn sure eating, and they numbers don't lie. That's the talk on death row."

Montega thought about his shorty Dee from Cali. He made a mental note to ask her if she'd heard anything about the White family when they went to dinner later on that night.

"I want you to listen to me, Montega, and don't take this personal, but don't come up here no more. I don't want you to see me like this. I want you to remember me how I was out there on them streets. And most importantly, take care of my baby sister. Treat her how I would but better, and guard her with your life. Promise me you'll do that for me, and we're squared off on everything."

Montega nodded. "On my mother."

"I love you, bro. You're the brother my mom shoulda had," Lil' Man said.

Montega nodded in acceptance. Lil' Man had been true right down to the very end, and at that moment, Montega swore on everything that he would honor his wishes. After Lil' Man got to talk to his brother, Ski-Mask, and cursed Nino out for the last time, they headed home. It felt as if Lil' Man had already died. To Montega, Lil' Man was his people, his heart, his brother, so his every request would be fulfilled, starting with Shug. Little did he know, Shug had his own agenda.

"Listen up. My reason for calling you all here on this cold, windy night is simple," Shug said to the group of henchmen surrounding him inside a South Philly warehouse by the docks on Delaware Avenue. He pulled out a picture of Montega that he got from Gee and held it up. "This is your target. Now, some of y'all already know what this dude looks like."

Shug made eye contact with an agitated Maniac before continuing. "As far as the rest, if you don't know him, now you do. His name Is Kenny Carter, but he goes by the name Montega. If you spot him anywhere, I want him dead—end of story. For the man that merks him, there's a quarter-mil waitin' for you."

Everybody's faces lit up when they heard the price tag that was on

Montega's head. "This dude drives a black '96 Impala SS. Remember that he killed Kev. There's already been several attempts on his life, so he's well-aware of shooters tryna run up on him. The object is to catch him by surprise. I don't care if he's pushin' a baby stroller; if you see him, shoot first, ask questions later. No one sleeps tonight until they find him. No one gets any pussy. All I want you to do is hunt… Hunt for this lone wolf. Now, roll out."

As the men rushed to their vehicles to search the city for the man in the picture, Maniac stepped to Shug, obviously angry. "I told you I could handle it myself."

"Yeah, well, obviously, you can't. Cuz still talkin'; he still breathin'. He still a pain in my ass. You wanna prove yourself? Bring his body back in a bag. And you can start at this location," he said, pulling a piece of paper from his pocket.

Maniac looked at it and frowned. "And what makes you think he'll be there?" Maniac asked.

"I don't," Shug said, spaced out. "But if I were in his shoes, I'd make sure I'm there on time."

Maniac nodded before getting into the car and driving off. If the location was accurate, there was no escaping death tonight.

Chapter Fifty-Six

Betrayed By A Jewel

"You killed my boyfriend..."

— BREEZY

The black Impala growled up to the restaurant on Chestnut Street in Center City. Montega scoped out the scenery. From the looks of it, everything seemed fine, so he drove around to find a nice place to park. The city was flooded with events that night, and the clubs were filled, making it hard for him to find a spot. He eventually found one two blocks down and around the corner on Manning Street.

He stepped out, dapper, in an all-black Ralph Lauren tuxedo with black and white wing-tip shoes. His cufflinks had the Silent King's logo on them. After setting the alarm on the car, he headed for the Capital Grill, where he was supposed to meet his future wife. For Montega, everything was starting to go well for him. The city was slowly falling in his hands, and he had money and a woman who he could have honestly brought home to his mother had she still been alive. He felt like nothing could go wrong.

Once he walked in the restaurant, he greeted the hostess and gave the woman his name so she could check the guest list. "Oh, here you are, Mr. Carter. Your date hasn't arrived yet, but we have your table ready in the back. Please follow me."

Montega followed the woman through the fancy dining area that resembled the Titanic's first-class dining room. They had live jazz, crystal chandeliers, and suave waiters—the works.

Sitting nearby, Breezy sat by herself, waiting for her date to arrive as well. She checked her watch again. It was now 8:00 p.m. So she sipped on her glass of wine and almost spat it out when she saw the hostess escort Montega to his table. She had to do a doubletake to make sure it was really him.

What is he doing here? she questioned herself.

As much as she despised him, she had to admit he was extremely handsome and looked great in a tux. Even some of the women with dates were checking him out on the low. Montega searched the room face by face to store them in his memory. When he came across the woman in the black see-through dress and black suede pumps, he had to make sure his eyes weren't deceiving him. Her natural hair was shoulder length and Indian straight, and her face was glowing without a single blemish.

"Breezy," he muttered to himself as he sat down.

When she caught his eye, he nodded out of respect. She returned a forced smirk and a short, girlish wave. Montega pulled out his cell and tried to call Dee's number but frowned when the operator said the number was disconnected. He immediately took the phone from his ear and checked the number, making sure he dialed the right one. "Disconnected?" he asked with a frown.

Even though he was disappointed, he decided to wait and see if Dee would show up. Ten minutes later, he concluded that she wasn't coming, which had him worried. He placed his elbow on the table and sank his cheeks into his palms, irritated. He had sat there for over half an hour, and, still, no call. It was then he had heard Samorah's voice in his head saying, *I guess nothing lasts forever.*

He started to call her and see what she had been up to, but his attention was drawn to Breezy, who looked to be arguing with someone on her cell phone.

"Bitch, I ain't know he was your husband. He told me he was single... Home-wrecker? Look, bitch, I don't know who you think you're talking to, but you 'bout to get your feelings hurt... What! Well, fuck you too."

Click!

Breezy shook her head while gently cuffing herself in the forehead. She couldn't believe the bad luck she was having lately. "No show?" a voice asked, standing on the other side of the table.

Breezy looked up and saw Montega. She was too upset to speak. She just nodded.

Montega looked down at the vacant chair and asked, "May I?"

Breezy looked at him suspiciously. As much as she wanted to tell him no, her mouth said, "Go 'head. I don't care. Did your date stand you up too?"

"Nothing lasts forever," he said with a pause and a thought. "Anyway, you ready to order? I'm starvin'." He picked up the menu and opened it.

"Order?" Breezy asked in disbelief. "Kenny, what are you doing? You know how I feel about you. You killed my boyfriend. Now, you're actin' as if everything is just peaches and cream. I hate you. Do you know that? Do you feel comfortable sitting with me with all these knives around?"

"I ain't got you hating me, shorty."

"Oh yeah?" Breezy said, snapping her head back. "Explain to me why not."

"It's simple. People fear those they hate," Montega explained. "You're too strong-minded and too bold to fear anybody. I watch you when you think I'm not lookin'. You might dislike my ways, but it's not hate. I know what hate is, and this isn't it," he said, looking over the menu. "Look. I know I've done some crazy shit in the past, but what can you do but love me or leave me the hell alone? And right now, it appears that we need each other's company. So let's not fuck it up with bad karma over what happened to your dude and my homie. If you haven't noticed, there's a black cloud hanging over my head. I'm paying my dues."

Just then, the waiter arrived to take their order. Breezy sucked her teeth, rolled her eyes, and then made herself order the Thai-marinated lobster with avocado, mango shrimp, and linguine. Montega had the chicken lasagna with garlic bread and a chef's salad. When the food arrived, Breezy's eyes lit up when she saw what he was eating.

Like a kid, she whined, "Ohhh, gimme some of that." Montega slid the salad over to her. "I'm sorry. That was so childish of me. I love salad though," she said, stabbing at the lettuce and stuffing it into her mouth.

"Don't tell me that's how you got all that back there, is it?" he asked, referring to her ass.

She slowly raised her middle finger at him. "Whatever, boy. Stop being so nasty," she said before retrieving her fork. "You know what you need to do? You need to take my advice and watch your back because Shug is still lookin' for you. And the only reason I'm tellin' you this is because you're my best friend's brother. So don't get smart like you did at the club a while back. Just take heed."

Montega dug his fork into the cheesy lasagna and watched as the colorful strings stretched to his mouth. He engulfed a forkful, chewed it, and said, "You think I haven't noticed? See, that's the difference between men and wolves. Shug sends goons to do his dirty work. I take matters into my own hands. Mark my words, Shug won't last, and neither will anyone else that's ridin' with him. I'm taking over this city, Bree, and I'm doin' it with a crooked smile. See?"

Breezy squinted at the handsome man in front of her as he smiled with confidence. She took a deep breath and drank some more wine. It was really helping her get through their encounter, perhaps more than she knew.

"I saw your letter, you know," she said, looking at him. He didn't stop eating, nor did he respond. "That is one clever hideout you have there in Awbury Park."

Montega looked up at her.

Seeing his discomfort, she said, "Relax. If I wanted you dead, you would be."

"That's relieving to know," he said, wiping his mouth and taking a gulp of wine. "So... how are you holdin' up?"

Breezy slowly snapped, slamming her fork to the plate when she heard the question. She stared at him as reality struck her. *Really?* she thought with hooded eyes.

Montega saw her sudden mood swing and quickly tried to fix it. "Look, shorty. I know we don't see eye to eye on things, and I know I might have done some bad shit, but—"

"Bad?" Breezy interrupted. "Kenny, you took away someone special to me. Then you expect me just to forget about it and move on, just like that. Are you serious?"

Montega shook his head. "You so selfish; it's a shame," he said with disbelief. "What about Razor, huh?"

Breezy quickly turned away with an attitude when she heard the name.

"Did he deserve what happened to *him*?" Montega asked, looking at her with pleading eyes. "It's part of the game, shorty. This is the way it goes. You kill my people; I kill you. Then somebody tries to kill me. It's called karma. You don't have to like it, but it will always be what it is. I'm sorry for what happened to dude, but I refused to get left stinkin' somewhere while someone else moves forward. Only the strong survive, and I'm still breathing."

Breezy didn't want to admit it, but he was right. Kev locked in his destiny when he killed Razor, and she knew that. *You live by the sword, you die by the sword.* Wiping a tear from her cheek, she tried not to breakdown. *Not in front of him.* "I still hate you." She sniffled.

"Awww, c'mon, yo. Don't cry. If it makes you feel any better, I'm sorry about bol. No, fuck that, I'm not sorry, but I am sorry about hurting you, and… and if you need anything from me, don't hesitate to ask."

"I don't want anything from you. Besides… I don't think you can handle what I need right now, Kenny," she blurted out unconsciously. She realized what she said and looked up in shock.

Montega's eyebrows rose, but he didn't know how to respond. He looked back at his plate and continued to eat. By the end of their meal, the wine had loosened the tension and allowed them to speak freely.

"This was really weird," Breezy admitted as she got up. "But I'm kinda glad it played out this way... I guess I can find a way to stop hatin' you so much."

"Thank God." Montega sighed. "Now I can cross the street without having to worry about you running me over."

Breezy giggled, remembering her attempted hit and run on him two years back. "You drove?"

"Yeah. Thankfully, I didn't get a ride from Jazz. My car is in the lot on the sixth floor. Why? Are you going to be a gentleman and walk with me?" she asked, picking up her fur coat.

"Do you want me to?"

"Do I really have to ask? Look at what I have on. All those crazy people out there this time of night and all this ass. I might get mugged."

Montega stared at her shapely figure and licked his lips. Breezy was thick and curvy, the way any man would want his future wife. Out of all his sisters' friends, she and Amber had the fattest asses. Too bad neither were meant for him.

"Aight, we out," he said. He got up from the table and followed her through the dining room to the exit. The fur coat was only a quarter length, leaving everything else in clear view. He watched as her ass bounced from side to side the whole way. The dress she wore left little room for imagination. He couldn't take his eyes off it until they got outside.

As soon as the cool air hit his face, he looked up and saw a flash of chrome in the dread head's hand standing across the street.

"There he is!" Gee shouted as three goons pulled out Mac-10s. Montega pushed Breezy to the ground.

"Get down!" he shouted while reaching into his tuxedo and pulling out two black Beretta M9s from their holsters.

The rapid fire from the Macs exploded from across the street. Montega fired two shots before ducking with a bruised Breezy on the other side of a parked car. The restaurant's front window shattered as the customers got down under their tables to avoid any stray bullets.

As Montega and Breezy took cover on the pavement behind the car, Gee abandoned his position, leaving his shooters, and crept across the street for a better shot. He was surprised by Montega, who fired four rounds into his chest from both pistols. Gee spun like a spinning top before hitting the ground, coughing up blood. More gunfire erupted from Maniac and two other machine guns, causing Montega to pose as a shield over Breezy as glass from the car window showered over their heads. Police sirens rang in the distance. Gee coughed up more blood before his body went stiff.

"Oh my God! Oh my God! We're gonna die!" Breezy panicked.

"Calm down and look at me," Montega demanded, cupping her face. Breezy looked Montega directly in his eyes and instantly saw his concern for her safety. She was able to calm down and listen to him.

"We're not gonna die, shorty," he said before stuffing one gun back in its holster. "They are. But you gotta listen to me. We can't stay here. We have to make it to my car. Now, take off your shoes. We gotta run. You go first, and I'll cover you."

"Fuck no, are you crazy? They have guns," Breezy said as her heart slammed inside of her chest.

"Look, Bree. If we stay here, we might as well shoot ourselves. Would you like me to shoot you? Because I'd be damn if I let them do it. Don't think about it; just run. Now go!"

Montega popped up, shooting at the henchmen who were trying to cross the street before the cops got there. Two shots from his gun struck one in the center of his chest, laying him out in the middle of the street. Breezy gathered up her courage to make a run for it and sprinted down the block. Montega fired four more rounds to keep Maniac off his ass then followed her. They spun the corner onto Sartain Street and continued.

"He's on the move! Kill him!" Maniac shouted.

Once Montega caught up with Breezy, he took her hand and guided her to the black car with Maniac and his men still in pursuit. Montega hit the remote start button, igniting the engine. The lights beamed on the outside as well as the dashboard, and the navigation screen inside. As Breezy rushed to the passenger side, more shots thundered with angry lead coming in their direction. Montega spun around with one gun aimed. Maniac stopped in his tracks and let the henchmen take the lead just as Montega took the shot.

Boom!

The hollow tip split the henchman's head wide open, splattering his brains everywhere as his body fell lifelessly. Target practice with Olivia paid off. Montega got into his car, shifted the gear into drive, stepped on the gas and peeled. Bullets pelted the tinted windows like a hailstorm. He and breezy ducked down, shielding their heads from harm's way, but nothing penetrated.

When Montega looked up to see that the glass hadn't broken, he sighed in amazement. "It's cool. The car... it's bullet-proof. That's why the windows don't roll down," he said, turning left down Camac Street then a right onto Spruce.

"Thanks. I really feel safe now," Breezy replied sarcastically.

The engine gargled 625 horsepower through the dual exhaust system.

Just when they thought it was over, two Jeep Grand Cherokee SRT-8's with 6.1 leader V8 Hemi engines appeared with shooters in ski-masks hanging out the windows armed with AK-47s spitting fire like blow-torches. Montega whipped another right turn on 13th Street and floored it. The Impala's powerful supercharged LT4 V8 Corvette engine raised the front up like a boat on the water. It raced across Market Street from one side to the other. The vibration trembled the interior like a NASCAR race car.

Montega swerved in and out of a few cars, causing the suspension to bounce. He took another strong right and almost lost control as he drifted onto Filbert Street, fishtailing the big body with spinning tires. The dual exhaust chrome pipes growled, and the motor screamed through the slits of the Ram air hood. Montega remained calm and in control. He checked his rearview every now and then until the two jeeps drew close once more.

"Shoot out the tires!" the driver instructed one of the shooters.

Montega whipped another left onto 9th street before the shooter could get a shot off. They flew past the Gallery just before he turned left once more onto Arch Street.

Eeeerrrbbb!

The tires screeched as they ate up the black street with a hunger for distance. Maniac and the rest of the henchmen did the same in the Cherokees. With the Convention Center on their right and the Criminal Justice Center to their left, they had no respect for minor traffic.

"Where are the cops when you need them?" Breezy asked, looking around.

"Fuck the police. Where else would they be?" Montega replied, veering in and out of traffic. "They somewhere eatin' a late-night donut or in the hood, fuckin' with some small-time drug dealer. One thing for sure. They ain't here."

As one of the Jeep Grand Cherokee's drew closer, the window rolled down again, and a henchman stuck half his body out, ready to shoot.

"Look at this dickhead," Montega said, looking in his side mirror. He slammed on the brakes and whipped right back onto Broad Street.

The Impala's wide ass drifted to the other side of the intersection. The Jeep Grand Cherokee lost control. It slid across the intersection and went head-first into a McDonald's that was on the corner of Broad and Arch Streets. A cop that was on post quickly got on his radio and called dispatch just as the other Cherokee SRT-8 came screeching around the corner in pursuit.

"What does he have in that bitch?" a henchman asked before rolling his window down to shoot. They could hear the engine from the safety of their own vehicle. It was deafening and exotic.

"Move out of the way and let me get him," Maniac replied, sticking the Uzi out.

Breezy ducked down again as bullets thudded against the back window. Montega turned left, swerving into oncoming traffic on Vine Street and headed for the Schuylkill Expressway. By that time, red and blue lights were flashing. Behind the Crown Victoria were three patrol cars. He whipped a strong right on 16th then advanced on.

"Put your seatbelt on," Montega advised as they turned onto a clear expressway.

Breezy obeyed, curious as to what he was up to. Montega put the gas pedal to the floor. The speedometer rose to 160 on the dashboard. Watching him from the passenger side, she noticed him flick on a switch under the dashboard. It was the switch that he had been dying to use. The red button on the steering wheel next to his thumb was blinking on and off.

"Kenny, what the hell are you about to do?" Breezy asked nervously.

"You ever been in a spaceship?" he asked.

As the Cherokee tried to gain speed, Montega hit the button and almost got whiplash. The car rocketed forward. Hitting speeds of over 180 miles per hour within seconds.

"What the fuck! Speed up!" Maniac ordered as he watched the black car with blue flaming pipes get smaller and smaller by the second.

"I'm goin' as fast as I can," his driver replied, looking at the dashboard.

Breezy watched with both hands glued to the armrest as everything went by so fast that she felt herself become dizzy. Bracing herself, she planted her feet to the floor. Montega, however, remained calm with one thing on his mind—getting away.

Once he'd done that, he could try to answer the question, *how did they know where I was?* He hated to believe it, but only one person knew his whereabouts, and that was the person he was supposed to meet. Dee. It hurt him to think that way, but if she was involved in this, then she, too, would have to die.

Chapter Fifty-Seven

Hate, Lust, And Revenge

"Why are you so crazy?"

— BREEZY

Kia sat on the comfortable leather sofa in her two-bedroom home in West Philadelphia, watching the *Channel 10 News*. She had been riding around the city all day with her girlfriends, Ebo and Amber, and she needed some rest. This was the only time she could get some peace. Most of her time was spent at her job, trying to sell houses that her brother's construction company built. It was a shame her boyfriend Larry went back to the Army. She really missed his company. He always kept her laughing.

She knew if a man wanted to win her heart, making her laugh would be half the battle. As Kia kicked her feet up with a bag of microwave popcorn, live footage appeared on the screen.

"*Channel 6* is live in front of a Chestnut Street restaurant, where just a few minutes ago, heavy gunfire erupted. As you can see, police officers are recovering two dead bodies. One was found in the street and the other between two parked cars. Police have yet to find a suspect, and there were numerous gunmen involved. Police believe that the shooting evolved into a car chase that left a mass trail of debris throughout the Center City area. Take a look at the footage picked up by the local street cams."

The black Impala sped across an intersection with two Jeep Grand Cherokees following. The windows were tinted black, making it impossible to get a visual on the driver.

Kia knew that car from anywhere. "Oh my God," she gasped out.

"This black Chevy Caprice or Impala was last seen traveling north on the expressway. Police say the car was under heavy gunfire before it evaded the suspects at high speeds. The Jeep Grand Cherokees seen in the chase also got away after a shootout with the police. We will bring you an update as information becomes available..."

Kia's mouth dropped, thinking about Breezy, who had said she had a date at that very same restaurant. And the black car... Could it really be her brother? She then rushed to the phone, but before she could pick it up, she heard a knock at the door. Knowing it had to be her best friends stopping by to tell her about the whole incident, she sighed, stopped, and turned for the door. Without asking who it was, she opened the door, expecting to see Breezy's face. To her surprise, it wasn't Breezy.

"Shug, how did you—"

Smack!

Kia spun and fell to the floor after getting slapped without a word spoken. Shug walked inside and kicked her in the gut. She rolled over as he shut the door behind him. "I'm gonna enjoy this," he said, removing his shirt.

As Kia tried to get up, Shug punched her in the face. She dropped back to the floor. He repeatedly hit her. Her vision faded. She was on the verge of blacking out. Grabbing her split, long, white T-shirt, Shug ripped it, exposing her bare breasts and red boy shorts. Shug licked his lips and unbuttoned his pants.

"I got a message I want you to give to your brother for me. Unfortunately, you won't be able to tell him, but by the time I'm finished with you, he'll get the point," Shug said.

"Fuck you!" Kia spat just before finally blacking out.

With a smile on his face, Shug said, "My point exactly."

MONTEGA

The black Impala came to a stop in front of Breezy's house. The sound of the transmission kicked in. The car went in reverse and parked. Breezy was so amazed with everything that she had just been through. It had her in shock. To be able to live to tell someone about a heavy gun battle and car chase would be exhilarating.

"Can I ask you a question?" She panted, looking over at him. "Why are you so crazy? I mean, those people were just tryna kill you, yet you're so calm about it right now. What you got? A death wish?"

Montega kept his eyes glued on the full moon that shined brightly in the cold, dark sky. "Sometimes, you gotta be a little crazy to survive in a crazy city like this. Yeah, you might think I don't have a clue, but I'm not stupid at all. I'm just real. If somethin' hurts me, I feel pain. If somebody tries to kill me, I'm bustin' at 'em, and if I feel I'm outnumbered, I'm runnin', point-blank. It's called surviving on instincts. My instincts are my best friend. They never let me down."

Breezy nodded in agreement. "You know, your sister really worries about you. I swear, if a person didn't know you two were related, they would think you were her dude the way she talks about you all the time. Perhaps more than she talks about Rafeek. You should be thankful for her. Not too many sisters give a damn about their brother."

Montega smiled as he thought of Kia. "That's my heart right there

—believe it or not. She know that too. I'd give my own life to save hers, and I can't say that about a lot of people right now."

"Wow, Kenny Montega does have a heart hidden somewhere in that chest of his," Breezy replied, patting his chest.

Montega grabbed her wrist firmly, and, just like that, time froze. The two made eye contact. Neither knew what the other thought, but their bodies were magnetic. Breezy blinked shyly, but before she knew it, their lips met. Tilting her head to the side slightly, she allowed his tongue to enter her mouth. Her heart pounded with both fear and desire. It was like being in some sort of weird dream. *Why is he doin' this to me?* she thought. The kiss was wet and aggressive but didn't last long. Just as quickly as it began, it ended.

Once she was out of the trance, she snatched herself away from him. She wiped her mouth while looking over at him, unsure of what she had done. Montega's tongue slithered over his lips, sucking her saliva from the surface. He still managed to remain cool. He took a deep breath and sat back in his seat. Breezy continued to watch him. She just couldn't figure him out. She had never met someone as bold, daring, confident, ambitious, and charming as he was. On the flip side, he was arrogant, foolish, and careless. Tonight, she was seeing a different side of him.

Montega drummed on the steering wheel, waiting for her to get out. Truthfully, he wanted to check on Dee.

"Do you want me to walk you to the door?" he asked, wondering why she hadn't made a move.

"No," she replied. "I want you to walk me inside."

Her reply caused him to look over at her to make sure he heard her right. She was staring at him with sultry eyes. He had seen these eyes before on most women he'd been with. He couldn't deny her.

When the two entered the house, Breezy quickly reset her alarm and turned on the chandelier in the dining room. Leaving it dim, she walked over to the stereo to turn on some music. It was way too quiet. "You can make yourself comfortable. I have some Coronas in the refrigerator. I have to run and freshen up," she said.

"I've heard that before. You don't have any machine guns lying around, do you?"

Breezy frowned. "No," she said, snorting out a laugh. "What type of bitches have you been dealin' with?" she asked before walking up the steps.

"The kind that set you up to get rocked by your enemy," he mumbled while pulling his guns out of their holsters.

He looked around the room then stuffed one into a crevasse of the sofa and the other under a wooden lamp stand.

He sat back down, exhaled, and thought about his time with Dee. Out of all the women he had dealt with, she was the most mysterious. From the moment he met her up until the second he stepped out of her limousine, he knew that what they had was too good to be true. Part of him wanted to believe that it wasn't. *Then why does it hurt so bad?* he thought with a sigh. He needed to get over her.

As the radio played a Beyoncé' melody, Montega walked through the plush dining room that Breezy had worked so hard to decorate and into the kitchen to grab a beer. He popped the top off the bottle with his teeth then began looking at the pictures on the wall. He came across a picture of Kev and Breezy together. She looked so happy—much happier than she was now. Then he came across a picture of Breezy and his sister at the club the night Razor was killed. He didn't even realize a smile was on his face until Breezy crept up behind him.

"Havin' fun?" she asked.

When Montega spun around, he was surprised to see her dressed in a T-shirt that came just below her thick thighs. What she held in her hand was even more surprising. It was Razor's Silent King chain. Pointing at it, he asked, "How did you get that?"

Breezy took his hand, turned it up, and placed the chain inside his palm. "After the incident happened, Kevin brought this to my house and had me put it in a safe place. I acted as if I didn't know who Razor was. Truthfully, I was hurting inside when he told me what he did. You probably hate me for this, but what's a girl to do when she's trapped between men and wolves?" she asked, putting her head down.

Montega looked at the chain long and hard. He then looked up at

Breezy, touched her chin, and lifted her head back up. "You can't do shit but survive, I guess. Like I said before, you gotta be a little crazy to survive in this city."

"I want to get crazy right now," she breathed out.

"Be careful what you wish for."

He moved in and began kissing her passionately. This time, she didn't pull back, nor did she stop him from pulling up the hem of her shirt. He went under it to squeeze on her soft, bare ass. When he realized she wore no panties, his shaft grew within his pants. Smoothly, he caressed her skin, molding her curves as he removed the shirt she had on and tossed it behind him. She was completely naked, standing before him with heavy, round breasts, wide hips, and a small waist. She stood bow-legged with a fat camel toe between her thighs.

She unbuttoned his pants and pulled them down so she could stroke what was hiding in his boxers. Once they were down to his ankles, she stroked his thick erection. Montega stepped out of the ring of clothes, picked her up, and slammed her against the wall, knocking down the picture of her and Kia. He held her up with his left hand and fed her treasures his dick with his right. With breaths of anticipation, Breezy invited him inside of her wet walls. His first thrust left her at a loss for words.

"Uhhh!" She exhaled. He rolled his hips into her again. Her body rose up the wall. Her breasts were pressed against his chest. A thrilling sensation went through her body, followed by chills that left her spinning.

Breezy clawed the back of his neck, leaving red marks on his skin as she panted. His back had already been brutally scarred from his previous mistress; now she was reopening the wounds. She clenched her teeth to keep from screaming his name. She opened her legs wide and then locked them behind his thighs. He dug deeper inside of her. She whispered his name in blissful passion.

"K-Kenny, ssss, oooh, Kenny. You feel so g-goooood!"

Montega held her up by her ass, slamming into her inner thighs on the wall.

"I... I want you to suck on my titties," she whined as she positioned one of her breasts to his face. "Please suck on my titty."

She closed her eyes and held her breast in Montega's mouth then threw her head back when she felt his tongue flicking across her nipple.

"Oooh, you gonna make me cum if you keep this up. I swear I'ma cum, boy!"

Montega pounded her against the wall, causing more pictures to fall to the floor. He couldn't hold her up much longer. His arms were beginning to tire. He then carried her to the dining room table. Breezy knocked the vase and the candle holders to the floor while Montega eased her onto her back.

Grabbing her waist, he pulled her to his torso. She twisted her face and clenched her teeth as her pussy pulsated with pleasure. With her hands pressed to his chest, she could feel his muscles going to work while he pulverized her insides. She then felt herself about to quake for the second time.

She moaned, "Nooo... ooooohhh, I fuckin' hate you! I swear I hate you!"

"I hate you too," Montega whispered as he plunged in and out of her juices.

"Let me ride it," she demanded.

"No," Montega replied, but Breezy wrapped her arms and legs around him and rolled both of them over. They rolled over until they both fell off the table onto the floor. Montega was now on his back with Breezy on top of him.

"Ya dick is so big," she said as she pushed her hips down on his waist, making him feel her inner muscles constrict around his shaft.

"Uhhh! Shit!" Montega moaned. "Fuck you doing down there?"

"Yeah, that's right. Keep crying, boy, because I'm 'bout to take you all the way there," she said, taking control. She was so wet that her cum dripped down onto his balls.

"Damn!" he gasped as he felt himself reaching his climax.

Breezy could feel it too, provoking her to ride him even harder. The feeling made Montega's toes curl. When Breezy saw his eyes start to roll in the back of his head, it made her orgasm intensify. She was like a rocket about to explode. Within seconds, her orgasm shattered.

"Oh, God, Kenny, ummm!" She squealed before falling off the saddle and onto the floor. She was out of breath, almost suffocating in the process. Montega turned over with a heavy desire to breath as well. He was covered in sweat.

They both looked into each other's eyes as a huge wave of regret crashed over them. It was the kind of regret that a person got after having sex with someone they knew they shouldn't have. Breezy gazed at Montega for a moment as her heartrate began to settle. Then she shook her head as if to say, *what have I done?* What was even worse was the fact that when she looked down at his dick, she wanted more… a lot more.

Chapter Fifty-Eight

Enough Is Enough

"What happened to my baby?"

(STACY)

Gi-Gi and Crystal pulled up to Kia's house early in the morning. They were supposed to be going to New York with their girlfriends, Amber and Ebo, to go shopping. Crystal got out and went to knock on the door. After several attempts, she got no answer. She then looked back at her cousin, who became impatient and shrugged her shoulders. *Kia's car is outside, so she's got to be in the house,* she thought.

Crystal tried the doorknob and found it unlocked. She opened the door and walked in. What she saw in the trashed living room caused her eyes to widen in horror. She quickly ran back outside to get Gi-Gi and call an ambulance.

Montega awoke bright and early, as always. He could never sleep with the sun up; however, he never expected to wake up next to the pretty face sleeping beside him on the living room floor. He slowly sat up to examine her naked body and immediately nodded his head. He had been knocking down one of the baddest chicks uptown all night long. In fact, he wouldn't have minded getting a morning quickie in if reality hadn't hit him. He had killed her boyfriend, his enemy, and in his mind, although she was beautiful, there was no way he could trust her. Without trust, there was no relationship.

Looking at her glistening golden skin, he realized that they would never have anything more than that one night. It was time to get the hell out of there. Silently, he gathered all his things and tiptoed to the door. Luckily, he made it out without waking her. Once in the car, he headed for the cave. The Impala was getting too hot. He would have to switch up and stick with the Charger for now. He stepped on the gas but was interrupted by the ringing of his phone.

"Hello?" he answered in his morning voice.

"Kenny, you gotta come to Einstein hospital now!" Crystal said frantically.

"For what?"

"Your sister... she... she got beat up real bad last night in her house. Your brother is up here snapping, so please hurry."

"What?" he gasped as his heart dropped into the pit of his stomach.

He quickly made a U-turn in the middle of the intersection. The Impala fishtailed, and its tires ate up the street. Montega took the lanes like a madman, swerving in and out of traffic. He couldn't believe his ears. The more he thought about his sister, the worse he felt. When he got to the hospital, Crystal, Amber, Jasmine, Ebo, and Gi-Gi were all there.

"Where the hell is my sister?" he asked, storming in.

Crystal pointed to the room. "The doctor said nobody's allowed in." But that didn't stop him.

When Taliban saw his brother heading for the room, he followed.

Montega shoved the doctor out of the way and entered the room with his brother. Kia was lying peacefully with IVs in her arm and a breathing tube in her nose. Her face was bruised, and bandages covered her wounded head. Montega filled with anger. As he stood there, looking at his helpless sister, Taliban paced the floor, enraged.

"I swear to God I'm catchin' a hommy today! Look what those muthafuckas did to my sister! I'm a kill 'em!" he shouted in rage.

A minute later, Stacy came rushing in, raising hell. "My baby! What happened to my baby?" she cried out as the security guard and the doctor came in the room.

Everything seemed to be in chaos. "Please, she doesn't need all of this commotion around her. What she needs is a lot of rest. And she won't get it if you all continue with this," the doctor said.

"Step out of the room, sir," the security guard said to Montega, reaching out to touch him.

"If you put your hands on me, it will be the last thing you do in this life."

The guard quickly withdrew.

"Doc, what happened to her?" Stacy said.

The doctor looked at Montega and hesitated before saying, "She was brutally raped and beaten."

Stacy fell to her knees dramatically. She put her face in her palms and cried. Hearing that, Montega turned and walked out of the room, knowing just who to blame for it. A plan formed in his head as he stormed for the exit. *Enough is enough,* he thought.

"Bro, wait up," Taliban said, following him.

"Nah, bol. You stay here with Kia just in case somebody tries something."

"What you mean, try something?" Taliban said, looking at him sideways.

"Did you see her face? Bol tried to kill her, dog. He must have thought she was dead. If it is who I think it is, he ain't gonna let her live to tell who raped her," Montega explained before heading out the room.

He got outside and into his car. The engine fired up, and the sound of tires sped off again.

Chapter Fifty-Nine

The Art Of Deception

"He's got a bulletproof Impala with an engine from hell..."

— CLYDE WHITE

In L.A., Diamond walked through the double doors of the cigar room to find her brother and Justin playing pool for money. They stopped to look up at her. She didn't look happy. "Well, it's about time you showed. I thought I might have to file a missing person's report. Was Philly that interesting you had to send your priest back home?" Clyde asked as he dropped a brick of cash on the edge of the pool table.

"You have no idea," Diamond replied. She walked to the bar to pour herself a vodka martini.

Clyde watched as his sister slurped down the drink like it was Kool-Aid. His eyebrows rose because he knew she didn't really like to drink liquor. "Rough flight?"

"I don't want to talk about it," she replied harshly while trying to breathe over the fumes of her cocktail.

Diamond was jumpy. She couldn't believe the whole time she was in Philly, she had been sleeping with the enemy. *How could I have been so naïve?* she thought to herself. She didn't want anyone to know that she had cried her eyes out the entire flight home. Her heart was broken, and she couldn't blame anyone but herself. It was true what people said about her. She made her own luck, as well as her own misery.

After telling Shug where Montega was last night, she thought she could get over the time they shared, but she was wrong. Instead, she felt something she hadn't felt since she was in her teens. She felt emotional. She couldn't understand how or why, but she had feelings for Montega. This was odd, being as though Wong Lee had supposedly shut off her emotions when he hypnotized her long ago.

Montega hadn't made it any easier for her. He had been nothing but the best to her. He treated her better than any man she ever had. He catered to her needs and did anything to make her smile. Ever since JR died, her whole world turned dark, but Montega brought light back to her life again. Now he was gone, and it was all because of her.

Thinking about his smile reminded her of someone from the past, someone from long ago. It was that thought that caused a tear to escape from her beautiful eyes. It trickled down her cheek and headed for her chin. Diamond caught it just before it fell. *Damn you,* she thought, cursing Montega for tricking her. She had to find the priest. She needed to make a confession.

"I talked to Shug this morning, you know," Clyde said, sinking the orange high ball into a side pocket. "He wanted to tell you that the information you gave him was right on the money."

Diamond's heart felt like it exploded. Her stomach clenched, and her emotions flared. Forcing a smile, she said, "Glad to be of some assistance."

"I'm curious about something though," Clyde said, looking over at her. "How were you able to track down Montega?"

Diamond shrugged. "Truthfully, Bain saw him first," she responded before turning her back to him to pour herself another drink. She closed her eyes, took another deep breath, and sighed, knowing that it was over. She told herself repeatedly that she had done the right thing. Regardless of her feelings, she couldn't mix business with pleasure. Montega had killed Tommy. Now he would suffer the same fate.

"Well, unfortunately, the target got away again."

"What?" Diamond asked, spinning around in shock. "You're kidding me, right?"

"That's what *I* said. Can you believe it? Shug sent his underboss along with six other shooters. Only his enforcer and three others survived. Montega killed Shug's underboss and two henchmen. Then, when the others tried to take him in that black Impala of his, their bullets were ineffective," Clyde said, almost as if he were reading a police report. "He's got a bulletproof Impala with an engine from hell. The guy seems to be one helluva driver. Not once did he lose control."

"Bulletproof?" Diamond repeated in disbelief.

"They say you can tell a person's character from what he keeps in his house, how he presents himself in public, and what he drives. You were right, Diamond. I think it's time that we take this Montega more seriously... before he does something that we may regret."

Diamond's mind was in a daze. Her anger was beginning to boil. She felt as if Montega had deceived her into falling for him, and no one deceived the Snow White Queen nor the Black Kiss of Death. The more her brother talked about him, the more she used her anger as a desire to kill him. This was a challenge—something that she never backed down from. Standing by the bar, she thought to herself, *I got close to him once; I can do it again. This time it won't be a kiss of passion. That is how it began.* She pulled out the poisonous black lipstick from her Gucci bag and thought, *this time, it will be a kiss of death. This is how it will end.*

Chapter Sixty

Leverage

"You turn me on..."

— APRIL "JUICY" MELENDEZ

Montega pulled into a parking space on Broad Street across from the Sneaker Villa store and killed the engine. Looking over at Juicy, he asked, "Are you sure dude play this spot like that?"

"I'm positive, papi," Juicy said, looking at herself in the sun visor as she played in her lustrous, reddish-bronze hair. "Stop doubting me. I told you my girlfriend works here. She and this puta talk all the time. He always stops by to see her."

"I think that's him right there," J-Rider said from the backseat as a Dodge Magnum pulled up to the store's entrance and double-parked. J-Rider was a slim guy, a few inches taller than Montega. He had shoulder-length individual braids and both arms completely covered with tattoos.

Montega watched as Spade put his hazard lights on then got ready to step out of the car once traffic permitted. The sunlight shined down on the city like a giant ball of fire, yet it was still freezing cold.

"See," Juicy said as she turned to look at Montega with a beautiful smile. "What I tell you?"

"Your mom should've named you Angel instead of April," Montega said, placing a hand on her cheek.

He then punched in the code and grabbed the silver Ruger 1911 .45 from the secret stash spot. "Get on the driver side, mami. When I cross, make a U-turn and pull up next to me." He fired the engine up again.

"Okay, but be careful," Juicy replied as Montega jumped out of the car.

As soon as the traffic cleared, Spade opened the driver side door and stepped out. He shut it just in time for Montega to walk up on him. Spade's eyes got wide as Montega pulled his pistol and clobbered him in the face with it. Everything happened so fast. Before Spade realized what was going on, he was being stuffed in the trunk of a car by two people.

J-Rider hopped out and helped Montega put Spade in the trunk.

"No!" Spade said as he struggled to get free. Montega slugged him again with the butt of the pistol. "Keep still, motherfucka!" He hit him again. Instantly, Spade saw blackness. His body went limp.

Once he was in the trunk of the car, the two got in, and Juicy sped off. "That was easy," she said as she headed for West River Drive. It was only a fifteen-minute ride, but the way Juicy drove, they got there in ten.

When they pulled into the park, the three got out and popped the trunk.

Spade jumped in fear. "Please don't kill me, cuz," he begged as J-Rider grabbed him by the collar and yanked him out. He flipped out of the trunk onto the grass.

Spade cried like a baby as he was placed on his knees to face Montega. "Please don't kill me. I won't be any trouble, I swear. That's you and Shug's business, cuz. Please don't do this."

"Relax, yo," Montega replied, checking his surroundings. "I'm not gonna kill you. All I want is information, then I'll let you walk. Now, where is Shug gonna be tonight?"

"C'mon, how am I supposed to know that?" Spade asked.

"Oh yeah?" Montega said, looking at J-Rider, who extended his weapon and aimed at Spade's head.

"I swear I don't know!" Spade shouted.

"Well, then you're no use to me," Montega replied, giving J-Rider the signal to rock Spade to sleep.

"Wait! I do know who can tell you!"

Montega put a hand up to stop his man from raising the murder rate. Squatting down so he could look Spade square in the eyes, he said, "Start talkin'."

"Maniac. He's Shug's enforcer. He knows where Shug stays. He can give you the info you need. I swear, cuz. I'm not lying."

Montega looked up at Juicy, who shrugged her shoulders. "Okay, Spade, this is how this is gonna play out. Like I said before, I'm not gonna kill you. You too pathetic to die by my hands. You make hustlers look bad in the worst way, especially hustlers from Philly. Look at you; all that money you made, and you still ain't worth one bullet. So if I catch you hustling in Philly again, they are gonna find your bones years from now at the bottom to the Schuylkill River. Do I make myself clear?"

Spade nodded in fear. He could see the darkness in Montega's eyes and knew not to play around. He had seen the same look of death in Shug eyes.

"Aight, get him up," Montega said to J-Rider.

"What you wanna do with him?" J-Rider asked.

"Put him back in the trunk until we confirm that Maniac knows what's up," Montega instructed.

Once Spade was back in the trunk, Montega turned to look at Juicy, who was biting down on her bottom lip. Her long, bronze hair blew in the wind. Her brown eyes studied him with hooded, curled lashes. "You turn me on so much, Kenny. You know that?" she asked, batting her eyes at him seductively.

"Chill, shorty, not right now. It's a war going on, if you hadn't noticed. Now come on and let's get this over with."

Juicy sucked her teeth, rolled her eyes, and pouted before getting back in the driver's seat. Once the gear was shifted into drive, they were en route to South Philly.

Chapter Sixty-One

The Hunter's Trap

"Didn't any one ever tell you to think with your head?"

— MONTEGA

Montega pulled up to Tasker Street and parked a block away from the corner Chinese store. Maniac was busy rapping with a couple of young bols about what happened on Chestnut Street the night before. The youngins were amazed by the story he told and the lies he added. The cold weather didn't seem to be affecting them at all. They wore heavy coats and leather jackets, skullies, and fitted caps.

Montega hopped in the backseat with J-Rider. "Aight, this is the plan. Juicy, you gotta get bol to follow you back here, then I'll pull out on his ass. J, you get out and sit on one of those stoops just in case he doesn't get in. Hopefully, the car doesn't spook him."

"And how do you expect me to get him to follow me back to *this* car?" Juicy asked.

"All you have to do is be you. Look at you; you got them tights, that little-ass shirt, and all that long hair. He'd be a fool not to bite. Once he get up on you and see how pretty you are, it's a wrap. Just give bol eye contact like you only want him."

"You mean the kind I give you 24-7, yet you're too blind to see it?"

Montega blushed before remembering something. "Oh, and go in the store and get some disinfectant and a couple rags for me, aight?" he said, going into his pocket to give her a few dollars.

Juicy smacked his money away. "I ain't broke, boy. Don't play with me like that," she said before grabbing her bag and opening the door. J-Rider shook his head and got out of the backseat. He tightened his wool ridge, threw the fur lining hood over his head, and posted up across the street where no one could spot him. Montega watched as Juicy tossed her shiny hair to one side of her shoulder and put on a fierce walk. He loved a woman who possessed the total package—long hair, pretty face, nice breasts, and all ass.

As she got to the next block where Maniac and the youngins were, she made sure she gave him heavy eye contact. Juicy walked into the store to get the things that Montega told her to buy.

"Damn, Maniac, she was all smiles at you," one of the young goons commented.

Hearing that, Maniac wasted no time crossing the street to pursue her. Juicy paid for the disinfectant and paper towels as Maniac came into the store. When she got her bag, she turned and bumped right into him. "What's up, baby? Where you headed?" he asked, undressing her right away with his eyes.

"Hi," she replied with a smile.

"Damn, you bad, ma. Where you from?"

"Southwest," she lied as she continued to walk out the door.

When he got a glimpse of her round ass in the black tights, he was hooked. Even though she looked a little younger than his usual freaks, he followed her out, making up in his mind that he had to bag this broad, freak or no freak.

"Damn, baby, slow down a little," he said, catching up with her. "I'm tryna get to know you."

"Well, I'm sorta in a rush. I have to clean up my kitchen so I can cook for this party I got going on."

"Yeah, you need some help?" he asked, seeing if she would bite.

Juicy licked her pink lips seductively while looking down at his print. "If you come over my house, I don't think I'd ever finish."

Her words sent a quick, sudden rush of blood between his legs. *I got one,* he thought excitedly.

"Ma, I promise I'll be a gentleman," he fibbed.

Juicy stared at him for a second. "Alright, hold this bag while I get my keys." She went into her pocketbook. When Maniac saw the black Impala, he quickly stopped like a deer caught in headlights. Juicy found the keys and hit the alarm button. The car beeped, and the alarm was deactivated. She looked at the suspicious look on his face and frowned. "What's wrong?" she asked, glancing toward the stoop at J-Rider, who was ready to give it to him if he backed out.

"This your car, ma?" he asked.

"Yeah, why wouldn't it be?" she said, walking around to the driver's side.

"Where did you get it from?"

"I got it from Manhiam on Monday."

Maniac knew that black Impalas with tinted windows were all over the city. In fact, he had mistakenly rocked three different guys because of that car. He knew this was the car but figured Montega got rid of it at the auction because it was too hot.

"You act like you don't like it," Juicy added while getting in the car.

Maniac checked the bodywork out. Nothing appeared to look marked by bullets, but the windows were so dark he couldn't see inside. Reluctantly, he got in. As soon as she shut the door, Juicy started the car. The doors automatically locked. Maniac recognized the sound of the exotic engine, but it was too late. Montega popped up from the backseat and pressed the gun to the back of his head. "Gotcha dumb ass. Didn't anyone ever tell you to think with your head and not with your dick?"

Maniac looked at Juicy and sighed with disappointment. "Fuck!" he said miserably.

"That's something we won't be doing, papi," Juicy replied with a girlish grin. She pressed the button on the driver's side panel and unlocked the back door.

J-Rider walked across the street and got into the back with Montega. He patted dread head down and removed his .45 ACP.

Maniac knew it would be over unless he could work out a deal. "Look, cuz, I'm not the guy you wanna kill. I'm just doin' what I'm paid to do, real talk. I ain't the one you lookin' for," Maniac said calmly with his hands up.

"Actually, you are the one I'm looking for. I talked to Breezy last night, and she told me you killed Razor and gave his chain to Kev. And you killed Gutter, so you have just as much to do with this as that fat pig you work for."

"I thought the nigga was you. Just like I thought the other one was you when I aired him out at the club," Maniac said boldly.

Montega looked at J-Rider, who had fire in his eyes as he cocked back the black Beretta 92FS .45 ACP and aimed it at the back of Maniac's head. Maniac flinched, but no one fired on him.

"Aight, playboy, you wanna walk like your man, Spade? Tell me where Shug rest his head, and you can walk," Montega said.

"Yeah right. Soon as I give him up, you'll kill me anyway," Maniac replied.

"No, you see, that's where you got me chopped. As soon as you tell me what I need to know, you're coming with us, then if you lie, I'm gonna use my chainsaw to cut you up in little pieces until you give up the info; then I'll kill you," Montega corrected him. "Right now, we're getting ready to release Spade. He's in the trunk."

"Do what they say, Maniac!" Spade shouted from the trunk.

Maniac thought it through for a second. He knew that if he told them and they took him with them, he could develop an escape plan. Shug's condo was in Upper Darby, which was a distance away. It would take all three of them to get through the front entrance alive. He gave them the information they needed. Montega nodded and looked at Juicy.

"You really love me?" he asked her.

"I put that on everything, papi," Juicy responded wholeheartedly.

"Then prove it."

Before Maniac could blink, Juicy whipped out a blue-steel, 6-shot .357 revolver, aimed at Maniac's head, and pulled the trigger.

Boom!

Chapter Sixty-Two

Clash Of The Bosses

"I make my own destiny…"

— MONTEGA

♫ **Machiavelli in this… Killuminati… all through ya body… It blows like a twelve-gauge shotty… Feel me… Come with me… Hail Mary. Run, quick, see… What do we have here now? Do you wanna ride or die? Die dah dah dah die dah dah dah…**

Montega pulled up to Shug's condo and parked in the alley on the side of the large, eight-story building. After Juicy blew Maniac's brains out, they pushed him out on Tasker Street as they drove by the corner where all the hustlers were posted.

Montega laughed as he watched them all scatter like roaches when they saw the car speed by. It took several rags to clean Maniac's brain fragments with the disinfectant, but with some elbow grease and a little help from Spade, the passenger's side was brand new again. True to his word, Montega let Spade walk before giving him his last warning.

Juicy put the car in park. Montega opened the stash spot once more to retrieve the small, black Beretta M9, along with an attachable silencer barrel. He screwed it on as J-Rider and Juicy strapped up.

The three then got out. Montega looked up to the ladder that led to each separate floor. "I'm going first. Y'all follow behind me," he said.

J-Rider cocked back his gun and nodded. Juicy's gun was ready. She had already decided that she would not go last.

Montega walked over to the dumpster, pushed it under the fire escape, and climbed up to the sixth floor. Maniac had told him that Shug kept at least ten shooters on guard, and most of them would be in the lobby. He had hoped this was true. Once he climbed onto the metal terrace, he pulled out his small pocket knife and looked down for them to come.

J-Rider was the first to grab the iron ladder, but suddenly, it collapsed from its position to fall away. Montega watched as J-Rider fell to the ground and quickly picked himself up. Montega's eyes reverted to Juicy's. He knew they couldn't help him now; it was all on him. Motivated, he turned.

"Kenny!" Juicy said, causing him to stop… "Te cuidas."

He nodded to her then cut all the wires for the security cameras throughout the building.

He tucked his knife away and pulled out a small crowbar to open the door to the sixth floor. He held his gun tightly, keeping a steady aim, as he swept the staircase. The lights were dim, which made everything a dreary twilight. After inspecting the staircase, he headed for the door to the hallway.

Peeking through the crack, he saw two men sitting outside Shug's condo, just as Maniac told him they would be. One was reading a 'Butt Man' magazine while the other slept. They were Shug's nightly bodyguards. The one reading suddenly lifted his head to take a quick survey of the hallway after feeling a slight draft.

Once he was satisfied, he raised the magazine again. Montega put his back against the wall. He held the gun up with both hands, took a deep breath, and popped open the door, firing once at the middle of the magazine. He moved forward quickly as the round was released.

The silent bullet struck the henchman's forehead dead center, jerking him back against the wall. His body went stiff. The blood from his head splattered onto his sleeping partner, causing him to open his eyes. He was staring into the barrel of Montega's 9mm. The Phantom had walked up on him so quickly and quietly; it was as if he was a real spirit. All that he heard was a sneeze.

Pssst!

Inside the bedroom, Shug had just finished knocking off some Russian chick he knew from South Philly named Raven. She had been denying him pussy for too long, and no one denied a boss. All it took was a little persuasion. Raven lay on her back, disgusted with the large man lying beside her. As Shug slipped his hands through her long, red and orange hair, she sat up. "I have to use the bathroom. I gotta pee," she said.

Shug snatched her up by the hair, almost pulling her off balance. He yanked her close and whispered coldly, "You better hurry up. And don't try no funny shit."

Letting her go, he watched as she slithered out of bed. He could feel himself getting an erection just watching her ass jiggle all the way to the bathroom. He then got out of bed and went to slip into some boxers. He turned on the lamp. That's when he saw the figure standing by the wall. He did a double take as the figure moved forward.

"What the…" he said, jumping back.

When he realized who the figure was, he sighed calmly and said, "Montega, I presume." He eyed the gun in the Phantom's hand, then he shook his head. "How did you find me?"

"Your bols ain't loyal; that's how I found you. It's funny though. I should've done this a long time ago to save the pain you caused me… The pain you caused my sister. You must feel real big, putting your hands on a woman, you piece of shit."

Shug put his hands up in defense, trying to stall for time as his eyes nervously scanned the room. "Now, hold on, tiger. That wasn't me. I don't abuse women. What you want? Some bread to clear all this up? I'll give you whatever. Just name your price. You know I'm good for it. Just… just relax, gangsta."

"I ain't no gangsta. I'ma… what they call it? A collector. And the only price I'm looking for is the one on your head," Montega replied, aiming at Shug's face.

"I'll see you in hell then, muthafucka," Shug said, accepting his fate.

"Enough talkin'." Montega placed his finger firmly on the trigger when the sound of a door knob turning distracted him.

"Did you say something?" Raven asked as she emerged from the bathroom.

Montega whipped his body around and shot in her direction. She spun and fell to the floor. Shug rushed forward at Montega just as he was turning back to him. He was able to get off one shot, striking Shug in the stomach, but it didn't stop him. Shug swung a hard-right hook to Montega's face, knocking the phantom mask off his head. He dropped his gun and stumbled into the dresser as Shug threw another wild haymaker at his face. He saw this one coming from a mile away.

Slipping under the punch, Montega came back with several powerful punches of his own to Shug's face. This only pissed Shug off. Shug grabbed Montega by the throat and launched him into the air. Montega's body came crashing down on the nightstand. As he tried to get to his feet, Shug grabbed him again and slung him into the glass mirror. His 183 pounds of speed was no match for 310 pounds of sheer power and brute force.

"I knew you was a weak-ass nigga. It'll be a cold day in hell if I ever let you think you can beat me in anything. Get up," Shug taunted as he approached.

Montega gripped a handful of broken glass fragments off the floor and threw them into Shug's face. Shug yelled as he tried to shield his eye. Montega took advantage of this opportunity and hit him with a haymaker, causing Shug to stumble into the sliding door leading out to the balcony.

Seeing he had him where he wanted, Montega rushed him at full speed. He tried to tackle him, but Shug countered by stepping to the side, grabbing Montega by the back of his shirt collar and sending him straight through the glass door and headfirst onto the concrete balcony. Montega rolled onto his back, dazed. He looked up at the night sky and saw the full moon glowing. It was a beautiful night to die.

Once Shug fully regained his vision, he walked out onto the terrace. The night air was chilly, and the wind blew viciously. He grabbed Montega by the collar and pulled him to the edge of the balcony's railing. Montega tried to fight him off in one last attempt for his life, but Shug was too strong.

"Now, you do me a favor, cuz," Shug growled out. "Tell that bitch Tee-Tee I said no hard feelings. It was just business."

"Why don't you tell her yourself, you fat fuck?" Montega spat as he gripped the small knife from his pocket and stabbed Shug in the right eye.

"Ahhhhhrrrrrggggghhhhh!" Shug shouted in pain. Blood squirted from the wound like a water gun. Shug lost his grip on Montega.

"Oh yeah," Montega said. "It will definitely be a cold day in hell… so dress warm." He slipped out of Shug's grasp. With every bit of strength he had left, Montega pushed Shug into the railing, causing it to snap. Shug fell six-stories down and splattered on the concrete below like a water balloon.

Montega, out of breath, bruised, beaten, and battered but not defeated, looked down at the dead body in disbelief, thinking, *I might not be the best fighter, nor might I be intimidating, but there's one thing I'm good at, and that's sending muthafuckas like you where you belong.* "Enjoy your cold day in hell, fat boy!" he shouted over the balcony before turning to go back inside.

When he entered, he picked up his mask and put it back on. After retrieving his gun, he noticed the Russian chick sitting on the floor. He hadn't actually shot her. He walked over to her to investigate. She was in such a state of shock that she couldn't move. Blood trickled from her cheek. She had been grazed by the bullet. She didn't even look up at him as she spoke. "I was gonna stab him with this knife," she said, showing him the small dagger she had hidden in the bathroom. "He made me sleep with him. He said if I didn't, he would kill my boyfriend. He did things to me that not even a whore would tolerate, and I hate him for that."

Montega looked down at the weeping woman as the tears streamed down her face. He knew he should kill her, but women and children were not part of the plan.

"You know, they say the person you hate is the one you fear the most. And the one you fear always seems to have one up on you in life. They somehow find a way to control you, even when you're not conscious of it. Well… not anymore. You don't have to fear him ever again. If I were you, I would get my clothes and get outta here quickly because the police should be on their way."

Montega backed into the darkness and left.

That night, after returning to his condo, he took the staircase to the rooftop where the Comcast Center looked over him from across the street. Looking out at the city, he felt like Scarface looking up at the blimp that read: **THE WORLD IS YOURS**. He thought to himself, *who would have ever thought this city would be mine? It's over.*

However, he just didn't know how wrong he was. It wasn't over. It was only the beginning.

Epilogue

Jasmine sat in the U.S. courthouse, waiting on the outcome of Mike's appeal. The courtroom was small and nearly empty. Someone had told her that the odds of winning an appeal in the federal system was very tough. Nonetheless, she sat patiently in an elegant, black dress. On her feet, she wore a pair of four-inch, rhinestone sandals that emphasized her statuesque features. Her dark, shoulder-length hair was swept up in a bun with a few strands that fell down her sensuous shoulders, and her vanilla skin glowed with radiant beauty.

Although she came to court confident and dressed to impress, inside, she was a nervous wreck. She hadn't seen her man since the day he turned himself in. The Feds operated with their own protocol and were nothing like the state and county systems she was accustomed to.

As the judge finally strolled in from the back, Jazz sat up and nervously uncrossed and recrossed her legs. Her sweaty palms left a fine film of perspiration when she brushed them across the fabric of her dress. The fat, bald, and disgusting judge slowly sat in his chair, put on his glasses, and carefully studied the paper he had in his hand.

When Jazz heard the bailiff announce the first case on the docket, butterflies danced in her stomach. Just then, a marshal escorted Mike into the courtroom. He had on the standard green jailhouse jumpsuit and cheap, blue Bruce Lee deck shoes. His hands were handcuffed behind his back, and he looked disturbed. He didn't have the smile that always melted Jasmine's heart. Instead, he looked defeated. She figured that part of his demeanor came from the bad news she had heard last night about his cousin Shug being found dead outside of his condo.

When Mike made eye contact with her, she knew that his problems were worse than what she imagined. He was supposed to be happy to see her there, confident he would win his appeal. Jasmine planned to take him home and never let go of him. But something wasn't right. He knew something that she didn't.

After the judge rattled off a hundred reasons why he wasn't going to grant Mike's appeal, he looked at Mike and had the nerve to ask, "Do you have anything you would like to say to the court, Mr. Harris?"

Mike shook his head no, which completely deflated Jazz. "Very well," the judge announced. "As I stated earlier, people like you pollute the city of Philadelphia. You are a menace to society, and the arguments that I have heard in this courtroom today have not altered my opinion. Therefore, I am going to deny your appeal."

Mike glared at the judge with a look of pure hatred and malice as he stood with the marshal. When he looked back over his shoulder, he saw Jasmine with her hand covering her mouth in shock. Tears welled in her eyes as she stood and walked out of the courtroom. Her happy ending had been destroyed in just ten minutes.

After leaving the federal courthouse, Jazz decided to vent the only way she could. She went to visit her girlfriend, Amber, uptown in Summerville. Jazz maneuvered the silver Range Rover Sport up Woodlawn. It was a little after 3 p.m., and the Pastorious Elementary School was just letting out. Children cluttered the streets, lugging book bags and lunch boxes. The speed limit on the one-way block had changed to fifteen miles per hour.

As she slowly rode by the red and brown brick building, she couldn't believe how crowded the neighborhood got around that time. This was the last day of school for the year. She made a sharp right turn onto Blakemore Street after noticing the young hustlers hanging out on the corner by the Chinese store.

Looking in her rearview, she didn't see any of the usual young bols out. Everything had changed since Mike went to prison. She got to the bottom of the block and parked then got out.

Amber lived with her aunt Lisa and her two brothers, Burl and Naheem. Their house was two doors down from where her girlfriend Kia's mom, Stacy, used to live and was covered with Christmas ornaments. Jazz stepped up on the porch and found the door open. She opened the screen and walked in to find a nineteen-year-old Naheem with his crew, Cyirl, Lil' B, Spizzo, Los, Quin, and Burl.

They were all sitting at the dining room table like it was some kind of summit. When Jazz walked in, they all turned and looked at her.

Jasmine stopped in the doorway as if she were intruding. Naheem, who had his back to the door, was the last to turn around. He was five years younger than his sister, Amber, but a year older than his brother, Burl. Jasmine always thought he was one of the most dynamic young bols ever to come out of the 'Ville since Kenny Carter, and he was also one of the cutest.

Although his brother Taliban had him beat because of his chunky cheeks, a light complexion, and was unique in his own way, Montega's pecan-tinted skin was slightly blemished with a few childhood scars, but he had a smooth, adorable baby face.

He was another one who enjoyed being inside his head. However, he wasn't comfortable around a lot of people, especially large groups, and would prefer to be invisible. After his mother's tragic accident, Naheem Paschel changed from an innocent, outgoing kid to a calculated street thug who adopted the nickname *9-11.*

"Jazz," 9-11 greeted her.

"Hey, Dink. Where's Amber?" Jazz asked, and 9-11 pointed upstairs.

Jazz set her purse on the table while giving Lil' B her usual suspicious look. Very few people liked Lil' B because he was just too sneaky. "What's up, Jazz?" he asked as if he were on great terms with her.

"Hi, Brian," she replied dryly as she walked up the steps to see her girlfriend.

Amber was in the backroom, getting dressed. She had just gotten out of the shower and slipped into a pink bra and thong set. She grabbed some lotion and jumped when Jazz burst in through the door. Jasmine snorted a laugh at her. "Scared ass. I ain't the police."

"Bitch, you play too fuckin' much!" Amber shouted.

"Who did you think I was?" Jasmine shifted her weight to her right hip with a chuckle.

"I thought you were Brian's perverted ass. I was ready to bust you in the head with this Victoria's Secret perfume bottle."

Jazz's face twisted up. "Bee *still* on that type of time?"

"Is he? Just the other day, he talkin' 'bout, 'Damn, Amber, if you wasn't my man sister.' I was like, 'Boy, if you don't get your little horny ass outta my face.' I swear I don't trust that boy. Anyway, what's been up, slut? What happened with Mike?"

Jasmine's face immediately frowned. She walked over to the bed and flopped down. Tears began to swell in her eyes again as if on cue.

"They denied his appeal. The fucking judge was talking shit, like my boo is a danger to the community. I can't believe he has to do five whole years inside that place. Amber, I'm scared out here. Shit is really crazy, and Reek; he ain't even returning my calls. I don't know what's up with him. He supposed to be Mike's man. He ain't even show up to his appeal hearing or let me know anything."

Amber squeezed her chestnut-brown, Coca-Cola bottle hips into the blue, fitted Seven jeans. "That's how these guys are, Jazz. They cool peoples when you out on the streets, but soon as you go in, they act like they don't even know you. That's corny. If it wasn't for Mike, these guys wouldn't have half the money they have now."

Jazz buried her head in her hands. Tears began to dribble out of her pretty eyes. "I don't know what to do, Amber. I need him out here with me. The house we got is just too much for a single woman to keep up with; not only that, but it's hard with all this temptation and shit. I hate sleeping alone."

Amber sympathized with her girlfriend. She walked over and sat on the bed beside her. Placing an arm around her shoulder, she said, "It's gonna be okay, Jazz."

"No, it's not gonna be okay, Amber. Five years is long as shit when you just did a bid with him. What am I supposed to do out here without him for that long? I can't believe this is happening to me."

Amber was speechless. All she could do was give Jazz a shoulder to cry on. She knew Jasmine was strong because if it were up to her, she would have said fuck Mike, or so she thought.

Down in the living room, 9-ll set a Nike duffle bag on the table in front of the rest of his homies and unzipped it. Everyone rose to see the guns inside. He pulled one out and said, "I hope y'all ready for this. If this Luchiano nigga got as much money as y'all say, then y'all better be prepared to do whatever it takes, no matter what. Now, let's roll out."

Together, the young wolves took the guns and headed for the mission—something that would change their lives forever...

To Be Continued...

QUESTIONS FOR THE READER

1. What truly drives Montega and why?

2. What does Diamond have planned to unite the Mexican cartel?

3. Out of all the women in his life, who loves Montega more and why?

4. Out of all of Montega's friends who is most likely to turn on him?

5. In relations who is Diamond to Montega?

6. As deadly as Diamond is, why would she take a priest as an advisor?

7. What are the names of the men that are true to Diamond?

8. Why did Montega's Impala get impounded?

9. What was the name of Million Dollar Mike's first girlfriend?

10. Fun Question: Can you use your pointer finger and go around the maze without going backwards to get to the 'M'? Try it. Take pictures and send them in for us to post on our instagram page of your success!

NOTE FROM THE AUTHOR

For years, I've been told I would never amount to anything in life if I didn't get my act together. And for years, I've struggled with trying to balance myself on this unstable current called life. Life can be cruel at times; it can be harsh, filled with pain, danger, and deceitfulness. And if you accept these problems in your life, then you are what you eat.

On the flip side of things, life can be happiness, fun, full of growth and development, unconditional love, and desire. The only way to achieve this is to believe in ourselves and use our minds to get us there. We can only go as far as our minds take us. It's like we start off with the mind state that we are born to lose, but in all actuality, if we believe in ourselves, we'd see that we were really built to win. I created the slogan: **Beware of the wolf** not to scare people but to warn them about me… to warn them that I've gotten my act together, and I'm coming for this world with everything I have like a skilled predator with a hunger to succeed.

Now I'm susceptible to teach myself anything. I'm prone to learn anything. I can achieve what I set out for just so long as I put my mind to it. I make my own destiny, and I encourage you all to do the same. The first step to becoming whatever it is you choose to be is: mind over matter.

Until Next Time...

Beware of the wolf,

Keon Smith

ABOUT THE AUTHOR

"At first I had just wanted to be heard, now I want to become an immortal author."

— KEON SMITH

My journey in writing started from a dream, when I awoke, I attempted to write down what I saw in my sleep. That dream became reality -my latest novel the BLACK KISS OF DEATH; the first of a 9 book series, the MONTEGA Chronicles.

Keon resides in the city of brotherly love and has two beautiful girls along with 24 manuscripts on the verge of being published so that his goal might yet be fulfilled.

facebook.com/KeonSmith
instagram.com/keonsmith_author

SKYLER PUBLISHING GROUP

The Higher Heights Of Contemporary Storytelling

Be sure to LIKE our Skyler Publishing group page on Facebook!

Be sure to FOLLOW our Skyler Publishing group page on Instagram!

facebook.com/skylerpubgroup

instagram.com/skylerpublishinggroup

CPSIA information can be obtained
at www.ICGtesting.com
Printed in the USA
LVHW030154251121
704426LV00001B/46

9 781730 934308